"Who the hell are [...] loaded pistol spo[...] slowly spreading across his face. He took a step to one side, his gun half raised. The other two desperados started to spread out, but the Ranger's voice stopped them.

"Stand fast, boys," Burrack growled at the two with dark warning in his eyes. Then he turned his full gaze upon the other one. "I'm covering for the Sheriff Mace Jenkins. Raise that pistol another inch and watch me blow your heart all over the wall."

There was mettle in the Ranger's voice, enough that the young cowboy hesitated for just a second. The Ranger saw the opening and took it. . . .

"Cotton leaves his readers with more than a memorable story . . . devilishly inventive . . . numerous twists and turns . . . a unique voice, style, and mission as a writer."
—Wade Hall, Professor Emeritus of English, Bellarmine College, *Kentucky Courier-Journal*

Justice

RALPH COTTON

Ø
A SIGNET BOOK

SIGNET
Published by the Penguin Group
Penguin Putnam Inc., 375 Hudson Street,
New York, New York 10014, U.S.A.
Penguin Books Ltd, 27 Wrights Lane,
London W8 5TZ, England
Penguin Books Australia Ltd,
Ringwood, Victoria, Australia
Penguin Books Canada Ltd, 10 Alcorn Avenue,
Toronto, Ontario, Canada M4V 3B2
Penguin Books (N.Z.) Ltd, 182–190 Wairau Road,
Auckland 10, New Zealand

Penguin Books Ltd, Registered Offices:
Harmondsworth, Middlesex, England

First published by Signet, an imprint of Dutton NAL,
a member of Penguin Putnam Inc.

First Printing, April, 1999
10 9 8 7 6 5 4 3 2 1

For Mary Lynn . . . of course

And in fond memory of Ralph Compton,
one of the good guys

We all miss you, mi amigo

PROLOGUE

Something about the three riders told the Ranger they were *wrong* the minute he'd seen them ride into Bannet. Had that been four days ago?

Yep, four days . . . He was certain of it. And that worked out just about right, *time-wise*, connecting them to the missing stagecoach, he thought, as he checked the big pistol in his hand.

He'd kept a close eye on them these four days. What more could he have done? They'd broken no law in Bannet that the Ranger knew of—until now that is. Now they were all three at the Metropolitan Saloon whooping it up, getting drunk, acting crazy, shooting their range pistols. . . . *Celebrating something?* He wasn't sure; but all the same, this was a good time to question them about the missing stagecoach.

He spun the cylinder on his big pistol, clicked the hammer down on a live round, holstered it, and turned to his partner, Maria. She stood near the door with her rifle in one gloved hand and her battered Stetson hat in her other. "Let's get this wrapped up and get on the trail." He looked at her. "We've been in town too long as it is."

She nodded, tossing her long hair back and placing the hat on her head. "But how do you *know* they are a part of it?"

"I just *know*."

At first glance, to anybody else, they were just three

cowhands down from the high grasslands. But that wasn't what the Ranger saw. He saw trouble.

"You *could* be mistaken." Maria checked her rifle, levering a round up into the chamber. "And what if you are? Innocent men will die."

"I'm not mistaken, trust me. They're part of the reason the Bannet stagecoach is missing. I'd bet a month's pay on it."

It wasn't anything in particular that he could put his finger on, and it was certainly not something he could explain; but there was a small voice inside him that always seemed to tell him when a man was *wrong*. He'd heard that voice loud and clear when these three young men rode in, low in their saddles, appearing to gaze straight ahead, while beneath their hat brims he'd seen them checking out the Bannet stage office. They'd been hanging around outside the office the morning the shotgun rider hefted the strongbox up to the driver. *Yep, they had a hand in things . . .*

"The dispatch rider did not say the stagecoach is *missing*," Maria said, "only that it is *late*. There could be any number of reasons."

He picked up his gray sombrero from atop the battered sheriff's desk and ran a gloved hand along the brim. "One day is *overdue*. Two days is *late*. Three days or more is *missing*. This one's been gone *four* days." He held up four gloved fingers as he spoke. Then he adjusted the sombrero down on his head. "Are you ready or what?"

"*Sí.*" Maria let out a breath and wiped a hand along her rifle barrel. "I suppose I *could* blame Sheriff Jenkins and his *snakebite* for all of this."

"You could," the Ranger said with a wry smile, drawing the edge of his duster back behind his pistol butt. "But it makes no difference now." It was true that had the sheriff of Bannet, Mace Jenkins, not stepped on a big bull rattlesnake and taken a dose of venom deep in his right leg, the Ranger and Maria would never have been asked to keep an eye on the town in the first place.

"We agreed to do it. So here we are," the Ranger added. He looked deep into her dark eyes for a second as his hand reached out and paused on the doorknob. "Are you ready?" He asked again, although he wouldn't have had to. Maria was always *ready*—it was her nature, the same as his. And as he looked at her, he saw the uncertainty had gone out of her eyes, replaced now by calm, cool resolve.

"I *am* ready." She spoke in a firm tone, nodding for emphasis; and they said no more as they stepped out onto the boardwalk and heard pistol shots followed by drunken laughter coming from the Metropolitan Saloon.

At the sight of the Ranger and Maria stepping down off the boardwalk and heading toward the pistol fire, an old teamster who'd been loading a freight wagon quickened his task, shoved the tailgate shut, bolted it with a nervous hand, leaped up into the wagon seat, and slapped the reins to the mules' dusty backs. The mules brayed and bolted forward, their haunches lowering against the heavy load.

Outside the Metropolitan, Sheriff Mace Jenkins stood back with a group of townsfolk gathered behind him. A crutch stood firm beneath his right arm. His face looked pale and slightly green under his swollen eyes. This was the first time the Ranger had seen Mace Jenkins up and around since he and Maria had arrived in Bannet.

"Howdy, Sam." Mace Jenkins spoke to the Ranger in a weakened voice. "I heard you was here looking after things for me." He shook his head. "You know I hate asking ya. I'd be in there in a streak ... wasn't for this danged snakebite."

"I know it." The Ranger looked around at the crowd

as another volley of pistol fire and drunken laughter spilled from within the saloon. The crowd shied back a step, then started to edge forward again. The Ranger stayed them in place with a raised hand. "How many times does this make for you, Mace? Three? Four times? I've never heard of a man having such a terrible problem with reptiles."

The sheriff looked down at his thick swollen calf, the trouser leg torn open at the seam. His toes stuck out of a thick bandage, rosy and puffed. "Only three times," he said, a little embarrassed. "That other time was just a sand lizard—made me sicker than a dog, though."

"Still, three times is a lot." The Ranger shook his head, drew his pistol, and let it hang down his side. "You oughta learn to put your boots on before you traipse out to the jake late at night." He nodded down at the swollen foot. "Seems like a reasonable practice, all things considered."

"I know it . . . I just can't seem to get the hang of it." He leaned a bit, unsteady on his crutch, glancing up and down the dirt street. "Where's your little woman?"

The Ranger winced a bit. "Do yourself a favor, Mace. Don't let *her* hear you call her that. Believe me, it'd be a lot worse than a snakebite." He nodded toward the saloon as another volley of shots resounded from inside. "She's fanning the back door . . . in case one of them gets a case of *rabbit* fever at the last minute and makes a run for it."

"That's good thinking," the sheriff said. Then his eyes lowered, and he added, "Heck, I'm ashamed to say it, but I can't even help ya haul them to jail, the shape I'm in. The doctor's saying he'll have to move me over to Humbly come morning. Talking like I might lose this leg if things don't take a turn for the better. I'd hate spending the rest of my life paying full price for a pair of boots and only able to use *one*."

"Well, let's hope you don't have to." As the Ranger spoke, he noticed the encroaching crowd had milled forward once more, and he moved them back again with a raised hand. "I just found out the stage to Circle Wells is missing. The one that left here four days ago."

"*Four days?*" The sheriff raised his brow. "Why'd they wait so long reporting it?"

"Telegraph lines are down north of here," the Ranger said. "The message had to go to the next office south and come back up here with a dispatch rider— all the way from Humbly." He nodded toward the saloon. "I've got a feeling these cowboys had something to do with it."

"Oh?"

"Yep. They slipped into town four days ago. I figure their job was to check things out, then cut the lines on their way out of town." He offered a grim smile. "They'd have gotten away with it if they hadn't stayed and took to drinking."

"My God. Then maybe I best get me a shotgun and go in there with ya, snakebite or not." Mace Jenkins rocked on his crutch under his right arm. "I can shoot left-handed, in a pinch."

"No. You stay here, Mace. I'll question them." The Ranger stepped away toward the Metropolitan Saloon. "Try to keep these people back if you can."

"I will. You be careful in there, ya hear?" The sheriff's words disappeared beneath another volley of pistol fire. The crowd gasped and shied back a step. "You heard the Ranger," Mace Jenkins called out to the townsfolk gathered behind him. "Get on back, now. Act like you've got some sense."

The Ranger walked forward, up onto the boardwalk, and stood for a moment outside the bat-wing doors of the Metropolitan Saloon. Looking in beneath a drifting cloud of powder smoke—getting a feel for things—he let out a breath and laid his left hand on the top edge of a door. This was what he didn't like about towns, he thought. There were always drunks with smoking pistols in a town—always one more head that needed cracking, one more hard case that needed a good stiff boot in his ribs. He didn't see how lawmen like Mace Jenkins stood it.

With his pistol still hanging down his side, cocked now, the Ranger stepped in through the doors, seeing the backs of the three young men as they laughed among themselves. They huddled close, like wolves hovering over a fresh kill, reloading their pistols, laughing under their breath. The smell of burned powder filled the saloon.

Against the left wall, twenty feet away, the bartender stood as stiff as an oak plank. A dark circle of urine covered his striped trouser legs and formed a spreading puddle on the dirty floor. On his head sat a half-empty beer mug. Sweat ran down his cheeks. Fear had his eyes glazed, bloodshot, and bulging.

"Game's over, boys." The Ranger spoke in a low calm voice, moving slow, stepping sideways across the floor toward the bar, where bottles lay on their sides in puddles of rye whiskey and broken shot-glasses. "Holster them range pistols before somebody gets hurt."

"What the—?"

They spun facing him, their eyes wild and whiskey-lit. Pistols raised in their hands. Two of them had only half reloaded when the Ranger's voice caught them by surprise—still gripping loose bullets in their gloved hands. One of them *had* finished reloading, and he'd snapped the cylinder shut as he turned. He would have to go down first, the Ranger thought, looking at them, putting it together in his mind. He caught a glimpse of the bartender dropping down and scooting along the wall toward the rear door.

"Who the hell are you?" asked the one with the fully loaded revolver, a bemused smile on his face. He took a step to one side, his pistol half raised. The other two started to spread out, but the Ranger's voice stopped them.

"Stand fast, boys." The Ranger spoke to the two with dark warning in his eyes. Then he turned his full gaze to the other one. "I'm covering for Sheriff Mace Jenkins. Raise that pistol another inch and watch me blow your heart all over the wall."

There was mettle in the Ranger's voice, enough that the young cowboy hesitated for just a second. The Ranger saw the opening and took it, giving them a chance to think about it. "You don't have to die here, none of you. All you've got to do is holster up your shooters, answer a couple of questions for me, and be on your way."

"Questions?" The one with the fully loaded pistol cocked his head slightly. "What kind of questions?"

"I know you, mister," said one of the others before the Ranger could answer. "You're that Ranger, *Sam Burrack*, ain't ya? You're the law dog that shot Montana Red, Hurley Yates, and all them others up in the high country."

"I've shot a *few*." The Ranger raised his pistol slowly as he spoke and rested his forearm down on the bar, the tip of the barrel pointing at them. "Now, holster up."

"I said, what *kind of questions*," the first one asked again. His pistol hadn't wavered an inch. He'd make the first move; the Ranger knew it. "Maybe we don't *feel* like answering questions to some damned *law-dog* Ranger. *Now what?*"

The Ranger let the challenge pass, and said in a level tone, "The Bannet stage is missing *four* days now. Don't suppose you boys know anything about it? Or about the lines being cut a few miles out of town?"

The Ranger watched their eyes for a reaction. He saw none. He'd have to press them harder, get them talking, make their words trip them up some way before they made a move with their pistols. But before he could say another word, the one with the full load spoke out, his words catching the Ranger by surprise for just a second.

"Yeah, we know *all* about the stagecoach, Ranger," the man sneered. "That was our gang that robbed it. *So what?*" His knuckles stood out white around his pistol butt, his finger tense across the trigger.

Their gang? Here it came. The Ranger was ready for it; but he needed to find out as much as he could before he killed them. "Oh? You boys are desperados then." Even as he spoke he felt the play starting. The two to his left grew more restless now, nervous. Their half-loaded pistols were angled downward, but ready to swing up at any second. "This *gang* of yours, anybody I might've heard of? Nobody famous, I don't suppose."

He saw a nerve twitch in the jaw of the man with the fully loaded pistol. "Not yet," the young man said, his gun arm poised like a coiled spring, the tendons in his neck standing out, a vein in his forehead pulsing. *Here we go* . . . "We're the Half Moon Gang," he added, his voice going thick, his boot toe bracing down on the floor, ready, set. "After *today*, we'll be the ones known for killing you here in this—"

His words cut short as the streak of fire shot off the bar top from the Ranger's pistol. The bullet punched a hole through his heart and slammed him back against the wall. *"Get him, Sandy!"* one of the other two cried out, both of their pistols coming up, cocking . . .

Out in the street, Sheriff Mace Jenkins felt the crowd move back, this time farther than before, as three more shots followed the first one they'd heard only a second ago. But Mace Jenkins stood firm in the ringing silence, his good leg trembling a bit in his trousers. *Dang this snakebite!* His left hand searched inside his coat and came out with a small Uhrlinger pistol. He fumbled with it—awkward in his left hand—aiming it toward the slow sound of boot-fall and ringing spur coming forward from inside the doors of the Metropolitan.

"Sam? Are you all right in there?" The sheriff called out as the bat-wing doors creaked open. The crowd gasped and seemed to hold its breath as one of the young men staggered out onto the boardwalk. He stopped and weaved back and forth, his pistol hanging loose in his fingertips. Blood frothed and bubbled from his shattered lung, and ran down the bib of his dusty shirt. Words came from his bloody lips as if spoken through a mouthful of wool. "Kill . . . all you . . . dirt stickers." The crowd stepped farther back. Mace Jenkins cocked the small pistol.

But then the young man faltered and sank straight down on his knees, his pistol falling from his fingers; and he rocked back and forth, then pitched forward off the boardwalk, facedown into the dark mud along the hitch rail, where moments before a big dun gelding had relieved itself. The horse nickered and drew quarter-wise against its tied reins.

"Lord have mercy," Mace Jenkins whispered, lowering the pistol. His eyes went back to the doors of the saloon as the Ranger stepped through them, replacing the three spent cartridges in his big pistol. Powder smoke drifted above his shoulders. He stepped forward and down off the boardwalk as Mace Jenkins came closer.

"Are you okay, Sam?"

"I'll do," the Ranger said, a slight strain in his voice. He reached down, took the dead man by his shirt collar, raised him from the filth, and propped him back against the boardwalk. "This one's name is

Sandy . . . ever seen him around here before? Or heard of him?"

"No, I surely haven't." Mace Jenkins leaned forward on his crutch, looking closer. "Young fellow, ain't he."

"Yeah, he is." The Ranger let out a breath. "All three of them are." He heard Maria's footsteps coming around the corner of the alley, and saw her move up beside him as he wiped a streak of mud off the dead man's face. "They're part of a bunch that calls themselves the Half Moon Gang. Ever heard of them?"

"Naw, sir, it doesn't ring a bell." Mace Jenkins shrugged, looking down at the dead man's face.

"That's what I was afraid of." The Ranger raised a boot toe and rolled the face back and forth, giving the sheriff a better look.

"Nope." Mace Jenkins shook his head. "A new gang, you suppose? That's the worse kind to deal with. Young toughs out to prove themselves. They'll wear a fellow out." Jenkins looked down once more at the dead face, the bloody mouth gaping, half filled with mud. "Wish I could help ya."

"They *are* the reason the stage is missing—one of them bragged about it." The Ranger's eyes cut to Maria, now standing beside him. Then he looked back at Mace Jenkins.

"Dang it! And here's me, stove-up with a bad leg." Jenkins shoved the small pistol back inside his coat and ran a hand across his forehead. "I swear, Sam. How'd you find out so much from 'em in such a short time?"

"Just a good listener, I guess." The Ranger turned to Maria. "Looks like I was wrong about one thing, though. None of them made a run for it like I thought they would."

"*Sí* . . ." She gave him a skeptical look. "Or maybe you knew they wouldn't . . . but you did not want me in there?"

"Don't start on me." A trace of a smile came to the Ranger's lips. But then he winced a bit as he raised his pistol and holstered it. Maria saw his expression change, and she stepped closer.

"What is wrong? Are you hurt?" She reached out toward his side, where he'd hugged his forearm against himself.

"Just a graze." The Ranger collected himself. "It'll be all right. We've got to get out of here and find the stage . . . could be folks stranded out there somewhere—no water, no food."

"No!" Maria took a firm stand. "We go *nowhere* until the doctor has taken a look at your side."

"Don't make a big thing of it, Maria." The Ranger's voice went lower, a little embarrassed in front of the sheriff. "We'll get right out there and right back. This ain't my *first* missing stage."

PART 1

A Coming Storm

CHAPTER 1

Doss Edding slid his big paint horse to a halt at the head of the other riders. He was wild-eyed drunk, feeling bloody and mean. The stagecoach robbery had only quelled his inner demons for a day. Now the whiskey had his mind boiling once more, and the demons were out, raging and dancing on his jangled nerve endings with sharp-clawed feet.

"There she is, boys, the ole Cottonwood Bank." His big paint horse stepped high-hoofed, spinning a full turn beneath him. He swung a gloved finger toward the small town below them, less than a mile away in a dusty basin. "Ain't she the sweetest thing you ever saw in your life?"

Doss wore a long black riding duster that belonged to his father, Matthew Edding—an old Civil War style that his father had worn back during his days with the Southern guerilla forces. Doss had taken the duster from his father's closet. Something about wearing it gave Doss a powerful feeling, even though it drooped a bit on his narrow shoulders.

"*Um-hmm*, like a peach on a tree," Little Tommy Caldwell answered, sitting beside him, his wide hat brim pulled up flat in front and held there by a woman's silver broach he'd found among the stage baggage. "Let's shoot 'em all, Doss!" He whipped a glance around at the other young men, yanking his battered range pistol from his belt. "Huh? What do

ya'll say? You want to shoot 'em all? Every damn last
one of 'em? I'll do it . . . don't think I won't. I sure
enough will!"

"Shut up and give me that whiskey bottle, Little
Tommy. You're too quick to wanta jump up and shoot
somebody," said Newt Babbage. Newt, a tall, thin
young man, sat wobbling atop his horse. He wore a
woman's plumed hat atop his battered Stetson, tied
there by a silk sash. The woman's hat was among the
spilled baggage along the trail after the stage robbery.
Newt Babbage took it as a trophy. He adjusted it with
his grimy fingertips as he reached out for the bottle of
rye in Little Tommy's hand. "You can't even *see* nobody to shoot 'em, without your wire rims."

The riders laughed, Little Tommy along with them,
pitching Newt the bottle of rye. "Oh? Well, now, I just
happen to have them babies with me, right here." He'd
rummaged in his duster pocket as he spoke, and came
up with a pair of dirty wire-rim spectacles. He hooked
them on behind his ears and squinted, batting his eyes,
which now looked three times larger. He jiggled the
pistol in his hand, grinning. "Now that I can see you,
Newton, tell me again that I'm too quick to wanta shoot
somebody. I *double-dog* dare ya."

"I've never known what that meant, a *double-dog
dare*." Newt Babbage threw back another shot of rye, a
trickle of it cutting through the dust down his chin. He
wiped it away with the loose end of the silk sash.
"And don't *point* that pistol at me, Little Tommy," he
said, adjusting the woman's hat atop his sweat-stained
Stetson, "I'm apt to wet my *poor* self." A ripple of
drunken laughter moved across the riders.

Dusty Charlie Allbright, the oldest of the Half Moon
Gang by a couple years, heeled his horse a step forward, swiping the bottle from Newt Babbage's hand,
saying over his shoulder as he passed him, "You *are*
apt to, Newt. You look like a whore anyway, with that

stupid hat. Tommy's liable to pinch your cheek if you ain't careful."

"What do you mean by that?" Little Tommy's eyes swam back and forth, glazed by whiskey. "Huh? What?" He glanced at the others. "What's he mean, *pinch Newt on the cheek?*"

"Aw, hell, Tommy, hush."

The riders laughed again, this time a bit louder, as Dusty Charlie stopped beside Doss Edding and gazed toward the town of Cottonwood. "Well, let's do it up if we're going to, Doss . . . before I get too sobered up. It won't come up here to us." He turned up a shot of rye, then without looking back, held it out behind him until a dirty hand snatched it.

"You drink all of that bottle, Harper, and I *will* shoot somebody, sure enough . . . *right here.*" Little Tommy's eyes looked deep and strange, swimming behind his thick spectacles. "You better listen to me, Lew, you fat turd, ya. I want a suck of rye before I do another thing."

But big Lew Harper didn't lower the bottle until it was empty. Then he let out a whiskey hiss, followed by a watery belch, and pitched the bottle over on Little Tommy's lap. "There, suck on *that*, and your sister too," he said.

"Well, *shii-itt*," Little Tommy said, slinging the bottle away. "I ain't got no sister—if I *did*, I *would*." He chuckled to himself, looking at Doss to see if Doss had gotten a laugh out of it. But Doss didn't seem to get it, or else hadn't been listening. Tommy thought he might remind Doss of it later, maybe tonight around the campfire. Yeah, he might bring it up again, remind everybody of how he'd said it—some smart remark about a sister he didn't even have—just before they'd gone down and robbed the bank . . . see what Doss thought of it then.

"All right, let's get serious now. Everybody ready or

what?" Doss Edding called back over his shoulder. "Newt? Tommy? Harper?"

The others either nodded or answered in turn. "Good," Doss called out. "Here we go—"

"I'm not ready." The quiet voice of Jesse Tiggs cut him off. Tiggs sat atop his horse, back a couple of steps from the others. They all turned in their saddles, facing him. He'd raised a boot and crossed it over his saddle, his gloved hands crossed at the wrists, resting easy on his saddle horn with a rolled cigarette curling smoke between his fingers. His wide-oval sat tipped back on his forehead—a bit too high for the time of day.

"What're you talking about, Jesse? Of course you're ready to go." Doss Edding glared at him.

Jesse Tiggs shrugged. He was the newest member of the Half Moon Gang, the next oldest after Dusty Charlie Allbright. But Tiggs had a way about him that made him seem much older than the others. He considered himself a straight-up gunslinger, and there were three dead Mexicans down in Sonora to prove it, if anybody wanted to check.

Just in from the border towns a few weeks back, Tiggs had learned to carry himself with the easy swagger of a stone-cold killer. The polished wooden handle on his long-barreled .45 carried an inlaid silver rattlesnake, coiled, with its rattler up, its fangs bared. "I've got eight hundred dollars in my pocket from the stage job," he said, a thin smile on his face. "That's enough money to last me till something better comes along."

"Bull, it is!" Doss Edding kicked his horse a step closer to Jesse Tiggs, the others shying to the side. But Tiggs didn't stir an inch. "Once a Half Moon, *always* a Half Moon," Doss Edding added, his voice coming back down at the sight of Jesse Tiggs' flat expression.

"You took an oath, same as the rest of us. I never figured you to crawfish on us!"

Tiggs didn't so much as flicker an eyelid. "Yeah, well . . ." He looked off, sucked air through his teeth, and turned back to Doss Edding. "You wouldn't believe how many oaths I've sworn and broken." He grinned, but it was a cold, closed grin—no mirth there at all. "Oaths are like a young woman's heart. I *swear* one and *break* one every other turn in the road."

"Not this oath, you don't," Doss Edding said, shooting Dusty Charlie a glance.

Dusty Charlie edged his horse closer, alongside Doss, his eyes fixed on Jesse Tiggs, a shotgun from the stagecoach raising slightly from his lap. "Doss is right," he said heavily. "This is one oath that doesn't get broken."

Little Tommy, Newt Babbage, and big Lew Harper just watched. The thin smile stayed on Jesse Tiggs' face. His wrists remained crossed on his saddle horn, the cigarette smoke still slowly curling from his lip. But Dusty Charlie's shotgun stopped rising from his lap when Jesse said in a low tone, "I don't know how fast you *think* you can swing iron, Charlie. But I bet every dollar in my pocket, you'll be dead before you can cock a hammer."

Dusty Charlie tensed, his hand tightening around the gun stock.

"Whooa! Everybody take it easy here," said big Lew Harper. "We're all part of the same bunch. Let's not get turned agin one another."

"I'm not turning against anybody." Jesse Tiggs spoke, keeping his eyes on Dusty Charlie, who settled down under Jesse's cold gaze. "But I'm heading back to the ranch. Oath or no oath, I'm sitting this one out."

"This ain't no *dance*," Doss Edding hissed. "You're either with us or agin us."

"Make sure you hear me good, Doss," Jesse Tiggs

said. "I'm gonna back this horse up and leave.
Whether I'm *with* you or not is a matter for me to decide. Whether or not you want me *agin* you, is something you better think about real careful like, before
you try to stop me from leaving." That's it, he thought,
keep them unsettled, not knowing the next move. These
boys hadn't been around the way he had . . . and they
wanted no part of him.

"Damn it, I swear, Jesse, what's got into you?" Little
Tommy asked.

Jesse looked back and forth among them, seeing that
none of them were about to call his play. He chuckled
under his breath. "Boys, I'll just be honest with you.
This is not my style. I'm out to make money the *easy*
way . . . without having to look over my shoulder for
the law. You boys didn't even cover your faces on that
stagecoach job—lucky nobody lived through it. You're
out to make names for yourselves as thieves and murderers. Not me. I'm a gunman, boys, and damn proud
of it. This desperado stuff don't interest me. If I
wanted to do something *daring*, I'd go look up Wyatt
Earp and shoot some holes in his head."

"So? What's wrong with making big names for ourselves? We're as tough as anybody else." Doss Edding
stared at him, as Jesse dropped his boot back down to
his stirrup and backed his horse away a few feet.

"Sure you are," Jesse said, smiling. "But the kind of
big names you're looking for end up on small tomb-
stones." He turned his horse sideways to them, and
stepped it farther away. "See you at the ranch—if
you're still alive."

"If my daddy's back from Riley, you better not tell
him what we done out here," Doss Edding called out
to him.

"Hell, I ain't crazy, Doss," Jesse Tiggs said. He tightened his hat down, kicked his horse into a canter, and
moved away shaking his head. See? Those boys were

idiots, Jesse thought. Young Doss, stupid and mean and full of rye whiskey—out here showing off in the ole man's war coat, saying Jesse better not tell his daddy. How long did this fool think it would be before his ole man knew what he'd done? They didn't even wear masks!

"I oughta blast him one," Dusty Charlie murmured under his breath, watching Jesse Tiggs leave.

"What's got into him, anyway?" Lew Harper scratched his jaw.

"Who's *Wyatt Earp*?" asked Little Tommy.

"Shit. Forget about him. He didn't do nothing anyway on the stagecoach job—just sat back and looked tough." Doss Edding yanked his reins, turning his horse toward the trail down into Cottonwood. "Now, come on, let's go get us some *fun fun fun!*"

"Hold up, Doss." Dusty Charlie grabbed Doss's horse by its bridle. "What if that crawfishing dog *does* go tell your pa what we've done? I don't want your ole man down my shirt over this. I'm supposed to be looking out for you."

"You heard him," Doss Edding said. "If my ole man hears what we did, he'll have every hand on the place pistol-whipping Jesse all the way to the Mexican border. Now, we going to rob this bank or *what?*"

"I am," Little Tommy answered. "I'll live a Half Moon, and die a Half Moon." He lifted his hat with its pinned-up brim and swung it above his head, rearing his horse up, then gigging it forward as it touched down.

"Hell, me too, I reckon," said big Lew Harper. "It don't make no never mind, one way or the next."

"That's more like it!" Doss Edding yelled, spurring his horse forward onto the trail. "When we get down there, don't none of yas lay a hand on sweet little Jimmy French. That sissy little peckerwood is *mine-all-mine.*"

Dusty Charlie brought up the rear when the others

had moved forward onto the thin trail. His shotgun in hand, he gazed back over his shoulder at Jesse Tiggs, until Jesse disappeared in his own wake of dust.

As the train slowed to a stop at the rail station in Humbly, Matthew Edding sat staring through the dusty window at the endless swirl of sand and wavering heat in the distance. A hundred yards out, a dry hot wind formed low dust devils on the desert floor. Sand twisted and spun among stiff branches of parched mesquite brush. A pale stand of wild grass whipped in a circle, clinging by hard fixed roots to its stark existence on the flat belly of barren earth.

He liked the feel of this land and its coarseness. There were no false promises out there. He respected the land for its brutal honesty. Out there the essence of mortality remained forever at work, all forms of existence constant in its struggle—its unending waltz on the earth plane.

Matthew Edding was a self-educated man in the things that mattered in his portion of the world, and he'd wasted no time seeking deeper meaning of the things that made up the larger world around him. Yet, as he looked out across the land, he couldn't help but feel some moral essence play itself out in that fiery basin—something as simple and as arcane as the dirt, he thought, but something deeper than man's mortal comprehension.

What he knew *about* life, he'd learned *from* life. And life had been a harsh teacher in this unyielding land. Like the cholla, the mesquite, and the sinewy wild grass, he'd held his spot against all elements, against all comers. *Thirty-five years.* . . .

He ran a hand across his weathered cheek and watched a lone coyote raise up as if from the bowels of the earth. It moved across the sand through a veil of dust—an ancient apparition—as the wind lessened, as scrub junipers lying sideways in submission now righted themselves and seemed to shake themselves out, and once more make their stand in the wavering heat. Thirty-five years of struggling upward, he thought, and now having to bow to the forces at work around him.

"Damn it, Doss." He hadn't meant to say the words aloud, but he did. Now that he realized it, he tossed a glance to Carl Statler and Joe Baylor, his two ranch hands sitting in the seat across from him. They stared at him with expectancy, a little surprised at the sound of his voice after such a long silence.

A second passed as a jet of steam streaked up and drifted past the window. Then Carl Statler managed to say, "Can't nobody blame you for what Doss done You've done the best you can, Matthew. He's a grown man now."

A grown man . . . Matthew Edding only nodded, if you could call it a nod. It was more like an uplift of his chin, a mere acknowledgment of Statler's words, but no attention paid to them, as he cut his eyes away from the two men and back out across the sand basin south of Humbly. What did these two men know about his son—about Doss being a grown man. At Doss's age, Matthew Edding had fought a terrible war, had stood face-to-face with gunmen in too many dirt streets to remember. He'd outrun a posse. He faced the Apache, and had cheated a gallows.

What had his son Doss ever done? Matthew Edding hated admitting it to himself, but what was his son good for? *Nothing.* . . . He let out a breath. Sure, Doss could ride, rope, and handle a herd as well as any man. Matthew had seen to it that his son learned these things no sooner than he was old enough to walk. He'd raised Doss as best he could on his own, after his wife, Sarah, had died giving birth to the boy. There'd been no woman to replace Sarah, not up on the high grasslands. Maybe that had been the problem. *Well, part of it anyway. . . .*

"Joe," he said without facing Baylor or Statler, "get on back there . . . unload the horses. This train leaves for Circle Wells in four hours. I plan on being *finished* here, and being *on* it."

"Sure, Boss," Joe Baylor said, already coming up from his seat, taking his rifle down from the overhead baggage rack.

When Baylor was out of sight, and as other passengers rustled and stirred upward from their seats, Carl Statler leaned slightly forward and said, "Boss, I didn't mean to speak out of turn. It's just that I can tell you're troubled about all this. The judge had no right asking ya to do such a thing—"

"The judge is a fair man," Matthew Edding said, cutting Statler short. "I can't fault him. In fact, this could have gone a lot worse."

"But Flores is a Mex," Carl Statler said, shaking his head. "It just don't seem *right*, a man like you having to make resta—resta—resta-whatever-the-hell ya call it."

"Resti-*tution*," Matthew Edding said, standing up from his seat, adjusting the silver latigo on his string tie. "And it is right that I do it. The Flores family are good people. Doss was wrong doing what he did. Now I've got to step in." He picked up his tall Stetson from the seat beside him and tapped it against Statler's leg. Statler stood up with a slight grunt. "Come on, Carl, let's get it done. This better be the last time I have to save Doss's behind."

"I'm sure it will be. Doss is just got a lot of gravel in his guts. What young man don't have at his age? This will be a lesson well learnt for him . . . don't ya reckon?"

Matthew Edding let his gaze drift once more out across the endless swirl of dust and heat before stepping into the aisle. "I hope so, Carl . . . I sure hope so."

CHAPTER 2

Once the doctor at Bannet had cleaned and dressed the bullet graze on the Ranger's side to Maria's satisfaction, the two of them headed out onto the upward slope of flatland north of town. For three hours that evening they'd followed the tracks of the Bannet stagecoach until the shadows of night grew long across the trail. They made camp alongside the wagon tracks, spent the night, and at first light the next morning set out again, the tracks leading them ever upward into the rocky badlands.

It was afternoon when they'd rounded a turn between two large boulders and the Ranger spotted the big dusty stagecoach horse grazing on a clump of grass alongside the trail. This was the safety horse that the stage always brought with it over the rough stretch of rocky terrain between Bannet and Circle Wells, in case one of their regular horses faltered on them, pitched a shoe, or picked up a sharp stone in its hoof.

From the looks of things, this extra horse was all that had survived whatever deadly game had played itself out here on the high switchbacks of the badlands hills.

With its broken lead rope pulled down sidewise and dangling in the dirt, the safety horse raised its head and sniffed toward the Ranger and Maria as they rode closer. Past the safety horse, the wheel tracks they'd been following snaked forward another forty feet, then took a sharp turn off the trail and over the edge of the canyon. *Found it* . . . The Ranger let out a breath, stilled himself, and prepared his mind for what came next.

He knew what to expect at the end of those wheel tracks. Indeed this *wasn't* his *first* missing stagecoach. Somewhere below on the canyon floor would lie the broken, splintered remains of man's toil and handiwork. Whatever care and craftsmanship had gone into creating the old high-spring Studebaker comfort coach would now be reduced to twisted steel and shattered rubble—only to mold with the earth around them.

Now that's handiwork from hell, he thought, looking around, trying to picture the dark scene the way it had happened. His mind caught the sound of gunfire and screams; he saw the frightened horses plunging out into clear thin air, their bodies writhing, their hooves struggling to take purchase beneath them but finding none. Nothing lay below them but a long drop into endless death as they whinnied loud and long to a silent sunlit sky.

As his dark thoughts and darker images settled, above the canyon, buzzards circled and dipped down out of sight. Beyond them in the far distance, a thin gray cloud streaked on the southern horizon. Weather coming, from a long ways off.

The horse he rode was a hard-boned white Spanish barb with a black circle around one eye. He stopped his horse on the trail, and turned back to Maria as she looked past him at the safety horse and shook her head. She heeled her bay gelding and rode forward to him.

"Looks like a rough one." He ran a gloved hand along the white barb's damp withers, patting it, settling it down. The white barb stepped high-hoofed in place, feeling edgy, wanting to move on. The Ranger stiffened the reins and checked it down.

Maria lifted the brim of her Stetson, let air under it,

then adjusted it back onto her head. "This is all so ugly, so senseless. If they only wanted money, why didn't they just take it and go?" She gestured a hand along the trail behind them. "Why all this?"

Envelopes from a spilled mailbag fluttered in the hot breeze. Pillaged baggage lay scattered along the trail. A hundred yards farther back, they'd found the opened strongbox, where in a last desperate attempt to save themselves, someone, most likely the shotgun rider, had hurled it from atop the stage.

The Ranger did not answer her, but instead only looked at her for a second before turning away. He heeled the white barb forward to a small dust-covered object lying in the middle of the trail where the stagecoach had taken its sharp turn. He stepped down as Maria moved her horse closer; when he'd picked up the crumpled rag doll and shook it free of dust, he almost wished he'd kicked it to the side—hidden it from her somehow.

She had asked him *why*. But to him, the *why* was not important. She knew *why* . . . and so did he. The men who'd forced that stagecoach off the edge of the canyon were not seasoned professionals. He pictured the faces of the three drunken cowboys he'd killed back in Bannet—how the one had bragged about robbing the stagecoach. *Stupid, violent . . . this Half Moon Gang.* Whoever they were, they were newcomers to crime, still learning their trade. *Sloppy at their work . . .*

Instead of *why*, he thought about *who*; and he tried to get an image of the kind of men who would do such a thing. These were all young men, he figured, young and wild and not very smart—like the ones back in Bannet. No doubt they'd fueled themselves on hard liquor first, something to raise their courage and at the same time keep them from seeing themselves for what they really were. These men would be snakes and cowards of the lowest order. He'd bet on it. They hadn't been at this gruesome business long—but they'd been at it long enough that *money alone* no longer mattered to them, if it ever had in the first place.

How did he come to see all this about them, from one lone safety horse and a set of stage tracks? He had no idea, gazing down at the dusty rag doll in his gloved hand, turning it, pressing it slightly, feeling its soft body give beneath his thumb. But this was the picture he conjured up from his instincts, and he wouldn't second-guess it. His instincts seldom steered him wrong. These men were strictly out for blood sport. Money had been only the twisted justification for their deed, merely the kindling that sparked the fire inside them.

Dangerous young men . . .

Now that their fire had spilled out and touched the world around them, it would feed on, raging out of control until someone dropped a hammer on them. Well, that would be his job—his *role* in this streak of madness. And he had no qualms about it, as he studied the rag doll in his gloved hands, its flat stitched smile, its blank button eyes. Somewhere below, over the edge and down on the canyon floor, lay the cold tiny hands that had nurtured this doll. He gazed away and swallowed hard, his expression hardening before turning back to Maria.

Maria had been with him only a short time. While she'd seen her share of outlaws and hard cases, she was still stunned by senseless brutality of this sort. But the Ranger had long lived close at hand to men like these. In a dark world of bloodshed and violence, he had long come to reconcile within himself, as all lawmen must, that there were no boundaries—no bottom to the lower depths of man's depravation.

He no longer asked himself *why*, and now he no longer wondered *who*. All he cared about now was *when*—when could he get these men in his gun sights.

The opportunity couldn't come soon enough to suit him.

Early on, as a younger man, when he'd taken on the mantle and calling of the law, he'd made up his mind that man's action and deeds would not shock or surprise him. It hadn't yet. Perhaps this resolve was all that had kept him alive many times throughout his life, up on the high badlands. To be shocked or surprised by the action of man left him at a disadvantage of sorts, he'd always thought. And in his business, he could not afford to be at a disadvantage.

He acknowledged that man at his best was by far God's most noble creature; yet he accepted that at his *worst*, man was the true incarnation of all demons the imagination could conjure up from its darkest depth. Man was still the only species he'd ever encountered who killed simply for the sake of killing. There lurked in man a taste for blood and carnage that went far beyond mere survival.

Somehow in man's twisted thinking, taking life became a means of righting wrongs done to him—wrongs both real and imagined. When fate, or luck, or circumstance acted in ill favor toward man, there lay a terrible dark force beneath man's outward personage that compelled him toward violence. What other animal possessed such a perverse nature as that? None that he knew of.

Only the devil. . . . The devil in skin, he thought; and he ran a gloved hand along the deep scar on his weathered cheek and gazed over to the edge of the canyon. Always, in confronting a gang of men such as these, he found that one stood out foremost in his evil and brutality. Sometimes it was the leader, but not always. With a young upstart gang like this, it could be someone that even the others least expected. Which one would it be? he wondered, already anticipating their capture, already trying to fashion an image of these men in his mind. But *why* they did it wasn't important. Not now, not ever.

Asking *why* was merely Maria's first step in accepting the reality of man's latest cruelty to his own kind. He had accepted that reality two days earlier, when the stage lines had wired Bannet and reported the stage missing. Four days meant more than a broken wheel or a downed animal, or even a rock slide or a closed trail. He had known what they would find out here before they'd ever left town.

"You can stay back here and hold the horses." He handed the rag doll up to her.

She held the doll for a second, staring at it with a hollow expression. Then she shook her head slowly. "No." She stepped down from her saddle and let out a breath. "I will see whatever there is to see here, and I will take that picture with me when we hunt these animals down."

"Suit yourself, then." The Ranger spoke under his breath, knowing that it would do no good to try and dissuade her.

They led their horses off the trail, following the wheel tracks right to the edge, where the weight of the stagecoach as it shot out into thin air had caused a break in a short pile of loose rocks. Overhead, the buzzards squawked and scolded and batted upward and hovered as if in protest—how dare they disturb what man's dark nature had provided.

"Watch your step," the Ranger cautioned. They'd left their horses back up the steep slope and moved down on foot to the next lower edge. Leaning forward, they looked farther down and saw the strewn wreckage: a dead horse here, another there, and the glistening swollen body of a man whose clothes had been shredded, ripped away, and slung aside by scavengers. The body of another man lay facedown, this one broken and twisted backward at the waist, a length of his raw white spine glistening in sunlight. A black swirl of flies droned above him.

At the next drop to the deep canyon, half of the crushed stagecoach lay on its side, teetering on the edge of the cliff. A woman's naked arm hung out and over the passenger step. The arm was blood-streaked and bruised, but not swollen like the bodies of the others. "I better get a rope and get down there. From the looks of her, she could still be alive."

Maria stood beside him staring, shaking her head slowly. "But—But how could she be?"

"Hey." He nudged her arm to get her started. "I don't know *how*. That's God's business. It's his game, we're just the players."

"*Sí*," she said, as if snapping out of a trance. "Perhaps if the woman is alive, so is the child."

They hurried, scurrying over loose rock and brush, back up to the horses. "Maybe, but let's not get our hopes up." The Ranger glanced back down at the stage, seeing it seem to slip forward an inch or more closer to the edge of the canyon.

At the horses, the Ranger took down the rope from his saddle, tied one end of it around an upthrust of rock, made two turns around his saddle horn across the back of his white barb, and pitched out the rest of the coils. With the rope from Maria's saddle tied to the end of it, doubling its length, he stepped down to the next level of the canyon. There, he took up the slack, threw the rope around his waist, and stepped down backward, feeding the rope hand over hand around him.

Above him, Maria steadied the white barb with one hand on his bridle and her other on the taut rope, as if gauging its strength through the tightness of it. Down the steeper slope the Ranger moved, through loose rock, through the cloud of flies and the strong smell of death beneath him, until he reached the battered half of the stagecoach.

"I'm there," he called out to Maria, his voice echoing across the open canyon, his boots back-stepping beneath him as loose rocks trickled down off the edge.

At the sound of the Ranger's voice, the woman's hand moved. It was only a slight flicker of movement. But that was enough. Hope surged in his chest. "She's alive!" he yelled out, quickly taking up the ten or so feet of loose rope beneath him, throwing another turn around his waist and back-hitching it.

Glancing up behind him, he saw where the wreckage had slid forty or more feet, perhaps all at once, perhaps over the course of time since the wreck.

"Hang on, ma'am, I'm coming." He scooted closer to the wreckage, and had just reached up toward the hand, when he saw the coach bob up and down just slightly up off the steep ground, suspended, held there only by its weight against a boulder at the canyon's edge. He heard a low groan from inside the wreckage and saw the woman's arm move, the hand trembling as it forced itself to reach out to him.

"Don't move, ma'am!" he yelled as the wreckage raised higher with a creaking sound, then settled back down an inch. Loose rock spilled from beneath it. *My God!* He dared not touch her yet, lest the shift of her weight send her tumbling over the edge.

He scooted forward, snatching up the broken brake handle from the ground—something to shore up the wreckage long enough to get her out—down to where the front of the coach lay tight against the boulder. He looked down over the edge. His breath stopped in his chest. *How in the world . . . ?*

The body of one of the team horses lay swaying against the canyon wall, wrapped in a tangle of traces and harnesses, impaled on the broken wagon tongue, the narrow strip of steel along the wooden tongue badly bent, some of its rivets gone, but still holding the tongue together. He shot a quick glance to where the back of the tongue and the front of the wrecked coach lay held together by a steel pin. The thick wooden plate on the bottom of the coach was separating farther from its nails and bolts with each bob and sway of the wreckage.

"Ma'am! Lay real still! I'll get you out!" He scooted back up from the edge to the rear of the wreckage, where the side of the coach lay crushed, no more than two feet high. He lay flat and looked in, across the splintered remains of a broken seat. And there he saw her lying sidelong and upward, her arm over the edge, still waiting for his hand. "I'm back here, ma'am! Don't move yet. It'll make the stage slide! Lie still!"

He started to ease himself into the crushed wreckage. But at the touch of his hand, it creaked upward, and settled forward another inch. He jerked back. "What is going on down there?" Maria called out from above him.

He didn't answer—there wasn't time. He tied a short loop in the end of the rope, lay back down, and pitched it inside toward the woman. "Ma'am, put your hand through the loop! Hurry! You've got to help me!"

Her voice was barely more than a whisper. "My— My daughter."

"*What?* Is the child in there? Is she *alive?*" The wreckage creaked up and down, and moved forward another inch. "Loop it around her!" Again the wreckage creaked and groaned. "Ma'am, hurry! Help me!"

He saw her arm raise, then fall, then reach over the broken seat toward the rope. The wreckage slipped forward an inch, then another. *No time!* He shot a glance up behind him toward the edge. "Hold tight, Maria! I'm going in!"

Maria heard him, but she had no idea what he

meant. She felt the weight on the rope tighten; and she steadied the white barb against it.

The Ranger flattened and crawled in between the crushed walls of the coach, the wreckage slipping farther when his weight went into it. "Grab the rope! Please!" he yelled at the woman, seeing her hand search back and forth, seeing her face, bloodstained and exhausted, barely conscious. He felt the wreckage jar forward and knew the boulder holding it was pulling free from the sandy ground.

He tried to crawl forward more, everything bobbing and sliding now—but her hand found the loop, and grasped onto it. *Thank God!* He snapped the loop tight around her wrist, and jerked back on the rope, pulling her toward him as the wreckage rose and settled forward.

"I've got you, ma'am!" For just a split-second, he saw her eyes, *pleading,* flashing an ember of hope at the sound of his words.

He felt the boulder pulling loose now, yanking the woman forward as the wreckage spilled away. This time it wouldn't stop. Gravity had it, free and clear. With all his weight and strength, he laid back on the rope in one last hard pull. Straightening back on the slope, he dug his boot heels in, the rope across him, pressing into his leg.

A last hard tug struck the rope tight with a loud twanging sound, like the snap of a bowstring. But he held firm, the tendons standing out in his neck, the rope digging into his gloved hands. Then he felt her weight ease upward above the edge as the wreckage crashed down the canyon wall with a rolling echo. Light as a feather now . . . and not a second too soon, he thought.

Above him, Maria felt the extra pull on the rope and saw the saddle slip sideways on the white barb's back. She drew the horse quarter-wise and forward, the horse knowing what to do and bracing himself. She let out a tense breath when the rope slackened a bit. But then her breath tightened again when she heard the Ranger yell out in a tortured voice, "Noooo! God, nooo!"

His words echoed along the canyon as Maria ran along the rope to the edge and looked down. He looked small down there, writhing on the steep slope of ground, his sombrero off and lying upside down beside him. He yelled loud and long again. For a second, she couldn't imagine why. But her eyes followed the rope to its end at the edge of the canyon; and for another second all she could do was wince and look away.

The Ranger rolled back and forth as he yelled, his arms tight across his stomach as if staving off terrible pain. "*Sante Madre*," she whispered and made the sign of the cross, then forced herself to look back at the end of the rope, at the woman's severed arm, where it lay pale and blood-streaked in the harsh glare of sunlight.

CHAPTER 3

Robbery hadn't entered Jimmy French's thoughts that morning when he'd hung his bowler hat on the wooden peg in the small cloakroom of the Cottonwood Bank—why should it? The bank had never been robbed. There was no reason to think it ever would be. Everybody knew that the bank owner and president, Mr. C. G. Hutchinson, had built the building with security foremost in mind.

Both teller windows in the Cottonwood Bank were secured with strong drop-forged steel bars shipped all the way from an ironworks in Pittsburgh, Pennsylvania. A time lock could be activated on the big Mosler safe with a simple flick of the wrist, making the vault impenetrable. On a shelf above each teller window, a Smith & Wesson .38 caliber pistol lay at arm's reach. Who in their right mind would consider such a thing?

Besides, everybody knew *everybody* in Cottonwood. Nothing ever happened here. Few strangers passed through. Now and then one of the ranchers in the area might bring some new ranch hand to town along with his regular crew. But they were all just hardworking drovers with no ambitions toward fast money. They weren't criminals. They drank and gambled and tossed off their wages while their boss took care of any business he needed to transact. Jimmy French doubted if any of them had ever seen the inside of the bank, let alone harbored any thoughts about robbing it.

It had been Jimmy's good fortune in life, going to work for the bank, finding a job that kept him indoors, out of the crushing heat. Banking was stable year-round work, rain or shine. As Mr. C. G. Hutchinson had told him a year earlier when he'd hired him for the position, banking was not merely a *job*, banking was a *career*.

And so it was.

All Jimmy had to do was keep his boots shined, keep his mind sharp, and learn everything he could about handling other people's money. A *responsible* position, a position of community trust. Banking was for Jimmy French the gentle, calm life he'd always sought for himself. The Cottonwood Bank was his place in the world.

He'd been small and frail as a child, and unlike other boys his age in the territory, he'd never adjusted to this harsh land. It was not his fault, and it most certainly wasn't his choosing. He simply wasn't right for this place and time, and he knew it. He was a timid young man, and this world frightened him. It always had.

Sure, he could handle a horse if he had to—and if it was well saddle-broken. He could chop wood. He could do most of the things that ordinary life here on the desert frontier required of him. But these things were not part of his makeup. They did not come natural to him as they should have.

Jimmy kept this way of life at arm's length as much as possible. His father had always called him a *fingertip* worker—this in a world carved out *by* and *for* the *two-fisted*, the rough and tumblers of this wild young land. *Well, so be it,* he thought. Banking had become his salvation, Mr. C. G. Hutchinson his mentor, his patron saint.

Today was a slow day, and Jimmy worked alone in the bank, sitting behind the desk going over the deposit ledger. When the bell above the door jingled and danced on its coiled spring, he stood up, smoothing a hand back along his hair, and walked over to the two dusty men who stepped up to the teller's window. With their faces shielded by their lowered hat brims, they milled slightly, one whispering something to the other under his breath.

"May I assist you, gentlemen?" Jimmy French smiled, and smoothed a hand down his vest.

"You sure can, you little pansy, you." Doss Edding and Dusty Charlie raised their faces, Doss speaking in a whiskey slur, a nasty grin on his dirty face. Dusty Charlie stood with a strange glint in his dark eyes. Jimmy was taken aback by Doss's words. He stopped cold and started to step back, the way a person shies from a growling dog. But then he froze, raising his hands instinctively as he heard the pistols cock and saw them swing up and level on his chest through the iron bars.

Right outside the bank, Little Tommy, Newt Babbage, and big Lew Harper sat their horses, holding the reins to the other two horses. Little Tommy fidgeted and wiped a dirty hand across his mouth. "Why don't I make a run over to the saloon and get us something to drink real quick? It don't take all three of us to hold these two horses, does it?"

"They told us to stay right here," big Lew Harper said. "So I reckon we better do like we're supposed to."

"Aw, hell, Lew," said Newt Babbage, the woman's hat hanging lopsided atop his Stetson. "It's going to be a long dry spell if we don't get something to drink here. Tommy'll hurry. Won't ya, Little Tommy?"

"I always do," Little Tommy said, grinning, his large, whiskey-lit eyes swimming back and forth behind his thick spectacles. "If I don't get some whiskey in me, I'll go crazy as a June bug. You had to show off, and finish off that last bottle . . . big tub of guts that you are." Even when Little Tommy Caldwell smiled, there was something unsettling about him, as if in a flick of an eye his smile could turn into something ugly and wrong, something vicious and out of control that a person would not see coming until it was too late to stop it.

"I did what anybody would do under the circumstances." Lew Harper nodded toward the saloon up the street. "Go on, then. Just don't be all day about it."

"This is *kind* of you, Lew—really, truly, *kind*," Little Tommy mocked him. "I mean, taking charge like this? When we all know that Doss and I are the ones what started this whole—"

"Tommy? Are you going or not? We're gonna *need* some whiskey before the day's over." Newt Babbage saw the same swirl of madness in Little Tommy that everybody else saw. His way of dealing with it was to not let it get started. The more Little Tommy was allowed to get out of control, the harder it became to settle him down. Little Tommy's mind was like a marble rattling in a tin bucket, Newt Babbage always thought. You had to grab the handle—keep the bucket steady.

"Yeah, all right." Little Tommy still smiled. "Just felt like we all need to know who's *who* here." He backed his horse a step and reined it around toward the saloon, his battered range pistol out of his waist and hanging in his dirty hand. See how they treated him if he let them? Harper had no right acting like he was in charge. The one thing Little Tommy didn't need— wouldn't stand for—was somebody stepping above him. The Half Moon Gang *had* been his and Doss Edding's idea from the start. He wasn't about to let peckerwoods like Harper and Babbage forget it . . .

Now, what's this? Sheriff Brady Martin stood with an oily cleaning rag in his hand; and he saw Little Tommy move along the dirt street with his range pistol out. A bit tipsy in his saddle, Brady Martin thought, watching Tommy through the dusty window of his office. He'd better go say something to this boy, get that gun out of his hand. Little Tommy Caldwell was dumber than a chunk of coal, but like any cowhand, he could get as wild as a buck deer on a bellyful of cheap liquor. Sheriff Martin didn't want to spend the afternoon hearing a store owner gripe about getting a window light shot out. This was an election year, after all.

He pitched the oily cleaning rag on the windowsill, swung his wide-brimmed hat off the rack beside the door, and stepped out onto the boardwalk. Before he'd stepped down into the dirt street and headed over toward Tommy, he saw the other two on their horses in front of the bank. Newt Babbage? Lew Harper? Yep, and they looked to be in no better shape than Little Tommy, Brady Martin thought. Damn it.

Newt Babbage wearing a woman's hat? What was this all about? Damn it! Here it was the middle of the day—the middle of the week. What are these boys doing here anyway . . . Well, he wouldn't stand for it. They couldn't sit there, drunk as they were, blocking the hitch rail to where none of the bank customers could use it. C. G. Hutchinson would throw a fit if he heard about this.

Inside the bank, Jimmy stood with his hands high, close to the .38 Smith & Wesson above the teller window. Doss Edding and Dusty Charlie, both drunk, trained cocked pistols on him. Jimmy wouldn't dare reach for that .38, though. The thought never even occurred to him. He wouldn't know how to use it—if he did, he couldn't just pull a trigger and shoot somebody, see their skin break open, blood flying everywhere.

With their free hands, Doss and Dusty Charlie snatched up the money Jimmy had taken from the teller drawer and laid up on the counter for them. "I said *all* the money, didn't I, huh?" Doss jiggled the pistol in his hand. "Now, get over and open that safe! You better *pray* there's plenty of money in it."

"But I—I can't, Doss." Jimmy French's voice trembled now that he realized this was really happening. "It's locked. Mr. Hutchinson locked it this morning, before leaving for Riley. He's going there to meet with your father, don't you know—"

"Shut your mouth about my daddy!" The rye whiskey had Doss's blood aboil. "You best open it, or I'll blow your head off. You think I'm fooling?"

"No, Doss, I believe you—but I can't open it, I swear. Why are you doing this anyway? For God's sake, Doss! You're able to get whatever you ask for here . . . you always have been!"

"It's none of your business *why*! Let us in there, you little sissy-boy. I got to see for myself. If you're lying, you're dead, right here on the spot!"

"I'll lose my job, Doss." Jimmy French's voice became a whimpering plea.

"Then, I'll just kill you anyway—"

"Let's take what we've got here and go, Doss!" Dusty Charlie cut a quick glance back over his shoulder at the front door.

"Hell, no!" Doss tightened his grip on the cocked pistol. "I never liked this sissy little peckerwood anyway."

"Wait, Doss, *please!* I'll do it! I'll let you in!" Jimmy felt his stomach rush upward. A sick weakness swept through him. He stepped over and unlocked the oak door.

"That's more like it," Doss said, pushing through, almost knocking Jimmy French off his feet. "Now, stay out of our way. You're being robbed by the *Half Moon Gang,* in case you're wondering!"

"The Half Moon Gang? I've never heard of—"

"You have now . . . so shut up!"

Outside, Sheriff Brady Martin stopped midway in the dirt street. Something felt wrong here all of a sudden—something about the look in Lew Harper's and Newt Babbage's eyes when he'd called out their names. Babbage raised a shotgun from across his lap.

Brady swung a glance at Little Tommy as Tommy staggered across the boardwalk into the saloon, leaving his horse unhitched, its reins dangling in the dirt. Then Brady flashed a glance back at the two sitting outside the bank, holding the reins to two *other* horses, one of them the big paint that belonged to Doss Edding. *What the . . . ? Was Doss Edding in there? Taking care of some business for his father? Then, why the shotgun? What was this?* He stood stunned for a second seeing the shotgun still coming up, in slow motion, from across Babbage's lap. *Aw, naw! Jesus, no! That shotgun . . . !*

Cold realization moved up the sheriff's spine. He fell back a step, his gun hand instinctively going down, reaching for the pistol at his hip, but feeling instead . . . an *empty holster? Oh, God!* His pistol lay back in his office, on his desk, where he'd been cleaning it earlier. The shotgun was up now, the butt coming to rest against Newt Babbage's shoulder, Babbage's thumb going over across the twin hammers, cocking them back.

Sheriff Martin broke back, turning—he had to get to his desk, had to get his pistol—ducking his head, and running toward his office as he yelled, "They're robbing the bank! Stop them! They're robbing the—" His words stopped short beneath the blast of the ten-gauge, the load of shot hitting him shoulder level in the back. The dirt street seemed to spin for a second, as Sheriff Martin spilled forward, breaking the hitch rail and landing half up on the boardwalk in a spray of blood.

A woman screamed. Along the streets heads poked

out of open doors. George Frocke, the mercantile owner, heard Brady Martin call out before the shotgun stopped him. He ran out and saw the sheriff's body lying broken on the dirt street. "Oh, Lord, no!" He ran back inside, jerked a rifle from beneath his counter, and shoved bullets in it with trembling fingers.

"What was *that?*" His wife, Emma, called out, running from their living quarters behind the store.

"A bank robbery! They shot Sheriff Martin! Stay down out of sight!"

"They'll kill you, George! You can't go out there! George!" She tried to grab his arm, but he pulled free.

"The heck I can't!"

In the bank, Doss and Dusty Charlie swung toward the sound of the shotgun. "Well, dang it all to hell!" Doss ran around to the front window, looked out, and saw the nervous horses stepping high-hoofed in place, Newt Babbage fanning the shotgun back and forth along the quickly emptied street. A skinny hound came forward from under the boardwalk across the street, barking, its hackles up, lunging at the horses' hooves. "Newt's killed ole Brady deader'n a mackerel," Doss called back to Dusty Charlie, seeing the sheriff's body across the street.

Lew Harper swung his horse around, saw Doss through the bank window, and yelled, "Hurry up in there! Let's get out of here!" Beside him, Newt's horse reared, nearly spilling him, as the hound lunged in and out between its hooves. "You damn flea-bit hound!" Newt brought the shotgun up into play, shooting the dog as his horse touched back down and spun a turn beneath him.

Doss turned, running back behind the counter. "Let's go! Newt's shooting up the town . . . dogs and all!"

"What about him?" Dusty Charlie asked, nudging his pistol toward Jimmy French, Jimmy's face trembling, stark-white. A cold string of saliva swung from his chin. *Don't let them kill me! Don't let them kill me! Please, God! Please, God!*

"I meant to stick him in the safe—" Doss shot a cold gaze into Jimmy's eyes. "You *sure* you can't open it? Tell the truth!"

"No, Doss, I swear!" Jimmy's voice quivered. *Please, God . . . Please, God . . . Please, God!*

"All right, then, come on." He jerked Jimmy forward and shoved him through the doorway. "You're coming with us, you sissy *peckerwood!*"

"That's crazy, Doss!" Dusty Charlie yelled, but even as he did, he helped Doss grab Jimmy and pull him toward the door.

At the saloon, Little Tommy had heard the first blast of the shotgun as the bartender stood four bottles of rye on the bar. "Uh-oh," he'd said, as the bartender and the other two customers flinched at the sound of the blast. "Got to go. Put these on my tab, Lawrence. I'll pay you my next time through. You be sure and remind me."

He snatched up the bottles in the crook of his arm, the pistol still in his hand.

"What's going on out there?" The bartender gave him a suspicious look. "You've got no tab here, Little Tommy Caldwell!" He'd switched his gaze past Tommy and out toward the street. Another blast of the shotgun in the street sent him reaching down under the bar for his sawed-off ten-gauge shotgun. "I'll get to the bottom of this . . . you bet!"

"I bet ya don't." As he raised up, Tommy shot him once, between the eyes, the bullet streaming a red ribbon of blood out the back of his head and breaking the big mirror on the wall. The shotgun flew away and knocked out a stack of clean shot glasses.

"Lord God! Tommy!" The two old men stood stunned, their mouths gaping.

"What're ya'll *looking at*?" Tommy's large eyes swam behind his thick spectacles.

"Tommy, you just killed a man—ole Lawrence! He never hurt a soul in his life!"

"I know that! I'll *shoot you* too." And he did. He shot them both, one in the leg, the other in the shoulder. Then he turned and ran, laughing, out onto the boardwalk, as the two old men sagged along the bar.

"Come on, Tommy," Lew Harper shouted, waving his pistol back and forth, the reins to the two horses being snatched from his hands as Dusty Charlie grabbed them.

"He can't see shit," Lew said to Newt Babbage. He called out to Tommy again as Tommy hit the street, snatching up his reins, and swinging up, dropping a bottle of whiskey on his way.

A rifle shot rang out from somewhere across the street and shattered the bank window. "Cover me," Doss called out; and in a crouch, shoving Jimmy French before him, he hurried across the dirt street and snatched the reins to the dead sheriff's big roan gelding from around the hitch rail. The animal whinnied, pulling away from the sound of gunfire.

"Don't shoot," a voice called out from along the street, "they've got the bank teller! They're holding Jimmy French!"

Tommy moved his horse along the street close to the boardwalk, taking his time, his arm full of whiskey bottles, his pistol waving back and forth. At the mercantile store, George Frocke raised up from behind a barrel. "Tommy, get down, boy! What's wrong with you? They're robbing the bank!"

"You don't *say*?" Tommy laughed, shot him once in the chest, then still laughing, kicked his horse forward to the others. "You see ole George Frocke back there? That idiot tried to warn me—told me there was a *robbery* going on. Can you believe that?" A shot rang out from an upstairs window across the street. "I shot his damn heart out."

"Come on, Tommy! Let's go!" Lew Harper fired his pistol at the window.

"Don't shoot, *for God's sake*," the voice called out again. "You'll hit the teller! Everybody hold your fire!"

"He's right," Doss yelled out down the dirt street. "Let's not get Jimmy killed here. This is a dangerous bunch. Let 'em go!" Then he leaned close to Jimmy French's ear, Jimmy murmuring mindlessly, *Please, God . . . Please, God,* praying over and over under his breath.

"Come on, *pretty* Jimmy," Doss sneered, shoving Jimmy French up on the horse and climbing up behind him. "You're riding with me today, all comfy-cozy like."

Even in the midst of the melee, Little Tommy Caldwell had managed to open a bottle of whiskey, pulling the cork with his teeth while his horse spun in the street. As his horse settled, he blew the cork away—*Where's Doss?*—threw back a swig, and looked along the street just as Doss sidled up to him on the dead sheriff's roan. "Looky here," Little Tommy said. "There's half a dozen guns pointed at us right now. You worried about it?"

"No. I ain't worried." Doss Edding smiled a crooked whiskey smile.

"Let's ride," Dusty Charlie said, "while they're still afraid of hitting the bank teller!"

"All of you throw down your guns," called a voice from across the street. "Turn Jimmy loose. We *know* every one of you. You won't get away with this."

"You go straight to hell," Little Tommy bellowed at the empty street and fired three quick rounds.

"I'm telling your daddy on you, Doss Edding," a woman's voice cried out. "You oughta be ashamed of yourself—"

"Damn you!" Doss gigged his horse forward, into the middle of the street, raising his pistol to Jimmy French's head. "Don't you see what's going on here? Do you want this boy to die? Because he will, sure as hell!"

Jimmy French saw the faces. They peeped from around corners of buildings, out of shadowed doorways along the boardwalk. He saw the fear and pity in their eyes, him sitting helpless, a cocked pistol against his head, roughly pushed to one side.

"We're leaving here!" Doss yelled, his sweaty left arm up around Jimmy's chest, his hand tight on the reins, holding Jimmy pinned against his chest. Jimmy could smell the sour whiskey on Doss's breath, close to his ear. Jimmy felt sick, scared, helpless; but most of all he felt ashamed—the townsfolk seeing him this way.

"Yeah! We're leaving!" Little Tommy yelled. "And we dare any of you pig lickers to try and stop us!"

Doss waited for another second as silence fell along the street. The others had moved their horses in behind Doss, all of them using Jimmy French as a shield now. "Now, that's more like it," Doss yelled along the dirt street. "Everybody stay down till we're gone!"

Little Tommy added, "All of you remember . . . you've just been visited by the Half Moon Gang! It's something you can tell your grandchildren about someday."

Two townsmen lay behind a water trough up the street with pistols in their hands. "What'd Little Tommy say? The *have what* gang?" one asked the other.

"I don't know," the other man shrugged, "something about a *half-moon*? I've never heard of them. Bunch of drunken knuckleheads, if you ask me—Doss strutting around like he's *something*, in that ole Civil War coat. They'll all hang for this."

"Let's go, Doss," Dusty Charlie said in a hushed voice, "before they get to feeling bold again."

"Yeah." Little Tommy laughed, his arm cradling the bottles of rye whiskey. "While they're all too afraid to shoot at us."

"Thank *sister-boy* here for that," Doss said, chuckling. "I knew he'd come in handy for something." He grinned and pressed his sweaty jaw against Jimmy's, and rubbed it up and down, the pistol still cocked against Jimmy's head. "We might just have us a *bunch* of fun with *pretty* Jimmy before we kill him. Bet you'd like that, wouldn't ya?"

They turned their horses and pounded out of town, whooping and firing back as they left. Before their dust had settled, the townsfolk were out in the street, two of them running over to the wife of the dead clerk, who sat wailing, cradling his head in her bloody lap.

"Have you ever in your *life* . . ." An old man stood in the middle of the street, scratching his weathered jaw. A shotgun hung in his hand. "Them boys have lost their minds."

"What in God's name made them do such a thing?" A woman asked, stepping up with a small pistol in her hand. "It ain't been no time since that Doss boy was buying rock candy from me . . . his pa toting him around on his shoulder, and all."

"Sheriff Martin's dead," said a man, running out from where Sheriff Brady Martin lay in a dark pool of blood. "I swear, I had just been talking to him less than an hour ago."

"I expect we need to get up a posse, don't we," the old man said, still scratching his jaw.

"Little Tommy kilt George Frocke! Kilt Lawrence White in his own saloon, and shot the two ole book peddlers, Nick and Vernon, all to hell," a young man said, running up, his breath heaving.

"Are they still alive?" the woman asked, poking her pistol down into her apron pocket.

"Yeah, but they're wounded, and madder than hell. Vernon said they weren't bothering a soul—just looking at some picture books they was wanting to sell in the saloon. Little Tommy shot 'em cause they *looked* at him."

"This ain't right." The old man shook his head. "We best get up a posse . . . anybody think so?"

"I don't hardly know what to do," the young man said, still breathing heavy, "with Brady Martin dead and all."

"You've no business chasing out after that bunch of murderers," the woman said. "Judge Lodge'll be here tomorrow. You better hear what he says first."

"You suppose so, Wanda? Just wait for the judge?" The old man cradled his shotgun and let out a resigned breath.

"Yep. Wait for him." She hiked her dress and apron, and turned in the street toward the sound of the woman wailing outside the mercantile. "Right now, we've got ourselves some *serious* burying to do here."

CHAPTER 4

For a long time that evening, the Ranger had sat in silence staring out across the wide canyon. Although it must have been the right thing to do, it seemed strange to Maria that he had taken the woman's arm, wrapped it in a shawl, and buried it alongside the trail, near the point where the stagecoach had gone off the cliff. Then he had taken a seat on a rock and had made no effort toward gathering their ropes, or striking a camp, or anything else. When Maria had done these things herself, she went to him and said, "It was not your fault, you know."

"Fault is not what's on my mind," he answered without turning his eyes from the gaping void before him. Somewhere, five hundred feet below them at the bottom of a sheer rock wall lay the shattered remains of the stage and its contents. "But I'll always wonder if maybe I could have saved her . . . had I done it different."

"Do not wonder," she said. She'd started to lay a hand on his shoulder. But she stopped herself. "What was to be, had to be. We arrived only in time to witness it, not to change it."

"That's true, as it turns out," he said, still not facing her, his gray sombrero hanging from his hand beside him, a light breeze lifting a strand of his hair. He raised a corner of his wide bandanna and ran it across his face. "I keep seeing that last look in her eyes . . . me telling her I'd get her out of there. She mentioned her daughter . . ." He stopped speaking and shook his head slowly.

A silence passed as evening shadows drew long across the sand, scrub mesquite, and juniper. At length Maria crossed her arms, and said in a quiet tone, "I have built a fire and boiled some tea. We must rest tonight, and get an early start back come morning." She paused for a second, then added, "Unless you think we should stay on the trail, and track this Half Moon Gang."

Only then did his face turn from the canyon to her, a glint of something sharp and dark in his eyes, his eyes mantled beneath his lowered brow. "Oh . . . I think it's safe to say, I'll be on this trail until it ends."

"I thought so." She nodded, turning south, hearing the faint sound of thunder somewhere along the far edge of the earth. Then she turned back. "You realize your jurisdiction ends less than a hundred miles north of here?"

"Really? I hadn't thought about it. But it doesn't matter. In a case like this nobody cares about jurisdiction." With that he stood up, and they walked back along the trail to where the horses stood picketed among pale clumps of grass near a small fire. On their way, the Ranger lifted his face to the sky in the direction of the looming dark cloud on the southern horizon. "Feels good like this, right before a storm. The breeze stays warmer well into the night."

"*Sí.*" Maria lifted her face and felt the breeze push her hair back. After a moment of silence, she mentioned in a quiet voice that since they were supposed to be keeping an eye on Bannet while the sheriff went to Humbly for medical treatment, they could contact the Ranger outpost and have someone else sent out to deal with the Half Moon Gang.

"Now, why on earth would you say a thing like

that?" He watched her as they both sat down near the low fire.

"Because I have never before seen you act the way you acted back there. It frightened me."

"Frightened you? I can't believe that. Nothing frightens you."

"Oh? Well, you are wrong. I get frightened . . . like everyone else. And when I saw you sit and stare and act as if you would never get up again . . . that frightened me."

"I'll be all right—I mean, I *am* all right. It just threw me for a loop there. Taking a life is something I've learned to reconcile with myself. Saving a life is something I've come to think of as God putting me in the right place at the right time. But *losing* a life that way? Feeling it slip out of my hands? That's a whole different thing. There's nothing I can think of that's ever made me feel so small and helpless. For a while there, it was as if I didn't exist—not in any real way. Not in any way that mattered."

"But now that feeling has passed and you are free of it? Now it will not bother you again?"

"I'd be lying if I said it won't come to my mind. But I'll be all right with it. That's all I can tell you."

"All right. Then, we will say no more about it . . . unless you need to."

"I don't need to. All I need is to get on this trail before it gets too cold to follow."

They drank tea and ate warm beans from two small tins the Ranger had taken from his saddlebags and opened with his boot knife, then heated above the low fire. After they'd finished their food and poured more tea, they sat quietly in the small circle of firelight with a blanket laid out between them. On her side of the blanket, Maria laid out her rifle, inspected it, and began wiping it down with a cloth. On the Ranger's side, he'd already taken out his big pistol and broken it apart.

Maria watched him as he picked up the pistol cylinder and rolled it back and forth between the palms of his hands and down his forearm, looking down through it into the firelight. She continued wiping the barrel of her rifle; and when he had examined and cleaned each part of the pistol and clicked it back together, he looked up at her and said, "These are all young men we'll be looking for."

"Oh?" She didn't want to remind him that he'd said that before. Instead she sat quietly and watched him raise the pistol near his ear.

"Yep. They're all young and crazy"—the Ranger listened to the metallic click of each turn of the cylinder beneath his thumb—"and they're all out to prove something to one another . . . to *themselves*, you could say." He studied the pistol in his hand, turning it back and forth in the glow of fire. "They've been thieving for a while. But I'd bet the Bannet stagecoach was the first killing they've done."

She sighed and cradled the rifle across her lap. "Then it will not be their last."

"No," he said. "They've gotten their taste of killing. Now they'll go on with it till we stop them." He loaded his pistol, holstered it, and reached around for the big Swiss rifle leaning against a rock. "Stealing was just their way into the game. Their way of seeing what they could stomach." He brought the rifle around and laid it on the blanket, firelight shimmering on the smooth stock. "The taking of inanimate *things* was only practice for these boys. It's the taking of *life* that's fanning their fire."

Maria only listened as he worked this out in his mind; and as she listened, she knew that while most of what he was saying would turn out to be true, he spoke about it to keep from thinking about the woman

in the crushed stagecoach, and the bodies that lay cold
and starkly exposed, before heaven and earth on the
canyon floor.

"I thought we were going to shoot everybody in Cottonwood?" Little Tommy Caldwell spoke to Doss Edding as they stepped down from their winded horses.
"Ain't that what you said we'd do?"

Somewhere along the trail, they'd stopped long
enough for Dusty Charlie to shinny up a telegraph
pole and cut the wires running out of Cottonwood.
While the others waited, Doss switched over to his
own horse. He'd tied Jimmy French's hands together
with a strip of rawhide and led him along on the dead
sheriff's roan beside him. For miles, Jimmy had
flopped up and down and swayed back and forth in
the saddle. Now Doss raised a boot and kicked Jimmy
off into the sand, then stepped down with the others.

"That's what I might've *said*, but it didn't work out
that way, *all right*?" Doss's voice sounded testy and
sharp, thick with rye whiskey. "We will next time,
though." He stepped around his horse to where
Jimmy French lay coughing in a swirl of dust. "Right,
pretty Jimmy?" Doss dragged him to his feet, saying,
"Come on, now," threw an arm around his neck, and
squeezed him down in a headlock until Jimmy bowed
at the waist and followed him along, back to where the
others stood passing around a bottle.

"What're we going to do with this idiot?" Newt Babbage asked Doss, passing the bottle on to Dusty Charlie. The woman's hat now stood sideways against the
crown of his Stetson, covered with dust.

Tommy Caldwell nodded toward a tall cactus.
"Want to take his britches down, tie him to that *cacti*
yonder, and shoot at his little wee-wee?" The others
laughed. Little Tommy moved around behind Jimmy,
reached between his legs, grabbed his crotch, and

shook him back and forth. "Except I bet he *ain't* even got no *wee-wee!*" He hooted, turned Jimmy's crotch loose, and drove a fist into Jimmy's stomach, sending him gasping to his knees. "Whooie! Get you *some*, Jimmy, Jimmy, *Jimmy!*" Tommy taunted him.

Dusty Charlie shook his head, threw back a drink of whiskey, and said to the others, "We better get serious here, and figure what we're doing next. In case you don't realize it, the Half Moon Gang is out in the open now. We've declared ourselves murderers and fugitives. They ain't going to just forget what we done back there."

Doss glared at him, his eyes red-rimmed and blurred. "First they got to prove we done it."

"Prove we done it?" Dusty Charlie just stared at him in disbelief. So did the others, even Little Tommy.

"Dang it all, Doss," said Newt Babbage, "they seen every last one of us . . . they *know* every one of us."

Doss's face reddened. "Seeing and knowing is one thing. *Proving* something is a different thing altogether." He tapped a finger to his head, his eyes wide and fiery. "I've been thinking a lot lately, about how the law works? You see, the law ain't all that smart. All we got to do is stick together, and it's their word agin ours. We all swear for one another that we were somewhere else at the time, and they can't do a thing!" He spread a crafty grin.

The others gazed back and forth with puzzled expressions, until Lew Harper shook his big head. "Lord, boys, we're as good as hung."

"I'm telling you, it'll *work*," Doss said. He shoved Jimmy with a boot, sending him sprawling to the ground, where he landed with a grunt. "The James Gang has been doing it this way for years," Doss added. "You never hear of them going to jail, do you?"

The others still stared, puzzled. Little Tommy grinned; and while he really hadn't given it any thought, he was always eager to agree with Doss Edding. "He's got a point there. If the Jameses can do it that way, so can we."

"Jesus," Dusty Charlie whispered under his breath, turning and walking his horse away from the others.

"But we *ain't* the James Gang," Newt Babbage said. "The James Gang ain't never been *caught*."

Doss glanced back and forth among them, his head starting to hurt, feeling pressured. "Then, neither will we," he said. "We're the Half Moon Gang from now on. We just got to stick to it."

"Danged right," Little Tommy said, taking a bottle from Lew Harper's hand and tossing back a drink. Whiskey sloshed down his chin. "Too late to turn back now." He ran a dirty hand across his lips, looking back and forth. "Anybody got anything to eat?"

They all looked at one another again. Newt Babbage shrugged and said, "I've got a few coffee beans in my saddlebags, if anybody feels like busting 'em up. We can boil us up a pot."

"What about ole *sister-boy* here," Little Tommy said, nudging Jimmy French with the toe of his boot. "Want me to shoot him? It'd be less trouble."

"Naw, leave him be for now," Doss said. "We'll have us some fun with him later. He ain't gonna be no trouble. He's scared to fart above a whisper."

Jimmy French lay in a ball on his side, his tied wrists up in front of his dirty, sweat-streaked face. He'd managed to stop murmuring to himself, but still couldn't control his trembling. They meant to kill him. He was sure of it. And from the things Doss kept saying, he could only imagine what terrible things they would do to him first. He dared not move a muscle or let them see him looking at them. They were completely crazy, he thought, and the least little thing might send them into a bloodletting rage.

He listened to them talk back and forth as they picketed their horses to graze, and gathered and broke kindling for a fire. As darkness set in, he saw their faces in the glow of the flickering fire. The whiskey bottles passed back and forth, and soon he heard an empty one hurl toward him and crash to the ground near his head. They laughed and talked about a stagecoach they'd run off the edge of a canyon, getting real excited about a woman screaming from inside it.

Jimmy shivered in the chilly night outside the warmth of the fire; and only as the coolness of night set in did he feel how wet the rawhide on his wrists had become from his sweat throughout the day. They felt cold and clammy now. He stretched his hands against them and felt them give. His heart pounded hard in his chest. What if they saw what he'd done? Almost against his will, he stretched the strips some more, until he was sure they could slip over his hands, if he dared risk it.

Late into the night, after another empty bottle had clinked against the ground, he slipped his hands free and lay breathless for a second. At the fire, the only ones still awake were Doss and Little Tommy. And in a moment, Doss stood up on drunken legs, and said, "Go on and turn in, Tommy. I'm gonna check on my girlfriend."

"Me too . . ." But Little Tommy made no effort to get up. His head only bobbed on his chest, and fell sideways.

Jimmy watched as Doss staggered over and stood above him, chuckling under his breath as he adjusted his double holster belt, the butts of the two pistols glistening in the darkness. Jimmy shuddered and clenched his jaws, ready to leap up and make a run for it, his fear the only thing keeping him from doing it.

"I hate boys like you, *pretty* Jimmy," Doss whispered, stooping down beside him, his right hand resting on a pistol butt. "Little puny-looking peckerwoods . . .

running around, just *looking* for it." His words slurred, thick-coated in rye whiskey. He weaved back and forth on his haunches, one hand still on his gun, his other coming out to grip Jimmy's dirt-streaked cheek harshly. "Well, now you're gonna *get* it," Doss spat at him.

Looking for it? Gonna get it . . . ? Doss was insane! Jimmy had to make a move, whether he lived or died. As Doss leaned his face down to Jimmy's, Jimmy eased a trembling hand to the butt of Doss's free pistol just beneath Doss's sight.

Jimmy heard the sound of the pistol barrel slice through the air, heard it crack hard against the side of Doss's head, right on his temple. He'd never raised a hand against anyone in his life—for a second he didn't realize he'd actually done it. But Doss let out a deep grunt and fell slack atop of him. Jimmy froze for a second, his breath tight in his chest, certain that now the whole camp would rise up from their drunken sleep and kill him. *Oh, God!*

But none of the others stirred. He shuddered and trembled, and somehow forced himself to roll Doss off of him. Rolling away with Doss's pistol in his hand, he scrambled up to his feet as he made his way, stumbling and falling toward the picketed horses. "The hell's going on?" A slurred voice called out from the fire. *Oh, God! Oh, God!* He fumbled with the rope hobble on the hoofs of the first horse he came to. "Doss? What're you doing?" the drunken voice called out.

In the darkness, when the hobble fell free, Jimmy raised up and found the bit hanging loose down the horse's jaw. He slipped the bit into its mouth, reached up, fastened the loose side of the bridle, and swung himself up into the saddle. "Help . . . me," Doss Edding called out to the others in the darkness, "he's . . . got away." Jimmy batted his heels to the horse's sides, his feet not even in the stirrups, and reined it out across the dark night.

"There he *goes!*" Little Tommy yelled in a drunken voice, coming up to his feet, his pistol raised out of his holster. "He's getting away!" He staggered, and emptied his pistol toward the sound of fleeing hoofbeats, hearing Jimmy French let out a loud yelp.

"Jesus!" Dusty Charlie leapt up to his feet. So did the others, ducking sideways as Little Tommy's pistol exploded within their midst. "What's going on?"

"Jimmy's kilt Doss and got away!" big Lew Harper yelled, scrambling at his feet for his rifle.

"Hold on, damn it!" Dusty Charlie shoved his way past Lew Harper and Newt Babbage, and ran over to where Doss wobbled on his knees, a ribbon of blood streaming down the back of his neck. Dusty Charlie slid to a halt, his mouth gaping as Doss fell over on his side. "My God, Doss . . . what're you doing out here?"

"Nev— Never mind me. Jimmy's getting away." He wallowed back up on his knees, and to his feet, clutching his gun belt at his waist. Dusty Charlie just stared, with his pistol half raised.

"He didn't get nowhere's," Little Tommy said, him and the others coming over to gather and stare at Doss Edding. "I hit him a good one."

"You sure?" Newt Babbage asked, wiping a hand on his face, trying to wake up. "You can't see shit, you know."

Little Tommy's eyes looked beady and small without his thick spectacles. "Damn right, I'm sure—heard him holler. Go out there and see for yourself."

As they stared at Doss Edding, he stood straightening his trousers, and said, "He snuck one of my pistols and cracked me with it—" Doss's words stopped short, trembling. "Why? You saying I'm *lying?*" His eyes darted across the others, wide and desperate-looking in the darkness. "You accusing me of something here? Saying there's something wrong with—"

"Easy, now, Doss," Dusty Charlie said, seeing

Doss's left hand go to his side, that holster empty. "Ain't nobody said *nothing* . . . but *you*." Dusty Charlie spread his hands, looking at the others. They milled, avoiding Doss's wild-eyed stare.

"I swear, Doss," Newt Babbage said, quietly, after a tense silence, rubbing his nose and looking down. "Don't know what gets into you sometimes."

"Damn you all!" Doss yelled. "Nothing's gotten into me! Somebody get out there and drag Jimmy back in here! Hang him from a tree! If he's alive, cut his damn throat!"

The others shied back a step. Big Lew Harper eased over to the fire and looked around for some whiskey. He wasn't about to go traipsing out looking for Jimmy French. If Doss wanted him, let Doss go get him. Harper was sobering up some now, his head pounding like a drum inside. He'd started having second thoughts about this whole Half Moon idea.

Little Tommy and Doss Edding went searching for Jimmy French out into the desert night, calling out his name, while the others moved back close around the fire, each of them avoiding the question in each other's eyes, until Dusty Charlie walked back into their midst. "He was drunk, all right. He went to take a jake, and Jimmy French got the drop on him. Let's not make a *thing* out of it. Get on out there and help them find that boy. He couldn't go far, if Tommy put a bullet in him."

But Jimmy French had not even slowed down when one of the bullets from Little Tommy's pistol sliced through his side. Having found his stirrups, he laid forward on the dead sheriff's roan and pounded out across the sand. The sharp pain in his side racked throughout him with each rise and fall of the horse; but he dared not slow down. And he dared not swing around and head back for Cottonwood, lest Doss and the others be spread out in search for him.

Blood ran warm down his side, and he had little

doubt that he would soon die in the saddle. Before him in the darkness, as if in wait, lay gullies and canyons that could swallow horse and rider straight down, hundreds of feet. Out there prowled dark creatures of his every nightmare, desert creatures of venomous fang and deadly claw who harbored nothing for man save for the taste of his flesh. Yet he rode headlong into these things with no hesitation, throughout the night, finding the possibility of what *might* lie ahead no less formidable than what he *knew* lay behind him.

At dawn, the big roan had slowed to an aimless walk, with Jimmy lying limp on its back, one rein dangling, dragging loose across the sandy ground. When the horse found water in a small rock basin and leaned down to drink, Jimmy pitched forward and out of the saddle, landing in a splash at the horse's hoofs. The horse sidled off a step, continuing to draw water as Jimmy came to with a start, wallowing and thrashing until he brought himself up onto dry sand.

He spit and strangled, and coughed up sandy water. Then, running a trembling hand over his wet face, he looked around, feeling dizzy and weak from his loss of blood. *Jesus.* . . . He'd made it! Still alive! It was hard to imagine that in spite of all that happened the night before, he'd lived somehow. He almost doubted it at first, until he looked up and saw in the east the thin silver glow along the far horizon where morning spread its light, quiet and still. *Thank you, thank you, Jesus* . . .

And he collapsed back onto the ground, wet and shivering, feeling warm blood start to ooze once more—brought on by his fall from the horse. He could have laid there for hours, but when his hand went to the reopened wound and came back up sticky and covered with fresh blood, he forced himself up onto his knees, feeling his heart start to race in fear.

Easy, now. Be calm . . . He hooked a hand into one of the stirrups and pulled himself up. *Don't panic. Not*

now. He looked back into the purple darkness of
dawn. Somewhere far back and to the south, a low
rumble of thunder hung in the sky. They could be
close right now, he thought, somewhere back there, on
my trail. A picture of Doss Edding's face flashed
through his mind—wild-eyed, drunk, and crazy. *Can't
stop now . . . got to keep moving*. The town of Bannet lay
at least a day's ride south of him. He had to make it
there. Had to get help, to stay alive. How long did it
take for a person to bleed to death? he thought as he
pressed on.

CHAPTER 5

Nobody in their right mind would put a horse forward that hard, the Ranger thought. Not in this kind of heat. He gazed down through mid-morning sunlight at the long drifting wake of dust. From where he and Maria stood atop a smooth rock shelf, the sand flats below swirled and wavered like a white-hot griddle. "Something's bad wrong down there," he said. "Look how he's pushing that poor animal."

When he looked at Maria beside him, she nodded, still gazing down. She brushed a gloved hand across her face, pushing aside a loose strand of dark hair. "Do you suppose this is one of the killers we're tracking?"

"Could be." The Ranger narrowed his gaze on the distant figure. "We'll soon find out."

"*Sí*. We'll find out." Maria's voice sounded resolved; and she turned with her reins in her hand, mounted her bay gelding, and gave it heel.

Below them on the flats, the big roan pounded on, sweat-streaked and blowing white froth. Jimmy French saw nothing before him, save for the endless sandy earth, the rising pulse of heat on the desert floor. And even these things stood tilted and pitched before him, his eyes unable to fix them into place. There was no blood left in his veins, he thought, feeling the beat of his heart try to lift something up inside him—something that simply wasn't there. He was dying now. He was certain of it.

Earlier, at dawn, beside the rock basin, he thought he might have beaten death. But he'd been wrong, merely denying it to himself. Death had him, even then, and had only been playing with him. Now that he knew he was dying—and had accepted it—death was not nearly as bad as Jimmy French had always imagined it would be.

The closer he drew toward death's dark scythe, the more clearly he came to understanding death. There was nothing to fear; and if there was nothing to fear *now*, right here, where death stood so close before him . . . then, had there ever been reason to fear death throughout his short life? *No.* He understood that now.

The roan's hoofbeat fell steady and straight beneath him. He swayed, clinging to the saddle horn with both hands.

Last night, when the bullet had first sliced through his side, terror came upon him in a crushing wave. So had pain. But no longer. All he'd felt for the past few moments had been some false sense of purpose that commanded him to live; and even that inner force had weakened, less important now as he drifted in and out of consciousness.

All he felt was some sense of lingering regret. There were things he'd done that he wished he *hadn't*. Like letting Doss Edding and Dusty Charlie back behind the counter. He'd only done it out of fear for his life; as it turned out, hadn't they killed him anyway?

Better he should have died there in the bank, taking his chances, making his stand, maybe reaching for the pistol above the teller window. He might have stopped everything right there, and saved some good people's lives at the same time. And so what if he'd failed—it would still have saved him the suffering, the pain, the humiliation. If he could only go back, do it all over. But he couldn't, of course. Living further was out of the question.

It came to him as he swayed in the saddle and felt the horse pounding on, his bloody shirt sticking to his wounded side, that only in these last moments of life had he come to know and appreciate the meaning of living. It seemed unfair, ironic, that now, as all his fears had vanished behind him in the dark night shadows, with those fears went life itself. Life was terribly unfair . . . leastwise for the living, he thought.

Well, what did it matter? What had anything *ever* mattered? He would die out here, from a bullet wound in his side. Eventually, he supposed, someone would find his dry-weathered remains, perhaps days or weeks from now. Jimmy French, the timid young man who'd worked at the Cottonwood Bank. Or perhaps they *wouldn't* find him that soon. Perhaps a thousand years would pass before anyone found his ancient bones—someone in the distant future, someone foreign to this world as he knew it. They would have no idea who he'd been, or what he'd thought and felt during his short time here.

He pictured himself a loosely framed bundle of bones, picked over on the desert floor, until a shifting blanket of sand wrapped him and wed him deep within the earth. If he was found years from now, he wondered what this world would look like. *Would there be settlers here . . . people having found a way to withstand this fiery sand basin? Who knew? What did it matter . . . ?* He drifted deeper into the long dark tunnel, the big roan pounding on.

When the Ranger sidled his white barb up and caught the big roan by its bridle, Jimmy had no idea the horse had slowed beneath him, and could barely discern that four gloved hands had reached out and brought him down from the saddle, out of the harsh sun, and into the shade of a tall-standing cactus beside a rise of broken rock.

Whoever these persons were, Jimmy French felt like telling them they were meddling where they didn't belong. Death had everything worked out for him. He'd made his peace with all things. Why don't they just go away? Couldn't they see he was dead . . . well, nearly so anyway. He felt himself struggle slightly.

"Easy, now, young man," a stranger's voice said to him. "Looks like you've caught yourself a pistol slug in your side." Jimmy French could hear the voice wavering back and forth, for a second sounding close to his face, then far away as if from within a deep cavern. "Not the worst I've ever seen," the voice added. "We'll get some water in you . . . get you rested here a few minutes."

Oh, sweet Jesus . . . Jimmy French felt his head raise slightly, and he blinked his eyes—eyes that he'd closed with no intention of ever opening again. Why couldn't this man leave him alone? He was *dying!* He'd gone past all earthly restraint. All thoughts had settled. But now he'd been disturbed. The process had been halted. Would he have to start all over? Go through all that again? He closed his eyes and tried to drift back to that point where death had taken him.

"Here, swallow this," the voice said, coming in a bit more clearly. "This water will help some." Jimmy felt his lips part against the moist canteen, felt tepid water run down his throat. He gulped, once, twice, three times. Then the canteen was taken away. He would not open his eyes . . . maybe this person would go, and let him return to the business of dying.

"While he's asleep, I'll take this old boot knife and cut that bullet right out of him," he heard the voice say to someone nearby. "Might have to go in deep. It'll hurt something awful, but he won't feel a thing. I'll just dig right down in there . . ."

Dig in there? Cut? A knife going in deep? He didn't want to hear such talk as this. He wanted peace, silence, clear beautiful words of solace . . . dreams of the dying, here at the end. He didn't want this, not this, not now!

"Yep," the voice added, "let's get his shirt cut away, so I can get in there at it."

Please! Go away . . . let me die here. He let his mind drift once more, felt his shirt pull away from the wound. *No, please . . .*

"He's a young man. He can stand this. Here we go. I'll get in there deep, maybe have to scrape around on his rib bones till I find what we're looking for—"

Jimmy French's eyes snapped open. His hand raised from his chest, shielding himself. "No, wait . . . please." His voice sounded weak and shallow. He looked back and forth between the two faces, a woman and a man; then he drifted for a moment, caught himself, and forced himself to stay conscious. "Who? Who . . . are you?" he asked, then collapsed back into the woman's gloved hands beneath his head.

The Ranger sighed in relief, poured water onto the faded bandanna in his hand, and wiped it across the young man's forehead. Jimmy French saw no knife in the gloved hands, only the canteen and bandanna. "Thought we was about to lose you," the Ranger said. "But it looks like you'll make it now. You've lost some blood. It's a clean wound, though, straight in and out."

"You're—You're not . . . going to cut into my side?" Jimmy French raised slightly from the woman's hands, but the gloved hands pressed him back down with the wet bandanna on his face.

"Naw, I'm not going to cut in there. I only said it to get your attention, to keep you from slipping farther away on us."

"Then . . . I'm going to live?"

"Unless we've laid you down on a rattlesnake." The

Ranger offered a tired smile, "Yep, I believe you're going to be all right."

"But, I was . . . dead," Jimmy French said in a weak, halting voice, this time not trying to raise up, as the Ranger poured more water on the bandanna, "really . . . truly, dead."

The Ranger squeezed the bandanna over the wound, and pressed it down gently. "Naw, you just thought you were. The fact that you can say it, means it wasn't so."

"No . . . I was, really."

"Well, you just rest. Losing blood can play some strange tricks on your mind. I've had it happen myself."

"You . . . have?" He looked closer, saw the glint of the badge and the butt of the big pistol, and said, "You're him . . . aren't you? You're the . . . Ranger? The one— the one who—" He struggled, trying to raise up.

"Easy, now." The Ranger pressed him back down again. He glanced at Maria, then back down into Jimmy French's eyes as he slipped Doss Edding's pistol from the waist of Jimmy's trousers and turned it back and forth in his hand. "I'm the Ranger," he said. "We'll talk some more after you've rested a spell."

"It's . . . not mine," Jimmy said in a halting voice, trying to nod toward Doss's pistol.

"Oh?" The Ranger looked at the pistol closer, saw the initials *DE* on it. "Then, that's just *one* more thing we'll have to talk about."

While Jimmy rested in the shade, Maria prepared tea, breaking up some jerked beef into it as it boiled, turning it into a strong broth. When it had cooled some, Jimmy managed to drink down two cups of it, at first feeling his queasy stomach try to surge it up. The Ranger had told him that this too was a sign he'd lost a lot of blood.

Jimmy relaxed and let the tea settle until after a while he felt his strength returning, felt his mind clear a bit. He was alive. What had he been thinking? He tried to recall some of the strange thoughts he'd had only a short time ago, about living and dying. Now, even the remnants of those thoughts slipped away from him, seeming to sink away to some deeper level of his consciousness, as he told the Ranger and Maria all that had happened in Cottonwood the day before.

As he'd given the Ranger the names of the robbers, the Ranger had taken out a pencil stub and a folded piece of paper from inside his duster and had Jimmy spell each name for him as he wrote them down.

"I never hit anybody in my *life*, even with my fist," he said, when he'd finished his story, "let alone with a pistol barrel. I was awfully afraid . . . didn't really believe it could knock him out."

The Ranger folded the list of names, put the list inside his duster, and patted a hand on it. "Surprised yourself, huh?" He studied Jimmy's eyes, seeing no sign of deception in them, only a hesitancy at the part where he'd stalled and skipped past the way he'd gotten the drop on Doss Edding. "A person can do a lot when they know their life is on the line." He reached out, patted Jimmy on his shoulder, and gave Maria a sidelong glance.

Maria caught the message in the Ranger's glance. She stood up with an empty cup in her hand. "Well, then, I will go see how your horse is doing. You have ridden him very hard. Don't you know better than to do that in this heat?"

"Yes, ma'am, I do . . . and I'm truly sorry." Jimmy watched her turn and walk away. He looked back at the Ranger. "I didn't know what else to do. If you hadn't stopped me, there's no telling . . ." His words trailed.

"But we did stop you." The Ranger smiled. "So put

that part out of your mind." He glanced at Maria, a few yards away now, checking the big roan.

"If you catch them, will I have to—" Jimmy continued, thinking about his treatment at the hands of Doss Edding and his gang. "That is, if they go before a judge? I don't want to ever tell what happened in front of anybody."

"Don't worry about it," the Ranger said, taking Doss's pistol from inside his belt and studying it in his hand.

"You mean about telling it?"

The Ranger smiled a thin smile, picturing the face of the woman in the crushed stagecoach. "No. I mean about them ever going before a judge. It's unlikely that'll ever happen."

"You mean, when you catch them . . . you'll"— Jimmy swallowed a dry knot in his throat—"you'll kill them? What if they surrender?"

"They won't, from what you've said about them. This Doss Edding is as crazy as anything I've come across lately. Sounds like he's got no idea what's real or what's not. He'll have to be put down, hard." He shrugged. "The others are not much better . . . falling in with a fool like him. They'll go down the same way."

"Those things he accused me of being"—Jimmy French's face reddened and drew tight—"I don't want you to think the wrong thing. It's not true what he said."

"I never thought it was." The Ranger twirled Doss Edding's pistol around on his gloved finger.

Jimmy just watched as the Ranger rose to his feet and shoved the pistol back down in his belt. "We don't want you running into that boy again. He's got to want to kill you now." He nodded toward Maria. "As soon as you're able to ride, she'll take you on to Bannet."

Jimmy shook his head. "I'm not afraid of them anymore, any of them—especially Doss. I don't know why, but for some reason, there's nothing about them that scares me now."

"Well, it still wouldn't hurt to get a doctor to take a better look at that wound." The Ranger patted himself on the side. "I took a graze myself. He fixed me right up."

"But you said my wound looked all right." Jimmy managed to raise up on his elbows.

"Yep, it does." The Ranger saw something at work in this young man's mind, something he couldn't quite understand. "But I'm not a doctor. Might get infected on you, then you'd be in big trouble out here." He nodded toward the south, where the long dark cloud lay on the horizon. "Besides, we got weather coming before long."

Jimmy French considered it for a second, then looked up at the Ranger. "You'll go face them alone? Just you? No posse or nothing?"

"It's what I do." The Ranger tossed the question aside. "Meanwhile, you can get rested up in a cool bed, instead of—"

"How can you do something like that?" Jimmy cut him off. "I mean just ride up to a gang of killers that way?"

"Through much prayer and meditation." The Ranger smiled.

"Doesn't it bother you? Aren't you afraid? They could *kill* you."

"I suppose they could . . . but only *once*," the Ranger said, "and then I reckon I wouldn't even know about it for long, would I?"

Jimmy felt a trace of the fading thoughts he'd had earlier. They tried to return to him now, something in the Ranger's words bringing them back, renewing them with clarity. *Yes!* This was how he'd been think-

ing earlier. This was how he'd felt . . . something free
and bold about facing death, death no longer frighten-
ing him as he'd felt it so close at hand. Doss and the
others could have killed him, but *only once.*

"You've *always* thought that way, I mean about
dying?" Jimmy asked the Ranger, the Ranger cocking
his head a bit to one side with a curious expression on
his face.

"If you're strong enough ask these kinds of questions, I reckon you're strong enough to ride on to Bannet," the Ranger said. Then he turned and walked over
to Maria.

Jimmy French lay propped on his elbows, things
working through his mind, as he watched the way the
Ranger spoke to the woman, who just nodded and
lifted a saddle up onto the big roan. *Only once,* the
Ranger had said. Jimmy liked that.

"Only once," Jimmy repeated under his breath.
Then he settled back against the rock and pictured
Doss Edding, standing in front of him, a few yards
away. Doss's feet spread shoulder width, his hand
went back for the pistol at his hip. Jimmy stood there,
with all the time in the world, his hand going back
steady and calm, sweeping around his own pistol . . . coming up with it, cocking it on the upswing.
Only once . . .

Doss Edding's eyes went wide and frightened there
at the end. Jimmy caught a glimpse of the townsfolk,
the look on their faces as they'd seen him helpless in
the street beneath Doss's sweaty arm. And he caught a
glimpse of Doss humiliating him, calling him names,
holding him close like a craving bastard dog marking
something that belonged to it. The pistol bucked in
Jimmy's hand. *Doss, you sick son of a bitch!* Jimmy
thought, liking the feel of the harsh words in his mind.
You could have killed me, but you missed your chance. Now

it's my *turn.* Jimmy's pistol shot back into his holster before Doss's body even hit the ground.

He closed his eyes for a moment, the wound in his side no longer mattering to him, the fang and claw of the desert no longer something to fear, rather something to be akin to, something to draw strength from. He'd faced death out there, and he'd lived through it. He was not as fragile as he'd always thought; this land was not as harsh and brutal as he'd always feared it to be. A man could stand up to it. Could face it and not let it beat him. He just did exactly that. He was alive! Damn it all! *I'm coming for you, Doss ... real soon, I'm coming for you.* He smiled to himself, feeling stronger.

CHAPTER 6

The two men had talked idly about the things they knew best: money and law. C. G. Hutchinson smoked a cigar, relaxing the last few miles from the railhead at Circle Wells. Territorial Judge Winfred Lodge drove the two-horse buggy along the rocky dirt trail. Their meeting in Riley had gone well for all parties concerned. Now Judge Winfred Lodge gazed ahead, attending the reins. C. G. Hutchinson blew out a long stream of cigar smoke, giving some thought to what their next step should be in establishing a rail line from Circle Wells to Cottonwood.

"Why don't I have the bonding papers drawn up as soon as we get to town," Hutchinson spoke, spitting a fleck of wet tobacco from his lip. "You can sign off on them first thing in the morning. That way it's all legal and done on *our* end, in case you get called away for a while."

"Certainly," said the judge, "unless there are more than the ordinary number of cases to be heard in Cottonwood."

Hutchinson smiled, his chin going back into the roll of flesh beneath it. "Oh, I don't think you'll have to worry about that. Brady Martin keeps Cottonwood as tame as a lapdog."

"That's just the way I like it." Judge Lodge flicked the reins on the horse's rumps. "We need tough, strict laws out here, and tough, strict men to enforce them."

A brief silence passed as Hutchinson puffed on his cigar, surrounding his head in large plumes of thick cigar smoke. "I can't express my gratitude enough, Winfred"—he took the cigar from his mouth, examined the ashes on the end of it, and tapped them off into the air—"for all you've done . . . stepping in, doing a little *personal* favor for ole Matthew Edding. His cattle shipments are the ticket to this whole project. Wouldn't be much point in the railroad bringing a spur this far, unless there's something to haul out of here."

"The law can be a bit flexible at a time like this," Judge Lodge said. "Mind you, his son will have to keep his nose clean from now on . . . I hope he understood that. As soon as I get back over that way, I'll see to it the charge is dropped."

"Indeed, you made it perfectly clear to him." Hutchinson raised an ankle and rested it across his knee. "His son, Doss, is not what you'd call a *bad* boy . . . just, well, *headstrong*, I suppose you'd call him. He may have fallen in with a rough crowd, been mislead by them. You know how that can happen."

Judge Lodge nodded. "Yes, I do, and it played a part in my consideration. That, and your personal reference on the boy's behalf."

Hutchinson grimaced for a second, then covered it over with a tight smile. "Well, I can see him doing *some* of what the old Mexican accused him of—the part about riding in, shooting up the place. These cattlemen get *cross* when they find their calves in someone else's pen. Can't blame them for that. Thank God no one was injured, of course."

"Yes, *definitely*." The judge nodded. "The boy was real lucky there. I wouldn't have *considered* dismissing it if anyone had been shot . . . intentionally or otherwise." He turned his gaze to Hutchinson. "And I *will* follow up, to be sure Matthew Edding went by and made restitution, as he promised."

"Aw"— Hutchinson tossed a hand at the thought—
"you can rest assured of it. I daresay, he headed there
no sooner than we boarded the train at Riley. Matthew
Edding is a man of his word. You'll see how quickly
this rail spur comes in, with his help."

"And his *money*, put forth on the bonds, of course?"
The judge glanced at him again.

Hutchinson smiled a fleshy grin of satisfaction. "Yes,
and his money, indeed."

A silence passed, then Hutchinson spoke in a lowered tone. "You know, for handling the bonds, my
bank stands to make a *modest* profit, not to mention
how much this rail spur will benefit the entire
town . . ." He let his words trail, and puffed on his thick
cigar.

"And?" Judge Lodge gazed ahead at the rocky dirt
trail.

"Well . . . let's just say, I see nothing *untoward* in my
offering you something in appreciation for what
you've done."

"I'm not that kind of official," Judge Lodge said, a
slight twitch moving across his heavy jaw.

"Nor am I that kind of businessman, or *citizen*,"
Hutchinson added quickly. "But it does no harm to
mention it, does it? Just between the two of us?" He
leaned a bit closer, taking a fresh cigar from inside his
coat pocket and offering it over to the judge. "Eh? Does
it?" He nudged his elbow against Judge Lodge's forearm.

A faint, tolerant smile spread across Judge Lodge's
face. He took the cigar, looked at it in his hand, then
turned his gaze ahead, flicking the reins, as they
rounded the trail down toward Cottonwood.

Over the years, Paco Flores had seen Matthew Edding
no more than a half dozen times. Yet each time they
met, Paco could always tell right away whether it was

a business or a social call, depending on what name Matthew Edding called him. Edding had called him Señor *Flores* five years ago, when Paco and his sons had rounded up eighty head of Edding cattle they'd recaptured from rustlers near the border. Two summers back, Matthew Edding had called him by his American name, *Frank,* when the eldest of the Flores sons had kept young Doss Edding from getting his belly sliced open in a barroom brawl in Riley.

But today? Today it had been simply *Paco,* when Matthew Edding and his two men rode in slowly and spread their horses out, a few feet apart in the dirt yard of the Flores Hacienda. *This is not good . . .* Paco rubbed his chin, watching the four men stare down at him from atop their horses. He knew why Edding was here. He had expected this visit for the past two months, ever since he'd gone to the sheriff in Riley and brought charges against Doss. But what else could he have done? It was only out of respect for Matthew Edding that Paco or one of his sons hadn't killed Doss and left him lying where he fell. *That* loco *bastard . . .*

"You shamed me and my boy, Paco." Matthew Edding spoke down to him, his chiseled features shaded by his wide hat brim, his string tie fluttering on a hot breeze. "I've been asked to come here and make things right . . . so I will. But you never should have gone to the law on this. Since when have you and I not been able to deal with one another?"

Paco shrugged and spread his left hand, keeping his right hand free and close to the pistol across his stomach. "Señor Edding. Do you think I *wanted* to do this thing to Doss?" He hesitated for a second, weighing his next words. "But he was *loco,* him and his *compadres.*" He gestured a hand out toward the cattle pens a hundred yards away. "They shoot up my place! He killed two of my horses! He accused me of stealing your calves. He says he will kill me and my sons! What else should I do? I do not want to hurt him . . . for *your* sake."

Matthew Edding stiffened a bit at Paco's words. "For *your* sake, be glad you didn't." He stepped down from his saddle and walked over to Paco Flores. "Turns out those *were* Edding calves, Paco." His gaze bored into Paco Flores. Behind him the two men watched from their saddles.

"*Sí*, of course they were your calves." He gestured once more toward the pens. "They still *are*. That is why my sons brought them here. Nobody else's cattle would be on the high south range that time of year. They bring them *here*, as they have many times, to hold them for you. Is this not what we have always done for one another?"

Matthew Edding let out a tense breath. "Doss is my *son*, Paco. I stand behind his call."

"And that is only natural." Paco shrugged. "But please understand what I say, Señor Edding, because I say this to you as a friend. Your son Doss, he is a troubled young man. You do not see his many problems."

"Whatever *problems* he might have is *Edding* business, his and mine. So don't ever bring the law into play on him again. Do you *comprende*?"

"*Sí* . . . I try to understand." Paco shook his head slowly. "But I would not be honest if I didn't tell you, that I hear things about Doss . . . bad things, things I do not *want* to hear about him."

Bad things? About his son? Matthew Edding's jaw tightened. He glanced around at his men, then back to Paco. "Where are your sons today, Frank?"

Now it's Frank, Paco thought. What next? "Out on the range, of course." He tilted his head a bit to one side, his hand still near the pistol on his stomach.

Matthew Edding took note of the look in Paco's dark eyes. Again letting out a tense breath, he stepped sideways to Paco and raised an arm up across his shoulders, "Frank, my ole friend," Edding said, nudging Paco forward, farther away from the shaded porch, "let's not talk to each other this way." He swept his free arm out, taking in all of the open range to the west and the south of them. "How much cattle do you have out there? Two, three, maybe four hundred head?"

"Perhaps that many." Paco looked into Matthew Edding's eyes close up.

"Good, good, then. You're doing real well for your family here," Edding said, nodding. "And even though you're Mexican, haven't I always treated you and your boys with respect, like you're just as good as the rest of us?"

Paco just stared at him.

"Well, it's true. You know I have." He let his arm fall from Paco's shoulder, but kept it near beside him, folding his hands behind his long riding duster, gazing out across the land. "Times when a buyer comes around, looking for a small purchase—I don't want to fool with it? Go see my friend Paco Flores, I always say to them . . . and I point them your way."

"*Sí.* We have always dealt fairly with one another." Paco nodded.

"Yes, we have." Matthew Edding turned his caged glance back to Paco. "And you know all about me . . . what I was back in the war, and for a long time afterward, until I got into cattle."

"I know you were one tough *hombre.* I know you rode with a gang of bold *pistoleros, sí.*"

"*Desperados,* that's what we were—you needn't be afraid to say it. I know what I was back then. And I know what I am now. All I want is to give my son a better life than I had. It's the same thing you want for your boys, isn't it?"

"This is so." Paco nodded. "We all want better for our children. It is the way things are."

"That's right, it's the way things are. I raised Doss to

be tough. Even though there was a softness in him after his ma died, I got it out of him. *Worked* it out of him. *Browbeat* it out of him. At times, I reckon, I even *whipped* a lot of it out of him. But he's as hard as a stick of hickory now . . . like a man out here has to be. Sometimes he gets a little out of hand, and I know it. But be that as it is . . ."

A silence passed, then Matthew Edding continued. "I talked to the sheriff in Riley, and to the territorial judge. Told them I'd come on out here—set things right with you." He nodded over toward the cattle pens. "I want you to keep those calves and let this thing pass."

"No, Señor Edding. They are yours. I cannot—"

"I insist, Paco," he said, cutting him off. "Keep the calves. But don't ever raise a hand or bring a charge against Doss. Or we'll have trouble, you and me . . . *bad* trouble."

Paco Flores resolved himself to saying nothing more, except, "I understand."

And moments later, when Matthew Edding and his men rode away at the head of a drifting stream of dust, Rosa Flores stepped out from where she had stood inside the partly opened door of the hacienda. She gazed out after their wake of dust with the shotgun in her hand, her free hand above her eyes, shading the sharp sunlight. "What will you tell our sons to do, the *next* time Doss does such a thing?" she asked.

"They will know what to do. And they will do what one must always do when an animal has lost its mind and comes at them."

She bowed her head slightly, brushing aside a loose strand of hair moved by the hot breeze. "You did not tell him what you know, about the thing his *loco* son did to the little girl down *Mejico*." She made the sign of a cross over her breast. "Perhaps you should have."

He looked at her, his eyes growing darker, a furrow rising in his brow. He winced. "How can I tell a man such a terrible thing—tell him that his son is a *mon-ster*?"

"But he should be told. It is only right that he should know."

"Perhaps he *already* knows . . . as any father knows, somewhere deep down in his heart."

At the head of the wake of dust, Carl Statler turned to Matthew Edding as they rode along, "Alls you had to do was say the word, Boss. We would've stopped his clock then and there."

"You know it," Joe Baylor said, on the other side of Matthew Edding. "To tell the truth, I was kind of hoping you'd give us the go-ahead. Damn Mex, accusing Doss of stuff he never done." He shot a guarded glance over to Carl Statler. Statler only looked away. Nobody said it out loud around the *boss*, but everybody still knew there was something wrong with Doss Edding.

Matthew Edding glanced back and forth at each of them, then looked ahead toward the town of Riley, miles into the distance. "Flores is a good man." Matthew Edding looked embarrassed. "He only did what he *thought* was right, at the time. I can't fault him for it. But it would've been better all around, had he come to me instead."

"Whatever you say, Boss," Carl Statler said. "Just want you to know we're behind you, Joe and me."

Matthew Edding didn't seem to hear him. He gazed straight ahead, saying, "As soon as we get back to the ranch, I'm gonna have a long talk with Doss—put a rake handle across his back if I have to."

"It always worked on me." Statler grinned. "My ole man could've won ribbons for how he swung a rake handle."

"Mine was always hell with a buggy whip." Joe Baylor looked at Matthew Edding for some sort of approval.

Still staring ahead, Matthew Edding replied, "Another thing. Gather up Little Tommy's belongings and pitch them out in the dirt . . . same with Newt Babbage, and that fat bastard, Lew Harper. They're bad influences on Doss. None of them's worth their pay to begin with. I want them paid off and out of there, first thing."

"It's done," said Statler. "What about Dusty Charlie? He's going off all the time with Doss, drinking and that."

"No. Dusty Charlie stays." Matthew Edding glanced at him, then cut his look away. "I told him to stay close to Doss, keep me knowing what the boy's up to. He's a good hand anyway. Get rid of the others. They're too young and green to know anything. I'm tired of my boy being misled by them."

"Now I believe you've got the right idea," Joe Baylor said. "Get rid of the source, and Doss'll fall right back in line. Little Tommy can't look straight down and see *dirt*. Harper's too fat to keep fed. And Babbage is *barely* smart enough to keep from getting shit in his whiskers. Only good *new* man we've got is Jesse Tiggs."

"Yeah? Tiggs is turning out all right?" Edding asked, shooting a sidelong glance at Carl Statler.

"Sure is," Statler said. "He's as good as any old hand on the place. He's a loner, but that never kept a man from doing a good day's work. Strikes me as a man wanting to better himself."

"See?" Edding raised a gloved hand. "That's the kind of person you want your son to take after—not a bunch of low-handed trash like those others."

They rode in silence, the three of them taking note of the dark cloud off in the south, a *bit* closer today than it had been yesterday, and *much* closer than the day before. After a moment, Joe Baylor cleared his throat and asked in a nervous voice, "Boss, can I say something about Doss . . . without you getting offended, that is?"

Matthew Edding shot him a glance. "That all depends. What is it, Joe?" Even as he asked, Edding stopped his horse and turned it quarter-wise toward Joe Baylor, his gloved hand coming to rest against the butt of the big Army Colt on his hip. The worn wooden handles on the pistol stood out foremost in Joe Baylor's vision, sunlight glinting off the trigger. Matthew Edding had worn that same big Colt since as far back as either of these men could remember.

Baylor swallowed a hard knot in his throat. Past Matthew Edding, he saw Carl Statler shaking his head, squinting, telling him *no . . . don't do it!* "Well, Joe, speak up." Matthew Edding stared at him through cold, hooded eyes.

"*Uh—*" Baylor stalled. "Well, that is, it's just— you know"—he shrugged—"raising a young boy on your own and all . . . no woman to help you with him. I just wanted to say, that *uh—* I don't envy you a chore like that." He glanced past Matthew Edding, seeing Carl Statler look relieved. "And that—well, I admire you for doing as fine a job as you've done."

Matthew Edding sidestepped his horse, his eyes staying locked and cold on Joe Baylor. "And that's it? That's what you thought might *offend* me? That's all you wanted to say?"

"Well, you never know what might offend a man." Joe Baylor offered a weak, nervous smile, shrugging again. "But heck, yeah, that's *all* I wanted to say."

"I thought it was probably just something like that." Matthew Edding dismissed it, his hand easing off of the pistol butt. His eyes stayed on Joe Baylor a second longer, then he turned his horse. Carl Statler looked at Joe Baylor and ran a hand across his brow. "Come on," Matthew Edding called back over his shoulder, "let's get to Riley and catch that train to Circle Wells. Looks like a storm's coming our way."

CHAPTER 7

Doss Edding didn't like the way the others had looked at him ever since last night. Were they really looking at him differently? Yes! He believed so. And what had Little Tommy meant earlier, at daylight when they'd finally quit searching for Jimmy French's body? "Looks like your *girlfriend* got away from you," Tommy had said to him, his big bloodshot eyes swimming behind those wire rims.

All right, Doss himself had called Jimmy his *girlfriend* earlier, but that was different somehow. He'd been drunk, joking. Just good manly sport. That was before he'd let things spin out of control, and let Jimmy get the jump on him. Why had Little Tommy brought it back up? What had he meant by it? Doss had asked him, but Tommy only looked confused and said, "Dang it, Doss, what's got you so *jumpy* all of a sudden. Ain't I the best friend you've got, or ever will have?"

Had he appeared jumpy, nervous, maybe looking like he was trying to hide something from the others? Why had Tommy said *that? Damn Little Tommy anyway!* Doss felt his face redden, thinking back on the night before. He pictured Jimmy French lying there in the dark, helpless and scared. He liked that part. But then he pictured *himself*, squatting down, leaning forward. *God Almighty!* What had he been thinking? What in the world had come over him?

He shook the picture from his mind, and ran a hand across his brow. *Well? So what? Anybody might joke around like that, drunk on whiskey . . . mightn't they?* He looked back at the others, all of them except Dusty Charlie lying stretched out—hung over—on the ground, beneath the thin shade of a cottonwood tree. Dusty Charlie sat on a short rock, gazing toward him, with his rifle lying across his lap.

Doss yanked his reins, bringing his horse around. "What're *you* looking at?" Doss shouted as his horse bolted forward the few yards, then slid to a halt. The others stirred and raised up, seeing Doss's wild-eyed expression as he stared down at Dusty Charlie.

"Just looking, Doss, that's all." Dusty Charlie spit and ran a hand across his mouth, his eyes staying on Doss Edding, making him even *more* edgy.

"I'm just looking too." Big Lew Harper chuckled, rising to his feet. "Just looking for something to *drink*." He looked all around at the others, fanning dust from the seat of his trousers. All of them looked sweaty, sick, and miserable. He added, "If we don't get something else to drink, we might just as well call it a run, and head back to the barn."

"Yeah, I might could eat a bite or two myself." Newt Babbage lay flat on his back, his knees raised. The woman's hat still sat broken and dirty on one knee. "I don't recall the last time we et anything." He flipped the dusty plume and watched it flutter in a hot breeze.

Little Tommy chuckled under his breath, rolled over on his side, and lowered his hat brim over his face.

"Boy, oh, boy." Doss spoke in a flat tone, finding a reason to cut his gaze away from Dusty Charlie to the others. "This is the awfulest bunch of *desperados* I've ever seen."

"How many *have* you ever seen?" big Lew Harper asked him.

"Humph." Doss stepped his big paint horse back

and forth in place. He hiked the broad duster collar up around his neck. "I'll tell you one damned thing. When my daddy rode guerilla with that bunch back in Missouri, they never complained all the time about something to eat, or running out of whiskey. They went and *took* what they wanted. Nothing held them back."

"Yeah, well, that was *them*." Newt Babbage stretched his long frame, and settled back down, stifling a yawn. The woman's hat fell onto the dirt beside him. "I expect your daddy could eat a fresh steer every day now, if he had a mind to. So could you. Your daddy's got more dang money than anybody in the territory."

"You saying something about my daddy?" Doss snapped his horse around toward Babbage. His eyes bored into him.

"Why, no, I'm not." Newt raised up onto his elbows and looked up at him. "I'm just saying he's rich, is all. What's bad about that?"

"Nothing that I can think of," Lew Harper chuckled.

Doss shot Harper a cold stare. "Nobody asked for your two cents on the matter."

Newt Babbage cut back in. "I'm saying while we've got *money* in our pockets, let's go somewhere and *buy* us a hot meal, and get some more whiskey. This outlawing ain't much fun sober, on an empty stomach."

"I've got an idea." Little Tommy grunted, rolling up onto his knees. "There's a brand-new whore over in Dunley. I heard one of the Circle E cowhands talking about her the other day. Said her name's Darlene, and she's bigger than the side of a barn—got freckles all over her, even on her teats. Said she came there to draw back some business."

"I— I don't know about Dunley," Doss said. "There's lots of places we could go besides *there*. Dunley's ain't nothing but a wide spot in the trail."

"But we're talking about a *brand-new whore* there," Newt Babbage said. "You *do* like whores, don't you? One with freckles all over her?"

"Dang right I do . . . freckles or not!" Doss felt his face redden. His voice sounded unsteady to him.

"Then, *Dunley's* where she's at." Lew Harper spread his hands to the others. "We go there, get us a nice bath, food, whiskey, and get checking her out—"

Dusty Charlie cut him off. "Am I the only one here who knows we're wanted by the law?" He stood up, letting his rifle hang in his hand. "Boys, I'm telling all of yas, we've got a rough row to hoe from here on. Get it into your heads! We're going to be hunted all across the badlands. Can't any of you see it? This thing is nothing to take lightly."

"Yeah, we all see it," Little Tommy said, standing the rest of the way up, poking a finger up against the bridge of his spectacles, pushing them up. "But I don't reckon being *wanted* means we gotta quit drinking, or whoring, or doing what we want to do, does it? Ain't the best part about being outlaws, the fact that we don't have to give a damn about nothing?"

Jesus . . . Dusty Charlie shook his head and let out a long breath. Maybe he *did* need a drink . . . a bunch of drinks come to think of it. He heard the low grumble of thunder in the south, stronger today; and he walked over to his horse, shoved his rifle down into the scabbard, and turned, as Doss Edding stepped his paint horse over near him.

"What's bothering you?" Doss asked, looking down at him.

"Nothing," Dusty Charlie said, "*nothing* at all." He looked over at the others. "Everybody wants to go to Dunley? Hell, let's get to it. I admire a freckled whore as much as the next man. Nobody else cares—then neither do I."

"You don't have to act like this about it," Doss snapped at him.

"Like what?" Dusty Charlie stared up at him.

"You know . . . like something's stuck in your craw. Like you've got something to say, but won't come out and say it. If something's on your mind spit it out."

Dusty Charlie looked away from him, seeing the others move to their horses and take up their reins. "Forget it. Let's go on to Dunley . . . we've got rain moving in." Without another word to Doss, he stepped up in his stirrup and swung onto his saddle. Things weren't working out the way they should here, he thought, turning his horse, kicking it out across the sand. Maybe he'd better give this whole Half Moon idea a little more consideration.

The others trotted their horses forward in turn, Doss staying back until all but Little Tommy Caldwell had passed him and moved on. He hadn't wanted them behind him, watching him, maybe whispering something about him behind his back. When Little Tommy reined up beside him, Doss flagged him ahead. But Tommy wouldn't leave. "Go on, get out of here, Tommy." Doss sawed his big paint horse back and forth on the trail, waiting for Little Tommy to pass.

"You might want to stay close to me awhile, Doss." Tommy spread a sly grin.

Doss Edding felt Tommy's large eyes searching his from behind the thick spectacles. Something in Tommy's stare made him uncomfortable. "I said, get on up there with the others. I don't need you always under my feet."

"Yeah?" The sly grin didn't waver. Tommy sidled his horse closer. "Well, maybe I got something here you've been wanting all morning." His dirty hands lifted his canteen strap from his saddle horn. "Something I didn't want the others to know about . . . just between us."

Doss just stared at him as Tommy twisted off the cap of the canteen and held it over to him. "Take a sniff, then tell me if I'm wrong."

"Hell, Tommy." Doss smiled now, holding the canteen beneath his nose, catching the smell of rye whiskey. "Why didn't you say so in the first place?" He threw back a long drink, let out a whiskey hiss, and held it on his lap. "After last night, I've been jumpy as a squirrel. Can't help it." He calmed a bit. "Don't pay no attention when I get like that."

"See . . . I don't forget my best pal." Tommy reached over, lifted Doss's canteen from his saddle horn, and hung it on his own. "You just keep that canteen for a while. I've had enough whiskey to last me to Dunley."

"Yeah, good idea." Doss threw back another drink, and let out another hiss. "If it weren't for me and you, Tommy, I'd hate to think what would happen to this bunch. We got to keep an eye on one another, don't you think?"

"We always have." Tommy adjusted his hat down on his forehead.

Ahead of them, Lew Harper called back, "Are you two coming with us or what?"

"Come on, Tommy." Doss heeled his big paint horse forward, Tommy falling in beside him. "We'll just keep this to ourselves. What the rest of them don't know won't hurt them."

"That's what I been telling myself all day." Tommy stayed his horse close beside him. "Hadn't been for you and me, there wouldn't be no Half Moon Gang. Right?"

"That's right," Doss said. "We started it. The rest of them wouldn't even *be here* . . . wasn't for us."

"We could go right back to just you and me," Tommy said. "Remember how it was last year? The way we'd sneak off, steal something here, something there? I liked it that way, just the two of us. Didn't no-

body know nothing about us. Only ones we answered
to was each other."

"It was good all right." Doss ran a hand down the
front of his father's faded Civil War duster. "But that
was different. We're a whole gang now. I've got re-
sponsibilities—gotta see to it things go right for all of
us. That's how it was for my daddy back when he was
a long rider."

The whiskey spread warm across his chest, soothing
him; and when they came up to where Lew Harper
had stopped and looked back for them, Doss kicked
his paint horse harder, shooting past him, then past
the others, only slowing a bit when he looked back and
saw Dusty Charlie a few yards behind him. "Well,
what're you bunch of crumb-bums waiting for.
Quicker we get to Dunley, the quicker we can raise
some hell."

"I swear," Newt Babbage said to Lew Harper as
Harper rode up beside him, "I never seen a man
change back and forth so much in my life." He reached
up and yanked the silk sash, freeing the woman's hat
from atop his Stetson. He tossed it away into the dust
where it spun and flattened as Little Tommy's horse
came past and stepped on it, mashing it into the dirt.

With the thunder grumbling closer out of the south,
the Ranger wasted no time getting under way. As soon
as Maria had helped Jimmy French swap his saddle
over to the stage horse and the two of them headed
back along the trail toward Bannet, the Ranger turned
his white barb, and picked up the tracks out across the
stretch of flatland, leading the dead sheriff's roan
horse behind him. From what Jimmy French had told
him about the Half Moon Gang, they were a bunch of
wild young men off on a killing spree. He pictured
them as drunk and stupid—something almost pitiful
about them in a way.

But being stupid and drunk didn't mean they were any less dangerous than any other band of prowling animals. As far as *pity*, he'd show them no more than they'd shown the innocent people in the stagecoach, or the dead townsfolk they'd left lying in the dirt in Cottonwood. Behind him, the thunder growled and rumbled across the sky.

Maria and Jimmy French would catch some of the storm before they swung wide of it and on to Bannet. Yet the Ranger had no choice but to send them on. If he didn't stay ahead of the storm himself, the rain would wash away the tracks. Then he could be weeks on the trail of these murderers. "Come on, Black-eye, let's get to it," he said to the white barb, heeling the horse, speeding it up; and he rode off across the hot sand.

CHAPTER 8

"Thank goodness you were able to make it here this morning, Matthew." C. G. Hutchinson's words were partly lost beneath the loud clap of thunder above Cottonwood. "Please come in. I have a nice hot pot of coffee already boiling."

For the past two days, the dark cloud from out of the south lay long and low above the sandy basin. It spilled itself on the small town as if with a vengeance. Thunder rolled off like cannon fire along the high ridgeline. Lightning licked down from the blackness and danced among swaying juniper and pine.

"Of *course* I made it here." Matthew Edding's face looked drawn and tired. "No coffee for me. I didn't come all this way for coffee." Only the night before had he arrived back at his ranch, thinking he'd straightened out Doss's problems. Now this. He closed the door to the sheriff's office as an orange streak of lightning twisted and curled away behind him.

"You better hope to God you know what you're talking about, Hutchinson . . . blaming my boy for what happened here. Old man Tomblin said there's already talk of a hanging, once they catch him." He turned and stood facing Hutchinson with a rifle in his gloved hand. Rain streaked down his slicker and dripped from his hat brim.

"Oh, dear," C. G. Hutchinson said. "I'm afraid it may have been a mistake, sending Tomblin out to tell you about this." He chafed his hands together, nervous but in control, having spent the morning deciding the best way to handle things. "Rest assured, though, no one here is talking about hanging your son. You have my word on it."

Matthew Edding's hand tightened on his rifle stock. His words were low and tense. "With or *without* your word, banker, I'll kill anybody who threatens my boy's life. *You* can rest assured of that." He turned slowly, looking around the dead sheriff's cluttered office. "Where's Judge Lodge? Old Tomblin said the judge would be here."

"As it turns out, Judge Lodge won't be joining us today." Hutchinson gestured him over toward a wooden chair. "But believe me, it's better just the two of us meet. This allows me the opportunity to tell you what I've come up with on your and Doss's behalf. It's good news, I assure you. You'll be relieved to hear it."

"Oh? I could use some good news right about now." Matthew Edding stepped over near the chair, but didn't sit down. On the battered desk lay the paperwork for the surety bonds. He glanced at the papers and at the ink pen and dipping well beside them. "I see you've gone right on . . . *business* as usual."

"Well, yes, in fact I have." C. G. Hutchinson stepped around behind the sheriff's desk, clearing his throat. "And I think you'll appreciate *why*, once you hear me out. I believe we can settle your son's trouble without things getting any more out of hand than they already have."

Matthew Edding just stared at him.

"You see, Matthew, I've spoken to everyone here about what happened, and it *may* be questionable as to whether or not Doss was actually involved in this terrible incident." He paused to let his words sink in . . . to check the expression on Matthew Edding's face and see how he took it.

Edding's expression didn't change a bit. "Tomblin said there were three people killed, counting Sheriff Martin . . . and your bank teller taken hostage. Said the whole town saw it. So either it happened or it didn't. Don't fool around with me."

Hutchinson raised a stubby finger. "Yes, it's true the whole town *saw* it happen. But in a situation like this, it's difficult to tell *what* people actually saw. The mind can play tricks on you at such a time. It takes a clear head in charge, to sort things out and let people know what truly went on. Now that folks have settled down a bit, I've been piecing this thing together, and getting quite a different picture." He lowered his finger, smoothed his hand down his vest, and added, "I don't mind telling you, Matthew, I've gone all out for you here . . . and this whole thing does not look as bleak for Doss now as it first seemed to."

"How so?" Matthew Edding continued to stare at him, a bit distrusting.

"Because, you see . . . Doss didn't *shoot* anyone. No, sir. Everyone in town agrees on that." Hutchinson shook his head. "One of your cattle hands killed Sheriff Brady Martin, and it was Little Tommy Caldwell who killed those other two people. Granted, your son was *with* them. He was seen holding young Jimmy French at gunpoint. But that fact *alone* shouldn't cause us to jump to conclusions, should it?"

Matthew Edding cocked his head slightly to one side, seeming to loosen up some. "Go on, Hutchinson, I'm listening."

"First of all, let's just consider it *preposterous* that Doss would have a hand in robbing my bank." He shrugged his thick shoulders. "I mean *really*—why would he? I daresay, the thousand dollars taken was a mere *pittance* compared to the amount you have on deposit with me." He smiled, but it was flat, business-like. "As far as I'm concerned, your son had always had access to triple that amount anytime he chose . . . on his *name alone."*

"I see." Matthew Edding started getting the picture. "Then, as far as the bank robbery, you won't be bringing charges against him?"

"Absolutely not." Hutchinson beamed, tossing a hand. "Let's just call that a misunderstood transaction. It could happen to anyone."

"All right . . ." Matthew Edding moved over a step to the wooden chair, unbuttoned his slicker, shook it out, and sat down, cradling the rifle in one arm. "So how *do* you call this whole thing? How do you see it working out?"

"Strictly between us" —Hutchinson spoke, lowering his tone, leaning a bit closer to Matthew Edding across the desk— "I can see how Doss might have been with the wrong crowd at the wrong time. Since no one has spoken to him, who's to say? He might have gone to the bank to withdraw money in your name, not realizing the ones he was with had planned to rob it. What if, having seen it happening—having seen Sheriff Brady Martin get shot down in the street and hearing gunfire from the saloon— Doss had to do some fast thinking? Perhaps he decided the *only* way to save other innocent lives was by pretending to hold our teller hostage and get these killers out of town without further bloodshed? Can you see it? Couldn't it have happened that way?"

A silence passed as Matthew Edding just stared at him for a second. Then Edding spoke in a low tone. "You can *actually* sell an idea like that to this town? To Judge Lodge? Make them all *believe* it?"

"Listen *carefully* to how I'm saying this, Matthew." Hutchinson leaned even farther over the desk toward him. "I would never ask anyone to *deliberately* lie, and I'm not *suggesting* your son concoct a story to escape justice. Heaven forbid." He raised his bushy eyebrows in mock righteousness, but then leveled them down quickly across his brow. "But based on your reputation, and all the good you've done"—he waved a hand down toward the paperwork—"not to *mention* what good you're about to do. There's no reason this town can't be persuaded to go along with it."

They sat in silence for a moment, Matthew Edding considering it, until C. G. Hutchinson cleared his throat and spoke in a lower, more guarded tone. "If you were to find your son before the law gets to him, and if he were to tell you that something like I've suggested is what really happened here, I'm certain that would be the end of this entire *ugly* incident."

"And the others? Newt Babbage, Little Tommy Caldwell, Dusty Charlie, and Lew Harper? What if they tell a different story once they're caught?" Matthew Edding asked, running a wet-gloved hand along his jaw.

"That *could* get sticky," Hutchinson said, "although I'm sure if it came to Doss's word against a band of saddle tramps, there's no question whose word we'll take." He smiled, spreading his hands. "We have every reason to be optimistic, with Judge Winfred Lodge presiding. I daresay, if Doss explained what really happened, this would go no further than a simple *legal* inquiry . . . in the privacy of this office." He tapped a finger on the desk.

"And your *teller*, Jimmy French? What about him? Has he shown up yet?"

"No. But I'm certain he will." C. G. Hutchinson considered it for a second, then added, "Unless, of course, Doss simply wasn't able to keep the others from doing the poor boy harm."

"Do you suppose they let him go, but maybe he's gotten rained in somewhere?" Matthew Edding asked, working it out in his mind now, seeing more and more the possibility in Hutchinson's plan. "That's quite a wash out there. A person could get swept away. Anything might have happened."

Hutchinson shrugged once more. "Be that as it may, *if* and when Jimmy French returns, rest assured, he'll see things in the best interest of the bank . . . *and* of the town. Don't forget, young Jimmy works for *me*. He's a rather timid, *pliable* young fellow. He'll do as I tell him."

"You better be right on all this, Hutchinson," Matthew Edding said. "I've got men out in this rain right now, searching for Doss to bring him to me. I was going to send him to Mexico until I found a way to get this straightened out. If he stays here and turns himself in on *your* say-so, I'm holding *you* responsible. Make sure this goes the way you say it will. Judge Lodge struck me as the kind of person who can get pretty harsh if he's a mind to."

"Yes, right you are. But you needn't do something as drastic as sending Doss off to Mexico . . . that *barbaric* wasteland. I've spoken at length with Judge Lodge. He's a reasonable man." As he talked, Hutchinson's fingertips went down and brushed across the paperwork for the rail bonds. Idly, he turned them to face Matthew Edding, and slid them forward across the desk. "Judge Lodge realizes that the law must always be subject to extenuating circumstances." He smiled now, sliding the pen and inkwell forward.

Matthew Edding took off his wet glove and laid it on his knee. He leaned forward, then stopped before picking up the pen. "But the law is *still* the law . . . or at least it was the last time I noticed."

"Well." Hutchinson smiled with confidence. "The law *is* merely a body of rules by which we live, provided it serves the good of *all* concerned. But let's face it, there's *nothing* carved in stone about it —*hasn't been*, not since Moses came down from the mountaintop."

Outside, thunder jarred the buildings along the boardwalk.

"Still," said Matthew Edding, "I'd feel better if I
heard something from the judge himself about this."

"Trust me," Hutchinson said, "I'm handling this.
Because of his legal position here, the judge will not be
able to say anything one way or the other until the
time comes. But I believe you'll be amazed at how easily this *ugly* little incident can all be put to rest, once
we set our minds to it." He nudged the pen forward
another inch, until Matthew Edding reached down,
picked it up, and dipped it into the well. "You *did* get
everything straightened out with the Flores family, I
presume?"

"Yes, I took care of it, just like I said I would."
Matthew Edding spoke, with his head bowed above
the paperwork; and when he'd finished signing the
bonds and the transfer of his personal funds—
$200,000 to be held in escrow— he laid the pen down,
let out a long breath, and added, "I'd also like to pay
for the funerals of the ones killed here. Will you see to
it? And express my condolences?"

Hutchinson winced a bit, reaching over, pulling the
signed papers back across the desk. "I'm not sure
that's a good idea, Matthew. Your generosity, although well intended, could be misconstrued by others —an admission of some kind of wrongdoing on
Doss's part."

Matthew Edding shook his head, "Since when has
an act of kindness become so difficult? I've bought
goods and supplies from George and Emma Frocke
ever since they opened their store here. Can't tell you
how much whiskey I've bought from ole Lawrence
White over the years. Seems like I could at least do
something to offer my sympathy—"

"No, please." Hutchinson raised a hand. "Let's let
this thing run its natural course. This is not about *peo-*

ple, it's about the law now. Emma had sufficient funds to bury her husband. If not, I would have *gladly* provided her a loan. The town paid for Brady Martin . . . as far as Lawrence White, there was enough money in his cigar box under the bar. Right now, it's best we let everything settle."

"I suppose you're right." Matthew Edding stood up, taking his rifle in his hand. "Just wish it wasn't this way."

"It's the *only* way, right now," Hutchinson said, also standing up, smoothing his vest down over his stomach. "The best thing for you to do is find Doss before someone else does, some outsider who might not agree with our thinking." He rolled a hand. "Keep this a *local* problem. Talk to Doss —make sure it happened the way I've suggested."

Matthew Edding nodded. "I'll find him before anyone else, Hutchinson . . . you can count on it. The less people involved in this the better."

The Ranger rode on through the gray downpour with his duster collar raised against the slantwise sheet of whipping rain. He'd lost a full day, taking shelter back beneath a cliff overhang until the worst of the storm had passed. Now the tracks he'd followed were gone, washed away—not so much as a hoof scrape on rock. There was no point in even searching for a sign. Where gullies had stood hollow and dry two days ago beneath a baking sun, swollen streams now rushed, full of swirling brush tangles and scrub trees torn loose by their shallow roots.

He might have outrun the storm had he pushed Black-eye and the dead sheriff's roan a lot harder. But he'd learned the hard way long ago, that a man in this country with a blown horse was no better off than a man on foot. So he'd holed up, letting Black-eye and the tired roan rest themselves while the storm raged.

Then he'd pushed on, slow and steady along an upper-ridge trail. More than once he'd had to side the horses close to rock walls and move behind gushing falls of runoff water, lest the force of it wash them over the edge.

When the trail dropped down onto a rocky stretch of sodden flatland, he stopped the horses beneath a cottonwood tree and gazed out through the whipping rain. To his right and a day's ride behind him, would be the town of Cottonwood—a good place to dry out, get a hot meal, a warm bed for the night, grain for the horses. But the men he hunted wouldn't be there. *Where would they have gone . . . ?*

He waited for his inner voice to speak to him, that small quiet voice made up of experience, instinct, part of the land itself. At some point in every manhunt that voice led the way; yet today it said nothing, as if having backed away from the weather, it would now lay silent until the weather passed. He waited, searching the rain and the muddy trail into the short gray distance. *Nothing. . . .*

He breathed a deep breath, and after a moment, patted the white barb on its wet withers. "Take us on, Black-eye," he said beneath the roar of pounding rain, "your guess is as good as mine." Ahead and higher up lay Dunley, a mining town where the silver mines had played out and closed, and where all that remained were a few claim pickers who worked the loose spillings on hands and knees—*bucket miners*, he thought.

When he'd chucked the white barb and the horse stepped off in that direction, he let it walk on aimlessly, not knowing why, until a few yards ahead he spotted the wet muddy plume of a woman's hat pressed down by the rain. *Well, I'll be. . . .* Swinging both horses sideways on the muddy trail, he dropped

down from his saddle, his boots raising a short spray
of muddy water.

He picked up the hat, shook mud from it, and
stepped back over to the white barb, holding the hat
up in his gloved hand. "See, Black-eye? See why I keep
you around?" He grinned beneath the sagging brim of
his dripping sombrero, stepped back up into his wet
saddle, and heeled forward in the pouring rain. "If
there's anything else you know, I wish you'd tell me
now."

While the Ranger pushed on through the mud and
the rain, back in Cottonwood, Judge Winfred Lodge
stepped out of the back room of the sheriff's office no
sooner than Matthew Edding had closed the door behind himself. "I don't like this kind of *underhanded* ne-
gotiation," the judge said, looking down at C. G.
Hutchinson with a grave expression. "This goes
against everything I've ever stood for."

"Trust me, Your Honor." Hutchinson leaned back in
his chair, a confident smile on his broad face. "We both
know that all things in life are negotiable. You know as
well as I do, that with a sharp lawyer—the kind a man
like Matthew Edding can *afford*—if this thing *did* go to
a trial, it could *very well* come out the way I'm suggesting it happened." He smiled. "Look at all the time
and expense I've just saved us." He rolled a thick hand
as if tossing the matter aside. "Consider this as sort of
a *bargain* for everyone concerned."

"The law is not something to be *bargained* with." The
judge spoke as he leaned forward, glanced at the
signed papers on the battered desk, and shook his
head. "This whole thing could come back and ruin
us . . . not to mention the fact that Doss Edding will
still be running loose. How do we know he won't do
the same thing again?"

"What are you worried about, Judge?" Hutchinson

rose from his chair and adjusted the lapels of his suit coat. "You heard what Matthew told me. He straightened out that little matter with the Flores family just like he promised you. He'll do the same with the people of Cottonwood. As far as Doss ever being involved in anything else"—he shook his head—"put it out of your mind. That boy will be afraid to spit in the street from here on."

"You better be right on this, Hutchinson," the judge said. Outside, thunder rolled and grumbled overhead.

"Oh, I'm sure I am right." Hutchinson shrugged, gathered the paperwork, folded it, and shoved it inside the inner pocket of his lapel. He patted a hand on his chest. "Besides . . . now that we have what we need, so what if his son does go wrong again? The law will simply deal with him *then*, instead of *now*."

He moved around the corner of the desk, placed an arm up around the judge's shoulder, ushering him toward the door. "*Winfred*, let's get out of this drab little hole and go to my office at the bank. We'll discuss how quickly you can handle the arraignment once Matthew finds Doss and brings him here." He reached out, turned the knob, and opened the door, while lightning twisted and glittered and flashed away into the gray sky. "Believe me, nothing will go wrong here. Meanwhile, I have some delightful sherry I'd like you to sample."

CHAPTER 9

Maria and Jimmy French did not have to take shelter from the weather. Their trail to Bannet had swung them wide away from the brunt of the storm itself, but not from the rain. The weather had only slowed them down.

Instead of catching the rain in wind-driven sheets, they'd caught it in a heavy deluge. It came almost straight down around them, flattening tall stands of grass to the earth and cutting rivulets down slopes of sandy rock land. More than once Maria had asked Jimmy how he felt. Each time he'd only nodded, staring ahead in the rain with a tight expression on his face. *What was going on behind that fixed stare?* she wondered . . .

The rain had lessened by the time they came to the rail siding four miles north of Bannet. Maria looked up and around at the dark cloud behind them, knowing that by now the Ranger had been hit hard by the storm. She shook her head, then turning forward again, nodded toward a rail shack a few yards ahead, where smoke curled from a tin stovepipe.

At a hitch rail, four horses stood huddled together with their heads lowered. "We will stop here for a while and dry off." Maria's voice raised above the sound of rain pelting the metal roof like steel darts. "Perhaps they will have some hot coffee." Beside the shack, water spun down a drainpipe, spilled over the edge of a filled rain barrel, and streamed away.

As they pulled forward, stepped down, and hitched their horses, the door to the shack swung open and a voice said, "It's the woman, Maria . . . and some fellow."

She glanced up at the smudged face of an old hostler standing in the open doorway. "Here, let me help you," he said, stepping out into the rain as she and Jimmy French reached down and freed their saddle cinches. "We've got the ones you've been looking for inside." The old hostler chuckled, sounding excited. "Yes, indeed! Philburn, Bertrim, and me—we caught 'em no more than an hour ago—the murdering dogs."

"What?" She gave him a puzzled look as she swung her saddle off onto her shoulder.

"I said . . . we've caught the ones who robbed the Bannet stage. We've got living proof they done it too. If there's any reward, we'll get it, right? Won't we?"

She didn't answer.

The old hostler reached forward to take Maria's saddle, but she stayed him back with a gloved hand. "Suit yourself, then," he shrugged and stepped along with her to the door of the shack. "Now, as far as that reward goes . . ."

Jimmy French followed with his wet saddle cradled in his arms.

"What are you talking about? How did you even know the stagecoach was robbed?" Maria asked the old hostler, stepping into the shack ahead of him.

"Because he confessed the whole thing to us . . ." As the hostler pointed and rattled out his reply, she didn't really hear him. But she didn't need to—she saw for herself. Near a woodstove, two men sat with rifles across their laps, tin cups steaming in their hands. They sat smiling at her. On the floor between them lay Two Dogs, the white-haired old Indian who worked in

Bannet mopping the bar and chopping wood. Blood ran from a gash on his weathered forehead; a noose hung around his thin neck. He raised slightly and looked at her through swollen eyes.

One of the men held the rest of the rope in his free hand. He jiggled it and chuckled as he spoke. "You might've missed the catch, little lady, but you've sure made it here in time for the hanging."

Maria swung a glance at Jimmy French, seeing the stunned look in his eyes. He shook his head, no. This old Indian had nothing to do with the Half Moon Gang.

Dropping her saddle, Maria stepped over quickly, jerking the rope from the man's hand. "You fools! This man has done nothing wrong."

"Easy, now!" one of the men cried out, all of them rising, spilling coffee, as she pushed among them and dropped to her knees beside the old Indian. "He admitted to it . . . confessed to robbery *and* kidnapping! There must be a lot of reward money in it."

She snatched the noose from around Two Dogs' neck and flung it away. "Don't talk to me about reward!"

The men shrugged, looking at one another. "That's the danged truth of the matter, little lady," one of them called out as she reached over to the Indian's feet and grappled with the tight strip of wet rawhide binding them together. "And here's the *living* proof of it."

She couldn't loosen the knot by hand, so she reached behind her back and drew the long knife from its sheath. Then she stopped with the knife in her hand as she caught a glimpse of the small child standing forward from among the men, staring terrified at the blade. *Santa Madre* . . . One of the men stood behind the child, his thick rough hands on her tiny shoulders.

"Don't be afraid, little girl," the man spoke down to

the child in a soothing voice. "Nobody's gonna hurt you here. Us boys will see to that."

Maria lowered the knife, looking into the child's frightened eyes, the child standing with a blanket drawn around her, her tiny hand clutching it close at her throat. Her pale blond hair hung in wet strands. "Oh, my, no," Maria said, her voice going soft, looking into those young frightened eyes. "No one is going to hurt you."

She turned quietly, cut the rawhide from around Two Dogs' ankles, then turned back to the child. "See? I only do this to let the man free." Her hand went behind her back and sheathed the big knife. "Where did you find this child?" She asked the three men, looking from one to the other.

"We found her with him." The nearest man spoke down to Maria, seeing the question in her dark eyes. "Him and his murdering friend came slipping toward Bannet with her a while ago. Didn't know we'd be here. He denied it at first . . . but we got the truth out of him. Old Philburn there recognized the child." He pointed to the man wearing a battered bowler hat. "He saw her getting on the stage the other day in Bannet, with her mama. He heard her mama tell the driver they were on a trip north to surprise the little girl's grandfather."

"Come here, child," Maria whispered, struggling to keep her eyes from going moist, drawing the little girl against her, rubbing a hand gently down the back of the child's damp hair. A silence passed, then Maria raised her face back up to the men, looking back and forth among them. "Two Dogs did not rob the stage-coach. We know who did it. The Ranger is on their trail at this moment."

The three men milled and looked at one another. Philburn nudged a finger against the brim of his bowler hat and glanced around at Jimmy French. Jimmy nodded firmly, confirming Maria's words.

"Well, Lord have mercy," Philburn said. Beside him, the old hostler rubbed a dirty hand along his smudged jaw and shook his lowered head. The third man looked away with a huff, slapping a disappointed hand on the wide leather chaps he wore. "Damn it all."

Maria turned, with the child still pressed against her bosom, and looked at Two Dogs. His eyes were pleading, but honest. "I know you did not rob the stage. So tell me what happened . . . where did you find her?"

Two Dogs shook his head slowly, nodding at the child, until Maria turned and passed her back to the man, saying to him in a lowered tone, "Take her to the other side of the stove. Help her dry her hair." And as the child moved out of sight, Maria turned back to the old Indian as he raised himself up on his elbows.

"My grandson and I . . . saw the stagecoach . . . being robbed. Saw it leave the trail and go over the cliff." He spoke in a halting voice, a cut on his lip opening and closing with each word.

"Bring him some water," Maria called over her shoulder, loosening the bandanna from around her neck. She heard someone step across the floor toward canteens hanging from a peg on the wall. "Go on, Two Dogs, tell me everything."

"We watched . . . from far away through my grandson's looking glass. When the door came open on the stagecoach . . . the little white girl flew out among the rocks." He shook his head. "The robbers did not see her."

It was Jimmy French who leaned down with the canteen and handed it to Maria. She noticed he had taken her rifle from her saddle scabbard and held it cradled in his arm. She wet her bandanna and pressed it against the gash on Two Dogs' forehead as he continued speaking. "When they left . . . we went down . . . and brought the child with us . . . to take her to Bannet. My grandson said it was the best thing to do."

Maria ran the wet bandanna back across his tangled white hair, wiping a smear of blood from it. "And your grandson? Where is he now?"

He nodded past her to the three men who stood huddled together, listening. "They shot him . . . but he got away. He is out there somewhere . . . wounded."

Maria turned a dark stare toward the three men. "You pigs! Do you see what you have done here! You have beaten this man and shot his grandson . . . for no reason, none at all."

They milled and looked away, Philburn shrugging once more, saying, "Now, how was we supposed to know all that, little lady? Here comes two Injuns walking in the rain—one carrying a little white girl under his arm? We didn't know the stagecoach had been robbed yet, but we knew it was *missing.* What was we supposed to think?" He tugged down on the brim of his wet bowler hat.

"You might have thought like any decent human would think," Maria said, her eyes ablaze, "that it happened as he just said it happened. You could have at least asked!"

"We did ask, after the other one got away and we caught this old bird." The man in the wet bowler hat pointed down at Two Dogs. "He admitted it to us."

Maria looked back at Two Dogs. He shook his head. "I tried to tell them . . . they heard only what they wanted to hear. I too could have gotten away. But then . . . what would become of the child?"

"The men who robbed the stage," Maria asked. "Did you recognize any of them?"

Two Dogs gave her a guarded glance, looked past her at the man in the leather chaps, then back into her eyes, nodding.

"What? Who'd he say they were?" a voice asked behind her. She turned to the man. They'd all leaned for-

ward to hear, but now they moved back a step from
Maria's glare.

"He did not say who the robbers were . . . only that
he recognized them."

"Well, little lady." The man in the riding chaps
spoke to her, a portly man with a wet gray mustache.
"Maybe we didn't do everything quite the way we
should, but if this Injun really didn't do it . . . we've
got a right to know who did."

"Who are you, mister?" Maria asked with a harsh
scowl fixed on the man.

He shrugged. "Me? I'm Giles Bertrim—cook for the
Circle E, Matthew Edding's spread, up on the high
range. I just happened into this." He jutted his chin.
"I'm the one who shot the other Injun, but don't go
blaming me for any wrongdoing. I only did what anybody else would." He wagged a dirty thumb toward
the old hostler. "He said something about there maybe
being a reward?"

Maria ignored him. She glanced at Jimmy French
and saw him nodding slowly. Two Dogs wasn't about
to identify any Circle E riders in front of Giles Bertrim.

"I understand." She spoke to Two Dogs in a quiet
tone, seeing the look in his dark eyes. "Are you able to
ride into Bannet?"

Two Dogs nodded.

"Just you hold on a minute there, little lady," Giles
Bertrim said. "We're gonna hear what he's got to say,
before anybody goes anywhere."

"No." Maria stood up, helping Two Dogs to his feet.
"We are all going to Bannet."

"Not me, little lady." Giles Bertrim stepped in front
of her, blocking her way as she tried moving forward.
"I'm needed back up at the spread. I got a job to do.
You ain't telling nobody what to do here. Far as I
know this whole thing you're doing is just a way of
beating us out of that reward."

She looked from one to the other and started to speak, but stopped short as she heard Jimmy French lever a round up into the rifle. "She said you're all going to Bannet," French said in a stern tone. "Now, get moving."

Bertrim chuckled. "Wait a minute, boy. I know you . . . you're that little bank teller from over in Cottonwood. Hell, don't go getting cocky here. You ain't nobody." His hand moved an inch toward the pistol on his hip.

"Maybe I'm nobody," French said, the rifle coming up, Maria seeing the tip of the barrel level at Giles Bertrim's head, "but I'm the nobody getting ready to put a bullet through your face."

Even Maria stiffened at the tone of Jimmy French's words. "Easy," she said to Jimmy, almost whispering, her gaze straight ahead on Giles Bertrim. "Mister Bertrim *is* going with us, aren't you, Mister Bertrim?"

Giles Bertrim's hand had jerked away from his pistol butt as if it were a snake. "Why, yes, ma'am." He swallowed and looked back at Jimmy French, who still had one eye closed, sighting along the rifle barrel. "No offense intended, boy—I mean, *young man.* Just trying to settle things here. There's been a lot gone on."

"Yeah," said Jimmy French, "you just had to *test* people a little bit first—see who you could buffalo and who you couldn't. Move your scrubby arse right now, or I'll kill you anyway."

"Lower the rifle, Jimmy, please." Maria kept her voice calm and steady as the men moved back wide-eyed. "There is a child here."

Jimmy French felt the tightness in his finger across the trigger. He had to force himself to let off it. When he did, he let out a shaky breath, his arm going almost limp at his side, the rifle nearly falling from his hand. *My gosh! I did it. It worked . . . actually worked!* He kept a firm gaze and looked from one to the other of the men standing before him. He wished there was a way to test the steadiness of his voice before he spoke. But there wasn't. So he said in a clipped tone, "Anybody else have a problem doing what this woman asked?"

Hands went chest high in obeisance, wet boots scuffled across the plank floor. "Here," Jimmy added, to Maria, putting his free arm around Two Dogs' shoulders, "let me help him. You get the little girl."

Maria only glanced at him for a second, then reached over and took her rifle from his hand. She stepped over and gathered the child in the blanket, picking her up. "Don't worry, dear, we will go to Bannet and find a way to get you to your grandfather. Do you know his name? Can you say it?"

The child nodded, still looking frightened. When she spoke, her voice trembled near Maria's ear as Maria held her close.

Two Dogs leaned against Jimmy French, noting the bullet hole and the trace of a bloodstain still on Jimmy's wet shirt. "You are wounded yourself. How will you help me?"

"It's just a scratch. Don't worry about it," Jimmy said, hefting Two Dogs' weight against his wounded side. Jimmy saw the child whisper once more in Maria's ear—Maria not hearing her clearly the first time. But then as they headed for the door, he saw Maria shake her head, and he asked, "What did she say? What's her name? Does she know her grandfather's name?"

"*Sí*, she told me," Maria said, carrying the child against her bosom. "Her name is *Justice*. Luckily, I know her grandfather. He is a good man. He will be glad to know she is safe. She is the granddaughter of the territorial judge, Winfred Lodge."

"Yes," Jimmy French said, "I've met Judge Lodge. He is a good and honorable man."

CHAPTER 10

The Half Moon Gang trudged several miles through the storm, their collars upturned against wind-driven rain, their horses bowing their necks against the force of it. They'd taken a higher path to avoid rushing streams that only hours ago had been dry, cracked gullies in the hard, sandy dirt. Above them, thunder slammed with the impact of field cannon, the sound of it seeming to break the sky apart higher up in the bellowing black heavens. Lightning licked down and twisted and curled.

At the crest of a ridge overlooking the nearly abandoned mining town called Dunley, Little Tommy reached an arm back and waved the others to him. "Here she is, boys. Let's get down there and shake something loose!" He yelled above the rage of the storm and saw the bleary images emerge toward him from the gray swirl like apparitions come forth from a netherworld. "Quit acting like a bunch of wet-nosed peckerwoods."

At the head of the other riders, big Lew Harper leaned in his saddle toward Newt Babbage beside him. "Look at him. He loves this kind of stuff. Crazy as a bedbug, and blind as a bat."

"I'd be careful with Little Tommy if I was you," Newt Babbage said. "I don't think he likes you much anyway."

The two stopped as Doss Edding and Dusty Charlie moved past them on the mud-slickened trail. Then

Harper turned back to Babbage. "I know it, Newt. You saw how he acted about me saying it was all right for him to go get the whiskey back in Cottonwood. Hadn't been for you cutting him off . . . I believe I'd had to fight him."

"That's something I wouldn't want to do. Only way to whip somebody like him, would be to kill him." Newt Babbage tightened his hat brim farther down on his forehead, and reined forward. As Harper fell his horse in beside him, Babbage added, "How are you feeling about everything?"

"What do you mean?" Harper drew his head down into his upturned collar.

"I mean, about the way things are going. To tell ya the truth, I'm starting to wish I'd never got involved in none of this. The way Doss acted last night, I wonder if maybe he ain't just a little bit, you know—?" He held up a wet-gloved hand and circled a finger around his temple.

Lew Harper stared straight ahead, his voice going low even though no one could hear them above the pounding storm. "It wouldn't surprise me none." A silence passed, then he asked Newt, "Have you ever thought about living in *Mejico*?"

"Yep, I have." Newt Babbage nodded. "Lately, I've thought it more and more." They rode on in silence until they came to where Dusty Charlie and Doss Edding had drawn their horses up alongside Little Tommy Caldwell. Down in Dunley, all that could be seen of the small town were a couple of battered tin roofs through the grayness of the storm.

Doss Edding looked at them from beneath his sagging wet hat brim, the soaked Civil War riding duster clinging to him. "You two are getting like old women, gossiping all the time. What're you talking about that you don't want the rest of us to hear?"

Harper and Babbage stared at him, unable to clearly make out his words beneath a clap of thunder. They looked puzzled, and before either of them could answer, Dusty Charlie cut in, gesturing a dripping gloved hand toward the town below. "Doss, can't you talk about this down there, where it's dry?"

Doss glared at him for a second, then took the lead down the slippery path, Little Tommy following close behind him. As Lew Harper and Newt Babbage moved into line behind Little Tommy, Harper cut Dusty Charlie a glance. "You know what we've been talking about, don't you?"

"All's I know is I'm soaking wet outside, and dry as a bone inside. Let's go if we're going." Dusty Charlie heeled his wet horse forward.

Lightning licked down and flickered across their faces. Harper looked at Babbage. "He knows . . . I can tell he knows. He's been thinking the same thing . . ."

On the empty muddy street they pulled their horses abreast and rode forward slowly, the rain whipping against them, their horses sloshing through the churning water. Overflowing rain barrels stood below corners of roof overhangs where water roared down in braided streams. They moved their horses to a hitch rail out front of the only saloon in town—a tilted wooden shack with a faded overhead sign batting sidelong on the wind.

"There better be a whore here, after all this." Doss glared at Tommy Caldwell, stepping down and spinning his horse's reins.

Inside the saloon, the bartender stood pitching wet logs into the open door of a potbellied stove that stood in the center of the floor. Under the cover of the storm, he hadn't heard them until they spilled through the door. Now he turned and saw them shaking themselves and slapping water from their wet hats. "Get on over here, boys. Get yourselves dry. I'm stoking this fire up. Looks like that storm's about blown itself out."

Water ran in thin streams through cracks in the ceiling. On the floor around the stove, dirt had turned to mud in a soupy mix of cigarette butts and curled wood shavings. "We heard you got you a new whore here," Little Tommy said, stepping forward toward the stove, rubbing his hands together. The others followed him.

"You bet I do." The bartender grinned across stained, crooked teeth. "A big ole strapping red-haired gal all the way from Indiana." His voice rose above the storm. "Darlene? You up in there? Got some cowhands out here wants to meet ya."

A thick voice called out from a room off the side of the small saloon, "Liquor 'em up, Earl, I'll be there directly."

Little Tommy grinned, nudging Doss with his elbow—"Told ya, didn't I?"—getting excited, wanting the others to get rowdy along with him.

"You sure did." Doss turned to the others. "Better make yourselves at home, boys. That whore don't know it yet, but she's got a day's work cut out for her with me. I'm going at her first. Any objections?" He looked from one face to the other. They only glanced among themselves and shrugged.

"Make me no difference," Lew Harper said, "so long as I get me a turn at her."

"All right, then!" Doss grinned and spun in a circle, letting out a whoop. But the grin looked waxy and nervous. The others milled and looked around at the dingy wet saloon. "What's wrong with this bunch?" Doss laughed. "We came here to drink and raise hell, let's get to it!"

"That's the spirit!" Earl the bartender chuckled. He swung the stove door shut, dusted his hands together, and stepped away quickly, moving around the end of the bar to a row of whiskey bottles. "You boys dry out some. I'll bring the whiskey to yas."

When Earl brought out glasses and a bottle of rye whiskey and tried to pass the glasses around to them, Little Tommy shoved the glass aside and snatched the

bottle from his hand. "Now, bring my friends one." He
pulled the cork with his teeth, spit it away, and threw
back a long guzzle.

"Why, sure thing." The bartender scurried away once
more, and this time came back passing out full bottles to
the others.

As they tossed back a few drinks, Doss had gone into
recounting a time when he and Little Tommy had gotten drunk and stolen a couple of horses. By then, Darlene the whore had thrown back a blanket that served to
separate her room on the side from the rest of the saloon.
"All right, I'm perked and ready here. Give your dollar
to Earl and get on in here."

"He's first," Little Tommy said, pointing his bottle at
Doss Edding.

"Then come on, hurry up." Darlene raised her big
bosom toward Doss and smiled. "The roof's leaking
over the bed."

The others looked at Doss; but his face reddened, and
he shouted at her. "Can't you see I'm in the middle of
telling something here? Don't tell me to hurry up,
whore . . . I'll knock your damn teeth out." Doss turned
back to the others, grinning, puffing out his chest. "Ain't
no damn whore tells me—"

Darlene glared at him for a second, then stepped forward from the blanketed door. "Why, you puny little
bastard. I'd like to see you try!"

Doss looked stunned. His grin sagged. His hand went
to the pistol on his hip.

"How about *I* go first?" Lew Harper stepped between
them as Darlene started across the wet floor.

"Yeah, Lew, you go on." Doss's voice sounded
strained. "Break her in for us." He raised his voice to
Darlene. "You best save some of your strength, whore.
I'll be on ya all day once I get started."

"Ha!" they heard her say, flipping the blanket to one
side and shoving Lew Harper into her room.

Doss's eyes flared; but Dusty Charlie spoke quickly, asking him to go on and finish the story. "What'd you and Little Tommy do next?"

"Yeah, go on, tell him, Doss." Little Tommy grinned, his eyes glinting large and punch-drunk behind his thick wire frames. "This is the best part."

Doss took a breath and settled, and wiped a nervous hand across his lips. "Well, anyway . . ."

The storm lessened as they drank and joked and swapped stories, each adding something the other might not have seen happen when they'd run the stagecoach over the cliff. When Lew Harper stepped back in through the blanket, grinning and running a hand back along his tangled wet hair, they looked at him and hooted, then laughed and threw back drinks. Tommy handed him a bottle of rye, slapped his wet back, and asked him how it was; but Harper only blew out a breath and said if Tommy wanted to know, he'd have to pay his dollar and find out for himself.

Newt Babbage nudged Doss and asked, "Are you going next?"

Doss glanced over and saw Darlene standing in the doorway with the blanket pushed to the side. "Well? Who's ready?" Her huge breasts were bare now, pale white and slick with rain water and sweat. She held up a stained gray bed sheet against her, covering her large belly. Her red hair lay in wet strands on her shoulders.

"Don't rush me, Newt!" Doss rounded his shoulder away from Newt Babbage and threw back a drink of whiskey.

"All right, just asking." Newt stepped back with a raised hand.

Little Tommy said to Doss as Newt moved away toward Darlene, slipping his galluses from his shoulders, "Tell about how you and me gave the Floreses hell over them winter calves."

"Yeah, that's a good one."

* * *

By the time Newt Babbage had returned from beyond the blanketed doorway, Doss Edding was staggering in place, babbling in a slurred voice about what it took to run a gang like this. The others only nodded and drank. They'd moved from the woodstove over to the bar; Doss only threw back a drink and kept talking as Babbage took his bottle of rye and moved over and leaned on the bar beside Lew Harper.

Little Tommy didn't interrupt Doss. Instead, he slipped away from beside him without Doss noticing and walked toward Darlene. She stood completely naked now, smiling a wet smile, drawing Tommy to her with a crooked finger. "What's wrong with your friend?" she asked, letting the blanket fall when she'd followed Little Tommy into the small room.

"Not a damn thing, I don't reckon." Tommy's large eyes swam behind his spectacles, looking her up and down. Then he grabbed her by the clammy loose flesh of her sides and pulled her down onto the soggy mattress.

While the wet mattress bounced and sloshed and creaked in its rope frame, at the bar Doss Edding had taken his pistol from his holster and swung it above his head. Good and drunk now, he let out a sound that was something between a laugh and a scream, and pulled off two rounds into the loose plank ceiling. "If there's a better man than me in this damned place, he better *speak now* and I'll forever hold his peace!" Doss looked around at the others and added, "I'm going in there next. Anybody got any objections?" His eyes were bloodshot and swirling.

"I already been." Newt Babbage puffed on a short cigar, dismissing it.

"Me too," said Lew Harper.

The two of them only shrugged and tossed back another drink from their bottles. Dusty Charlie stood beside Doss at the rough-planked bar, constructed of long pine boards atop wooden barrels. "Hell, Doss, you been saying you're *next* ever since we started. Either go on back there or hush about it." He tossed back a long drink, let out a sharp hiss, adding, "You coulda gone first like you *said* you was." Behind the bar, Earl the bartender stood watching them, his friendly smile gone now, a nervous look taking its place. Rain dripped down onto his shoulder. Having heard the way Doss was talking, babbling about robbing and killing, all he wanted was for these boys to pay up and leave.

"Well, this time I mean it," Doss said, spinning his pistol and holstering it "I wanted to make sure she's worth fooling with. Let the rest of ya take a crack at her first." He offered a stiff grin. "Ain't that the smartest way to do it?"

"Whatever you say, Doss." Dusty Charlie, Babbage, and Harper shot one another guarded glances, then looked away.

A tight silence passed until Little Tommy staggered through the wet-blanket partition. "She said, anybody else who's interested better come on now whilst she's still in the mood." He laughed, looking over at Doss and Dusty Charlie. A nerve twitched in Doss's tight jaw. Dusty Charlie just stared at him.

"Go on, Dusty," Doss said. "I reckon you're in a bigger hurry than I am."

"I'm in no hurry at all," Dusty Charlie said. "I might not even do it at all."

"What?" Doss looked at him. "We came all this way . . . now you ain't even interested?"

"Never mind about me." Dusty Charlie threw back another drink, let out another hiss. "You go ahead, if you're going to. I'm doing some drinking and thinking."

"Thinking? About what?" Doss asked.

"Just thinking." Dusty Charlie glanced at Harper and Babbage, then looked down at the wet bar.

Darlene's thick gravely voice called out from beyond

the blanket. "What's it gonna be out there, fellahs? Once these bloomers come up, they're staying up till it stops raining. I ain't gonna lay here and *drown* waiting on you raw-ass cowboys."

"Shut up! We ain't no damn cowboys!" Doss shouted toward the blanket, his face turning red. "I'll be there when I'm good and ready!" He ran a moist hand across his face. "No half-a-dollar whore's telling me what to do."

"Half a dollar? Huh," she called out from the doorway. "Where'd you go to school?"

Dusty Charlie gazed away through a dirty window into the blowing rain. Thunder crashed, but farther away now, the worst of the storm moved on. "Rotten, dirty whore," Doss grumbled under his breath.

The others looked at him, Little Tommy snickering, putting on his mud-streaked spectacles, his small weak eyes growing large behind them. "Dang it, Doss . . . you're acting like you ain't never skint it back on a—"

"Watch your mouth, Tommy," Doss snapped. "I have, plenty of times. I just don't like being crowded about it." As he spoke, he took money from inside his riding duster and slapped it down on the bar. The bartender snatched it up. "There, now," Doss said, "I'm going. Is everybody happy?"

The others only stared as he stepped across the mud-streaked floor and flipped through the blanket in a huff. As the blanket swung shut behind him, Newt Babbage looked at Dusty Charlie and asked in a lowered voice, "What exactly *are* you thinking about, Dusty?" As he asked, Lew Harper leaned in closer with them.

Dusty Charlie let out a long breath, looking back in from the storm. "I'm thinking we've all got on a *bad* drunk and done some terrible things," he said.

"Bull!" Little Tommy snatched a bottle off of the bar and swigged from it. Rye whiskey dribbled freely down his chin. "This ain't the first raid we was ever on."

"But it's the first time we've killed anybody," Dusty Charlie said. "It's one thing to rough up a few heads in a saloon brawl or steal a few head of Mexican horses across the border." He threw back a drink, then added, "But, boys, we've got big trouble here. Jesse Tiggs was right. We set out making a name for ourselves. Now we've done it." Thunder rumbled above them.

"Jesse Tiggs ain't nothing but a lot of bluff talk with a fancy gun," Little Tommy said.

"Then, why didn't you tell him so, Little Tommy?" Dusty Charlie stared at him. Tommy looked away and sulked.

"Anyhow, I want out of this. What about you?" Dusty Charlie spoke, looking down at the bar top.

Harper and Babbage looked at one another for a second, then back at Dusty Charlie. Lew Harper said in a low tone, "We've been thinking about it ever since we ran out of whiskey back on the trail. This thing has gotten too big—bigger than I ever thought it would. We started off just drinking and raising hell on the weekends. Now look at us."

"Yeah," Newt Babbage cut in, "Doss didn't know where to stop. He's got a daddy can buy his way out of stuff. What have we got? I ain't got nothing or *nobody* to help me out."

"Newt's right," Harper said. "I believe it's time we clear out of here. To hell with this Half Moon Gang idea. I'm thinking about Mexico myself."

Dusty Charlie nodded, then looked at Little Tommy. Little Tommy just stared, working something out in his mind. After a second, he threw back a drink and spread a wide drunken grin. "Not me, boys. To hell with the rest of yas. I'm in it till the last dog's hung."

CHAPTER 11

.

As Dusty Charlie, Lew Harper, and Newt Babbage slipped out through the open doorway of the saloon toward their wet horses, Dusty Charlie glanced back once and shook his head. "Ole man Edding will skin me alive. I've never mentioned it to any of you, but Matthew's been paying me extra to look after that boy for him. I hate going back on my word."

"Are you kidding me?" Newt Babbage asked with a bemused look on his face. "There ain't nobody can look after Doss Edding. He's plumb out of his mind." He adjusted the soaked saddle and tightened the cinch. "I reckon Matthew Edding knew it to begin with, or he wouldn't have asked you to do it in the first place."

Water ran from Dusty Charlie's sagging hat brim. "Let's just get out of here before Doss sees we're gone. I don't want to have to fight him if I can keep from it. Tommy could be in there telling him right now." He stepped up into his saddle, the other two doing the same.

"Don't worry about that." Lew Harper spoke as they swung their horses around on the muddy street. Lightning snaked down in the distance, followed by a clap of thunder. "Tommy won't say nothing till he's sure we're gone. He's glad it's just the two of them again."

"You're right, Lew." Dusty Charlie let out a breath

and looked at the other two, chucking his horse forward. "There's something not right about Doss and Little Tommy. I've been seeing it for a while. What happened with the bank teller just cinched it for me."

"What are you saying, Charlie?" Lew Harper asked as they put their horses forward together, keeping them as quiet as possible along the muddy street.

"I don't know," Dusty Charlie said, drawing his collar up against the blowing deluge, "just that something wasn't right about that deal the other night. You saw the look on Doss's face—it was about more than just scaring the kid." He slid them a shielded glance from between his raised collar and his sagging hat brim. "He had something in his eyes, like they were on fire with evil burning inside him."

Newt Babbage cocked his head. "Me and Lew were saying the same thing earlier. Dusty, do you suppose Doss and Tommy have plumb lost it?"

"I don't know what they are . . . and I don't care." Dusty Charlie nudged his horse forward. "I'm just glad to get shed of both of them."

"Lord have mercy." Lew Harper whispered under his breath, letting dark possibilities cross his mind. Lightning twisted and curled.

Once past the edge of town, they kicked their horses up into a trot, the animals splashing mud and drawing their heads sideways against blowing sheets of rain. "I know one thing . . . I'm never getting drunk again," Newt Babbage said. They rode on for nearly a mile without speaking another word, moving farther away from beneath the main body of the storm, feeling the thrust of it lessen against them.

Ahead of them atop a low ridge, the Ranger looked down and saw the three soaked riders moving along the puddled trail, coming up into the rocks toward him. Was it them? Were these men stupid enough to backtrack themselves after robbing a bank—after the

stagecoach killings? I'll soon find out, he thought, stepping his horse back, searching through the pouring
rain, looking for any others that might be lagging behind. *Only three of them . . . ? What about the other two?*

Moving up onto the narrow trail, Dusty Charlie
looked forward into the silver-gray rain, then fell his
horse back from the lead and let Harper and Babbage
move past him. Water ran silty and swift down a deep
ditch along one side of the trail, roaring over rocks and
splashing high. Lew Harper glanced at Dusty Charlie
and asked him above the roar of water, "What're you
pulling back for? There's room up here."

"Nothing, go on ahead," Dusty Charlie called out,
also raising his voice above the hard rush of runoff
water. "I'll keep up with you. This horse ain't acted
right since we left town. Think he's getting a pulled
tendon."

"That's all you need right now," Lew Harper
grunted, chucking his horse forward, moving on.

Rounding a turn where the trail spread out and leveled for a few yards, they snapped up sharp on their
wet reins, stopping short at the sight of the lone rider,
who sat his horse crosswise in the middle of the trail
before them.

"Whooa, Jesus!" Newt Babbage cried out, startled.
His horse bumped sideways against Lew Harper's.
Harper's horse shied away, nearly spinning beneath
him. He settled the horse and held it in place.

"Evening, boys." The Ranger spoke in a level tone
from ten yards away. His wet sombrero brim raised
up slightly, just enough to reveal his eyes. Rain fell
straight and steady, plastering his duster tails down
the white barb's sides. "Hope you can help me out
here."

They glanced past him, to where his spare horse
stood tied to a short jut of rock—Sheriff Brady Martin's roan. They glanced back to him, taking note of the

big pistol lying across his lap. Beads of rain stood on the pistol. "Who are you?" Newt Babbage asked, his hand dropping down close to his holstered .45 range Colt.

The Ranger's wet gloves were off, and sticking out of his duster pocket. He raised a hand into his duster, took out a folded piece of paper, and tapped it toward them. "I'm looking for five men who came this way earlier," the Ranger said. "Tell me if any of these names sound familiar to you."

Lew Harper whispered back over his shoulder, "Get up here, Charlie, *quick!*" He stepped his horse to the side, enough to let Dusty Charlie come forward between them. But Dusty Charlie didn't come forward. Instead, he backed his horse a cautious step and turned it sideways on the trail.

The Ranger began calling out the names in a clear voice above the rain and the rushing water. "Doss Edding, Tommy Caldwell, Newt Babbage—"

His words stopped. Lew Harper's hand jerked for the .45 on his hip as the Ranger's big pistol fired from across his lap. The shot lifted Lew Harper from his saddle and pitched him sidelong into the roaring stream of runoff water. Newt Babbage's horse nickered and reared as he tried to raise *his* pistol. But the Ranger's white barb stood still as a stone, the Ranger's next shot hitting Babbage like the blow of a sledgehammer, centered on his chest, sending him backward. Babbage's free hand stayed taut on the reins, his weight going back, pulling the rearing horse back with him.

Both horse and man tumbled backward and down in a tangle of leather, hoof, and stirrup. Muddy water splashed high. The Ranger sent his white barb forward with a tap of his heels, his pistol up now, seeing the third man spin his horse back down along the mud-slick trail. Dusty Charlie disappeared around the turn in a muddy spray.

It figures . . . That one had looked a little older. A little wiser? Maybe so, the Ranger thought. This one had let his buddies take the lead once they'd moved up onto the narrow trail. But he wouldn't get far. The Ranger had the edge now. And he wasn't about to lose it.

He lowered his big pistol and checked his white barb down beside Babbage's horse as it stood up shaking mud from its back, its saddle hanging far down one side. He grabbed the horse by its bridle and settled it, spinning its reins around his own saddle horn. He stepped down from atop the white barb, putting the folded wet paper back inside his duster, his big pistol still in his hand. Rain fell heavy and straight, and he took his gloves from his duster pocket, put the left one on, and snugged it up with his teeth. Then he took a deep breath and looked around.

Newt Babbage's body lay twisted and broken on the muddy trail, the weight of the horse having come down hard on him. The Ranger only toed him with his boot, then stepped over to where Lew Harper lay flat on his back, gasping, the lower half of him bobbing in the muddy stream. "Which one are you?" The Ranger asked, stooping down, looking Lew Harper in the eyes. Rain pelted the muddy stream.

"Pull . . . pull me out." Water swirled across his thick chest. His large stomach rose and fell with each labored breath. He batted his wet eyelashes and coughed up a belch of dark blood.

"Why? You ain't going nowhere, *yet*." The Ranger rested down on his haunches, his arms out across his knees. He jiggled the pistol in his hand. "Besides, the last time I tried pulling somebody out of something, it didn't go all that well."

"What—? What do you mean?" Lew Harper

gasped, the muddy water washing away red across him, one hand struggling to hang on to a rock against the downward-rushing stream.

"Never mind." The Ranger shook his head. "Which one are you? Babbage? Harper? Allbright? Caldwell? Not Doss Edding, are you?"

"Har—Harper. Lew . . . Harper." Blood spilled from his thick lips. "That's . . . Newt Babbage." His eyes moved in the direction of the body on the muddy trail.

The Ranger nodded back along the trail. "What about the one who ran?"

"Dusty Charlie," Harper gasped. "Please. This water's . . . about to wash me away."

The Ranger shrugged. "And you're the ones who raided the bank in Cottonwood and ran the Bannet stage off a cliff, right?"

"We . . . was drunk, is all. We never . . . would've done it, otherwise."

"Save it for the devil," the Ranger said, remembering the dying woman's eyes in the wreckage of the stagecoach before it had made its long final plunge. "Where's the others? Down in Dunley?"

"Yeah, Dunley—" Harper's voice sounded weaker, more and more strained now as he spoke. "Two of them's down there."

"Good." The Ranger nodded and stood up. But he stopped. *Two of them?* "That's all of you, then, right? All five of you?"

"I told you . . . everything. Show some mercy."

"How many are there in this Half Moon Gang? I'm told there's five of you."

"Yeah, five, now . . . one quit on us." His eyes pleaded.

"Who was he? When did he quit?"

"Before the robbery." Harper shook his head. "He didn't do nothing in Cottonwood."

"What about the stagecoach? Was he there?"

"He . . . he didn't do nothing there. Come on, Ranger, I'm dying." He held on to the rock and raised his free trembling hand up toward the Ranger. "Please help me!"

"Well, all right." The Ranger took his muddy wet hand and jerked him a few inches out of the swirling water. Then he turned him loose. "So you want mercy, huh?" The Ranger looked down at him as he took two bullets from his belt and reloaded the big pistol. "Here's all the mercy you'll get from me."

"Don't! Please don't shoot me no more!"

"I'm not going to." He checked the pistol, slipped it back inside his duster, and holstered it. "I'm gonna give you a few minutes to die on your own while I strap your friend's body across his horse. If you ain't dead by then, I'll kick you out into the water and let you ride these sharp rocks down to the flatland." He leaned slightly and added in a lowered tone, "Now, is that *mercy*, or what?"

"That ain't mercy . . . it ain't even human. Please!" Harper's voice trembled.

"It still amazes me sometimes," the Ranger said, "the way you thugs always expect mercy—as if the world owes it to you." He shook his head. "If you're smart, you'll get to dying real quick. I don't have all day to fool with you."

Lew Harper looked up at him, seeing only harsh resolve in the Ranger's eyes. There was no point in pleading. Harper swallowed a tight knot in his throat and closed his eyes tightly as the Ranger turned and stepped away, over onto the muddy trail. "I—I'll try," Harper said in a faltering voice.

"Better try real hard," the Ranger called back over his shoulder to him. And a few moments later, when the Ranger had finished raising Newt Babbage's body, dropping it across the wet horse's back and strapping it down with a length of rope, he stepped back over to

Lew Harper, leading Harper's horse by its reins. When he poked a boot toe against Lew Harper's ribs, Harper didn't move. *Yep. Good enough* . . . He was dead now.

The Ranger stood for a second looking through the pouring rain along the thin trail down toward Dunley. The third rider had few options—either he'd headed straight back to Dunley to warn the others, or he'd cut out, back through the storm and across the high range to the west, letting the weather wash away his tracks.

But there was one other thing the third rider could have done. He might have taken position up in the rocks and waited for an ambush. But the Ranger doubted it. From what he'd learned so far of the Half Moon Gang, they weren't the smartest, and they definitely weren't the toughest he'd ever seen. Stooping down, the Ranger hefted Lew Harper's body beneath his limp shoulders and dragged him back from the rushing water. With any luck, this would all be over by the end of the day.

CHAPTER 12

Doss swung his pistol in a rage. "Damn them all to hell! Why didn't you come and tell me, Tommy?"

Little Tommy shied back a step, his drunken eyes swimming behind his spectacles. "Forget about them, Doss." He talked quick, his words thick with a whiskey slur. "Think about it. It'll be better this way. You and me understand one another. Can't you see it? Just the two of us together . . . like it started out? We can bring in some new Half Moon members anytime we're ready. You see where I'm at, Doss. You know where I stand. I'm staying with you no matter what . . . pals to the end."

"But they swore an oath, just like my daddy and his guerilla riders did back in the war! They can't just turn tail on us like this."

Tommy tried a sheepish grin and shrugged. "Looks like they've already done it, buddy."

"Like hell!" Doss swung a bottle of rye off the bar and threw back a drink. "They're gonna *pay* for this, Tommy! I *swear* they are! When I give my word, I *keep* it. I'd never run out on a partner. Never have, never will!" He pushed himself away from the bar, snatching Little Tommy by his coat sleeve. "Come on, we'll find them peckerwoods and show them we mean business. This ain't something they can quit anytime they feel like it!"

The bartender had slunk down behind the bar while

Doss Edding waved his pistol. Now he ventured up as the two men left the saloon. "Darlene? You all right in there?" His voice called out in a hushed tone. Outside, the tail end of the storm grumbled and drifted north.

"Hell, yeah, I'm all right," Darlene chuckled, and in a second her mud-streaked hand pulled the wet blanket to one side as she stepped through it, adjusting her wet dress down over her plump body. "Easiest three dollars I ever earned—except for this blasted rain. You oughta fix this roof."

"I know," the bartender said, his eyes still wary and fixed on the open doorway until he caught sight of Doss and Little Tommy gigging their horses away from the hitch rail. "I'm going to fix it, once business picks up." Then he let out a breath, hearing the two horses splash away along the mud street. "Now, there was a strange bunch. What were they talking about—the Half Moon Gang? Ever heard of them?"

"Nope." She shook out her wet red hair and pulled it back with a thick hand. "But that last one said he's the leader . . . if you can believe that." She cocked her head slightly, reflecting on Doss Edding. "He's a weird one. I don't think he had an idea in the world what he was doing back there. He wouldn't even take off his duster."

"Oh?" The bartender raised a wet eyebrow. "You mean, he didn't even . . . ?"

"Not with *me*, he didn't." Darlene smiled a thick-lipped smile, stepped over and raised a bottle of rye from atop the bar, and threw back a shot. "Crazy as a loon." She shrugged, letting out a watery belch. "But God love 'em, they're all a little bit crazy . . . ain't they."

Outside, at the far end of the mud street, Doss Edding reined his paint horse up at the sight of the rider moving down the trail toward them. "Hold on,

Tommy!" At a hundred yards, through the rain and
the gray swirling mist, he barely made out the high
crown of the gray sombrero; but behind the rider, he
saw the three-horse string, two of them with bodies
draped across their saddles.

"What is it?" Tommy asked, checking his horse
down, squinting through his mud-smeared spectacles.

"A rider," Doss said, trying to make the figure out
more clearly. He did not recognize the Ranger, but on
one of the horses behind him, Lew Harper's body
bobbed up and down, too big to miss. "Jesus, Tommy!
He's killed Lew—and somebody else!" He yanked
back on his reins, his horse hunched down, back-stepping, raising mud. "Lord God! It's the law—a lawman!
Tommy, they're on to us!"

"All right, take it easy. How many are there?"
Tommy squinted, unable to see that far off.

"I don't know—oh, God! Maybe one, I can't tell."
Doss's voice had broken, shrill and trembling.
"What'll we do?"

"Just one?" Tommy gave him a bemused look.
"Then, we'll kill him. That's what we'll do."

Ahead of them, the Ranger stopped his white barb
and stared through the rain at the two horsemen stirring back and forth in the middle of the street. *Here we
go. . . .* He heeled Black-eye forward, pulling the three-
horse string behind him. If these men were the ones he
was after, he'd soon know. They'd make a move before he got much closer.

"He's seen us! Let's get out of here, Tommy, quick!"
Doss yelled, panicking, trying to turn his paint horse
as Tommy snatched it by its bridle.

"No. We'll shoot him," Tommy said. "Just watch
me." He turned loose of Doss's bridle and raised his
pistol from his holster. Doss shot a glance at the rider
pounding forward, growing larger now, more clearly
visible, a wake of water spraying up behind him.

"You can't even *see* him!" Doss jerked again on his reins. He had to make a run for it, with or without Tommy. Maybe Tommy could buy him some time here.

Tommy squinted, sighting along his pistol barrel, holding the pistol with both hands.

"Stick with me," Tommy said, "I've got him."

Doss moved quickly, slamming his horse against Tommy's while Tommy stood high in his stirrups, both hands out before him. Tommy's pistol fired a wild shot. Doss straight-armed him out of his saddle, snatching the reins to Tommy's horse as Tommy splashed down into the mud. "Kill him, Tommy! I need both horses! Kill him while I get away!"

"Wait, Doss!" Tommy slipped and slid, coming to his feet, his pistol in the mud, his wire rims down there with it somewhere.

"Can't wait!" Doss turned, nearly shaken out of his wits, heeling his big paint horse away, leading Tommy's muddy horse behind him. "Kill him, Tommy! I won't forget you for this!"

"Dang it, Doss! What are you doing? Don't leave me this way!" Tommy looked all around, then bent and searched the mud frantically for his pistol and spectacles.

The Ranger gave the white barb more heel. "Come on, Black-eye," pounding faster through the muddy water, seeing the rider on the paint horse turn and take off with both horses, the other fumbling in the mud. Yep, these were his boys all right, he thought. The Half Moon Gang, young, stupid, and here at the end, cowards who couldn't even stand up and face what was coming to them. He cocked the big pistol forward, leveling it in a full run, splashing mud, closing fast.

Before him, at a distance of forty yards, Little Tommy found his pistol and came up from the ground with it, slinging it back and forth to free mud from it.

He raised it toward the sound of the closing hooves. But it was too late. The Ranger let the hammer fall, the shot hitting Tommy high in his right shoulder, spinning him, pitching him down in a spray of muddy water.

"Damn it!" Tommy squeezed out his words, his breath having left him at the impact of the .45 slug. He tried to focus his weak eyes on the blur of man and horses as the Ranger pounded past him. Then the Ranger stopped and turned his string around in the middle of the street, seeing that the other rider had pulled too far away, gaining a solid lead out toward the high buttes southeast of town. No problem, he thought. The Half Moon Gang was finished now—only two of them left, and those two on the run in different directions. He had a pretty good idea where Doss Edding would be headed. The other one he'd track down and kill at his own pace.

Little Tommy ran his hand back and forth in the mud searching for his spectacles, cursing, clenching his teeth against the pain in his shoulder. "I'll kill you!" His pistol had flown out of his hand and once again lay lost in the mud. "Don't come any closer," he yelled as the Ranger stepped down from his saddle and walked toward him, leading the horses. "I've got another gun here," he lied. "You better stop—I'm warning you!" Tommy's eyes squinted at the blurred figure. "Damn it, I mean it! You stay the hell away from me!"

"Which one are you?" the Ranger asked, taking out the list from inside his duster and glancing down the names he'd marked off with a pencil stub. "Doss Edding rides a brown and white paint horse. Reckon that makes you Tommy Caldwell?"

"Who's asking?" Tommy raised his weak eyes, searching upward, squinting through the falling rain. The Ranger spread open his duster, showing the badge on his chest. Little Tommy spit and ran a muddy hand across his eyes. "Ha, mighta figured—a damn law-dog Ranger. To hell with you! I ain't answering nothing to nobody, so you just as well not ask—"

His words cut short when the Ranger stopped two feet away and kicked him in his jaw with a muddy boot. Before Tommy could right himself, the Ranger stood the boot down on the back of his neck and jammed the side of Tommy's face down into the mud. "I won't ask again, then." His voice stayed calm. "The next sound is me sending a bullet in the back of your head." The big pistol cocked and lowered. His finger tightened on the trigger.

"Yeah, I'm Caldwell, dang it! Tommy Caldwell!" Mud flew from his lips. "Now, go on and shoot me. I don't give a damn!"

The Ranger stood still for a second, thinking it over. He might need to wait, see what else this one might tell him about the others.

"See? You can't just shoot me, can you? That's what I thought. You law dogs are all alike—can't just shoot a man for no reason, not if you're any kind of lawman."

"I can't? Now, where on earth do you boys get such foolish notions." The Ranger shook his head, let out a breath, and raised the pistol, letting down the hammer with his thumb. He took his boot off Tommy's neck, holstered the big pistol, reached down, and grabbed Tommy's coat collar, jerking him up from the mud. "Come on, now. You're not hurt that bad, a tough boy like you."

Tommy staggered to his feet. "I demand to know why you shot me. You've got nothing on me, law dog! I know the law . . . you're gonna pay for this!"

"Save it for the hangman," the Ranger said and shoved Tommy toward the open door of the saloon, where the bartender and Darlene stood staring out at them.

"I knew they was trouble the minute they rode in," the bartender called out, Tommy staggering toward him, dripping blood as the Ranger pushed him on. "Wouldn't have let them in if it hadn't been storming so hard. Can't refuse anybody shelter, you know."

"Is that a fact?" The Ranger thrust Tommy inside with one last hard shove, then walked in leading the muddy string of horses behind him. The bodies of Newt Babbage and Lew Harper lay limp across the wet horses' backs, dripping bloody water onto the mud floor. "Then I don't suppose you'll mind my horses drying out a little in here."

"Hold on here," the bartender said, him and Darlene fanning to the side as the string of horses passed them. "You can't bring this mess in here. I'm trying to run a business, for *crying out loud!*"

The Ranger ignored him, reaching down to where Tommy had fallen on the floor. He yanked Tommy up and flung him backward into a wet wooden chair. The chair legs sank down in the mud. Tommy grunted, pressing a wet hand to his bloody shoulder. "You hear me?" the bartender shouted, moving over behind him. "This ain't allowed here. No horses . . . no dead bodies. They've got to go. This is a place of business here!"

The Ranger turned, raising his sombrero brim, taking note of the empty mud-stuck saloon. "I'm all the business you've got right now, so settle down and show some manners." He looked around again, shaking his head. "We'll be out of here before you know it, once this boy quits bleeding and the rain lets up."

"It'll be tomorrow before the rain lets up." The bartender's eyes widened.

"I know." The Ranger glanced again around the muddy saloon. "I don't like it any better than you do. So let's just be polite and stay out of each other's way."

Darlene moved forward, eyeing the Ranger and the dull glint of the badge on his chest behind his open duster. "Earl, do you know who this is?" Her words sounded hushed. "This is *him*, Sam Burrack . . . the *Ranger*. The one who killed Bent Jackson, Montana Red, and all them others!"

"Well, help my time." The bartender moved closer for a better look as the Ranger leaned and tore open Little Tommy's shirt. "You're not him, are ya? Are you sure you're him?"

"I oughta know." The Ranger spoke without turning to him. "While you're not busy, why don't you look after these horses for me." He glanced at Darlene. "And why don't you see if you can rustle up something to eat. You don't mind, do ya?"

"Nothing's free, Sam Burrack," she said, cocking a hand to her thick hip.

"I know it." The Ranger poked a finger against Little Tommy's bleeding wound as he spoke to her. "I'll pay up before we leave."

"Oh?" She smiled. "In that case, there's lot's of ways we could pass the time." She moved forward a step, but the Ranger held her back with a hard stare.

"I didn't come here to play, ma'am," he said. "As he said, this is strictly business here. Just pull me up some food and coffee."

"Hold it." The bartender stopped Darlene as she turned to move back toward the other room. "Ranger, you can't come in here giving orders. You don't even have jurisdiction here. You've stepped way over the line."

"So did these bummers," the Ranger said, raising Little Tommy's muddy chin. He shot the bartender a strong glance. "Now, how's those horses doing?"

CHAPTER 13

Doss Edding's big paint horse splashed on through the pouring rain. Doss lay low, casting glances back over his shoulder in the flickering streaks of lightning. Somehow in his panic he'd lost his grip on his spare horse's reins, and let the animal race away into the storm. Now Doss pounded on scared and alone, all of his partners gone, no more Half Moon Gang standing behind him. *Bunch of cowards . . .*

The gang had been his and Little Tommy's idea from the start; now Little Tommy lay dead in the street, he thought, looking back over his shoulder, seeing nothing behind him but the grayness of the low misty swirl. *Damn it! It wasn't supposed to have turned out this way.* He spurred the paint horse harder, the horse worn and wet and struggling through thick sandy mud.

He knew of no place to go but home, back to the ranch where his father would be waiting for him. Matthew Edding would rant and rave—Doss might have to take a beating—but in the end, his father would have to realize that there was nothing to do but help Doss escape from the law. Wouldn't he? Of course he would. What choice would he have—see his only son hang, watch him swing from the gallows? Doss thought about it as he pressed on. So deep were his thoughts, that he almost ran into Dusty Charlie as Charlie sidled out of the rain and up closer toward him. When Doss caught sight of him, he nearly spun his big paint horse away.

But Dusty Charlie called out, "Doss! It's me. Damn it, hold up!" Thunder rumbled overhead. He snatched at Doss's reins as the big paint horse reeled and reared, slinging mud. Lightning glittered and flashed across Doss Edding's frightened face.

"Jesus, Charlie!" Doss collected his horse, checking it down, Dusty Charlie reigning up beside him. Doss's expression turned relieved, then it came to him how Dusty Charlie and the others had run out on him and Tommy. He tensed. "Let go of my horse, damn you. I oughta put a bullet in you. Where's the others?"

"They're dead, Doss." Dusty Charlie let go of the paint horse's reins, both horses stepping back and forth in the mud. Rain pounded down. "A lawman killed them both—I barely got away myself. I was on my way back to warn you and Tommy."

Doss looked at him. "Like hell. You all three ran out on me. Tommy said so."

Dusty Charlie let out a breath. "All right, I won't deny it. We were heading to Mexico. But that's all changed now. Do you know who that is, riding that white barb horse? That big gray sombrero? It's that Ranger everybody's afraid of. He's kilt everybody he's ever hunted! We got to stick together now, or he'll kill us too." Charlie glanced around in the rain and mist. "Where is Little Tommy?"

"Dead in the street," Doss said, nodding back through the rain toward the town. "I tried to stay and help him, but he wouldn't hear of it. He made me take his horse with me and leave . . . he sacrificed himself just so's I could get away." Doss's eyes narrowed on Charlie. "That's what a true buddy will do. For two cents I'd go back there right now and kill that Ranger where he stands." He shook his head, slinging water from his soaked hat brim. "But that's not the way Tommy wanted it."

"Then, where are we headed?" Dusty Charlie asked, not believing a word about Little Tommy wanting to face the Ranger alone, but at the same time needing to partner with somebody should the Ranger come close to him again.

"To the ranch," Doss said. "We can shortcut straight across the badland hills and be there by nightfall. Nobody can track us through this rain. Daddy and his men can go with us, get us across the border. Even the Ranger won't mess with my daddy. Not if he wants to stay alive."

"That might be fine for you, Doss, but your daddy's gonna kill me for letting all this happen. He's bound to know about it by now."

"I'll handle my daddy," Doss said, adding an air of confidence he didn't quite feel. "If you're with me on this, I won't let you down." He pointed a finger. "Only don't try cutting out on me again, *ever*. You understand?"

"Yeah, I understand. Maybe I could lay back and wait till after you talk to him first . . . let him know what kind of spot we're on? Maybe you can settle him down some first?"

"No. We ride in together, and tell him how it is. He's got to help us." Doss reined his horse around on the trail as he spoke, feeling himself taking charge of something once more, and liking the feel of it. "Just stick with me, Charlie. The Half Moon Gang ain't finished yet—not by a long shot."

They pushed their horses on through the pouring rain until by evening the storm had played itself out. By then they'd crossed the low rolling badland hills, moved down onto the northern boundary of the Edding spread, and rested their tired wet animals down to a walk. In another hour the rain had stopped altogether, and they caught sight of the Edding hacienda in the near distance.

"Well, looky what's coming here," Jesse Tiggs said, more to himself than to the four other drovers standing on the low plank porch of the bunkhouse. He took one last draw on his cigarette and flipped it into a mud puddle, watching Dusty Charlie and Doss Edding come across the stretch of sparse grassland from the north.

Word had spread about what Doss and his friends had done. Matthew Edding had sent some of his men to search for Doss the day before. None of the remaining cowhands wanted any part of this kind of trouble. "Lord, here they come," said one of the other hands. "There'll be hell to pay here before long. Think I'm gonna draw back and make myself scarce for a spell."

"Believe you're right," said another, moving down off the plank porch toward the horses at the hitch rail. "I just remembered where I saw some strays before the storm. Anybody want to ride with me . . . take a look?" When the other three stepped off beside him and began unhitching their horse's reins, he called toward Jesse Tiggs, "What about you, Jesse? Better come on with us. Things are going to get rough around here for a while."

Jesse grinned, and said without taking his eyes off Dusty Charlie and Doss Edding, "Naw, it don't take all four of us to round up a handful of strays. Think I'll stick here and watch the fireworks."

"Careful you don't get caught up in something you can't get shed of," one of them said, mounting and turning his horse from the rail.

"I never do," Jesse said, flashing them a smile. As they turned and rode off, he took the bag of tobacco from his pocket, rolled another smoke, lit it, and leaned against a porch post smoking, running things through his mind until Doss and Dusty Charlie rode up into the muddy yard. How far would Matthew Edding be willing to go to save this idiot's life? he wondered. More importantly, how much would he be willing to spend?

"Well, now," Jesse said, smiling, when the two moved their winded muddy horses up to the hitch rail, "if it isn't the infamous Half Moon Gang, in person. Looks like you boys have had quite a turn at it."

"We've got problems, Tiggs," Dusty Charlie said in a solemn tone, stepping down from his horse. "All *three* of us. So don't act like you're any better off than us."

"That's all a matter of how you look at it, Dusty Charlie," Jesse said, stepping off into the mud and laying a hand on the neck of Doss's paint horse, as if looking it over. "Where's the others?"

"They've all been killed," Doss said. "That crazy Ranger with the big sombrero killed them all . . . didn't ask if they were guilty or nothing else. It's the most unfair thing you ever saw. He's an animal!" He shook his head at the injustice of it. "He's got to be stopped."

"Then you shoulda stopped him." Jesse chuckled, shook his head again. "Hell, he did you two boys a favor. If they're all dead, there's no living witnesses to the stagecoach robbery," Jesse grinned, then added, fixing a firm gaze on them, "except for me, of course." His grin broadened. "You boys better be real good to me."

"What're you getting at?" Doss asked.

But before Jesse Tiggs could answer, Dusty Charlie said, "Don't talk crazy, Tiggs. You've got as much to lose as we do, if you open your mouth."

"Maybe, maybe not," Jesse Tiggs said, his palm coming to rest on the pistol butt at his hip. "Nobody can put me at the bank robbery in Cottonwood. Nobody except you two can pin the Bannet stagecoach job on me . . . and I could fix all that right here and now."

Dusty Charlie's eyes widened a bit. "This ain't the time to go falling apart, Tiggs. We got to all stick together . . . work ourselves out of all this someway. Mistakes have been made, but everybody deserves a second chance, don't they?"

"Second chance? Ha!" Jesse Tiggs nodded over toward the light shining from the window of the hacienda fifty yards away. "It sounds good to me. Now, let's see you sell the idea to ole Matthew. He's been real cross lately."

Doss Edding stood staring off at the same light, in the falling gray dusk. "He's—he's there right now, I reckon?"

"That would be my guess," Tiggs said, still grinning. "Come on, I'll walk you boys over . . . see to it you don't lose your way. I wouldn't miss this for the world." He nodded them forward and fell in behind them toward the hacienda.

Inside the hacienda, Joe Baylor and Carl Statler stood off to the side, rifles cradled in their arms, watching Matthew Edding pace back and forth in front of the open fireplace. On the other side of the large room, a plate of dinner sat untouched on a polished oak desk. Matthew Edding had been like a caged wildcat all day, waiting for word back from the men he'd sent out in the storm looking for Doss. So far, he'd heard nothing. A thick coffee mug stood hooked on his finger. He sipped and paced.

"You'd think with all the men I've got out there, we'd know something by now." Matthew Edding's eyes cut across Statler and Baylor, the two of them uncomfortable under his gaze, as if somehow it was all their fault. They glanced at each other hesitantly as their boss turned his eyes from them and began his pacing once more.

"It's been this danged storm, Boss," Statler ventured. "Couldn't nobody get nothing done. Now that it's over, I reckon we'll be hearing something most any time."

"Oh, you do, eh?" Edding stopped before the fireplace and spun toward him. Statler cowered back a step. But before Edding could say another word, the door to his office swung open and Doss stepped inside and stopped, his wet hat hanging from his hand. Behind him, Dusty Charlie moved in and to the side, followed by Jesse Tiggs. Tiggs stepped around the other two men and distanced himself a few feet from them.

Matthew Edding stood staring for a second, stunned speechless it seemed. Doss fidgeted in place. Then Matthew Edding took a breath and said in a controlled voice, "Where in heaven's name have you been, boy?" His eyes moved across Dusty Charlie and Tiggs, then to Doss as he took a step forward, holding out his coffee cup for Carl Statler to take from his hand. "I oughta beat you within an inch of your worthless life!" He stalked closer, his broad open right hand going back for a swing.

"Pa, wait! Please! Let me explain!" Doss Edding's wet hat fell from his hand, both hands coming up to protect himself. He looked small and fragile now, the mud-streaked Civil War duster drooping down off his shoulders—a child playing soldier in his father's old uniform.

"Explain what—?" Matthew Edding caught his son with a powerful open-hand slap across his face. "—How you've murdered and robbed innocent people?" His eyes were ablaze, looking Doss up and down. "And you wear *my* coat? My *war duster*? Why you—"

"No! Pa!" Doss reeled sideways, staggering, almost falling, until his father's backhanded slap caught him hard on the other cheek and seemed to right his balance for a second. Matthew Edding's big hand caught

Doss by the collar and shook him upright. Dusty Charlie winced, cowering farther to one side. Jesse Tiggs only smiled, his hand resting on the butt of his pistol as Matthew Edding's next hard slap resounded in the large room.

Dusty Charlie inched back toward the door, but a cold glance from Jesse Tiggs stopped him. With his hand on his pistol, Tiggs' gaze seemed to hold the others in place as Matthew Edding's powerful right hand rose and fell, time after time until Doss lay sobbing and pleading on the stone floor. "Get up and take it like a man!" Matthew bellowed down to his son. But Doss only drew himself into a tight shivering ball, and as Matthew Edding's boot swung back to kick him, Jesse Tiggs stepped forward, still wearing a slight smile, and placed a firm hand on Matthew's arm, stopping him.

"That's enough for now, Edding," Jesse said. "We got too much to do." Dusty Charlie, Carl Statler, and Joe Baylor stiffened at the sight of Tiggs grabbing Matthew Edding by his arm. Nobody treated the boss this way.

"What the—?" Matthew Edding reeled around, pulling his arm free, ready to swing at Tiggs. "You don't tell me when it's enough!"

"I just did," Tiggs said, his right hand still on his pistol, his eyes returning Edding's harsh gaze. "No point saving him from hanging if you're gonna beat him to death, is there?"

"Nobody's hanging my son." Matthew Edding glanced down at Doss, seething, then back up at Tiggs, seeing something in Jesse Tiggs' eyes that made him ask in a dark tone, "What's your business here anyway, Tiggs?"

"My business is helping you keep your boy alive, Edding." Tiggs looked down at Doss Edding sobbing on the floor. Then he shook his head and looked back up at Matthew Edding. "If you don't want my help, just say so now . . . I'll draw my pay and get in the wind."

Matthew Edding took a deep breath, running a hand across his forehead. He looked around at the others then back to Jesse Tiggs. "I don't need your help. It's all been worked out. My boy ain't gonna hang. He wasn't a part of the bank robbery."

"Oh?" Tiggs raised an eyebrow. "Then, you must be beating him for wetting the bed. Maybe you better talk to ole Dusty here."

Matthew Edding shot Dusty Charlie a searing glance. "Don't worry, I'll handle *Dusty*, next thing." Dusty Charlie swallowed a dry lump in his throat and stared down at his boots. Edding turned back to Jesse Tiggs. "Now, what's on your mind, Tiggs? Spit it out."

Jesse Tiggs gestured his eyes toward Carl Statler and Joe Baylor.

Matthew Edding caught the gesture. "Carl . . . you and Joe go check on the horse, or something. Leave us alone here."

"Sure thing, Boss," Carl Statler said. And when the two of them had left the room, Matthew Edding looked back at Jesse Tiggs while Tiggs reached down and pulled Doss up to his feet.

"Quit crying, Doss"—Tiggs brushed a hand across Doss's shoulder—"and tell your daddy who's on your trail. Tell him what happened to the others."

Nearly a full hour had passed as Doss pressed a damp bandanna against his red swollen cheeks and told his father everything about the stagecoach robbery, and the bank robbery at Cottonwood. He named the others, all except Jesse Tiggs—Tiggs standing nearby with his hand still resting on his pistol butt. When Doss finished, Matthew Edding turned to Dusty Charlie with his fists clenched at his sides. "I paid you good money to watch my boy. Now look what you've brought him to."

"But, Daddy," Doss said, "nobody made me go along with—"

"Shut up, boy!" Matthew Edding snapped, cutting him off, slamming a hand down on the polished oak desk beside him. "*Damn* you for pulling us into something like this. I've done everything a man can do to keep this kind of trash out of our lives! Now you've put us both in the middle of it!"

"I—I was drunk. I wasn't thinking." Doss cowered back a step.

"You weren't thinking?" Matthew Edding let out a deep breath, and ran a hand across his forehead. "All right, listen good. You didn't know about the robbery. You went to Cottonwood to pick up some money for me from the bank . . . you understand? The others started robbing the bank before you saw what was happening."

Doss looked confused; but Dusty Charlie saw right away what Matthew Edding had in mind. "Sure, Doss, remember? That's how it happened," he said. "You and me had no idea the others were planning to rob the bank. We just—"

"Who said you weren't in on it, Dusty?" Matthew Edding stood with his fists still clenched at his sides. "Keep your lousy mouth shut until I figure what to do with you!"

"You don't have to do nothing with me, Mr. Edding. I can head out, cross the border, and disappear," Dusty Charlie said sweating, considering what other grim options lay before him. "You'll never see me again . . . that's a promise."

Jesse Tiggs had rolled a smoke and lit it while Matthew Edding raged at the other two. Now he took a last puff, dropped the butt on the stone floor, rubbed it out with his boot sole, and said before Matthew Ed-

ding could answer Dusty Charlie, "That'd work fine
for you, Dusty. But how do we know you won't pop
up later, get caught by that Ranger? Start shooting
your mouth off about this thing?" He shook his head,
grinning. "Naw, you're a bad risk here, right,
Matthew?" Calling him Matthew now. "If the others
really are dead, Dusty here is the only living witness to
the stagecoach—the only accomplice left who can say
Doss was in on the bank robbery."

"Now, just a minute, Tiggs," Dusty Charlie said.
"What about you? Don't go acting like your hands are
clean! You're just as—"

His words cut short beneath the sound of Jesse
Tiggs' snakehandled .45. On the wall behind him,
Dusty's blood and brains splattered across an oil
painting of a cowboy riding a bucking bronco in the
sunset. Jesse's pistol spun back into his holster before
Dusty Charlie's body landed in a heap beside the open
hearth. "Lord God!" Doss shouted, his hands going to
his face.

"Damn it, Tiggs!" Matthew Edding's hand went to
the pistol on his hip, but stopped there. "What was
that for? What was he trying to say?"

Tiggs shrugged. "He'd say whatever he had to in
order to save his arse, I reckon. The fact is, I was right.
He knew it, so do you. Don't jump down my shirt for
doing what you know had to be done . . . if you really
want to save Doss." He shot Doss a glance. "Am I
right?" Doss lowered his eyes.

Matthew Edding clenched his teeth and thought
about it for a second. "God help you if you're string-
ing me along, Tiggs. If I find out you're a part of all
this someway, I'll—"

"You'll what, Matthew?" Tiggs smiled, a low dark
smile. "You'll take Doss in? You and your cow push-
ers?" He shook his head. "No, you don't want to ask
what I have or haven't been a part of. What man work-

ing for you stands a chance if you run into that Ranger? Sure, you might have the judge leaning your way. But what about the Ranger—crazy Sam Burrack? Can you stop him? Think he won't kill Doss, just because you've fixed things legally?" Tiggs chuckled under his breath. "The Ranger doesn't work that way."

"If he moves against us, I'll take him down," Matthew Edding said. "I've faced fast guns in my life. Besides, he's out of his jurisdiction."

"Then, you tell him that when he's leveling his big pistol down on Doss. Sure, you've faced your share of gunmen . . . twenty years ago." Tiggs shrugged again. "Hell, you didn't even see it coming, me burning Dusty down. You wouldn't have had time to clear leather if I'd been taking you down next. Let's just be honest here."

Matthew Edding stared, considering it, his hand working back and forth on the pistol at his hip. What about this Jesse Tiggs and his fancy pistol? Was there anything to him? Did it really matter if there was or not—so long as he served as a target between Doss and the Ranger? Matthew Edding eased his hand away from his pistol butt.

The door swung open and Carl Statler stepped inside with a cocked shotgun raised and pointed. "I heard a shot!" Carl swung the shotgun back and forth, then leveled it on Jesse Tiggs. "Everything all right in here, Boss?"

Tiggs shot Matthew Edding a questioning gaze and asked under his breath, "Well? Is it, Boss?"

Matthew Edding swallowed, looked at Dusty Charlie's body, then back to Carl Statler. "Yeah, everything's all right. Dusty admitted what him and the others done. We told him we were taking him in . . . he made a break for it. I had to shoot him." His eyes went to Tiggs as he spoke to Carl Statler. "Get some fresh horses ready, Carl. Enough for us three, and you and Joe. We're heading into Cottonwood tonight . . . get this thing over with in the morning."

As soon as Carl Statler lowered the shotgun and stepped outside, Edding asked Jesse Tiggs, "All right, how much is this going to cost me?"

Tiggs grinned, taking his time now, playing it his way. He took out his bag of tobacco and leaned back against the polished oak desk. "Oh . . . let's say two thousand dollars, just to be there, make sure everything goes smooth—kill the Ranger if he sticks his nose in. That's not so much, is it? To keep young Doss here alive, so maybe someday he'll father you a grandson?"

Matthew Edding glared at him. "Two thousand, then. But you don't make a move on anybody unless I say so. The Ranger might not even be around. If he is, you do your job, then light out of here. I'll never want to see your face again."

"No more than I'll want to see yours," Tiggs said. He moved over beside Doss and lay an arm up around his shoulder. "I'll need a thousand now, just to keep me interested. I'll take care of your boy for you . . . even wipe his nose if I have to." His grin broadened. "Have the other thousand ready when I put that Ranger down."

"Then let's get going." Matthew Edding adjusted the gun belt at his waist.

"Sure." Tiggs looked back and forth between the father and son, and he grinned once more. "You've got all night, Matthew, from here to Cottonwood, to make yourself believe Doss really is innocent . . . that it all happened the way he's going to say it happened." His smile faded, seemed to melt away, his face turning solemn. "And once you lay some money in my hand, I'll make myself believe he's really worth killing for."

PART 2

———◆———

Odds and Evens

CHAPTER 14

Morning sunlight glistened on the mud street of Bannet, as Maria, Jimmy French, and Two Dogs crossed the walk planks from the hotel to the telegraph office. Two Dogs carried the little girl perched on his hip in spite of his bruises and soreness. The town's doctor—the one who'd sent Sheriff Jenkins on to Humbly for his snakebite—had attended to Two Dogs and wanted to put stitches in the gash on his forehead. But Two Dogs would have none of it. So instead, the doctor had pressed the cut together, salved it, bandaged it, and wrapped Two Dogs' forehead in white gauze.

The young doctor had also treated Jimmy French's wound, bound gauze around his waist, and given him an extra supply of salve and bandages to take with him. "I don't suppose it would do any good to tell you both you need a week's rest, would it?" the doctor had asked, wiping his hands on a bloodstained towel. When neither Two Dogs nor Jimmy French answered, the doctor only sighed, "That's what I thought," and pitched the towel aside.

At the hotel, when the desk clerk had refused to allow Two Dogs to stay there, Maria had held the little girl forward, told the clerk who the child's grandfather was, and said that if Two Dogs couldn't spend the night, neither would the rest of them. "How will you explain to Judge Lodge that you sent his granddaughter off to stay in the livery barn?" She stood firm, until the clerk grudgingly took down keys from the wall behind his counter and laid them before her.

"I better not get jumped on for this," the clerk grumbled under his breath.

That had been two days ago, and now they walked along, each of them eager to get under way, back toward Cottonwood. The little girl clutched her battered rag doll against her bosom, its blank eyes seeming to take in the aftermath of the storm. During the two days, the storm had come and gone, and still the townsfolk struggled to free themselves from the mire. The sound of scraping shovel blades and sloshing mud floated in the air.

Outside the telegraph office, French and Two Dogs waited while Maria walked inside. Across the mud street, Giles Bertrim, the old hostler, and the other man from the railroad shack, moved along the boardwalk staring over at them. Bertrim held a shotgun across his plump stomach. He and the other two had been drinking steadily ever since they'd arrived at Bannet. With the sheriff out of town and the whiskey bolstering their courage, they'd grumbled about Maria forcing them to come back to town with her. Now their grumbling had turned back to talk of a reward, Bertrim still not convinced that Two Dogs hadn't robbed the stage.

"We'll have trouble before we leave here," Jimmy French said to Two Dogs in a quiet tone.

The old Indian saw the look of resolve on French's face and replied, "Most trouble will pass, if a man wants it to. Do you want it to pass, Jimmy French?"

French didn't answer, but only stood staring across at Bertrim and the others. The heel of his hand caressed the smooth hickory butt plate of the pistol at his waist. If he were to draw and make a fight with these three right now, he wondered what order it should be in. Bertrim would have to be first of course—him with the shotgun across his belly. But who next? The hostler? The other man? In a situation like this, perhaps you just had to see which one made the next move and be ready for it. He stared back at them and thought about it.

When Maria stepped back out onto the boardwalk, she shook her head and said to French and the old Indian, "The lines are still down. It could be another week." She thought of the Ranger somewhere alone on the badlands, and added, "We cannot wait here any longer." Her eyes went to Two Dogs. "We will take the little girl with us to Cottonwood, and search for your grandson on our way."

Two Dogs only nodded, then turned his attention back to the little girl in his arms.

"Take a look over there." French gestured his eyes across the street toward Bertrim and the other two.

"*Sí*, they are one more reason we must leave here. They are drunk now . . . drunk enough to get themselves killed if they are not careful." She stood gazing over at them with her rifle hanging in her gloved hand. "Be careful we do not let that happen. Stay wide of them." She started forward a step.

"I say we take them down, here and now."

Maria stopped and cut her dark eyes to Jimmy French, a little surprised. "Oh? Just like that? We would shoot these men because they are drunk and stupid?"

"They weren't drunk when they shot this man's grandson and were ready to hang him."

"I know," said Maria, "that is why I left a message for the sheriff when he returns. He will deal with them. This is his town, and his people."

"Yeah? Well, what about the ones who robbed the bank and took me hostage? Were they only drunk and stupid?" French stared away from Maria, over at Bertrim and his shotgun. "Look at the harm they did."

"If you do not see the difference between these drunken old men and the ones who robbed and killed innocent people . . . then you have no business carrying a loaded gun."

"Are these drunken old men any less dangerous than the others, once they pull a trigger?" French asked.

"All men are dangerous when they pull a trigger." Maria stared hard at him. "But we must do nothing to provoke them. We must wait and see what they have in mind before we take action."

"Sure." French's tone turned a bit sarcastic. "Let them make the first move?" He shook his head, returning her stare. "That makes no sense to me. I say, why take a chance on them? Why give them the advantage?"

"Decent people never have the advantage," Maria said. "But to remain decent, we accept this fact, and deal with the situation as best we can." Before French could say another word, she added, "Now keep your head and follow me," and she stepped back down onto the walk planks and headed toward the livery barn. Jimmy French and Two Dogs looked at each other and fell in behind her.

"Where are we going?" the little girl asked Two Dogs, gazing ahead at Maria's back, Maria's long hair tied back and swinging beneath her battered Stetson brim.

Two Dogs drew the child closer against him. "We will go find your grandfather. He will be glad to see you." As Two Dogs spoke, he glanced forward at the three men as they moved down onto the walk planks before them. Giles Bertrim stopped on the walk planks and propped the shotgun up on his hip. The old hostler and the other man, Philburn, stood beside him, looking drunk and a little uncertain. Jimmy French tried to step around Two Dogs on the narrow plank.

But Two Dogs slowed to a stop and held French back with his free arm spread to the side, blocking him. "Stand easy," Two Dogs said over his shoulder, "we have this child to think about. Let Maria handle this."

"Just stop where you are, little lady," Bertrim called out to Maria, his voice thick with a whiskey slur. "You're the one made us come here. Now we're all gonna wait till Sheriff Jenkins gets back from Humbly and sorts this thing out."

"You shot his grandson, Bertrim. Haven't you done enough?"

"Nope, not yet. We're gonna make sure that old Injun is as innocent as you say he is—see that there ain't some kind of reward for catching him. So you just stop right there and not get yourself hurt."

But Maria kept walking toward him, her rifle swinging back and forth with each step along the planks. "Get out of my way, Bertrim," she said in a low tone. When he refused to budge, she stopped three feet from him, and jacked a round up into her rifle chamber. "All right, then." She nodded her head. "You have a right to die where you stand." Her eyes slid across the other two men behind him. They stood a bit shaky on the walk planks. "But you have no right getting these two poor souls killed with you."

She leaned a bit and called out to the men behind him, "You can leave now, this instant, or you will have to die with this drunken fool."

"Hold on, now," Bertrim said, leaning with her, his shotgun unsteady in his hands. "We've gave it some thought. Maybe you know that Injun is guilty. Maybe you got some notion that you're going to collect the reward. Maybe there's more than we—"

His words turned into a deep grunt as Maria's rifle barrel swung up hard and caught him between his spread legs, in his crotch, lifting him up on his tiptoes. The other two jumped back a step. Bertrim jackknifed at the waist, his shotgun going off straight down, blasting a spray of mud, then falling from his hands as he clutched himself. His face went deep red, then purple. He wobbled in place until Maria's rifle butt snapped around and up, clipping his chin and knocking him off into the muddy street.

"You've killed him!" the old hostler cried out, his eyes bulging, bloodshot with whiskey.

"He is not dead. But he will wish he was when he wakes up . . . and so will you if you do not get out of our way." Maria's rifle barrel swung around and leveled on them.

The hostler's hands swung chest high as he stepped back, almost bumping the other man off into the mud. "Ma'am, you wouldn't pull this kinda stunt if the sheriff was here."

"And neither would you," she said, stalking forward, the two men backing away until they scurried up onto the boardwalk. "When Sheriff Jenkins gets here, he will deal with you. You would do well to sober up before then. Now, stay out of my way." Behind her, Two Dogs chuckled, holding the little girl against his chest, Jimmy French pressing him forward.

"Told you she would handle it," Two Dogs said without looking back.

When they'd reached the livery barn, Maria looked back and saw the two men drag Giles Bertrim up from the mud, silty water running from his whiskers. People had stopped their shoveling at the sound of the shotgun blast and now gathered, some of them scratching their heads, watching Bertrim cough up a brown spray.

She turned to Jimmy French and Two Dogs as they swung open the livery barn door and stepped inside. "They will sober him up and send him on his way in a couple of hours. Sheriff Jenkins will know where to find him." She looked at Jimmy French. "Isn't it better that he is still alive, and that our hands have not shed blood needlessly?"

French didn't answer. Instead he moved to the stalls where their horses stood watching them. Maybe she was right in this case, and maybe he would have agreed had he taken the time to think things out. But right or wrong, it wouldn't matter to him once he got a chance to stand face-to-face with Doss Edding. He meant to kill Doss, plain and simple. Nothing or no one was about to change that.

On the way to Cottonwood, Tommy Caldwell told the Ranger everything about the Half Moon Gang—the robberies, the murders. The only gang member he didn't mention was Jesse Tiggs. For all his threats and surliness in front of the bartender and Darlene the whore while they'd waited out the storm in the muddy saloon, once under way, alone on the trail, Little Tommy couldn't seem to keep his mouth shut. The Ranger didn't even have to ask. All he had to do was listen.

At a spot where they'd made camp above a rushing stream, the Ranger poured tea from a pot, and passed the cup over to Little Tommy. "Sounds like if you and Doss hadn't started the gang, those other boys would never have thought of it."

"Ha," Tommy scoffed. "They were just knuckle-headed cowboys, them others. Turns out I'm the real *desperado* of the bunch. Doss mighta been the one come up with the Half Moon idea, but I was the one with enough guts to pick right up on it—to make it work." He thumbed himself on his chest, sipped the tea, and jutted his chin, his eyes looking small and strained without his spectacles.

"Hadn't been for me, Doss wouldn't got this thing started on his own." He spread a slight crooked grin. "I've been a mean wild sumbitch my whole life. Everybody always said I'd hang before I turned twenty, if somebody didn't kill me first. Looks like I've proved them right."

"If that's what you started out to do, I reckon you've done it all right." The Ranger poured himself a steaming cup and sat back with it, his big pistol across his lap. "It's a shame so many innocent people had to die in the process."

"Innocent? *Shiiit*," Tommy sneered. "Innocent of what? Ain't nobody in this world innocent. They've all done something worth dying for—if they ain't yet, they soon would have, the way I figure."

The Ranger stared at him, picturing the woman's face the second before the wrecked stagecoach went sliding over the edge of the cliff. He felt the urge to raise the pistol from his lap and crack it across Little Tommy's smiling face. But he held his urge in check, and sipped the tea. "Figuring things that way, I suppose you also think it's okay, Doss leaving you standing in the street the way he did? Running out on you?"

"Hey! Doss did what he had to." Tommy stiffened a bit at the Ranger's words. "That's just how this game is played. It ain't important. The main thing is, I was the last one standing, and I never gave an inch, did I? Huh? I never turned tail. I showed my mettle, didn't I?"

"Yeah." The Ranger let out a breath. "You showed yourself all right. Maybe they can carve that on your headstone."

Tommy sipped the rest of his tea and tossed the tin cup to the ground. "You ain't my judge, Ranger. I see the way you're looking at me, like I'm some kind of trash. But the truth is, there ain't a man alive who don't wish he was a *desperado* like me. Most of them just don't have the guts to try it. Bet you've given it some thought yourself, ain't you? Tell the truth, now."

"You sure talk a lot, little Tommy," the Ranger said,

finishing his tea, slinging the last drop toward the ground. He stretched forward, keeping his eyes on Tommy, picked up the cup Tommy had tossed on the ground, and sat both cups near the low fire.

Tommy chuckled. "But you ain't answered. What's the matter, did I strike a nerve?"

"No," the Ranger said, picking up the handcuffs he'd laid near his feet. "Your question just ain't worth an answer." He gazed away for a second and ran a hand along the scar on his cheek. "All thoughts come to all men, at some time or another. It's how a man acts on them that counts. A man is what he does . . . not what he thinks of doing. What he thinks of doing is just dust on a passing wind."

"That makes less sense than anything I ever heard," Tommy said, raising his wrists as the Ranger reached out with the cuffs and spread them open. "Alls I know is, you're the law and I'm a *desperado*. But look who's more afraid of the other. You have to put cuffs on me before you can lay down and rest without being scared."

Now the Ranger managed a slight smile. "I don't have to cuff you, Little Tommy. This is just an act of kindness. I could drop a hammer on you and let you ride back to Cottonwood like your buddies there." He nodded toward the bodies on the ground near the horses.

"Yeah? Then, why don't you? What's kept you from it?"

The Ranger snapped the cuffs, and sat back. "If you could understand that, Little Tommy, the rest of this would have never happened."

The next morning, they started off on the last thirty-mile stretch of badlands toward Cottonwood, staying above the flats and gullies where the heavy rain had left the land sodden, and where rushing brown water filled crevices and creek beds and swept along tangled swirls of brush and driftwood in its swollen path. From the opposite direction, some of the men Matthew Edding had sent out looking for his son two days earlier had also weathered the storm, and taken to the same high rocky trail.

When the Ranger heard their horses' hooves clicking against stone, coming nearer, he led Little Tommy and the rest of his string to the side, into shelter between two tall boulders. "Lean forward," he said to Tommy, his voice low and quiet as he drew the reins to Tommy's horse and pulled it up close beside him.

"Do what?"

"You heard me." The Ranger's pistol came up from his holster. He reached over to Tommy and tapped the pistol on the back of his head until Tommy bent forward, low in his saddle. Then the Ranger spun one of the horse's reins around Tommy's neck, and half hitched it, drawing Tommy farther down, his face just above the saddle horn. And the Ranger sat holding the other rein in his free hand as the horsemen came forward around a turn in the trail.

"Morning, gentlemen," the Ranger called out when the four riders moved into sight.

"What the hell . . . ?" Their horses shied and scurried sideways beneath them. They reached for their pistols, but trying to calm their horses at the same time caused them to falter. In the second it took for them to gather themselves and the animals, they saw the pistol leveled on them, and they stopped cold, raising their hands away from their holsters.

"What brings you boys this way?" The Ranger offered a slight smile, his gloved thumb laying across the cocked hammer. Two of the horses carried a Circle E brand on their rumps. He took note of it.

"Why, we're . . . we're . . ." A rider wearing a bright blue bandanna stammered, catching sight of Little Tommy bowed over with the rein around his neck and

cuffs on his wrists. He swallowed hard. "That is, we're
out searching for strays . . . ain't we, boys?" His eyes
flashed across the other three bunched up around him,
then went back to the Ranger. The other three nodded
in agreement.

"I bet you are," the Ranger said. He gestured his
head sidelong toward the bodies across the saddles behind him, without taking his eyes from the riders.
"Looks like I've rounded up whatever strays you're
looking for. So I reckon you can go on home now."

"Lord God," the man with the blue bandanna said,
looking at the bodies. "You're that Ranger, ain't ya,
mister?"

Little Tommy lifted his weak eyes and cocked his
lowered head toward them. "You know damn well he
is! Why ain't you shooting him! Get me loose—"

"Shut up, Tommy." The Ranger cut him off, yanking
on the rein in his hand, then said to the riders, "Let's
not fool around here. You know who I am, I know
why you're out here. You're Circle E boys, looking for
Doss Edding. Am I right so far?"

"Ranger, we don't want no trouble here," the man
said.

Beside him, one of the other riders nudged his horse
forward a step. "But we've got a job to do, and we're
gonna do it."

"See," Little Tommy cut in. "Ole Matthew sent them
out to find Doss. What are you gonna do now, Ranger?
Now that the odds have changed some?"

"We ain't looking for Doss," the man said, "and
that's the gospel truth." He stared at the Ranger. "We
came looking for the rest of this bunch. You just beat
us to them."

"What?" Little Tommy tried to jerk his head up.

The Ranger yanked hard on the rein. "Keep still,
Tommy, maybe you'll learn something," he said.

"That's right," said the rider with the blue bandanna. "We *was* looking for Doss, that's true. But we ran into him and his daddy on the trail night before last. They've gone to Cottonwood with Jesse Tiggs and a couple others. Doss is gonna make a statement on what happened. Ole Matthew asked us to hunt the rest of this bunch down, either kill them"—his eyes skimmed across the bodies of Harper and Babbage—"or make sure they's already dead. Looks like Tommy here is the last of them."

"You're lying!" Tommy raged. "Doss won't do that! He won't make no statement against me."

"He's doing what he has to do, Tommy, like you told me," the Ranger said.

"No, I'm not lying." The man shook his head, still looking at the Ranger. "Matthew and Doss Edding wants this *Half Moon Gang* out of business as bad as the law does. Matthew's already kilt Dusty Charlie for trying to make a break. He said if we find any of the others still alive, he'd pay us three hundred dollars to kill them for him. Doss said the same thing."

A silence passed as the Ranger put the picture together in his mind. Then the man broke the silence. "The best thing for everybody is for you to hand Tommy over to us . . . and give us those two bodies." As he spoke, his hand had drifted a bit closer to his holster. So did the others. "I know your reputation, Ranger, but there's three of us. We're serious men."

"That's it," the Ranger said, nodding, "go on and lift them pistols up . . . only do it with two fingers, then pitch them out over the edge."

"You're crazy," the man with the blue bandanna said, making a grab for the pistol at his waist, "all we got to do is throw down on you all at once and—"

The blast of the Ranger's big pistol echoed out across the sky. The man lifted up from his saddle and flipped backward, bumping into another rider's horse before hitting the ground. The others scurried in place, struggling with their spooked horses, their hands once more moving away from the holsters, their eyes wide.

"Don't shoot!" one of them shouted. "See, look here." His thumb and finger lifted his pistol by the butt and tossed it quickly out over the edge of the trail. "You boys get shed of them guns! Hear me?" His eyes flashed to them. "This ain't worth dying over. He'll get his when he gets to Cottonwood! Matthew will take him down!"

"Shit," said one of the men, steadying his big gun while the other two tossed the pistols away, "I got a brand-new forty-dollar Colt here—damned if I'll throw it out on them rocks!"

"Sanborn, damn it to hell!" the man raged. "Throw that gun away or he'll kill us all, you stupid son of a bitch!" Spit flew from his lips.

"What about it, Sanborn?" The Ranger had cocked the big pistol again. Now he drifted it over, pointing it at the heavyset man called Sanborn, as Sanborn sat staring with a determined look on his face. "These boys just decided their life is worth more than three hundred dollars. You're saying yours ain't worth forty?"

"Come on, damn it, Sanborn!" the other man shouted. "We'll get our chance some other time. Don't act like an ass!"

Sanborn's thick jaws tightened. His eyes flashed across the others. Then he took a deep breath, let it out, and cursed under his breath as he lifted the new Colt by its butt. "I *hate* doing this." He seethed toward the Ranger, tossing the pistol away. "There . . . satisfied? I'll follow you to Cottonwood, Ranger. When this is over, I'll kick your behind five times over for every scratch on my new Colt!"

"Since you put it that way," the Ranger said, "now you'll all four have to step down and shoo them horses away. I won't have you on the trail behind me."

"Thanks a lot, Sanborn," one of the men grumbled, stepping down from his saddle. "You and your mouth!"

"Shut up, Herb." Sanborn raised his heavy body and stepped down with an enraged look on his face. "He was gonna make us do it anyway . . . wasn't ya, Ranger."

"Whatever you think." The Ranger unwound the rein from around Tommy's neck and stepped Black-eye out onto the trail, pulling Tommy and the string behind him. "If you boys are smart, you'll gather your horses and firearms and clear away from here. Don't come looking for me in Cottonwood, unless you want to die there." He sent the string ahead of him with a slap on a horse's rump, and fell in behind it, sitting half turned in his saddle, his big pistol still cocked toward them; and they all stood watching with their hands held chest high until he'd disappeared around a turn on the high rock trail.

CHAPTER 15

They left Bannet with Maria in the lead, followed by Jimmy French with the little girl now on his lap, and Two Dogs riding beside him on a crow-bait mule they'd purchased at the livery barn. They only stopped for a few minutes at the rail shack to see if Two Dogs' grandson might've ventured back there. But after looking around the shack, Two Dogs shook his head, and they rode on. A few miles past the rail shack, Two Dogs had taken the lead and picked up his grandson's tracks where the young man had stopped and rested in a pile of deadfall brush. Maria noted the look of concern on Two Dogs' face as he reached down and tapped his finger against the dark bloodstain on the ground.

They followed the young man's tracks up into a stand of scrub piñon at the top of a steep slope of rock, where once again they stopped for a moment. Two Dogs bent down and touched his weathered finger to another dried spot of blood on the face of a slanted boulder. Below them a hundred feet, Jimmy French held the horses and the mule, the little girl on his lap hugging her rag doll.

"He came past here after the rain." Two Dogs looked up from the dried spot of blood and up above the crest of jagged rock above them. His expression became more grim as he turned back facing Maria. For his grandson to have hidden and waited out the storm, and still be bleeding when he made this climb, could only mean that his wound was deep and serious. "He is a strong young man, my grandson. But he has lost too much blood." Then, in answer to the concerned look on Maria's face, he added, "I will go alone to the top and search the flatlands for him."

"We will go and help you," Maria said.

"No. You have much to do in Cottonwood. If my grandson is alive, I will be many days tending him. If he is dead, there are things that must be done to make sure his spirit knows where to go. Either way, this is for me to do alone. You take Jimmy French on and let him tell the townspeople what the outlaws did. Tell them how my grandson and I saw it, and tell them how my grandson carried the little girl to safety."

"It would be better if you were there to tell them these things yourself." Maria spoke in a soft tone.

Two Dogs shook his head slowly. "Jimmy French can tell them. If they do not hear the truth from one person, why would they hear it from two?"

She raised up from where she'd bent down beside him and gazed into the distance, then looked back to Jimmy French and the little girl on the trail below them. "Are you certain, Two Dogs? It doesn't feel right for me to leave you here, without water or food."

He looked up at her, his grim expression softening a bit as he wiped a strand of loose gray hair from his weathered face. "There is food and water all around me, and already I can hear my grandson calling out to the quiet spot inside my chest. He tells me to come forward alone."

"You mean . . . you think he is dead." She studied his face, seeing the resolve in his dark eyes.

"Yes, he has gone on, I think," Two Dogs said in a quiet voice; and he lowered his eyes and nodded slowly, running his palm back and forth above the spot of blood. "I am certain of it."

Maria stood in silence for a moment, the warm wind

broken and swirling among the rocks. "When this is finished, I will come back to Bannet and make certain Bertrim and the others pay for what they have done. You have my word."

"No," he said. "This was not an act of bad men . . . only blind men. I heard the words you spoke to young Jimmy French in Bannet. Your words were wise—trust them. My heart does not cry out in vengeance. It cries out in regret. Vengeance will not heal regret. Now, go . . . take the child to her grandfather. This is what my grandson wants you to do. This is what he tells me."

"*Sí*," she said in a soft tone; and before turning away, she placed a hand down on his shoulder.

"This rain was a bad one." Two Dogs looked up at her. He shook his head back and forth slowly, the warm wind licking at his long gray hair. "Always, I will remember this as a time of bad rain, and nothing more."

Maria left him alone and climbed down over the short rocks. At the bottom of the trail, she walked over to Jimmy French and took the mule's reins from his hand. She tied the mule to a short stand of mesquite and looked up to where Two Dogs sat rocking back and forth on his haunches.

"He's not going on to Cottonwood with us?" Jimmy French asked.

"No. He wants you to tell the people what happened, and how his grandson lost his life bringing the little girl in off the badlands."

"Don't worry, I'll do that," Jimmy French said. Then in a lowered voice he said, "Damn Doss Edding and the others. If I ever get my hands on them."

Maria stopped before swinging up into her saddle. "You just tell the truth about what happened. The law will do the rest."

"The law has been known to fail, sometimes." Jimmy

French watched her step up and right herself onto her saddle. She sidled her horse close to him and reached out for the child.

"But not this time. The Ranger and I will see to it."

Jimmy French had started to say something more, but he thought better of it as he passed the little girl over to Maria and watched the child settle onto her lap. He would keep quiet for now. He knew what he had to do. The woman didn't understand. Perhaps no one understood but him. This was a personal matter—between him and Doss Edding. He waited for a second until after Maria heeled her horse forward. He watched her ride forward a few yards, the little girl looking back at him over Maria's shoulder. Then, drawing a deep breath, he heeled forward himself and rode along behind her on the narrow trail.

Behind them, up in the rocks, Two Dogs watched them until they became small dots at the far end of a rise of dust. Then he breathed deep, slipped the long knife from beneath his ragged shirt, rose to his feet, and climbed upward along a footpath until he reached the top of the ridge that opened onto a stretch of flatland. Once there, he searched among a stand of thin young saplings, and when he'd found one that would measure two inches in girth, he bent down close to the ground and chopped it off.

This one would do, he thought, turning the sapling in his hand. He tested its strength across his knee, then sat down and peeled away its bark with the knife, keeping the longer strands and laying them out on the ground in the sunlight beside him. He cut a narrow notch in one end of the bare sapling; and when he'd finished inspecting it, and saw no more use of the knife, he broke the blade off at the hilt by pressing it down across the edge of a sharp rock.

The knife handle snapped free, and Two Dogs slid the blunt end of the blade back into the notch in the sapling. Maria had been right in what she'd said, he thought, as he picked up the strands of bark and began wrapping them around the end of the sapling, drawing the notch together tight around the knife blade. She was a good woman, so he had gone along with her. He had agreed with her rather than waste time and words trying to explain what must be done.

Two Dogs had learned long ago that in matters of justice, it was wise to remain silent. *But now*—He stood up and ran a weathered hand along the newly fashioned spear. Maria was gone. Her sense of justice was sound. But his grandson was dead; he knew it, and he would not insult himself or his grandson's spirit by waiting to see what the sheriff of Bannet or anybody else would have to say about it about a white man mistakenly killing an Indian.

He looked down along the trail running from Bannet, the trail Bertrim would be riding on his way back to the Circle E ranch. *Let the law devour itself*, he thought, gazing out through the sunlight with the wind pushing back his long gray hair. In the tightened grip of his aged hands lay the only justice he understood, the only justice he could abide by.

At dusk, the Ranger led Little Tommy and the string of dead bodies around a downward turn into a sparse grazing valley, where a few head of scraggly sheep lifted their chewing mouths and stared and bleated at them. "Damn sheep." Little Tommy sniffed toward them, raised his cuffed hands forming a pistol, aimed a finger at the blurry image of the animals, and clicked his thumb up and down. "First thing I ever kilt was a stinking sheep—blew its head off with a shotgun, just for bleating at me." He chuckled, his weak eyes looking small and drawn back in their sockets, malevolent, lost, and searching.

"Is that a fact?" The Ranger only spoke in passing as

he gazed ahead at the sun-bleached shack constructed of crumbling adobe brick and scrap wood, held together by wire and frayed rope.

"Yeah. But I quit killing sheep and took to killing the shepherds. Found it more to my pleasure." He laughed and ran his dirty shirtsleeve across his forehead.

As they neared the shack, a skinny young boy ran out barefoot and raised a battered old Navy Colt toward them. "Stop right there. Don't come no closer." His small hands struggled to steady the heavy pistol.

"Easy, young man." The Ranger brought his white barb to a halt. "I'm a lawman, bringing in a prisoner. Tell your pa I'm here."

At the doorway to the shack, a wisp of fine red hair pulled forward on the breeze before a little girl shied back out of sight.

"My pa ain't here, mister," the boy said, the weight of the pistol already causing it to droop in his hand. "He left before sunup . . . looking for strays, if the wolves ain't et them. Could be gone three or four days. Nobody's here 'cept Elsa and me. So ride on about your business."

"Ornery little peckerwood," Tommy sneered under his breath.

But the Ranger only smiled. "If that's what you want, young man, that's what we'll do." He gestured toward a slice of shade beneath a spindly piñon that stood beside a stone-rimmed well. "But would your pa object to us watering our horses and cooling them before heading on?"

The boy stepped back, lowering the heavy pistol. "Naw, I reckon not." Then he leaned slightly to one side, taking in the bodies across the saddles. "Them men there . . . did you—did you kill them?"

"Yep, I did." The Ranger stepped his horse toward the shade, looking out across the empty land to where a dust devil danced low to the ground. He caught a

glimpse of a child's dirty toe inch forward in the doorway, then jerk back out of sight. "Tell me something,
young man." He stepped down from his horse as Little
Tommy did the same. "You're only a couple of hours
from Cottonwood. Couldn't your pa have left both of
you there with someone?"

"We don't go to town, mister. Besides, I can take care
of things here. I've got this pistol and seventeen bullets.
Nobody better bother us if they know what's good for
them." He cut a warning glance at Little Tommy,
Tommy's weak eyes trying to focus on the Navy colt.

The Ranger snatched Tommy by his forearm and
shoved him over against the trunk of the piñon. "Well,
you don't have to worry about us. But keep that pistol
a safe distance from this prisoner." The Ranger looked
around again across the desolate land, thinking about
these two children alone out here for the next few days.
He shook his head and let out a breath. "Do you suppose your pa would mind if we spent the night here
under this tree . . . head out first thing in the morning?"

"Are you sure you're a lawman?" The boy eyed him,
taking in the Ranger's badge on his chest.

"I'm pretty sure." The Ranger smiled. "If I'm not, I
wish somebody would tell me."

"Well, then . . . I don't think Pa would mind." The
boy looked relieved. "We've got some dried shank of
lamb if you're hungry."

When the Ranger had watered the horses and the
boy had brought them strips of dried meat, they'd
eaten in the grainy light of a rising moon. When they'd
finished, they turned in for the night, the Ranger first
cuffing Little Tommy's hands around the narrow trunk
of the piñon. Before the first rays of morning light
reefed across the east, the Ranger had made his string
of horses and bodies ready for the two-hour ride into
Cottonwood.

It was just after sunup when the Ranger led his grisly

string of body-draped horses into Cottonwood. Already, the sharp rays of sunlight drew swirls of heat up from the empty dirt street. Tommy rode beside the Ranger, his hands cuffed, slapping at flies that drifted forward from the backs of the corpses and spun and darted about his dirty face. Tommy looked at the Ranger through weak eyes. "How come these flies ain't bothering you none?"

"There's an answer for that, Little Tommy, but you don't want to hear it." The Ranger looked all around at the deserted street and along the boardwalks, where a lone old man sat whittling on a short scrap of wood. A lank hound scooted forward from beneath a boardwalk. It stretched, shook itself, and trotted closer with its hackles half raised, its wet nose raised toward the smell of death atop the horses until it fell in alongside the Ranger's white barb and whined, wagging its knobby tail. "Never seen this town so quiet," the Ranger commented to himself.

But as the white barb snorted and walked on, the soft clop of the horses' hooves following behind it, heads began to venture out of doorways. A woman stepped out of a restaurant wiping her hands on her apron, staring toward the Ranger. The old man stood up slowly from his whittling and pushed up his floppy hat brim. Tommy chuckled under his breath. "These sheep-lickers will faint dead away when they see it's me out here."

"Keep your mouth shut to these folks, Tommy, or I'll crack your head with this rifle barrel." The Ranger saw townsfolk move out of the shadows of the storefronts and head down into the street toward them. "After what you and your buddies did here, you oughta hang your head in shame."

"Shame, my arse." Tommy spit. "I'd do it all over again, if I just had the—"

The Ranger's rifle came up from across his lap, dealt Tommy a sharp blow across his forehead, then lowered back down as Tommy wobbled in his saddle. "Open your mouth again," the Ranger said in a calm tone, "and I'll crack you in your teeth. Do you believe me now?"

Tommy seethed, but nodded, righting himself in his saddle.

Now the townsfolk moved forward, quickening their pace, then slowing and staying back as if in caution, seeing Little Tommy Caldwell and the bodies on the horses behind him. "It's that Ranger," a man said in a hushed voice.

"Then thank God," said Emma Frocke, appearing forward of the others, her face drawn and haggard, her black dress streaked with dust.

"You'll find this a sore and sorry place," said the old man who'd been whittling. He stepped out in front of the Ranger's horse with his arms spread, his pocketknife in his weathered hand. "For neither the law nor the Lord smiles on us anymore."

The Ranger drew his horse to a halt as the old man stood firm in front of him. "Shut up, Thurman," a voice called out. "You don't know nothing about stuff like this. You're just a preacher."

"I might be a preacher"—the old man swung his head toward the sound of the voice, then back to the Ranger—"but I know when my face has been spat in." His eyes glistened, red-rimmed and angry, and speaking up at the Ranger as he pointed his pocketknife toward Little Tommy, he added, "In this town they let killers like him go free. Did you come here to hang this piece of punkwood and set things right here? Or are you just one more of 'em?"

"What's bothering you, mister?" the Ranger asked, glancing past the old man and thirty yards farther up the street toward the sheriff's office. "I'm bringing in the men who robbed your bank."

Two men had just stepped out of the sheriff's office. One was a big heavyset man wearing a dark business

suit and derby hat. The other man wore a suit as well;
but with a thin string tie, and he adjusted a wide oval
Stetson down on his forehead. This one wore a tied-
down holster with the butt of a .45 sticking up from it.
As he caught sight of the Ranger, Little Tommy Caldwell, and the bodies behind them, his hand drifted up
and rested down on the pistol butt. The Ranger took
close note of it.

"Pay no mind to Thurman here." A man wearing a
clerk's apron stepped forward from the other townsfolk. "We've suffered a tragedy . . . some folks want to
make it a bigger thing than it is. They want to place
blame where it doesn't belong. Everything's settled
here. Thurman's a Bible thumper, just letting off a little
steam." He swung toward the other townsfolk and
called out in a louder voice, "Look, the Ranger's
brought in the whole Half Moon Gang! All of them
dead except little Tommy! But it looks like Little
Tommy's killed his last man! We'll get a hanging out of
this! Won't we, folks?"

Heads nodded in unison; voices grumbled.

The Ranger cut his glance away from the men out
front of the sheriff's office and back down to the townsfolk as Emma Frocke stepped closer and said, rushing
her words, "No! No! Thurman is right, Ranger. Nothing is settled here. Thank God you've come along." She
leaned forward and clutched the Ranger's boot. "Little
Tommy killed my husband! But Doss Edding was in on
the whole thing—and they're letting him go! He's
going free as a bird. You've got to stop them!"

"Going free?" The Ranger stared at her. "What are
you talking about? Doss Edding is the leader of this
bunch."

"She's beside herself with grief, Ranger. Can't you
tell? Her husband was killed here," the man in the
apron called out, then reached to take Emma Frocke by
her arm and pull her away.

"Let go of me!" she shouted, swinging her arm free of the man.

The man started to grab her again, but the Ranger's voice stopped him. "Leave her alone, mister," the Ranger said, raising the rifle barrel from his lap.

"Crack his head, like you did mine." Little Tommy snickered, then fell silent when the Ranger dealt him a cold stare.

"Who's in charge here, now that Brady Martin's dead?" the Ranger asked the townsfolk as he swept another glance up the street where the two men stood outside the sheriff's office.

"Nobody exactly," said a voice. "C. G. Hutchinson's been sort of leading things—just till we get everything settled. He's our banker."

"Oh?" The Ranger sat staring toward the sheriff's office. "Then, I take it he's one of those gentlemen standing there?"

"Yes," Emma Frocke said, "but don't listen to him, Ranger. He's on Doss Edding's side. He's the one letting him go!" Again, she leaned forward and clutched the Ranger's boot. This time he nudged her back gently.

"You'll have to excuse me, ma'am," he said when she'd moved back. Then he tapped the white barb forward.

"He's going free, Ranger!" she shouted as he moved forward, leading the string of horses and the dead men, and the swirling cloud of flies that followed him. "Do you hear me? They've let my husband's killer go free!"

"Nobody's going free, ma'am." He tossed a glance back at her. In that moment he saw in her eyes the same lost and pleading look he'd seen in the young woman's eyes the second before the wrecked stage made its final plunge over the edge of the canyon. "You've got my word on it."

CHAPTER 16

In front of the sheriff's office, the Ranger caught a glint of light reflecting off a gun barrel from atop the roof of the barbershop across the street. On the roof next door to the barbershop, he saw the tip of a rifle barrel ease back out of sight as he turned his white barb and led the string to the hitch rail. *Two gunmen high up* . . . How many more were scattered here and there, he wondered, taking in shadowed doorways, stacks of freight and delivery goods along the boardwalk.

Hired gunmen? No. Probably cowhands from the Circle E. There's been no time to bring in any professional killers. Whoever they are, here goes, he thought.

He moved his white barb close to the boardwalk, putting these men at risk should gunfire come from the rooftops behind him. C. G. Hutchinson took a step back. But Matthew Edding stood fast, his feet spread shoulder width, his right hand on his holstered pistol. He'd just seen what the Ranger had done, moving up close like this. Had he already spotted Baylor and Statler across the street? Edding believed so. This Ranger was sharp, no doubt about that—*eyes like a hawk* . . .

Behind Matthew Edding, the door to the sheriff's office creaked open and Jesse Tiggs stepped out, his right glove off of his hand and shoved down into his gun belt. The Ranger noted it, then turned his gaze to

Matthew Edding. Seeing the question in Edding's eyes, the Ranger answered it. "Yeah . . . I see the riflemen. I've been roof-topped before. I can live with it . . . can you?"

Matthew Edding ignored the question. "We know who you are, Ranger, and why you're here," he spoke out, as the Ranger rocked his white barb back and forth in place and let the lead rope to the rest of the string relax in his left hand. "We appreciate you bringing in the Half Moon Gang, but this is a bad time here in Cottonwood. It'd be better for everybody concerned if you drop those bodies off and move on." He nodded toward Little Tommy Caldwell. "We'll take care of that one for you. You can count on it."

Tommy Caldwell's beady eyes widened. His face went pale. "Mr. Edding, it's me, Little Tommy . . . Doss's best friend!"

"I see it's you, Little Tommy, you rotten piece of trash." Matthew Edding stared at him. "You've got no friends here." He shifted his gaze back to the Ranger. "He'll get what's coming to him, Ranger. Where did you catch him?"

The Ranger shifted the white barb quarter-wise to the boardwalk and let his right hand rest on his rifle stock, his thumb lying across the hammer. "Are you a lawman, mister?" he asked, then fixed a steady gaze on Matthew Edding, watching to see if Edding's eyes went to the rooftops behind him. They didn't.

"A lawman? Why, no, I'm not." Edding shifted a bit in place. "The fact is, we've lost our sheriff to that band of murdering cowards. For now, Hutchinson and I are doing our best, trying to maintain—"

"Then why are you even speaking to me?" The Ranger asked, cutting him off. "I only speak to other lawmen in matters such as this. Since you're not wearing a badge of any sort, keep your mouth shut."

Edding stiffened, fuming. Jesse Tiggs cracked a thin

smile, seeing what the Ranger was doing, already liking his style. He stepped to one side and moved forward, his hand relaxed and poised near his strapped-down .45, the silver snake on the pistol butt glinting near his fingertips. The Ranger lifted a brow toward him, his right thumb tight across the rifle hammer. *A silver snake? Come on, now. . . .*

C. G. Hutchinson swallowed a dry knot in his throat and ventured a step forward. "Now, see here, Ranger. Mr. Edding happens to own the Circle E, largest cattle spread in this territory."

"Then, he can talk to me about cows sometime, if I'm ever interested." The Ranger kept his horse shifting in place, knowing the difficulty it caused the riflemen over on the rooftops. His eyes cut across Edding and Tiggs and back to Hutchinson. "Are you a lawman?" he asked Hutchinson.

"No, sir, I'm Mr. C. G. Hutchinson . . . owner of the Cottonwood Bank. As a part of my civic duty, I'm seeing to it things go smoothly here until such time as—"

"Then, you shut your mouth too." The Ranger stared at him. "I'm not here to conduct any banking business either." He tossed a nod toward Little Tommy beside him, and at the fly-infested bodies covered with a thin sheen of road dust. "I'm bringing these men in for robbing the Bannet stage and killing its passengers. I'll only talk with someone of legal authority."

You have to hand it to this Ranger, Tiggs thought, he comes on strong and isn't going to back an inch. But Tiggs had done this same thing himself a dozen times. It was all just for show, wasn't it?

"Then, for the time being it appears you will have to deal with us," Hutchinson said, hooking his thumbs around his lapels.

"I don't think so," the Ranger said, "not just yet." He nodded back toward Emma Frocke and the rest of the townsfolk gathered in the street. "What was the

woman talking about . . . saying Doss Edding has been
set free? He's the leader of the Half Moon Gang." His
eyes cut back to Matthew Edding as he added, "He's
the one I'm still after." His eyes gestured toward the
door to the sheriff's office, and he asked Hutchinson,
"Is he inside?"

Hutchinson squirmed; a line of sweat glistened
down his plump cheek. What if they started shooting
from across the street? He was right in their line of fire!
Why had this Ranger pulled in so close this way? Why
wouldn't he settle that blasted horse? "Well, yes, Doss
is in there, but—"

"He's innocent, Ranger," Matthew Edding said, cutting Hutchinson off, his hand tensing on his pistol
butt. "He happens to be my son. So walk easy."

"Walk easy?" The Ranger cocked his head slightly.
"I'll walk easy when your son's in a box with the lid
nailed shut."

Matthew Edding tensed and moved forward.

Jesse Tiggs stepped forward too, the smile still on
his face, his left hand raised slightly toward Edding,
checking him down. "What Mister Edding is saying,
Ranger, is that this whole thing has been a misunderstanding . . . but now it's all been straightened out.
There's no trouble here, unless you plan on making
some for yourself."

"I bet you're not a lawman either, are you, young
man?" the Ranger said to Jesse Tiggs with a cold stare.
Beneath his words came the sound of his rifle hammer
cocking. The rifle raised an inch from his lap, the barrel pointing into the narrow space between Edding
and Tiggs. *Yep, a lot of brass in this crazy ole Ranger . . .*
Tiggs enjoyed this, seeing a man stand firm, knowing
he was covered front and rear. Killing this man was
going to be the most fun he'd had in a long time. *Easy,
now,* he cautioned himself, shrugged, and took a short
step back.

"Your son is a low, cold-blooded murderer," the Ranger said, speaking to Matthew Edding but keeping his eyes square on Jesse Tiggs. "I mean to kill him, or else watch him hang. It's that simple. Anything else you gentlemen need to make of it . . . do it now, while we're all of the same mood and manner." He snapped a nod back toward the rooftops. "I reckon them boys are anxious to get on down out of the sun."

At first Matthew Edding had wondered why Jesse Tiggs hadn't made his move. Wasn't that what he was paying Tiggs to do? But now that Edding had settled down for a second, he understood what the Ranger was doing. This Ranger had seen through their play right off, and even knowing their strength, he still wanted to call their hand and push it to a showdown. Just like that, Matthew Edding thought, no talk, no room for reasoning, knowing full well that gun sights were on his back.

What kind of man was this Ranger he'd heard so much about over the years? *Reckless . . . ?* Maybe, a little. But working his odds, keeping the horse moving, keeping Baylor and Statler unsteady, unsure of their aim. *Dangerous . . . ?* Absolutely, Edding thought. This Ranger worked quick, so quick that a man hardly had time to realize what he was doing until it was too late. He'd have to remember that. He hoped Tiggs was seeing the same thing here.

"There's not going to be any trouble, Ranger," Matthew Edding said, letting out a tense breath. "We are the law here. Now, ease your thumb off the hammer."

The Ranger narrowed his gaze. Matthew Edding was no fool; he'd just seen that. This man wasn't going to allow himself to be pushed into something. What about the young man beside him with a silver snake on his pistol butt? Yep, this one was a gunman—hired muscle. Since Edding hadn't had time to send out for a gunman, this one must have already been here. Already working for Edding, handling cattle? Then, maybe he hadn't been a gunman very long, the Ranger thought, already sizing up everybody, getting a feel for the situation.

But it didn't matter how long this young man had been hiring out his services. He looked cocky, confident. Edding could have unleashed him any second. Why hadn't he? The Ranger looked from one to the other, seeing the same faint smile on Jesse Tiggs' face, knowing Tiggs was checking him out head to toe.

A tense silence passed beneath the sound of buzzing flies. The hound that had first spotted the Ranger riding in came trotting along the boardwalk; but at the sight of the men, sensing the coiled tension between them, the dog slunk to a halt and slipped back and away. Then, behind Matthew Edding, the door to the sheriff's office creaked open once more. Judge Winfred Lodge stepped out, his reading spectacles in his hand.

"Sam," the judge said in a cautious voice, "I've been listening. You're out of line here. These men are telling you the truth. They do have legal authority here. I've granted it. Now, do as I say . . . uncock the rifle."

"What's the story here, Judge Lodge?" the Ranger asked without taking his eyes off Edding and Tiggs. Hutchinson didn't concern him. He'd already seen that C. G. Hutchinson had no stomach for his kind of business. "I've traipsed half the badlands catching up to the Half Moon Gang. Now the leader is being set free?"

"It's just like they said, Sam. This has been a terrible misunderstanding. Doss Edding got caught up and misled by a bad bunch. They used him to rob the bank here." He looked at Little Tommy Caldwell, and back across the bodies of Babbage and Harper. "As far as the Bannet stage—I have no idea. But this case here has been settled. We've had an arraignment. I saw no grounds to charge Doss Edding with bank robbery or murder. He's leaving here a free man."

The Ranger stared at him. *So you say . . .* "But I have a witness, Judge. A young bank teller by the name of Jimmy French. He'll testify that Doss Edding is the ring leader. And I've got Doss Edding's pistol. French took it off of him when he got away from the gang."

Behind the Ranger, the townsfolk had ventured forward. Now they stood close up, listening. "Jimmy's alive?" a voice murmured.

"Then your witness should have been here two hours ago," the judge said. "Sorry, Sam. This case is finished."

The Ranger noticed that in all the years he'd known Judge Winfred Lodge, this was the first time the judge seemed to have trouble looking him in the eyes. Somebody had gotten to this man. There'd been no justice served here. "Then, I'll kindly ask you to turn Doss Edding over to me, Your Honor. I'm taking him and this one back to Bannet to stand trial for the stagecoach robbery."

Matthew Edding tensed; the Ranger saw it. "Easy, Matthew," Jesse Tiggs said under his breath, noticing that even though the judge had told the Ranger to uncock his rifle, the Ranger's thumb still laid across the drawn hammer.

"No, Sam." The judge shook his head. "You and I both know you're over eighty miles out of your jurisdiction. If you want to take Doss Edding into custody for the Bannet stage robbery . . . you know the procedure. You'll need a signed order from Judge Morrison."

A signed order? "I'm not leaving without Doss Edding! Either in a saddle or over it, he's going back with me, to hang! Since when has jurisdiction and paperwork ever come into question in a murder case like this?" The Ranger felt his left hand tighten on the reins. "You didn't see the bodies picked over by buzzards, Judge. You didn't see the eyes of the woman who died asking about her child. What does jurisdiction mean to a woman and her little girl laying dead at the bottom of a ravine?"

The crowd murmured, restless behind him. Little Tommy slumped in his saddle, casting a glance back at the angry faces behind him.

"I understand how you must feel, Sam. But you know the rules. Do you have proof that Doss Edding had something to do with the woman's death?" the judge asked, taking note of the mob, now stirring louder. C. G. Hutchinson stood in silence—the judge was doing a fine job here.

"I've got this one," the Ranger said, tossing a side-long nod toward Little Tommy. "He was there. He admitted it—even bragged about it. Told me how him and Doss Edding founded the Half Moon Gang."

Matthew Edding's head bowed slightly, in shame, the Ranger thought. Beside him, Jesse Tiggs stood relaxed, enjoying the show, his eyes studying the Ranger's every move, every word. This Ranger was good. Shooting him would be a feather in any gunman's hat. He'd have to play it just right, though. When the time came, he'd milk it for all it was worth—get a good-sized crowd watching him. Then *bang!* He'd smoke this man to the ground.

"Is this true, young man?" the judge asked Little Tommy.

Little Tommy cursed under his breath, his eyes fixed on his saddle horn. "I ain't saying nothing about nothing anymore," he grumbled. Then he straightened a bit in his saddle, as if a light had gone on in his head, and he said to the judge with a trace of a smug grin, "I'd like to see anybody deny anything when somebody's pistol-whipping them . . . threatening them. Damn right I admitted to it—wouldn't you? To keep *this* man from killing ya? Look at my face, look at what he's done to me! He even broke my spectacles—and I'm blind as a bat without them."

"Save your breath, young man," the judge said. "You'll get no sympathy here." Judge Lodge looked at the Ranger. "I'm gonna ask you to turn him over to us, Sam, and ride on. He'll answer for the bank robbery and killings here."

"You've got some nerve," the Ranger growled, "denying me justice, refusing to give me Doss Edding for the stage robbery, then asking me to turn this man over to you? Do you really see me going along with this? I'm not leaving here without these killers!"

"You have no choice," the judge said, his voice taking on a stronger tone. "Aside from my great respect for you and your badge, you have no more authority here than any other man on the street. Am I making myself clear, Sam? You've upheld the law your entire life. Don't break it now."

The Ranger stared from one man to the other as a tense silence crackled in the air. He glanced back at Emma Frocke standing at the front of the townsfolk, her eyes reminding him too much of the woman's eyes who'd looked into his from within the shattered remains of the Bannet stage. And as he let out a tense breath and lowered the hammer on his rifle, he saw in Emma's eyes the same trace of vanishing hope, as if she herself had just gone over the edge of a deep canyon wall.

"All right, Your Honor," the Ranger said, letting the lead rope fall from his hand, "they're all yours." Without another word, he backed the white barb away from the string and turned it in the street, his eyes lingering for a second on Matthew Edding and Jesse Tiggs.

Judge Lodge winced and wiped a hand across his sweaty forehead. "It will all work out, Sam," he called out. "You'll see. This is for the best, believe me." But the Ranger ignored him and moved the horse across the dirt street toward the saloon. The townsfolk parted a way for him, watching him pass.

Jesse Tiggs stood with the same faint smile on his face, his gun hand poised but relaxed. So this was Sam Burrack, the Ranger he'd heard so much about in nameless border towns over the years. He couldn't believe what he'd just seen! The judge had backed him down? Just like that? Maybe this Ranger wasn't as tough as he'd seemed. Some tough words, just to let Matthew Edding know right off that he meant business. His thumb across that rifle hammer—just a threat? Sure, as it turned out, that's all it was, Tiggs thought. And to think the Ranger had even fooled him for a second—had him actually admiring his style. *Well, forget that.* . . . This would be the easiest money he'd made in a long time.

"That's not the last we'll see of him," Tiggs said in a lowered voice to Matthew Edding. "He'll make a play for Doss . . . you can count on it." But Tiggs didn't mean it. He only said it to keep this pot boiling, let Matthew Edding know he was getting his money's worth, let him and his idiot son sweat for a while. As far as Tiggs was concerned, he'd just seen the Ranger's whole hand—all talk, no action. *Disappointing in a way* . . .

"I know," Matthew Edding replied, his voice almost a whisper. "He won't stop. I just saw the kind of man he is. There's no way to stop him, except to kill him. And that's not going to be so easy."

Tiggs glanced at the worried look on Matthew Edding's face, and had to keep himself from chuckling. Was ole Matthew out of his mind? Couldn't he see what Tiggs had just seen? The way the judge had just handled the Ranger, had just put him in his place?

"Yeah, I'm afraid you're right, Matthew," Tiggs

whispered as the two of them stepped down and took the lead rope and the reins to Little Tommy's horse. "I suppose you're feeling a little better now about what you're paying me to take care of him, eh?"

Matthew Edding didn't answer, and Tiggs noticed that he didn't take his eyes off the Ranger until the Ranger had stepped down from the white barb, hitched it at the rail, and gone up on the boardwalk into the saloon. Edding walked to the middle of the dirt street and stood staring, his big arms hanging loose at his sides.

What was wrong with these old men? Tiggs smiled to himself. Had he been in the Ranger's place a while ago, there was no way in hell he'd let the judge or anybody else back him down. Not after coming on so strong that way. Maybe the Ranger was slipping. Sure, the Ranger might try to justify it by calling it his deep respect for the law, but Tiggs knew better. All he'd seen move away from the boardwalk was a brow-beaten old lawman who'd talked a good game and cocked an old rifle. *So what? What had it gotten him?*

Tiggs wasn't impressed anymore. Evidently, Edding was too worried about Doss to realize what had just happened. Yep, this would work out just fine, Tiggs thought, reaching up and shoving Tommy off his horse and onto the dirt street. "Come on, idiot," he said. "Let's get you inside . . . get you looking presentable for your hanging."

"How'd you manage to come out looking so good in all this," Little Tommy asked Tiggs under his breath. "You're as guilty as the rest of us."

"Guilt is only what you make of it." Tiggs smiled, and shot a glance toward the sheriff's office, where C. G. Hutchinson and Judge Lodge had just stepped inside, leaving the door open for him and the prisoner. "I'm surprised you've managed to stay alive this long,

Little Tommy . . . you and your buddy, Doss." He shoved Tommy forward. "Now, come on."

"Yeah, and I reckon you'd like to see them hurry up and hang me just to keep my mouth shut." Tommy spoke over his shoulder as Tiggs pressed him toward the boardwalk and the waiting jail. "But I stick by what I swore. Once a Half Moon, always a Half Moon. You don't have to worry, Tiggs."

"That's good, Tommy, real good," Tiggs said. But he could care less what Tommy said to these people here. Tiggs was sitting on a winning hand. The way he looked at it, he was in no hurry. He'd leave with two thousand dollars warming his pocket. He could kill that old Ranger anytime he felt like it.

CHAPTER 17

"What a scum hole," Little Tommy said, squinting his beady eyes as Jesse Tiggs opened the plank door that separated the sheriff's office from the two-cell jail attached to the rear of the building.

"Oh . . . I've seen worse." Tiggs looked around, smiling as he pushed Tommy forward. "Look at it this way." He stared into Little Tommy's eyes as he unlocked the barred door to the cell next to Doss Edding's. "You're not going to be here long enough to get homesick."

"Real funny, Jesse." Little Tommy turned, sticking his cuffed wrists close to the bars. Tiggs slammed the cell door, reached through the bars, and unlocked Tommy's handcuffs. "Any chance of me getting some grub?" Tommy rubbed his wrists and opened and closed his stiff fingers. "I'm hungry enough to eat the arse out of a running wildcat."

"I'll see if I can find you one." Tiggs grinned, brought the handcuffs out between the bars, and twirled them on his trigger finger. "Whatever I bring you, it'll probably be your last meal." His grin broadened. "They're doing up the paperwork right now. But I bet there'll be a trial *and* a hanging before the ink's even dry."

"To hell with them," Little Tommy spat, and rubbed his weak eyes with his thumbs. "Them and their damned stupid laws and rules . . . what the hell do they know about anything?"

"That's the way to look at it," Tiggs said. He nodded toward the other cell where Doss Edding sat in silence staring at them from a shadowed corner. "There's your buddy, Doss. He's waiting on some paperwork of his own. Maybe you *desperados* can get your heads together . . . swear another oath or two while you wait."

"You never understood what we were about, Jesse." Tommy's weak eyes searched the other cell for Doss Edding. "At least we're men enough to stick by what we believe in." He half turned and raised his voice toward Doss Edding's dark cell, "Ain't that right, Doss?"

When Doss didn't answer Little Tommy, Tiggs only chuckled and shook his head, stepping back and opening the plank door. "I can't argue with you on that. Whatever it is you boys believe in, it's way over my head." *These damned fools. . . .*

The two of them sat in silence for a full ten minutes after Tiggs had closed the door behind himself. They stared at the cracks of light through the planks and at the movement of Jesse Tiggs as he stepped across the sheriff's office. They were unable to clearly make out his voice as he spoke to the judge and C. G. Hutchinson.

"Think I'll walk over and join ole Matthew at the restaurant." Tiggs smiled at them, liking the way he could throw Matthew Edding's name out like that. "Told Tommy I'd bring him back something to eat. Can I bring you gentlemen anything?"

When both the judge and Hutchinson looked up long enough to shake their heads no, Tiggs smiled and adjusted his hat down on his forehead. "Suit yourselves, then. I'll be right back to keep an eye on our prisoner." He went to the door and left.

Beneath the sound of a ticking clock, the judge sat at

the battered oak desk beside C. G. Hutchinson. He examined page after page of the hastily prepared court order, Hutchinson craning forward, keeping an eye on things. From time to time, the judge looked over at the plank door. Then he'd shake his head, looking back down to the pen in his broad hand.

When he'd finished signing the papers before him, Judge Lodge leaned back and let out a sigh. "That about does it." He looked over at the front door as if able to see beyond it and across the dirt street, and he pictured the Ranger sitting alone in the saloon. "Poor Sam. I hate having to call him down that way over jurisdiction. He's right, you know. Jurisdiction has never been an issue when it comes to the killers and lunatics he's faced out there."

"Aw"—Hutchinson waved it away—"I wouldn't let it worry me if I were you. The Ranger has to realize times have changed."

"Have they?" The judge looked over at the plank door again, then stood up and wiped his hands together and adjusted his suit coat.

C. G. Hutchinson also stood up, clearing his throat and picking at the seat of his trousers. "Don't start having second thoughts, Your Honor. This is all turning out better than even I supposed it would. The Ranger showing up with Little Tommy almost threw me for a second . . . but if you think about it, this works out fine. Now the townsfolk can have their pound-of-flesh, so to speak. They needed somebody to hang for all this." He shrugged and tossed his plump hands. "Now they've got Tommy Caldwell. What could be more perfect?"

Judge Lodge looked at him with a trace of contempt in his eyes. "I keep thinking about what Sam said, about the woman and her child dying out there. He said he saw the woman's face, right before she died."

Judge Lodge winced. "That's the part about all of this that sours on my stomach."

Hutchinson smiled, jutting his heavy chin. "Come on, now, Judge. If you ask me, the Ranger is just taking his job too personal."

"Too personal? For God's sake, Hutchinson, Sam *saw her face*. Do you know what that means? That's as personal as it gets. You and I didn't see her . . . we're not as touched by it. Doesn't that mean anything to you?"

"Now, now, Your Honor." Hutchinson raised an arm and laid it over the judge's shoulder. "Of course it means something to me. But we're not circumventing justice by handling things this way." He leaned closer and added in a lowered voice, "We're just timing it in a way that works out better for the social fabric of this town, for *all* of us. You put the Ranger in his place by telling him pretty much the same thing, *respect for the law . . . bowing to authority*. These were your words, and they were true. Even he saw that, as bitter as it may have tasted to him. You're administering justice the same as always." He pinched his thumb and finger together and winked. "Only this time, you've changed it just a shade."

Judge Lodge moved from beneath Hutchinson's arm, over to the peg on the wall beside the door. "Perhaps you're right." He took down his hat and placed it on his head. "But I keep hearing Sam telling about the woman and her child. You've never been a family man have you, Hutchinson?"

"No. I've never had the luxury of a wife and children. Can't say I've missed it much, though. What about you?"

"My wife passed away seven years ago. I have a daughter and a grandchild. My daughter's husband died in military service a little over a year ago, fighting the Apache. Fortunately, my daughter and the child live in Ohio . . . far removed from this hostile land."

"Well, there, you see? No wonder you sympathize with the Ranger. But let's face it . . . people die out here every day. It's terrible, but it's a fact of life. You can't afford to take it personal, now, can you?" Before the judge could answer, Jesse Tiggs stepped back in through the front door carrying a tin plate full of beans and biscuits.

The judge let out a breath, looked at Tiggs' smiling face, then replied to Hutchinson as Tiggs moved toward the plank door, "I suppose not. Let's get court set up at the mercantile store. I want to wash my hands of this as soon as possible . . ."

Jesse Tiggs kicked the plank door closed with the back of his foot, stepped over to Tommy's cell, and slid the tin plate of food through the slot on the cell door. "There you are, Tommy, beans and biscuits, hot off the stove. If there's a better last meal on this earth, I don't know what it would be." He grinned, tossing a glance toward Doss Edding's cell.

"You're enjoying all this too much to suit me, Jesse Tiggs." Tommy moved back and sat down on the bunk bed in the corner. Then he fell onto the food like a starved animal. "If you ever was a Half Moon member at all," he continued through a mouthful of food, "you'd be figuring a way for me to bust out of here."

"Naw, the shape you're in? Wounded? No spectacles? How far would you get before that Ranger put a big hole in your back? Besides, Matthew Edding hired me to get Doss shed of all this mess. I gave him my word." Tiggs raised his brow, taunting. "You wouldn't want me breaking my word, letting old Doss end up beside you on the end of a rope now, would you?"

Tommy looked up from his plate and stopped chewing. "You're helping Doss? How?"

Doss's voice came from the dark cell for the first

time since Tommy had been brought in. "Shut up, Tiggs! If you're really working for my daddy—looking out for me—you better start acting like it. You've got no right tormenting Tommy just because he stuck it out when the going got rough, and you didn't."

"Help Doss how?" Little Tommy demanded again.

Jesse Tiggs chuckled. "Oh, I'm what you might call Doss's personal bodyguard, seeing to it that the Ranger or nobody else around here shoots him for what he done. I'm surprised he didn't mention it to you. He's real proud of it, I bet."

"I said, shut up, Tiggs!" Doss stood up, stepped out of the dark shadows, and moved to the front of the cell. His hands clamped around the bars. "If you know what's good for you!"

"Why, yes, sir, *Boss*." Jesse Tiggs spoke in a mock voice and backed away toward the door. "I'll just excuse myself and retire to the sheriff's desk. Bet you two ole *desperados* have a lot to talk about. If you need anything, just holler."

"What's taking my daddy so long, Tiggs? Tell him I want out of here! You hear me?" Doss rattled the door to his cell.

"He's finishing his meal right now," Tiggs said, his hand on the door. "He seemed a little upset that I left here long enough to get this food. He's real worried about that Ranger. Says it's best to let the Ranger cool down a little bit before we move you out of here. Then we'll take you out the back way and slip you out of town. Don't that make you feel big?"

"Damn it to hell," Doss cursed as Tiggs closed the plank door behind himself.

"Doss? What's the deal here?" Little Tommy sat the empty plate on the floor and moved forward, wiping his hand across his mouth. In the thin light, up close through the bars, he saw that Doss wore a wool suit, a white shirt, and a string tie. "Why are you all dressed up?" His weak eyes squinted, searching Doss up and down.

"You might as well know the whole of it, Tommy. I signed some papers saying you're the leader of the Half Moon Gang—that it was you and the others who made me do everything." He looked away from Little Tommy. "It says I was never a member of the Half Moons."

"But . . . but why, Doss? We agreed to live and die a Half Moon. Ain't that what I'm doing? Holding out till the end here?"

"Damn it, Tommy, I thought you was dead after I left you in the street. What was I supposed to do? Hang? For nothing? When all I had to do was put the blame on a dead man? What's the matter with you?" He fell silent for a second as Tommy stood staring at him, stunned. "Besides, my daddy made me do it. Wouldn't you have done the same?"

"Jesus, Doss . . . no I wouldn't! We took an oath, that no matter what, we'd declare ourselves to the end. That's what Sandy and the others did in Bannet. They never denied what they were. They went down with a fight. The Ranger told me so. I listened to what that banker said out front a while ago—how you told everybody you got caught up in this against your will. I said to myself, *way to go, Doss!* I just figured you'd found a way to beat them all. Damn. I never thought you was gonna deny who we are."

"And I'm not, Tommy, not for long anyway. But things are a mess here. Everything got turned around someway. It's that damned Ranger caused it all." Doss gazed away, unable to look into Tommy's beady eyes. "I just need some time to think things out, get another plan going."

"If you don't, then what . . . I just hang, and you go off like nothing ever happened?" Tommy shook his head.

"No . . . hell no! Is that what you think of me? That I'd do a pal that way? Once I'm out, I'll get you out, Tommy, that's a *promise.*"

"How? You heard Jesse. They're gonna try me and hang me before the ink's even dry—"

"Then, I'll bust you out." Doss gripped the bars. "Just go along with things. I'll get a gun to you somehow. Just be ready for it."

"When, Doss?"

"I ain't sure. But it's coming. We're still buddies— still the ole Half Moon Gang, eh? I won't let you down this time."

On the other side of the plank door, Jesse Tiggs had stood listening. *Complete idiots . . .* Now he shook his head at Doss' words and walked around the empty sheriff's office looking things over, getting a bit restless. He'd have to bide his time, he reminded himself. This was the big chance he'd been looking for. Once he took care of the Ranger, his name would be known all over the territory—maybe farther. This could put him right up there with William Bonney, Doc Holiday, and all the rest of the big guns.

Thinking about it, he drew his pistol, spun it, dropped it back down into his holster, and drew it again, this time faster. *Yeah, I'm quick enough,* he thought, turning the gun in his hand, looking it over. He held it up, blew a mist of breath on the silver snake handle, and polished it up and down his shirtsleeve. Then he holstered the pistol once more, spread his feet shoulder width, crouched a bit, and—*Damn . . . that was fast!*—the pistol streaked up into his hand, as if it had just appeared out of thin air.

He chuckled, spinning the pistol. He couldn't wait to see the look on that ole Ranger's face when he put it on him. And he couldn't wait to see the look on the faces of Matthew Edding, his idiot son Doss, and all these mindless townsfolk. He'd catch the Ranger standing out there in the street, maybe running his mouth to Matthew Edding, and he'd call out to him, *"Hey, Ranger . . . over here."*

The Ranger would turn, see him standing there about thirty yards away, sunlight glistening off the silver snake on his pistol handle. That would look good, he thought, dropping the pistol back into his holster, poising his hand near it. He'd make sure his voice was just loud enough to draw the town's attention, but not loud enough to give away what he was trying to do. No, he had to do this just right. *"Matthew Edding and Doss are leaving now, Ranger. It's just you and me . . ."*

Maybe Edding and his idiot son would just be cutting through the back alley behind the jail, hear his voice out there on the street, and stop just long enough to see him make his play—*that would be great!* Let ole Matthew see that his money had been well spent. He could just hear Edding telling the boys at the Circle E about it later, saying, *"I never saw anybody so fast in my life, boys. The Ranger barely cleared his holster before Jesse dropped him . . ."*

That was what being a *real* man was all about, that's what Doss and Dusty and Little Tommy couldn't understand. It wasn't about being known as a thief—a two-bit *desperado*. What kind of fool wanted a reputation like that? No sir. He grinned to himself. But to be able to stand out in the street, powder smoke curling up the back of your hand, a man lying there stone-cold dead, one shot through his heart. . .

Now, that's the way to be seen, he thought. Any damned peckerwood could rob a bank, chase a stage off a cliff. But to kill a man like this ole Ranger, a man known for having brought down some of the hardest killers in the territory? This was worth doing.

"You, Ranger, come on out here," Tiggs said aloud—practicing—there in the empty office. Then he relaxed, his feet still spread, picturing it all in his mind, just the way it would be—just the way he had it all planned. Getting a feel for it.

In the cells beyond the plank door, Tommy and Doss had heard Jesse's voice. "What'd he say?" Tommy's weak eyes searched the stripes of light through the cracks in the door. "Who's he talking to out there?"

Doss stood tense and still, his face taken on a worried look. "I don't know . . . the Ranger, I think. That's what it sounded like anyway."

CHAPTER 18

The Ranger sat alone at a table in the saloon where he'd been sitting for the past half hour, his rifle resting across the scarred tabletop. Behind the deserted bar, ole Nick and Vernon stood watching him, each with their wounds still bandaged. Nick whispered under his breath, scratching his scraggly beard, "Don't know if C. G. Hutchinson did us a favor or not, putting us in temporary charge of this place. Between ole man Edding, his gunslinger, Tiggs, and this Ranger, we could be smack in the middle of a shooting war here."

"I know it. But with Hutchinson's bank holding a mortgage here, he couldn't stand to see the place sit empty for long."

"All the same," Nick said, "it ain't Hutchinson's rear end that'll be sticking up in here when the shooting starts. It'll be ours!"

Vernon grinned, spat a stream of tobacco into a brass spittoon, and ran a weathered hand across his mouth. "We knew this book peddling was a tough business when we went into it. The main thing is we got our books in here, didn't we, eh?" He elbowed Nick in the ribs and winked. Along the front edge of the bar stood rows of leather-bound volumes—Shelley's *Frankenstein*, Melville's *Moby Dick*, Dickinson, Poe, Hawthorne. Stacked beside them were nickel novels about Annie Oakley, Kit Carson, along with Frank Tripplet's account of the James brothers.

"Yeah . . . but does any of this drinking crowd read anything?" Nick reached out and flipped a speck of dust off a thick volume of Shakespeare's collected works.

"What's the difference? Every book there has a picture of some kind or other in it." Vernon shrugged, slung a damp bar rag over his shoulder, and smoothed a hand down the beer-stained bartender's vest he'd found hanging in the stockroom. "We use our heads here, and someday there won't be a saloon west of the Missouri that won't have a row of our books in them." He picked up a bottle of rye and a shot glass, and started around the bar toward the Ranger's table.

"Still sounds a little far-flung to me," Nick said under his breath.

Vernon shot him a glance. "Think ahead, dang it. Don't this beat peddling door to door across the territory? Getting dog bit? Shot at? Getting an arrow in our backs? Farmer's daughters always accusing us of stuff? Yes, sir, it does," he answered himself, moving away.

At the Ranger's table, Vernon stopped. "Ready for that drink yet, are ya? Ole Nick and myself will have to be leaving here in a minute to go testify against Tommy Caldwell. Whole town'll be there. What about you?"

"I'm not going."

"Then, would you mind keeping an eye on the place?"

The Ranger only glanced up at him, and at the bottle of rye; then he looked away, across the tops of the bat-wing doors to the street. "Leave the bottle here. Sure, I'll keep an eye on the place."

When Vernon had stood the bottle and the shot glass before him, he cleared his throat and ran a finger beneath his damp collar. "Care for anything to read while you wait?"

The Ranger only stared up at him until Vernon raised a hand slightly. "Just thought I oughta ask." Stepping back, Vernon turned and shrugged—a *why-not* sort of shrug—at Nick as he walked back toward the empty bar.

The Ranger stared at the bottle and glass for a moment, then poured the glass full and started to raise it to his lips. But he stopped, letting out a tight breath, and sat the glass down and pushed it away with his fingertips. It wasn't a drink he needed right now. He needed to let the coiled spring inside his chest unwind. He needed to sit quietly and think, and not let this situation make him do something rash. He'd gotten a glimpse at what he was about to face. He needed to move slow now—slow and deliberate.

Moments ago, above the bat-wing doors, he'd seen the faces of Hutchinson and Judge Lodge as the men walked along the boardwalk across the street. Now he saw the judge come forward alone and step with caution through the creaking doors. The judge stopped and looked over at him before coming any closer. "Sam, I came to talk to you." He spread his suit coat open. "I'm not armed."

Not armed . . . ? The Ranger stared at him. "Since when have you ever had to say such a thing to me, Your Honor?" He raised a boot beneath the table and scooted out a chair for Judge Lodge as he came forward.

"Sorry, Sam. But I know the mood you're in." He stopped, looked down at the full glass of rye, and back to the Ranger's eyes.

The Ranger let out another forced breath, raised his gun hand from his pistol butt, and rested it on the table. "I'm not in any kind of mood. Have a seat." He nodded toward the empty chair. Judge Lodge sat, scooted forward, and folded his big hands on the scarred tabletop next to the rifle barrel.

"Well, it's obvious you're upset."

"Upset?" The Ranger managed a thin tight smile. "You haven't seen the upset part yet, Your Honor. I'm just holding back right now, seeing if maybe you've got some good reason for handling things the way you're handling them here." He tilted his head slightly, eyeing the judge. "Tell me I'm right, Your Honor."

The judge grimaced a bit and ran a hand across his face. "Sam, this whole situation is very complicated. I don't really expect you to understand."

"What is there to understand? Things always get complicated when we skirt the law, Judge. I've heard you say that very thing a hundred times. Isn't that why you've always said you'd never do it?"

"I'm not skirting it now," the judge said. But his words did not carry the amount of snap the Ranger would have expected had his accusation not been true. The Ranger noted it, and listened as Judge Lodge continued. "This is one of those rare cases where the facts are cloudy."

"Oh? Cloudy?" The Ranger nodded.

"Yes, cloudy. Look at it logically. There is no sane reason for Doss Edding to have robbed a bank that would have given whatever amount he asked for. Even the bank's owner insists on that. And since Doss Edding shot no one, and there was no one here to dispute his statement that he was forced into this and only acted in a manner that could possibly save innocent lives by getting the gang out of town when he did—"

"The more you talk, the more I'm offended," the Ranger said, cutting him off. "*You* know that boy is guilty, *I* know he's guilty, and everybody in this town including his *father* knows he's guilty! So let's not sit here rubbing one another's leg about the subject. Let's get down to the meat of it. I just want to know why you've let him off the hook?"

"Jesus, Sam." The judge shook his broad head. He picked up the shot glass full of rye, tossed it back, and inhaled sharply. "Give me some room on this one . . . that's all I'm asking of you. We're getting ready to take Tommy Caldwell to the mercantile store and hold a trial. Everybody is a little nervous about you. I came to tell you you're free to attend, but you'll have to check your firearms at the door."

"That won't happen," the Ranger said, laying a hand on the stock of his rifle on the table. "The way things are shaping up in this town, I'd advise everybody to arm themselves, and arm themselves well."

"I was afraid you'd react this way, Sam. But if you refuse to disarm, it's my duty to instruct you to stay away from the proceedings."

"Don't worry. I hadn't planned on being there. There's nothing there I want to see, especially if it involves Doss Edding standing up and lying—making a mockery of justice. You're right, though. It wouldn't do for me to be sitting there with a loaded firearm on me." The Ranger managed a stiff smile. "I'll just keep out of sight until everything's over."

"Then what?" The judge stared into his eyes.

The Ranger stared back with the same intensity. "Then I'll administer the law from my level—on the dirt—without all the pretense and paperwork."

As they spoke, Nick and Vernon had watched from behind the bar. Now Vernon ventured forward with a shot glass in his hand and a leather-bound volume of Shakespeare under his arm. He'd just sat down the glass and started to take the book from under his arm, when the judge waved him away without taking his eyes from the Ranger's. "Not now, Vernon," the judge murmured.

As Vernon shrugged and stepped away, the judge said to the Ranger in a firmer tone, "You have a clear warning, Sam. If you take justice into your own hands without jurisdiction, I'll have you before my bench." He pointed a finger for emphasis. "Don't make me do it this way, please!"

"Justice *is* in my hands, Your Honor. You put it there the minute I saw what a mockery this thing is. Don't ever forget, you're not the system, Judge. You're just one spoke in the wheel, same as me. The minute this system fails to work, every man and woman on the street has the right to take it out of our hands."

"You're talking *vigilante* justice now, Sam, and I won't stand still for it!" The judge slapped his broad hand down on the tabletop.

"Then you should've done your job right in the first place." The Ranger shook his head. "No, sir, I'm not talking vigilante justice. I'm talking pure justice—justice without all the whereas' and why-fors. Justice without the whitewash, and with all the fat trimmed off it. Every day Doss Edding stands breathing air on this earth is one more day he cheated that poor woman and her child out of. I won't stand still for that. You've cut Doss Edding loose for the bank robbery, but I'm taking him down for murder and stage robbery."

"Not here you won't."

"We'll see how it goes. If I don't get him here, I'll get him somewhere. Don't forget, the Circle E is on the border of my jurisdiction. The minute he steps across the line toward his father's ranch, he's fair game, far as I'm concerned."

"You can't bring him back here, Sam. I won't let you!"

"I don't plan on bringing him anywhere. I'm hoping he'll put up a fight. But if he doesn't, since jurisdiction had become such an issue all of a sudden, I'll take him

all the way to Bannet, let Judge Cletis Morrison try his
case. Maybe it won't be as complicated there."

Judge Lodge's face reddened, looking into the
Ranger's eyes. He let out a breath, slumped a bit, and
said in a hushed tone, "Sam, man to man, off the
record . . . I think Doss Edding is as guilty as the rest of
his buddies. But this was a hanging offense. I had to
give him the benefit of a doubt, before turning him
over to a jury."

"Save your breath, Judge. This was a clear-cut case
if ever there was one. Every judge who's ever heard a
case has had the power to tilt justice one way or the
other. It was your job to stand on equal ground—but
you let something get in the way. I haven't figured out
what it was yet, but it has something to do with that
banker, Hutchinson. And where there's a banker involved, there's money involved. Even a blind man
could see that." He started to pick up his rifle and
stand up from his chair. "Now, if you'll excuse me,
Your Honor, I'll go find me some grub and get back
here before the trial starts."

"No, Sam, wait, please." The judge's hand went out
and held his rifle barrel, pressing it back down on the
table. "I—I can't leave it like this between us. We've
always respected one another. Let's not lose that."

The Ranger eased back down into his chair. "I can
only respect you as much as you respect yourself,
Judge."

The judge looked at him. "I'll tell you what the circumstances were here. But believe me it's not about
money. Not money of any consequence to me person-
ally, at least . . ."

The Ranger sat quietly, listening as Judge Lodge
told him of how Doss Edding had started trouble and
shot up Paco Flores's ranch, and of how C. G. Hutchinson had intervened on behalf of Matthew Edding.
When he said that Matthew Edding had made restitu-

tion for what Doss had done, and that in return the charges would be dropped the next time he held court in that part of the territory, the Ranger only shook his head. "So, if it wasn't for his father's money and influence, Doss wouldn't have been running free—causing all the harm he's done."

"Doss is a young man." The judge spread his hands on the tabletop. "I saw no reason not to give him another chance."

"And because you did, you were ashamed to admit that while you were giving him a second chance, he was right out there killing and robbing."

"No . . . that wasn't it." The judge paused for a second, then in a lowered voice told the Ranger about the bond and the money in escrow to bring about construction for the railhead. When he'd finished he added, "So, all things considered, and the fact that there was an honest possibility that Doss had been an unwilling accomplice in the bank robbery and murders, I consider my decision to be just. Had I have known about the charge of murder and stagecoach robbery, and had you produced any witnesses to it . . . of course it would have been different. But without witnesses, or evidence of some sort, this is something we'll never know, will we?"

"No," the Ranger said, again standing, picking up his rifle from the table, "I suppose we won't."

This time the judge stood up as well and smoothed down his lapels. "I hope we've at least cleared the air between us, Sam. We're both reasonable men, on the same side of the law. This just happens to be one time we disagree." He spread his hands in a friendly gesture. "Next time, who knows."

"Yeah, who knows." The Ranger nodded, and adjusted his sombrero on his head. "But I'm still taking Doss down. You can wager on it."

"All right, I won't argue with you. Just give me your

word you won't do it here, Sam . . . or bring him back
here afterward. Under the circumstances, it wouldn't
be the wise thing to do."

The Ranger nodded. "I promise I won't make a
move until after they hang Little Tommy. That's all I
can give you." He took out a dollar from his pocket
and flipped it down onto the table for the bottle of
whiskey he hadn't drank.

"The boss ain't gonna like this one bit," Herb Wilson
said over his shoulder to Sanborn and Dowdy as they
rode into Cottonwood, leading the dead man's horse
with his body across the saddle. "Becker was a good
ole boy. Boss won't understand how we sat by and
watched that Ranger shoot him without us lifting a
finger." A rise of dust lifted above their horses' hooves
and drifted back behind them on the still air.

"Humph!" Sanborn spit a stream of tobacco. "Then
that's just too bad for Boss. I didn't see him out there
getting his brand-new pistol thrown on the rocks. Far
as Becker goes—he owed me seven dollars. Think how
I feel."

Five yards behind them rode three other cow hands
from the Circle E, who'd met them on the trail leading
a buckskin gelding that belonged to their missing
cook, Giles Bertrim. "I swear, Sanborn," said Dowdy,
"is money all you ever think about?"

"No, it's not. I also think about pistol-whipping that
Ranger as soon as I catch him—forty-seven-dollars'
worth, the way I figure it." He ran a hand across the
butt of his new Colt pistol and felt the scarred metal.
"Forty for the pistol and seven for what Becker owed
me."

Herb Wilson checked his roan down in the middle
of the dirt street and nodded toward the Ranger's
white barb hitched out front of the saloon. "If you

mean it, here's your chance. Ain't that his horse? He said he'd be here."

"Well, I don't know." Sanborn squinted in the sunlight, feeling a bit pressured all of a sudden. The Ranger had said he'd be here, but somehow that realization hadn't dawned on Sanborn until just now. "There's more than one Spanish barb in this country, I reckon."

The three other Circle E riders moved forward and stopped with them, everybody now gazing toward the saloon. "Yeah, but solid white? With one black-circled eye?" Herb Wilson stared at him, not letting him off the hook. Dowdy snickered under his breath. From the hitch rail where the white barb stood quarter-wise, the horse returned their stare; and as if knowing they were talking about him, he raised his head slightly and snorted toward them, stamping a hoof.

"I'd say that's your boy all right. Now, get on over there and get ta pistol-whipping him." Herb Wilson turned in his saddle to the others and added, "I'll go a dollar on the Ranger, boys."

"Now, that's a hell of an attitude for you to take." Sanborn fumed, watching Herb Wilson reach into his trouser pocket. "Before I bust him up, I best see how Boss feels about it, don't ya think?"

"Why?" Wilson grinned, mocking him. "Boss ain't the one what got his new pistol skint up—Becker didn't owe him no seven dollars." A ripple of muffled laughter stirred across the other men.

"All right, then, damn it! You want to see some blood?" Sanborn jerked himself down from his saddle and threw his reins up to Dowdy. "I'll show you some blood!"

"Anybody covering this dollar?" Herb Wilson said in a lowered voice as Sanborn stomped toward the saloon, slapping dust from his worn leather chaps. The others only shook their heads slowly.

Inside the saloon, the Ranger had started to step through the bat-wing doors ahead of the judge. But now, seeing Sanborn cross the dirt street, he moved to the side, saying, "After you, Judge. I'm not all that hungry after all—might just stay and browse through some books for a while."

Hearing the Ranger, Vernon poked Nick in the ribs and smiled. But when the judge stepped out onto the boardwalk and Vernon started toward the Ranger with a copy of *Moby Dick* under his arm, the Ranger moved to the side of the doors and raised a hand, stopping him. "Stay back," the Ranger said in a hushed tone.

From the street, the other Circle E riders watched as Sanborn stomped up onto the boardwalk, his new pistol drawn now, slapping the barrel against the palm of his hand, getting ready. Herb Wilson shook his head and closed his eyes as Sanborn threw open the bat-wing doors. Twenty feet farther up the boardwalk, the judge had turned at the sound of Sanborn's heavy boots and spurs. *What the . . . ?*

There came a short second of silence, then both the judge and the Circle E riders stiffened at the sound of hard wood against solid bone when the Ranger brought his rifle butt full swing into Sanborn's jaw, sending the big man back through the doors, off the boardwalk, and into the street, knocked cold.

Blood rained and splattered.

"And that's that," said Wilson, shoving his dollar into his pocket, swinging down from his saddle. "I knew I shoulda offered five to one."

"Is he dead?" Dowdy and the others stepped down, letting their reins fall to the street. They moved forward toward Sanborn with caution, yet not hearing a sound from the saloon save for the doors still flapping back and forth.

"No, but it'll be a while before he knows his own

name." Herb Wilson leaned down with two of the others and scooped Sanborn up between them. "There's the blood he was talking about, I reckon."

On the boardwalk, the judge stared for a moment longer, before stepping backward, turning, and moving away toward the mercantile store. "All right, Ranger," Dowdy called out to the swinging bat-wing doors, "you've won this time. Where's his new pistol? You've got no right keeping a man's—"

Dowdy's words stopped short, seeing the Ranger step out onto the boardwalk, his rifle in one hand, Sanborn's new Colt in his other. Without a word he stepped to the edge of the boardwalk, drew back the pistol, and hurled it away, high onto the tin roof of a building across the street. It bounced, clamored, and slid down the back side of the metal roof until it fell in the soft mud of a pig lot.

"You've got one hour to get him into riding shape. After that, if you're on the street, I'll kill every one of you." The Ranger looked from one to the other, Sanborn hanging limp between three of them, with blood running down his fractured jaw. Up the street, Tiggs and Matthew Edding had stepped from the restaurant toward the mercantile store across the street, headed for Little Tommy's trial. Other folks headed for the trial also stopped and stared, but the Ranger ignored them, keeping his gaze riveted on Tiggs and Edding.

"Those are my men," Edding said, clenching his fists at his side, taking a halting step.

"Easy, Matthew." Jesse Tiggs sidled close to him, with an arm raised in front of him. "This will keep. He's just baiting you again, can't you see that?" Tiggs chuckled, watching Sanborn's boot heels leave two jagged trails behind him as the others dragged him across the dirt street. "Keep calm."

Edding shoved Tiggs' arm away. "Don't tell me to keep calm."

"Hey, Boss." Tiggs shrugged. "He's just playing more of his game with us. That's all."

Matthew Edding turned a cold stare at Tiggs. "Game? Is that what you think? That this is just a game with him?"

They turned and stared until the Ranger stepped back through the bat-wing doors and let them slap shut behind him. "If you think this man isn't dead serious, you're wasting your life and my time and money." Matthew Edding rubbed the butt of the big Civil War pistol on his hip. "That man's mind is made up . . . he'll kill anybody who gets in his way."

Back inside the saloon, the Ranger had walked over to the bar, wiping a smear of blood from the butt of his rifle and inspecting the rifle stock. "You fellows might as well get going," he said to Nick and Vernon. "Looks like court's about to start." He leaned the rifle against the bar, slipped a leather-bound volume of *Marcy's Prairie Traveler* from the row of books, and began leafing through it.

Vernon and Nick had been staring at the Ranger since he'd cracked Sanborn's jaw. Now, seeing him take out the book, they grinned at each other. "That'll be another dollar for the book," Nick said, rubbing his hands together, "if you want to buy it."

The Ranger smiled to himself. "Tell me something. Why would a person pay good money for a book when they stand here and read one for free?"

Their smiles dropped, but before either one could say anything, the Ranger brought up a dollar and laid it on the bar. "Is there a back door out of here?"

"Why, sure," Vernon replied, thumbing toward the rear wall, "but you don't strike me as a man who uses a back door."

The Ranger leafed idly through the book without looking up. "I take whatever door will lead me where I'm going."

CHAPTER 19

Little Tommy Caldwell's trial would be swift and straight to the point. Before it started, Matthew Edding had gathered his men outside of the mercantile store and told them his plans. After the trial, all the men would circle their horses close around Doss, slip him out of town through the alleys, and get him past the Ranger. It seemed a simple enough thing to do, yet after talking to his men, Edding had looked them over, sizing them up. Concern clouded his brow. *All this worry over one ole Ranger . . .*

Dowdy and Herb Wilson were older men, nearly his age. They were top hands when it came to handling cattle. But neither of them were fighters. They had no stomach for it. Becker had been the only one who would use a gun on another white man. But the Ranger had made quick work of him, according to Wilson and Dowdy. He looked at Becker's body lying across his saddle. *Damn it . . .* The only ones he knew he could count on were Baylor and Statler, old friends who'd worked for him all these years. He hated offering them up to the Ranger, but he would if it came to it—them and Jesse Tiggs as well.

He looked at the other three men who'd joined Dowdy and Herb Wilson on the way to town. These were younger men, newer drovers just up from Texas. Good hard-working boys. But they knew they were at the top of their trade, and could pull out any day and find work in any direction. They owed him no loyalty, other than what they would owe to any rancher they worked for.

He doubted they would stick up for Doss if the going got very tough, no matter what he offered them. "Okay," he said to the men, "is everybody clear on what I want here?" There was no way to rally these men. This wasn't about the cattle herd being in danger, or the ranch itself, or even about his life, or their honor. Drovers didn't sign on for this kind of gun work.

As much as he hated to admit it, what he needed right now was a bunch of crazy young men like the ones the Ranger had killed: Dusty Charlie, Newt Babbage, big Lew Harper . . . and most of all, someone like that warped-minded Little Tommy Caldwell. They were the kind of trash that would jump at an opportunity for trouble, he thought—the kind you wouldn't mind putting between yourself and a bullet.

Edding took a breath. "Are we all set?" He fixed a gaze out across the men gathered before him . . . the same kind of gaze he'd given other groups of men years ago, back during the war, before leading them off into a life-or-death battle.

"What about Sanborn here?" Two of the newer men held Sanborn propped up between them. Sanborn was still knocked out, but babbling some broken words behind a string of bloody saliva.

"Somebody get a wet rag and stick it on his jaw," Matthew Edding had told them. "He'll keep till later." The Circle E men only shot one another guarded glances.

"Giles Bertrim is missing, Boss," Dowdy said, keeping his voice low to Matthew Edding. "These boys found his buckskin gelding wandering around—had a streak of blood on its saddle."

Matthew Edding glared at him. "And? So?"

"Thought I oughta tell ya," Dowdy said, shrugging. "He's been a real fine cook. Hate to think something's happened to him."

"It's not important right now. All that matters to me right now is my son Doss—and getting him out of this mess."

While Matthew Edding spoke with his men before moving into the mercantile store for the trial, Jesse Tiggs, Carl Statler, and Joe Baylor had walked through the alley to the sheriff's office. Now they slipped back along the alley, bringing Doss Edding and Little Tommy from their jail cells.

Doss walked along in his fresh clean suit, his string tie fluttering on a breeze. Little Tommy struggled beside him, in handcuffs and leg chains, dragging himself along in front of Carl Statler's and Joe Baylor's rifles. Tiggs was close behind him with his pistol trained on Little Tommy's back. Little Tommy had squinted at Doss and whispered, "What about now, Doss? While there's nobody here but us Circle E boys."

"No, not yet," Doss whispered back to him, staring straight ahead. "Stay calm, I'll get you a pistol and get you out of here."

Little Tommy raised his voice a bit. "But when, damn it! Turn me loose."

"I heard that, Little Tommy," Tiggs said behind him, poking the pistol barrel into Tommy's back. He grinned. "I'm offended that you'd think any of us here would break the law, eh, fellows?"

Statler and Baylor looked at one another and nodded. "You never was no count, Tommy," Statler said. "I knew it when I first seen you couldn't tie a back-hitch or a sway knot."

"I can tie either one now. I swear I can," Tommy said, hesitating, stumbling as Tiggs' pistol barrel pushed him forward.

Tiggs chuckled. "Don't worry about it. All your knots will be tied for you, today."

Doss Edding spun around. "Leave him alone, Tiggs! Or so help me God—!"

"You'll what?" Tiggs' eyes flashed cold into Doss's eyes. Baylor and Statler jolted to a halt. "You'll tell your daddy on me?"

"There's things I *could* tell him," Doss warned, trying to take a firm stand.

"Yeah? But they're things he already knows. He just can't admit them to himself—worried about his baby boy and all." Tiggs chuckled, shoving Tommy on, Doss having to walk backward for a couple of steps before turning to keep up. Then Tiggs, still chuckling said, "Doss, if you and your daddy only realized how much alike you are, it'd make you both sick to your stomachs."

Baylor and Statler moved forward once more, their expressions questioning one another. "I'm nothing like my daddy—and he's nothing like me! When this is over, I'll kill ya, Tiggs!" Doss raged, moving on through the alley.

"If you see anything happen that changes your mind, Doss, be sure and let me know." Tiggs grinned, picturing himself and the Ranger faced off in the street, the Ranger crumbling to the ground like a clump of dry earth—or like thin paper with a hole burned through it.

When they'd arrived through the back door of the mercantile store, the gathered townsfolk whispered back and forth as Doss and Tommy came forward. Doss stared down, his face red, Little Tommy glaring back at the crowd through his weak bleary eyes, showing them a sneer on his dirty face. "You rotten sons a bitches!" called the voice of an old man amid the surging crowd. Emma Frocke screamed, sailing forward, her fingers drawn into claws. She sank her nails deep into Tommy's face before Jesse Tiggs moved between them and tore her away.

Tommy spit blood from his lips. "Why, thank you, ma'am! That's the sweetest thing any—"

"Order in my court," Judge Lodge called out, cutting off Tommy and the jeers from the townsfolk. "I'll have *order!*" He rose halfway up from a straight-backed wooden chair, behind the table someone had set up as a makeshift bench; and he felled his gavel twice on the rough tabletop. "Everybody with issue will be heard *in turn!*"

The crowd almost settled, but then the old man cried out with spit flying from his lips, "Issue a rope around that peckerwood's neck! Hang him! Hang Doss too! The dirty bastards!"

Once more the crowd surged; but this time, before Judge Lodge could raise his gavel, a shot exploded up into the ceiling from Matthew Edding's pistol. The crowd gasped and cowered. C. G. Hutchinson, standing behind the dry-goods counter, felt his collar turn damp and clammy, and he ran a nervous finger around inside it.

Along the front wall of the store stood the Circle E cowhands, Matthew Edding in the middle, forward of the rest of them, his pistol still raised and smoking. Sanborn's limp body lay sprawled in a chair, his bloody swollen face staring blank at the ceiling.

"You heard the judge," Matthew Edding called out. "Now, quiet down. My son has been questioned and cleared of all charges. He's here to give testimony only. Is that clear?"

Eyes darted toward him, then back to the judge. "That will be enough, Mister Edding." The judge propped forward on his thick palms, the heavy wooden gavel sticking up from between the fingers of one hand. He narrowed his brow, "I, and I alone, will address this court, if you please!"

"Then, get ta addressing it," Herb Wilson called out from among the cowhands, his voice taking on a tougher tone in the presence of Matthew Edding—the Boss.

"Stand down, Herb," Edding said, cutting him a glance.

"Yeah"—Dowdy whispered to Herb Wilson, snickering—"you're just brown-nosing anyhow."

The judge stared from one face to another amid the townsfolk as they murmured and milled in place, until slowly they settled, and all that could be heard was Emma Frocke, her sobbing muffled against the bosom of another woman who held her close, shushing her and patting her back.

"Good, then," the judge said, lowering himself back down into the chair, "this court is now in session." He turned toward Tiggs, Baylor, and Statler, who'd gathered close around Little Tommy and Doss Edding. "Bring the defendant forward."

Little Tommy had made up his mind watching the angry eyes stare at him. If this was how it was going to be—to hell with it. He'd play it out hard to the end. He jerked himself free of Tiggs' hand, stepping forward on his own, his wrists cuffed before him. "Ain't nobody has to bring me no damn where."

"That's right, idiot," Tiggs said in a hushed tone behind him, palming Little Tommy on the back of his head. "You've brought yourself."

"Enough of that!" Judge Lodge glared at Jesse Tiggs. "I won't stand for a prisoner being mistreated in my court!"

"Well, excuse me, Your Honor." Jesse Tiggs grinned. "Are you nice and comfortable, Mister Caldwell?"

The judge glared at Tiggs for a second longer. Then, glancing down at the paper on the tabletop for another second, he looked up at Tommy. "Tommy Caldwell, you are charged with murder and bank robbery. Both charges are hanging offenses in this territory. Before hearing how you plead, it's my obligation to ask you—do you wish the services of an attorney to speak on your behalf?"

"Hell, no. Why would I?" Little Tommy sneered. Yeah, he was through worrying about it. They were going to hang him anyway. He'd show them he didn't give a damn.

"That's right—!" The old man called out from amid the townsfolk. "—What kind of lawyer would be low enough to speak for this no-good son of a—"

The judge's gavel rang out from the rough tabletop, cutting the old man off. "One more word out of you, and I *will* have you removed, sir!" Judge Lodge called out to him.

The old man shrugged and spread his hands, "What'd I do?"

Little Tommy went on. "I don't need nobody to talk for me. And I ain't pleading for nothing from nobody." He turned and glanced at Doss Edding with a proud look on his face. "I'm the one and only leader of the Half Moon Gang. I killed ole man Frocke, shot them ole book peddlers . . . robbed your damned bank. I'd do it all again."

The crowd jeered. Ole Vernon took a step forward, his fists clenched; but Nick grabbed his arm and yanked him back. "Easy, Vernon, he'll get his due. We got our business to run."

"If you want to see how a real *desperado* faces a hanging," Little Tommy called out to the jeering crowd in a raised voice, his beady eyes darting to Doss Edding, "then, come on! Hang me, you bunch of stupid lousy dirt-stickers! Let's get it done . . ."

Up the street in the saloon, the Ranger let out a breath. *See?* This is what I don't like about towns, he had thought a moment ago when he'd heard the pistol shot coming from the mercantile store. Towns were noisy and skittish, and it seemed to take forever to get anything done. He'd stood attentive for a moment and waited to hear more gunshots. When no more came, he'd shrugged, closed the copy of *Marcy's Prairie Traveler*, and opened the copy of Shakespeare's collected works. He smiled to himself. *Much ado about nothing . . .*

He had collected himself now, he thought, fanning the pages idly, stopping, reading a line here and there, then fanning on, his rifle up on the bar now alongside the leather-bound book. Since arriving and being confronted by Edding, his gunslinger, the banker, and the judge, he might have lost sight of himself and what he stood for there a second. But not to any great extent. He'd put it together pretty quick, and now he realized—let the rest of them go about whatever plans they had to make, come up with whatever schemes they could come up with—in the end justice would not be lost here. He'd see to that.

He reached over the bar, keeping one gloved finger on a page, marking his place; and he took up a beer mug, ran it half full from the tap, and sipped it through a low head of foam. Little Tommy Caldwell's trial, if you could call this a trial, should be winding down any minute. Then what would he have? *Let's see . . .* Tommy Caldwell would hang right away. No question about that.

Matthew Edding would try to get his son out of town the safest way possible, with all of his cowhands protecting the boy. They would be expecting the Ranger to make a move then, but that wasn't his plan at all. He'd promised Judge Lodge that he'd wait until after the hanging before he made a move on Doss, but he hadn't said how long. As far as the Ranger was concerned, his promise would be kept the second Little

Tommy's toes swung pointed at the dirt. Why wait any longer than that?

As soon as the hanging was over, he'd be ready. He'd grab Doss Edding before anybody knew what hit them. Then he'd go on about his business. Nothing fancy . . . just another day's work.

The Ranger nodded to himself and closed the book. What else did he have here? This Jesse Tiggs, a steely eyed young man with a silver snake on his pistol. What kind of real seasoned gunfighter would wear a gun like that? Nobody he'd ever come face-to-face with. Nobody out on the badlands. No, sir. Sure, he figured this Tiggs must be good with a gun, to even have the nerve to wear such a thing as that in public.

But he'd checked Tiggs out real good those brief moments on the boardwalk. This man had just enough experience to make him hungry for more. Tiggs wanted what all young gunfighters wanted, a big show, lots of onlookers. Tiggs has probably convinced Matthew Edding that he and he alone was capable of handling the Ranger.

Good enough . . . The Ranger sipped his beer and ran a hand down the scar on his cheek. And Matthew Edding? Edding already knew better. Matthew Edding had rode the long-rider trail years ago, the Ranger reminded himself. Edding knew the deal. He saw through this snake-handled gunslinger. But Edding could afford to use this man, Jesse Tiggs—could pay him enough to put him out front. So why not do it?

It wasn't because Matthew Edding was a coward. The Ranger had looked deep into Edding's eyes, and he'd seen what was there. This man Edding had the glint of killing in his eyes—murder from a long time ago. But Edding hadn't tested himself with a gun in a long while. He wouldn't bet his son's life on his gun skill if he could keep from it. Edding had spent these past years making up for what he'd done in the past. The Ranger understood that.

But running this through his mind, the Ranger knew that when it came to the showdown with Doss' life on the line, Matthew Edding would be the only man here that deserved a second thought. This man would fight to the death, nose to nose, gun sight to gun sight, and he wouldn't back off.

The Circle E cowhands were no problem. They would scatter and bolt. They knew Doss wasn't worth fighting for. Jesse Tiggs? *Well . . .* The Ranger sipped the beer, then swirled it around in the mug and finished it off. He'd soon see what kind of stuff that gunman was made of. Meanwhile, he wondered what was taking Maria and Jimmy French so long.

CHAPTER 20

"They're fixing to hang Little Tommy Caldwell straight away, in one hour," Nick said, stepping through the bat-wing doors. The Ranger turned sideways at the bar and watched the two book peddlers come forward, Vernon stepping wide, going back behind the bar. Nick moved up beside the Ranger and slapped a hand down on the bar top, beside the collected works of Shakespeare. "That's right, one hour. If he wants to make peace with the Lord, he better pray quick, and in several languages."

The Ranger nodded. "I don't suppose Little Tommy denied a thing?"

"Naw, sir, he was belligerent to the last letter. The way he acted, I'm surprised they didn't hang him right there—from a rafter in the ceiling."

"And what about Doss Edding? Did he even testify?"

"Nope, Doss never had to say a word. The judge said he wouldn't have to. Us neither, the way Tommy took all the blame for everything. He even spit at the judge and told him to get on with it." Nick paused, looked the Ranger up and down, then said in a lowered voice, "That Doss is guilty as sin. I don't see how his pa pulled this off for him. You're still going after him, ain't ya? For justice's sake?"

"Yep . . . for justice's sake." The Ranger thoughtfully drew a deep breath and let it out.

Ole Nick slid a glance to Vernon behind the bar, then looked back at the Ranger. "Well?"

"Well, what?" The Ranger looked at him.

"Well . . . you don't seem to be in much of a hurry to get it done. Doss and his daddy are up at the restaurant right now, waiting to see the hanging, with the Circle E boys drawn around them tighter than grass in a pig turd. Wasn't for you being here, this saloon would be packed right now."

"So you want me to leave?" The Ranger reached out and pushed the collected works of Shakespeare over toward the stack of books on the bar.

"No. We enjoy your company. I'm just saying, if justice is going to be served . . ." He let his words trail.

"Funny thing about justice," the Ranger said, picking up his rifle from across the bar and cradling it in his arm. "Sometimes it moves swift . . . other times it seems like it takes forever." He adjusted his sombrero on his head. "But the thing about justice is that it's always at work." He allowed a thin smile. "It just has to work at its own pace. We can't seem to speed it up or slow it down. Sometimes we can't even see it when it gets here. But make no mistake . . . justice always comes."

He moved from the bar toward the rear door of the saloon. "You paid for a book," Nick called out. "Don't go off and forget it."

"I'll pick one up later," the Ranger said, "when I've got more time to read." He stepped out into the alley and closed the door behind himself.

Nick looked at the long row of books, then around the empty saloon. He sighed, looked at Vernon behind the bar, and said, "You know who I bet would buy some books if I grabbed up an armful and took 'em to her? Emma Frocke . . . don't you think? After losing her husband and all?"

Vernon bit off a chew from a twist of tobacco and

moved it over into his jaw. "Settle down, Nick. This idea is gonna work. We just got to give it some time."

Out in the alley behind the saloon, the Ranger walked east, farther away from the mercantile store and the restaurant where the townsfolk and Matthew Edding, along with his men, had gathered for Little Tommy's hanging. Edding and his men would be watching the saloon, trying to keep an eye on his comings and goings—waiting for him to come out. So he needed to get the jump on everybody, show up where they'd least expect him.

At the far end of town he waited, peeping back along the street a hundred yards. He took his time, and when a breeze lifted a deep swirl of dust, he took off his sombrero, stepped out into the drifting brown cloud, and drifted with it across the dirt street, his long duster tails licking out around him. He did not move fast or crouch low. He moved with the flow of the wind.

While the Ranger slipped out of the dusty breeze and into the alley across the street, Jesse Tiggs sat on a nail keg, guarding Little Tommy in the stockroom of the mercantile store, a shotgun cocked and lying on his crossed knee. He twirled his snake-handled pistol idly on his finger. "You know, I got to hand it to you, Little Tommy. You're the most stupid peckerwood I've ever seen . . . but you do stand for your word, don't ya?" He grinned. "So far you're managing to swallow everything you bit off for yourself."

"Yeah," Little Tommy said, brooding, without turning his weak eyes up to Tiggs. "But don't write me off yet. I might still have an ace in the hole."

"Oh? Well, let me guess what that ace might be . . ." Tiggs stopped twirling his pistol, and pushed up his hat brim as if in reflection. "I've got it!" He tapped the pistol barrel to the side of his head. Tommy glanced up at Tiggs' bleary image, then back to the floor as

Tiggs said, "Why, Doss Edding! Of course! He's your
ace. I almost forgot—ole Doss could come busting
through the door any minute, pitch you a gun, and the
two of you ride off, guns blazing, into the wide sunset.
Now, damn, that's romantic." Tiggs grinned, and
twirled his pistol again.

"You don't know nothing, Tiggs."

"Yeah, you're right. What do I know"—Tiggs settled back on the nail keg—"except that we both started
out from the same point. Now look at us. You're going
to hang from a pole in a few minutes . . . I'm gonna
walk away a free man. See any difference there?"

"You're no different than me, Tiggs," Little Tommy
said in a low tone. "You were out to make a big name
for yourself, just like me and Doss." The conviction in
Tommy's voice caused Tiggs to tilt his head a bit, curious. "And you won't walk away from here free either.
You'll die here."

A silence passed as Tiggs only stared at him. Then
Tommy lifted his head to Tiggs. "That's right. You've
got yourself set on killing that Ranger—making yourself the cock of the walk. But it ain't going to happen.
He'll spit you out like bad breakfast. So laugh it up
while you can. You're as dead as I am."

"Aw, but you're wrong there." Jesse Tiggs leaned
forward a bit, raising the pistol. Cocking and pointing
it at Tommy's head from two feet away. "See, I've got
a talent, a skill that is in high demand . . . something
you and the others never had."

Hearing the pistol cock, Tommy raised his bleary
eyes and looked into the barrel. He didn't shy back
from it. "Maybe that's so. But you ain't going
nowhere. Yeah, I'm stupid. I know I have been all my
life. I'm stupid, and I can't see nothing worth a damn.
I made up my mind that nothing good was ever gonna
come to me—so I'd take whatever I wanted till they
stopped me. I wanted a name for myself, and I'll get it.

It won't be much, but it'll be what I expected. You? Sure, you're smart. You got good eyes, you got talent. But don't think that makes you any better off—"

"I'm tired of hearing you," Tiggs said; and he pulled the trigger as Little Tommy stared into the barrel. But before the trigger struck the bullet, Tiggs caught it with his thumb, then smiled. "Whew! That was a close call, eh?"

Little Tommy hadn't so much as flinched an eye. That bothered Tiggs. "*Shiiit,*" he hissed, lowering the pistol. "You damned idiot."

"Why? Was I supposed to be afraid you'd kill me?" Tommy chuckled under his breath. "So, what do you figure? I'm too stupid to be afraid? Or too blind to see what you did?"

"Probably both." Tiggs tried to shrug it off, yet something about Little Tommy talking this way unsettled him, and he shifted on his nail keg and changed the subject. "You know I'd offer to get you a preacher, but the only one in town is that old man—the old whittler who was cussing you at the trial." He grinned.

"Let him whittle, then. I don't want no preacher anyway. I know who I am, what I am, and where I'm going." Tommy ran a cuffed hand across his mouth and lowered his weak eyes to the floor. "Bet you wish you could say the same."

Out front of the telegraph office, where a line pole stood straight and high with a hastily tied noose thrown over its cross member, the old whittler had shown up with a banjo and sat down on a battered lard bucket. "There'll be no words of grace from me today," he'd said. He plucked the banjo one string at a time, tuning it close to his ear, then fell into a loud festive strum.

"I hate these kind of last-minute occasions," said a

woman's voice as she moved from the restaurant door through the throng of people. She carried a platterful of hot corn on the cob. Steam billowed. "I don't guarantee it's done all the way through. You'll have to take it like you get it, I reckon. Had no time to fry any chicken." Hands reached out. Coins dropped onto the wooden platter.

"It don't seem natural not being able to go to the saloon, like we could at any other decent hanging." Dowdy spoke to Joe Baylor above the ring of the banjo. "This whole thing seems wrong. Surely I could slip up there long enough to pick us up a bottle of rye."

Baylor's eyes snapped at him. "Boss says we stick here. So shut up and do it! You see any townsfolk going to the saloon? Hell, no! They all know that Ranger's there, wilder than a scalded bobcat. You want to be the one to fool with him? After seeing what he done to ole Sanborn?"

Near the telegraph pole, Sanborn rocked back and forth with a wet towel wrapped around his swollen jaw, chin to forehead, with his hat shoved down holding it in place. A glazed distant look clouded his bloodshot eyes. His nose had turned the color of fruit gone bad.

"I was there, Baylor, don't forget." Dowdy thumbed himself on the chest. "I saw it all. The Ranger could've killed Sanborn if he wanted to. So don't tell me nothing about it. Besides, them ole book peddlers are in there. They don't seem too worried about the Ranger." As he spoke, he leaned forward from the front of a building and gazed up the street toward the saloon. But nothing stirred in that direction but a twist of brown dust and a lanky hound with its back curved against the breeze.

"That's right, because them two ole peddlers are as crazy as he is. The point is, Boss needs us here to back his play. So shut up! Pay attention here."

Dowdy stepped back a step and turned to Herb Wilson on his other side. "If Boss wants a piece of that Ranger, I say he needs to call him out and get to it."

"What?" Herb Wilson looked up from sorting through a wad of wrinkled dollar bills in his gloved hands. In one palm he held a pair of worn ivory dice. "What are you talking about, Dowdy?" He blew on the dice and rattled them in his closed fist. "Think we can work up a game with this bunch?"

The banjo rattled loud and long, yet Dowdy lowered his voice even more. "I'm talking about this whole deal here," he said, leaning a bit closer. "We're supposed to be here backing the Eddings. But I say to hell with Doss and the horse he rode in on. He's as guilty as Little Tommy and the others. He deserves to be swinging from that pole his damn self, don't he?"

Herb Wilson only shrugged, detached from the matter. "Sure, I guess. Why not? I mean who cares about Doss one way or the other. Put him out of your mind." He rattled the dice, their sound muffled by his gloved hand. "You got any money?"

"A couple of dollars, but you ain't getting it. Sanborn borrowed four dollars off me to pay for his new pistol. Now it's gone, and he probably won't even remember the money." He shook his head. "I haven't done well working at the Circle E, to be honest about it. Now Boss is wanting us to fight that Ranger for him. Are you going to?"

"What? Fight the Ranger? Do I look crazy to you?" Herb Wilson stopped rattling the dice and looked at them in his gloved palm. "I saw the odds on killing that Ranger the minute he blew Becker out of his saddle. That ole Ranger's a tough piece of work. What about you? Are you going to fight him? Because if you are, stay a few feet away from me. I don't want to die catching a stray."

"No, I'm not." Dowdy looked all around at the

milling crowd, at ears of boiled corn raised to wet lips, then he added, "So what are we waiting for? Let's pull out of here, before we get in any deeper."

"Not yet," Herb Wilson said, looking away, eyeing a fellow in a faded silk vest who'd come stepping toward them through the gathering of townsfolk. "I'm drawing what pay the Circle E owes me before I go."

Dowdy pushed up his hat brim. "Then we'll have to ride along, all the way back to the ranch to get it."

"Big deal. That Ranger ain't going to make a move on us unless we make one first. He won't make a move period, till he's got everything the way he wants it."

"I hope you're right."

"Well, gentlemen," said the stranger in the faded silk vest, moving up to them. "Isn't this something— the whole town out like this." He gestured a hand and smiled. "And I see you have some dice there. I've always been fascinated by the clatter of those clever little cubes."

"Have ya sure enough?" Herb Wilson smiled and turned away from Dowdy, rattling the dice once more, this time toward the newcomer.

Dowdy stepped away, and looked over at Matthew and Doss Edding side by side out front of the telegraph office. He couldn't make out their words to one another, but it didn't appear to be a friendly conversation. He wondered how much pay he'd have coming right now, if he asked for it in the middle of the month this way.

The new cowhands from Texas had been watching the crowd and talking low among themselves. Now, at the sight of Herb Wilson and the stranger in the silk vest squatting down, counting money down onto the boardwalk, the cowhands nudged one another and moved toward them. Dowdy walked over near Sanborn—Sanborn didn't seem to recognize him right away.

Out in front of the telegraph office, Matthew Edding snatched Doss by his arm and spun him around. "Don't turn your back on me when I'm talking!" he hissed. "You're not going anywhere until this is over. You're gonna watch . . . and you'd better learn from it! I've put everything I've got, or ever will have, on the line for you. Do you understand that?"

Doss had been talking a bit firm to his father, but now, seeing the look in Matthew Edding's eyes as he'd jerked him around and spoke to him, Doss's voice trembled. "But . . . but, Daddy. Tommy has been my friend. I can't watch them do this to him. For God's sake . . . what are we doing here? You know the Ranger's coming for me. Let's go! Now! While there's a chance."

Matthew Edding pulled him close, face-to-face. "I'll tell you what we're doing here. We're making a show for these folks. Do you think they've forgotten? No! Right now, they've put it aside. They'll get some justice out of watching Tommy hang. But we've got to stand firm here—show them you've nothing to hide. We can't look weak, or tomorrow they'll start thinking about it all over again! They'll want your hide!"

"Then—then at least give me a gun. What if that Ranger comes over here, calls me out."

"If he does come now, the one thing you better not have on you is a gun. Are you a complete fool? You started this mess, but I'm cleaning it up. So keep your mouth shut and try to look like you've got some sense. Keep an eye toward the saloon if you want to do something." He settled a bit, took a breath, and brushed a hand across Doss's shoulder. "As soon as Tommy hangs, we'll gather the men around you and ride out. Jesse Tiggs is staying behind. He'll handle the Ranger."

Doss's face reddened. "Tiggs, Tiggs . . . that's all I've heard since we left the ranch—"

"And you better be glad of it," Matthew Edding said, stopping him short. "You think I give a blue damn about a two-bit gunslinger like Tiggs? Just do like you're told!"

The Ranger had crept through the alley behind the crowd, moving up and over the town garbage dump, through broken glass and past a busted rope bed frame. At the rear of the restaurant, he'd crouched down when a woman stepped out and slung a pan of water on the ground. Then he'd moved on as quiet as a ghost until he rounded the side of the telegraph office, moving toward the street with his back against the wall of the building. At the front corner of the telegraph office, he crouched down behind a rain barrel and listened.

He couldn't make out Doss and Matthew Edding's words beneath the sound of banjo music and the stir of the crowd, but that wasn't important. He knew what to do when the time came. He leaned back against the wall behind him and relaxed for now, his rifle standing propped between his knees. What in the world was keeping Maria? She and French should have arrived a day before.

PART 3

Last Dog Hung

CHAPTER 21

Maria and Jimmy French had stopped to water their horses at a small watering hole in a rock basin, and to let the little girl rest in the shade beneath a cliff overhang. Another fifteen miles and they would be in Cottonwood. As French filled his canteen, he looked back over his shoulder, saying to Maria, "It's been a rough few days for me . . . but I've learned a lot from it."

"And what have you learned?" She held the child on her lap and pressed a wet bandanna against her face.

He thought about it for a second, realizing that much of what he'd learned he could not express; things about people, human nature at its worst and its best. "I've learned a lot about myself. That I'm not nearly as fragile as I might have once thought." He smiled. "Being snatched out of my safe little day-to-day existence and thrown into a pack of rats like Doss, Tommy Caldwell, and the rest of them has given me a different outlook on life. I feel stronger now . . . for having lived through it, I suppose." He did not want to mention what he had in mind once he met Doss or any of the others face-to-face. She didn't need to know about it.

"Sí. Life is a great teacher of all things, both good and bad. A wise person understands the good of it and learns to be strong. A foolish person sees only the bad . . . and instead of strength they learn only bitterness." She watched him closely as he stood, capped the full canteen, and walked over to her while the horses blew and drew water, their saddles off and lying over in the shade.

He stooped down beside her, and she saw a shadow of thought move across his brow, as if he believed her words but did not want to fully accept them. But she wouldn't ask him what went through his mind. This was something he'd have to work out for himself. "One thing's for certain," he continued, "I've grown to admire you and the Ranger—the way you two live, the way you handle things. When all this is settled, I might decide to do something different. I don't know if banking will be exciting enough to hold my attention any longer. There's a big world out here. I think I'd like to see more of it."

She continued to rub the wet bandanna around the little girl's neck, cooling her. The child looked up into Jimmy French's eyes as he spoke. "Is it the big world you wish to see . . . or is it the ways of the world that has your interest?" Maria queried.

He seemed to consider it. "Maybe both, after all this."

"Then, be careful." She lowered the bandanna from the little girl's neck and held it in her hand, gazing long into Jimmy French's eyes. "The world itself is a magnificent thing to see. But the ways of the world can draw you to it like a flame draws a moth. If you are not careful, the ways of the world will burn you up."

"See? That's what I mean. You know this, I don't. And how will I ever if I don't experience it myself? I'd like to be like you and the Ranger—confident, no fear. That's the only way to live." He pictured Doss Edding from ten yards away, the two of them faced off in the middle of a dirt street . . . pistols blazing.

Maria only stared at him, seeing the distant look come into his eyes. After a silence she stood up and dusted the seat of her trousers, holding the little girl in the crook of her arm.

Jimmy French saw something had changed in her expression, and as he stood up with her, he shrugged. "Did I say something wrong?"

"No. But we need to move on to Cottonwood."

It was not what he'd said, but rather the look on his face that had bothered her. She'd seen that look on men's faces before. There was anger in Jimmy French that had to be reconciled, anger at wrongs done against him, events that he had not handled the way he thought he should have, looking back on them. Escaping from the Half Moon Gang had taken courage, she knew. Yet it was courage he'd summoned up with trembling hands. So he mistook his courage for blind luck. And that was not enough for him now. He needed more. He needed to see his courage as something calm and in control.

She was tempted to tell him that true courage always works with trembling hands, for what courage does it take to do something if there is no fear? But she wouldn't say this to him. He was still too consumed by the demons the Half Moon Gang had left dancing in his mind. He would see it himself perhaps, in time, if the lessons in his life taught him wisdom. For now she knew that perhaps he needed those demons. What else did this young man have to fill the ugly hollowness that shame left in its wake? The Half Moon Gang had shamed him . . . not by merely their actions against him, but by the way he'd allowed them to make him feel inside.

Little Tommy Caldwell stumbled out of the mercantile store, the chains on his ankles having pulled his dirty socks down, the toe of one sock dangling loose and catching on a nail head as he moved out onto the boardwalk. Jesse Tiggs steadied him with one hand up under Tommy's arm, his other hand carrying the short-barreled shotgun. "Easy, Tommy," Tiggs said, "let's stop for a second here." And he paused, gazing across

the crowd, while Judge Lodge and C. G. Hutchinson
loomed close behind him.

"What's the holdup?" C. G. Hutchinson asked, stepping wide of them as a soggy corncob sailed forward
from the crowd and bounced off across the boardwalk.
"Move along quickly, now!"

"Don't rush me, damn it!" Tiggs hesitated. He'd
never seen a hanging from this end, facing the crowd,
seeing it through the eyes of the man about to die. He
felt pressed, somehow smothered, by the angry faces,
the harsh voices, the raised fists. *Jesus* . . . He wasn't
sure what he should have expected, stepping out here,
but it wasn't this! There seemed to be no breathing
space out here.

Little Tommy didn't seem bothered by it. He
squinted at the jeering crowd and cursed the townsfolk
under his breath. Another soggy corncob sailed
through the air, this one clipping Tommy's face, and he
bent his shoulder around and wiped it across his wet
jaw. "Come on, Tiggs," he said, his voice cold and hollow. "Let's do this thing up. I don't want to wear everybody's dinner on my shirt." He jerked his arm forward,
Tiggs holding on to him.

When Tiggs still hesitated, Judge Lodge moved
around from behind him. "Well? Are you going or
not?" C. G. Hutchinson had already managed to move
along the boardwalk and disappear down into the
crowd.

"Don't rush me!" Tiggs' wild eyes flashed at the
judge. More corncobs sailed past them, bouncing off
Tiggs' shoulders, one barely missing the judge's face.

"Come on, Jesse," Tommy said, ducking his head and
leaning closer to Tiggs, "don't soil yourself here. Think
how bad that would look."

Tiggs' face reddened. "Come on, then, you idiot son
of a bitch!" He yanked Tommy along, moving down off
the boardwalk, the crowd surging but then parting as

the barrel of the shotgun swept across their angry faces. "Make us some room here!" Tiggs shouted, noticing that his voice sounded shallow and not at all the way he would have wanted it to sound. He had little control here—at least not the control he wanted, nor anticipated.

These people should be standing back at the sight of him, this shotgun in his hand. Maybe he wasn't standing as tall as he should be. He straightened himself, pulling Tommy forward, Tommy not seeming concerned as spit flew forward from the pressing townsfolk and ran down his dirty face. Some spit sprayed on Tiggs' face as well. *What was wrong with these people?*

As Matthew Edding, Doss, Baylor, and Statler had turned at the sight of the crowd parting for Tiggs and Little Tommy, the Ranger rose up from behind the rain barrel with his rifle cocked, and stood flattened against the side of the building in the shadow of the narrow alley.

Farther along the boardwalk, the dice shooters rose up, money in hand, dusting their knees, watching the dark shadow move across the dirt street. For the first time Matthew Edding noticed what the men had been doing. He seethed at the sight of it. *Gambling? Shooting dice while they were supposed to keep an eye out for the Ranger?* "Damn it, Statler," he said, "you and Baylor get over there. Tell them fools there's a ten-dollar bonus for whoever spots the Ranger when he comes this way!"

"Sure, Boss." The two men turned and ran the twenty-foot distance along the boardwalk, to the cowhands. *Damn it!* Matthew turned back to the crowd before him. Tommy's weak eyes searched upward toward him and Doss as Tiggs shoved him onto the waiting horse beneath the telegraph pole.

"Doss? Doss? Are you there?" Little Tommy called out above the din of the angry crowd. "Don't worry none about me, ya hear? Live a Half Moon, die a Half—"

His words stopped, cut short by the banjo that swung out from the crowd and busted across his back in a spray of splinters and snapping strings. The crowd roared. Tommy went down on one knee, Tiggs hovering over him. Spit flew.

"Daddy, for the love of God!" Doss cried out, trying to turn away. Matthew Edding grabbed him and straightened him forward. Behind them, the Ranger inched forward from the shadows.

In the street, only a few feet from the pole now, Tiggs swung the shotgun up, his thumb cocking the hammer as he dragged Tommy to his feet. *Damn this!* Why had he ever gotten into this part of it? He was a straight-up gunslinger! Not this! This wasn't getting him anywhere, not in anybody's eyes, especially his own! A blast of fire exploded upward from the short barrel. "Everybody get back!" Tiggs yelled, and slung the spent shotgun into the crowd, coming up with his snake-handled pistol. "I'm warning yas! Give me some room!"

The crowd gasped and fell silent beneath the rise of burned powder. Tiggs glanced around for Judge Lodge, but the judge had managed to slip past him, and now stood beside C. G. Hutchinson, near the hanging pole. *Damn all of this!* "Don't nobody move," he yelled, pushing Tommy forward. Beneath the pole, the horse stamped a nervous hoof and shook out its tangled mane.

"See, Jesse," Tommy said, regaining his breath, "just you and me out here—"

"Shut up! Damn you." Tiggs moved with him, the crowd silent but stirring closer. He shoved Tommy upward on the horse until Tommy hung halfway over the saddle. Then Tiggs flashed his pistol back at the pressing crowd. "All right, now! Give me room to hang him, for Christ's sake!" Tiggs yanked the key to Tommy's anklet chain out of his shirt pocket. He hurried, with a shaking hand, unlocking the chain and letting it fall to the dirt.

While everybody stared forward, the Ranger moved like a stalking cat around from the corner of the alley, and out onto the boardwalk behind the Eddings, his cocked rifle at port arms. Sliding a glance back and forth from beneath the lowered brim of his sombrero, he stopped close to Doss Edding's back—close enough to see the pulse beat in the side of Doss's throat as Little Tommy righted himself in the saddle with a sheen of spit and sweat glistening on his face.

Tiggs looked up at the dangling noose above Tommy's head, then all around at the crowd, feeling beads of sweat break loose on his brow. "Somebody help me here—get this rope around his neck!"

No one made a move. After a silent pause, Little Tommy said, "Well, shit," and reached up with his cuffed hands, and grabbed the dangling noose and slipped it over his head. A gasp went up from the crowd. Laughter rippled from the cowhands along the boardwalk. "You're supposed to cuff his hands behind him, you stupid peckerwood!"

Tiggs' face reddened. "Shut your mouth, Wilson!" Tension swelled in his chest and pounded like the fast beat of a drum. This looked bad out here— not at all how he wanted it to look to these folks . . . to Matthew Edding, to the other cowhands, to the Ranger. He glanced up the street toward the saloon. Was the Ranger watching? Damn, he hoped not. What was happening to him anyway? It was as if Little Tommy had cursed him some way, the things he'd said in the stockroom. Nothing had gone right since! *Okay, calm down.* . . . He bit his lip, flashing the pistol toward the cowhands. They stepped aside from Herb Wilson. Wilson shrugged tightly and stepped back.

Tiggs looked over at the judge and Hutchinson for some kind of direction, some advice, anything. The two

of them gave him nothing with their hollow stares.
Now what? Why didn't they let him know something . . . what he was supposed to do next? Had everybody washed their hands of this but him? *Jesus . . .* He
let out a tense breath and turned his face up to Little
Tommy Caldwell.

"All right, Tommy Caldwell!" Tiggs drew back a
gloved hand, ready to smack the horse's rump. At least
he'd make this look good. Take his time, sound calm,
look collected. "Is there any last thing you'd like to say
before—"

"Damn every one of ya!" Little Tommy screamed the
words, then let out a loud *Yiiii-hiiii*, and batted his dirty
sock feet against the horse's sides.

No! Wait! damn it . . . ! Jesse Tiggs stood stunned, his
hand drawn back to slap the horse's rump, the horse
gone off now from beneath Little Tommy. Little
Tommy swung back and forth on the creaking rope, his
cuffed hands standing flexed out before him like poised
talons on some strange twisted bird. *Jesus, no! Not like
this!* Jesse Tiggs' pistol hung limp in his gloved hand.

Townsfolk winced; they sliced their breath and
swiveled their heads away from the sight. "Lord God!"
one of them gasped.

"Let him swing," Emma Frocke spoke out in a dry
tone, her red-rimmed eyes taking it all in.

There hadn't been enough slack in the rope to break
Tommy's neck. He gagged and wiggled, a dark circle
creeping down his crotch, staining his already sodden
trousers. A flopping dirty sock kicked itself free, and his
bare white foot cramped downward in a tight arch. This
was no way to die, even for an idiot like Tommy Caldwell, Tiggs thought, watching him swing, hearing the
rope creak, seeing Tommy's eyes bulge from his blue
face—turning to a darker shade, then to purple. A vein
stood tight on Tommy's forehead as if ready to burst.

Little Tommy had held out till the end, but now that

the end drew tighter and tighter around his throat, instincts took hold inside him . . . and in reflex against the burning pressure on his face, his hands snatched upward over his head. He caught the rope and yanked himself up. "Damn it, Tommy," Tiggs screamed, "turn loose . . . let go!" He lunged forward snatching at Tommy's kicking feet.

On the boardwalk, Matthew Edding had inched a step forward, mesmerized. Doss jerked back from the sight with his eyes clenched shut. At that second the Ranger made his move, swinging his arms around Doss in a bear hug, the cocked rifle pointed up, the tip of it poking Doss beneath his chin, tilting his head back at a sharp angle. "Got ya," the Ranger whispered into his ear, stepping back with Doss hugged tight against his chest.

While this happened, the horse that had bolted forward from beneath Tommy Caldwell felt the weight leave its back and had slid to a halt ten feet ahead. Shaken by the noise of the crowd and by the sight of hands reaching out to snatch its reins, the spooked horse reared, came down in a spin and ran right back in the direction it came from.

Passing beneath Tommy's pumping feet, the horse veered into Jesse Tiggs and spun again. But not before one of Tommy's feet caught the saddle just enough to hurl himself upward, catching the rope in his cuffed hands and managing enough slack to throw the noose from around his neck. The crowd stared, stunned, not believing their eyes. Now the horse swept beneath Tommy for one more pass, and as if the whole thing were something rehearsed by a circus performer, Tommy came down into the saddle upright, and batted the horse forward, off along the dirt street.

"Tiggs! Damn it, man! He's getting away!" Matthew Edding swung his big pistol up as he yelled. Tiggs did the same. But neither man could risk a shot into the crowd as Tommy weaved the horse back and forth, ducking low in the saddle, and then speeding down the street in a wake of dust. Women screamed, jumping out of Tiggs' gun sight. Men fell back over one another. C. G. Hutchinson dropped down, his thick arms wrapped around his bald head. The judge stood rigid, his fists clenched at his sides, watching Little Tommy as Tommy let out a long war whoop and rode out of town.

Matthew Edding spun toward his cowhands, who stood on the boardwalk with stunned expressions. "Well? What are you waiting for? Get after him!" They didn't make a move. "What's the matter with you men?" he bellowed.

As he spoke, he saw them staring past him. Then he turned to see C. G. Hutchinson in the street, gazing past him as well. He turned toward Doss. "What's wrong with every . . . ?" His words trailed away at the sight of his son standing rigid in front of the Ranger at the corner of the alley, the Ranger's rifle barrel propping Doss's chin upward.

"One move and I'll kill him," the Ranger said. Yet, as he spoke, his eyes cut away for a split second to the drift of dust Little Tommy had left standing in the air. He couldn't let that one get away. A picture of the two children at the sheep rancher's shack flashed across his mind—the young boy standing up to Tommy, protecting his little sister, the heavy pistol in his hands. Tommy would be headed that way, and he'd make short work of those children. The Ranger couldn't let that happen, no matter how bad he wanted Doss Edding brought to justice.

The cowhands had collected themselves now and milled slowly forward. "Stand still!" Matthew Edding raised a hand toward them and spoke without taking his eyes off of Doss and the Ranger.

"Lord, Boss! What do we do? Do we take him down

or get after Little Tommy? Tell us something here!" Carl Statler's voice trembled.

"Forget Little Tommy. Nobody move." Edding's voice dropped low. Behind him in the street, the crowd caught sight of what was going on, and fell silent. "Turn him loose, Ranger," Edding said, his big pistol still in his hand, smoke curling up from the barrel. Now Tiggs moved forward from the crowd, his snake-handled pistol still in his hand.

The judge had turned and stood staring. "For God's sake, Sam! You can't do this. You gave your word."

"I told you I'd wait till after Little Tommy's hanging, and I did," the Ranger said. "It's not my fault Tiggs bungled the job." His eyes cut to Jesse Tiggs and saw Tiggs' face turn white. But even as the Ranger spoke, his mind was ticking like a clock, knowing Little Tommy Caldwell was getting farther and farther away with each rise and fall of his horse's hooves.

"You can't do this, Sam!" The judge stepped closer, seeing the slightest uncertainty in the Ranger's eyes. "Tommy's getting away. Do you want that on your conscience?"

The Ranger flashed a glance at the cowhands on the boardwalk, at Matthew Edding before him, at Tiggs standing in the street. "I've got no jurisdiction here, Judge, remember? I can't go after Tommy Caldwell." But he already knew he would have to. As he spoke, the picture of the two children came to him again. Some things had to come first in his life. Sure, he was going after Little Tommy. He just had to work through this first.

"Show some reason, Sam. You have no jurisdiction to arrest Doss Edding either. Let's not quibble over the law while that lunatic gets away! As an officer of the court, I'm asking you to turn Doss Edding loose and go after Little Tommy!"

"That's not an easy thing to do just now," the Ranger

said, noting the pistols in Tiggs' and Edding's hands. "I've got this one. This one is a bird in the hand—"

"You won't leave here with him, Ranger," Matthew Edding said, cutting him off. He braced forward a step, the pistol slightly raising. In the street, Tiggs did the same. The Ranger's rifle barrel stiffened higher, his gloved finger drawn tight against the trigger.

"Hold it! Everybody stand calm!" Judge Lodge said. "Sam. You are a lawman. You have no choice but to act in the public's best interest here. Now, turn him loose and get going. I'll have everybody toss their guns away." He started to turn toward the cowhands.

The Ranger looked towards them as well. "That's not necessary, Your Honor. I hope somebody here makes a move on me." His eyes then bored into Matthew Edding's, then glanced over to Tiggs. He said close to Doss's ear, "You're more trouble than you're worth." And with the quick flick of his rifle, he swung it from beneath Doss's chin, leveled it on Matthew Edding, and shoved Doss forward into his father's arms.

Doss's breath heaved in his chest. "Shoot him, Daddy! Now! Before he gets away—"

"Shut up, boy," Matthew Edding said, holding Doss against his chest. Tiggs and the cowhands had stirred forward a tense step. But a stern glance from their boss stopped them.

"This is the second time I've trained a rifle on you, boy," the Ranger said to Doss. "Don't forget what they say—third time's the charm." The Ranger backed into the alley, around the rain barrel, his rifle still cocked and aimed.

"Let me take him, Matthew," Tiggs said just above a whisper.

"No, not now. He could have killed Doss. Let him go. As soon as he's gone, we're getting Doss out of here."

CHAPTER 22

Seven miles out of Cottonwood, Maria and Jimmy French had jerked their horses to a halt on a raised stretch of rocky ground. Maria had been riding double with the little girl on her lap when the first drift of Tommy Caldwell's dust showed itself above the edge of a low cliff. As soon as Jimmy French saw the dust, he batted his horse forward a few feet closer to the edge of the cliff. He looked out and down, then called back over his shoulder to Maria. "It's one rider." Maria stepped her horse over beside him as he added, "He's bareheaded, and riding hard."

"Oh?"

Maria gazed out at the drifting streak of dust, seeing the rider at a distance of two hundred yards and closing fast. She had started to ask Jimmy French to take the child from her. But before she could say another word, French blurted out as the rider drew nearer, "My God! It's Little Tommy Caldwell!"

"It is? Then here, quickly. Take the child." She leaned toward him in her saddle, raising the little girl who lay sleeping against her bosom. But Jimmy French ignored her. Moving sideways away from her, he drew the rifle from Maria's saddle scabbard before she could stop him.

"Don't worry, I've got him," he said, pulling his horse's reins high and turning it with a tap of his heels.

"No! Wait." Maria turned her horse along with him.

"You do not know these kind of people. Take the child. Let me handle this man."

"Sorry . . . but Little Tommy is mine. All mine." He gigged his heels into the horse's sides and took off down a narrow path toward the lower sandy flatlands below them.

Sante Madre. . . . Maria took off behind him. But with the child waking and stirring against her, she had to keep her horse in check and move carefully down the loose sandy path. She called out to Jimmy French as he came out onto the flatlands in a full run. But he wasn't listening to her. Ahead, beyond a low rise, all they could see of Little Tommy now was his drifting dust. Jimmy French rode straight toward it.

Beneath French, the horse stretched out into a fast run along the sandy trail rising and falling before him as he ducked low in his saddle with Maria's rifle in his hand. He'd never fired a rifle from atop a horse—he had never fired a rifle period. So what? He wasn't afraid of Little Tommy. He wasn't afraid of anybody anymore.

Behind Jimmy French, seeing she had no chance of catching up or stopping him, Maria reined her horse off the trail and headed into the cover of high standing rock. That's where this fight would end up unless one of these men killed the other as soon as their paths met. This was unlikely, she thought, the two of them firing at one another from horseback. Once they clashed on the open trail, one of them would force the other to take cover in the high stretch of rocks. She would be there, waiting. But first, she had the child to think about.

Ahead of Jimmy French, and riding straight at him across the rise and fall of the land, Little Tommy could neither see him coming, nor could he hear the sound of French's horse's hooves above the sound of his own. What he could hear was Jimmy French's first rifle shot as it exploded at a distance of seventy yards. And upon hearing it, Little Tommy reined his horse down hard.

Tommy's horse slid and back-stepped, then sank down on its haunches, raising a cloud of dust. Veering the animal instinctively toward the hazy image of rock land to his left, Tommy kicked the tired animal forward, hearing a voice call out to him. "Tommy Caldwell? I've got you covered, Little Tommy. It's just you and me now. Make your stand!"

Ha! Make a stand? Right! Was this fool out of his mind?

Tommy made for cover in the sloping rock land, cursing his handcuffs, wishing he had a gun. The voice he'd heard didn't belong to the Ranger, but it did sound familiar. Who was it? *Damn it . . . !* He wished he could see something!

Another shot exploded behind him when he'd cut across thirty yards of sandy flatlands to the edge of the rocks. He slid the horse down to a halt, and flung himself out of the saddle. White froth bubbled and hung from the tired horse's mouth. "Come on, horse . . . just you and me."

He jerked the tired animal along behind him across jagged rock, climbing upward into the steep slope. The sole of his dirty sock snagged and tore on shale and sharp brush stubs. His breath pounded in his chest. Another shot exploded, this one pinging off a rock and ripping through the air beside him. Whoever that was, they couldn't shoot. He still had a chance here. Yanking the horse along, he climbed higher, moving into deep rock cover as he went.

"Stand and fight, Little Tommy! You coward!" Jimmy French yelled out into the upreaching rocks before him. He was down from his saddle now, walking toward the rocks, the rifle pointed forward waist high. He had no idea how many shots the rifle held. "It's me!

Jimmy French. Remember me? That worthless sissy from the Cottonwood Bank? Doss's girlfriend?"

Little Tommy stopped, having just rounded out of sight behind a tall leaning boulder. *So it's Jimmy French. . . .* He smiled to himself. *Well, now, sweet Jimmy.* Things were looking better and better. He yanked the horse up ahead of him and slapped his cuffed hands on its rump, sending it a few feet higher.

"Hello, Jimmy French, sister-boy," he called out, turning, squinting around the edge of the boulder. "I thought I killed you and was done with it. What brings you out here anyway? You miss me and Doss?"

"I'm here to kill you, Little Tommy. And Doss, too, when I find him." Jimmy French crouched into the rocks, seeing Tommy's horse move into sight above the leaning boulder. "Come on out and fight like a man!" Another shot exploded from the rifle. "I'm going to see you dead!"

Little Tommy chuckled under his heaving breath, sinking down and searching the ground for a hand-size rock. He couldn't see French from this far away, but if the rifle fire kept up, he'd track French by the sound of it. *Keep on shooting, Jimmy. . . .* That's all he needed until sweet Jimmy French got close enough for him to make his move. "Why, Jimmy boy. That's a terrible thing to say to me . . . after all we've meant to one another." His hand finally found a rock. "There's nothing wrong between us that can't be smoothed out, if we're both willing to try. I'm unarmed here, you know. Maybe we oughta talk things over."

Little Tommy laid his cuffed hands out on the hard ground before him, jiggling the cuff on his left hand back and forth, checking the tightness of it. He took a deep breath and held it. Steadying his left hand on edge, he raised the rock six inches—the length of slack in his chin—and slammed the rock down hard onto the joint of his thumb.

"I don't care if you're armed or not, Tommy. I'm coming in for you." Jimmy French stepped deeper into the rocks, climbing upward.

Pain shot upward from Tommy's crushed left hand; but he withstood it, clenching his teeth until it turned into throbbing numbness. Then, hearing French's footsteps across loose rock, he raised the rock and smashed it down again, this time feeling the bones in his left hand give way altogether. He rose up and leaned back against the boulder, his breath coming in sharp gasps, bouncing on his toes to keep from screaming out. He'd done it, though! He bet Doss or none of the others could have stood it . . . but he had.

The cuff slid down easily over the heel of Tommy's crushed left hand, and he held the chain tight in his right hand and swung the freed cuff back and forth, getting a feel for it. Now all he needed was for Jimmy French to come into view. He'd take that rifle . . . French's boots, anything else he needed. *Man, oh, man!* He'd give anything if the rest of the Half Moons were alive and could see this.

"Do you hear me in there, Tommy? Where are you? Show your lousy self."

Tommy smiled, wishing there was somebody beside him right then, somebody he could turn to and say, *watch this.* But he stayed as still as the stone around him as Jimmy French's voice and footsteps moved closer. Tommy judged the sound . . . twelve feet, then ten, then eight . . . six . . . five.

"You can't hide up there, Tommy."

Little Tommy braced himself, his crushed left hand tucked in, dripping blood against his stomach. The cuff hung from his right hand, drawn back, ready. Jimmy French was still talking as he stepped past the edge of the leaning boulder. But Little Tommy didn't hear his words—he didn't care. He saw Jimmy French now, close up, French's eyes searching ahead, not seeing him there less than four feet to his side.

All Jimmy French heard was the sound of something heavy slicing through the air, then the cuff chain slapped him hard across his face. The metal cuff swung around, hitting the side of his head like the blow of a small hammer. French reeled backward, the rifle no longer steady in his hands. The image of Little Tommy wavered before him, the chain slicing through the air again.

Jimmy ducked back and down, feeling the blow glance off his shoulder. He pulled the trigger on the unsteady rifle and saw a belch of fire streak into Tommy's side. Tommy staggered back with a deep groan. Jimmy went down to his knees, catching himself against the side of the boulder. *Oh, God! Why'd he do this? This was a terrible mistake. He shouldn't be up here! Tommy Caldwell would kill him for sure . . .*

Through a wavering haze, Jimmy French managed to work the rifle lever. Tommy staggered back and forth, but he hadn't gone down. Now he cursed and moved forward. "Damn you, sissy little peckerwood!"

Jimmy pulled the trigger, this time the tip of the barrel only inches from Tommy's stomach. *This would do it! It was over, thank God! But the rifle only clicked. Oh, Jesus . . . !*

"Give me that!" Tommy yanked on the rifle barrel, but Jimmy held firm, being pulled forward with it. The chain had gashed his nose and jaw, and he only saw Tommy as a shadow through a red veil. He lunged forward into Tommy's chest, both of them going down in a spray of dust and loose rock. They grappled and slid down against the leaning boulder, the cuff chain pounding into Jimmy's back, Jimmy with one hand tight around Tommy's throat, his free hand in a tight fist, pumping blows into Tommy's bleeding face.

On an edge of rock twelve feet above them, Maria sat

the little girl aside behind a low pile of rock. "Stay here, and cover your ears," she said, taking the little girl's hands and showing her how. And when she raised back up, her pistol came up from her holster. She fired a shot in the air. "All right! That's enough!"

The two only flinched for a second at the sound of her shot, then rolled and fought on. She waited, tensed, moving the pistol back and forth with them, looking for a shot. "Die, Sweet Jimmy! Damn you . . . to hell!" Tommy yelled, his breath all but gone. As he pulled away from Jimmy and came up almost to his feet, Jimmy lunged again, landing three feet short. Tommy staggered backward, the cuff swinging from his good hand. He drew back a dirty bare foot to kick French. But in that narrow space between them, in that second before either one could make another move, Maria saw her shot and took it.

From two miles away, the Ranger had heard the rifle fire and stopped his white barb on the trail. A moment passed, then he'd heard the two pistol shots. Now he kicked Black-eye out into a run across the flatlands. He'd been following Little Tommy's trail all the way from Cottonwood. Now the trail no longer mattered as he sped forward. Whatever the shooting was about, odds were strong that Little Tommy Caldwell played a hand in it.

The Ranger reined the white barb down when he saw the lone horse standing at the base of the steep slope of rock land. He recognized it as the same horse Jimmy French rode to Bannet. His eyes searched the rocky land as he stepped down from his saddle, swinging his rifle from across his lap. Maria and Jimmy French were up in there somewhere. Still, he better move with caution.

Instead of leaving Black-eye in the open with the other horse, he led them both just inside the first up-reach of rock and spun their reins around a bleached stub of juniper before moving up on foot. At the faint sound of a man's voice beyond the tall leaning boulder, he froze for a second, seeing Tommy's horse standing in the open above him. Then he moved around in a half circle, flanking the animal, wanting a better look behind the boulder before moving in.

In the small clearing behind the boulder, Maria and Jimmy French stood over Little Tommy Caldwell while Tommy lay gasping with his head propped up on a short smooth rock. His smashed hand lay limp in the dirt. His right hand with the cuff dangling from it scratched back and forth on the ground beside him. Blood pulsed from the bullet hole above his right ear with each failing beat of his heart. "This . . . don't hurt none . . . none at all. Ain't a one of yas ever . . . hurt me none," he rasped.

Jimmy French stood staring down at him, staggering in place, blood running from the swollen gash on his cheek, the imprint of the chain clear and blue across his bloody nose and forehead. Maria's pistol still hung in her hand. "Stay here with him," she said to French. "I must see to the child." She brought the little girl down to the small clearing with her and once more sat her out of sight—the child shaken by the noise of the gunfire and the violent tension seeming to permeate the air around her.

"Doss . . . was wrong . . . about you," Little Tommy said as Maria stepped away toward where the child sat with her hands over her ears. "Why didn't you . . . ever act like this, before?"

"I didn't have to . . . *nobody* should ever have to." Jimmy French ran a dirty hand across his forehead.

"Who knows . . . we mighta coulda . . . been friends," Little Tommy said. He winced and shifted a bit on the ground, reaching his good hand beneath his back. "My back . . . feels funny. Did she—?"

"No, she didn't. She only shot you in the head." Jimmy French spit blood from his lips.

While they spoke, the Ranger had worked his way down toward them, quietly through the rocks, keeping his eyes on Little Tommy.

"Well . . . since I'm dead . . . and gone to hell . . . I wanta tell you something." His weak and fading eyes gestured Jimmy French down to him. When French hesitated, Tommy chuckled faintly. "Don't be scared . . . I ain't . . . gonna hurt you."

Jimmy French's jaw tightened. "I know you're not going to hurt me." He bent down close to Little Tommy. "Now, say what you've got to—"

"Watch that hand!" The Ranger's voice spoke out above Jimmy French, just as Tommy's hand came from beneath his back with a four-inch sliver of sharp rock in his grip. French saw the Ranger's big dusty boot come out of nowhere to clamp down on Tommy Caldwell's wrist.

"My God!" Jimmy stood up and backed away from Little Tommy with an expression of disgust and disbelief on his blood-streaked face. "You were still going to kill me? Even now? Why in the name of God?"

"Because he's a born killer," the Ranger said, kicking the sliver of rock from Little Tommy's hand. "Eh? Isn't that right, Tommy Caldwell? Kill till the killing takes you away?"

Tommy strangled on a surge of blood, then settled himself and smiled a fading smile. "See? You . . . know me now . . . don't ya, law dog." His weak eyes swam across the bleary image of the Ranger standing above him.

"Yep." The Ranger pushed up the brim of his sombrero. "I've known you all along. You ain't my first crazy killer." His hand brushed idly across the scar on his cheek. "You're just the most current."

As they spoke, Maria had seen the Ranger, and now

she moved up beside him, leaving the little girl several feet away beyond a large boulder, where she would witness none of the carnage.

"I bet I'm . . . the worst though." Blood surged once more from Little Tommy's lips, the steady pulse of blood flowing slower from his head wound now.

"You need to hear somebody say it, don't you?" The Ranger stared down at Little Tommy's weak eyes as they seemed to sink farther away.

"I don't . . . need nothing. But it's . . . the truth."

"Well, listen up, then." The Ranger let out a breath. "I've got to hand it to you, Tommy Caldwell. You're the meanest, rottenest, most twisted piece of work I've come upon in my life. Killing you has been like killing the devil himself. How's that?"

"*Yeaaaah . . .*" Tommy managed a thin waning smile. His eyes grew smaller, more distant as they hazed over and slid shut. "Ain't it the truth . . ."

Jimmy French whispered under his breath, "Lord have mercy on him. Lord have mercy on all of us."

They stood in silence for a second, until Maria reached out and touched the Ranger on his arm. "I have someone here I'd like you to meet." She spoke in a soft voice, and gestured the Ranger away from the body on the ground. He stepped along behind her, his rifle in his gloved hand. Ten feet from the body of Little Tommy Caldwell, she stopped and turned and revealed a small child standing there. "This is Justice," she said as the child turned her face up to the Ranger.

"My, my . . . Justice. What a powerful name for such a pretty little girl." The Ranger raised a gloved hand near the child's cheek, close, yet not touching, as if needing to feel only the aura of something so precious—as if to touch it would surely cause it to vanish. Then he lowered his hand back a bit and looked into Justice's clear eyes as he said to Maria in a quiet tone, "There's more to this, isn't there?" Of course there was more. He knew it; and he took a breath, lowered his hand, and said, "Can you tell me now?"

"*Sí*, some of it." Her eyes flashed to the child, then back to his. "She is the child who was on the Bannet stage." She said it and watched his eyes for a second. "She is the granddaughter of Judge Winfred Lodge."

The Ranger tried not to look as stunned as he felt by Maria's words. Flashing a thin smile at the little girl, he said to her gently, "Well, then, Justice. We need to take you to your grandfather straightaway."

Jimmy French stepped over to them. Maria handed the child to him and fell in beside the Ranger as he started down toward where he'd left the horses. On the way down, she told him the rest of her story, about how she and Jimmy French had found Justice with the men at the rail shack, about Two Dogs and how the men had shot his grandson—about how the two Indians had seen the stagecoach robbery. When she'd finished, she stood watching the Ranger gather the reins to the horses, and she asked in a lower tone, "And what about the Half Moon Gang? Is this Tommy Caldwell the last of them?"

"No," he said, "there's still one more. Doss Edding is still alive. He was in town when I left there."

"What?" Maria looked stunned. "He is there, and you did not arrest him?"

"Yep, that's right." The Ranger gazed across the sandy flatlands as a strong breeze licked in, spinning up dust and shifting it about from place to place in a stir of dried brush and wavering heat. "Now we've got to take Justice to the judge and tell him what happened to his daughter."

Maria stood in silence with him for a moment. Then she said quietly, "Things have not gone well in Cottonwood, have they?"

"No, they haven't. You know I don't do well in

towns. I couldn't lay a hand on Doss Edding. The judge wouldn't let me near him."

"You mean—Judge Lodge? He protected Doss Edding?" Her eyes reflected the dark irony of it.

"Yep. Apparently Doss's father swings a lot of weight around there. And it's even worse than that." He told her everything else that had happened—how during the time Doss and his gang were robbing the stage and killing the judge's daughter, the judge was right then meeting with Matthew Edding to pardon his son for some other crime he'd committed. "So that's how things have gone on my end," he said when he'd finished telling her.

While he'd spoken to Maria, Jimmy French had gathered Tommy Caldwell's horse, hefted Tommy's body across the saddle, and came leading it down out of the rocks, carrying the child in his arm.

Maria shook her head slowly, thinking about what the Ranger had told her. "Now the very man who protected Doss Edding from you will be the one who cries the loudest for his blood."

"Something like that," the Ranger said, and he paused for a moment, running things through his mind. Then he looked at Jimmy French and at the child in his arms, and he let out a breath and said, "This job never gets any easier. Are we ready to ride?"

CHAPTER 23

On their way to Cottonwood, with Justice sitting on his lap, the Ranger thought about the strange turn things had taken now that the judge's daughter and grandchild had become a part of it. The order of law the judge had held him to was now the same law that, if followed in its rigid form, would free the man responsible for the death of the judge's daughter. Regardless of the outcome now, this was something the judge would have to live with the rest of his life. The Ranger let out a breath thinking about it.

Beside him, Jimmy French led Tommy's tired horse with Tommy's body lying limp across the saddle. Now and then, French would glance back at the body with an uneasy feeling. At one point when he'd glanced back, the Ranger had said, "What's the matter? He's still dead, isn't he?" On the other side of the Ranger, Maria smiled and leaned forward a bit, looking across the Ranger at Jimmy French.

"Yes, he is still dead," Jimmy French said, embarrassed, as he faced forward and shook his head. "For a minute there I began to wonder if anything would ever kill him. I've never seen anything like him ... beating his own hand to a pulp to get the handcuff off?"

"Wolves will do it," the Ranger replied, "so will a wildcat. Any critter will give up their paw to shed a trap. Men like Little Tommy die hard ... it's the way they have it planned their whole life, whether they realize it or not. You don't put a bullet through them clean and simple, and figure that's the end of it. They want it to be bad and bloody to the very end. It's the only way they know to leave some kind of mark on the world."

"But, no matter what else he might've been, he was a man, not an animal."

"Really? Maybe you didn't look as close as you should have," the Ranger said. "Little Tommy had no conscience, no reasoning, no remorse, and no concern— not for his life or anybody else's. I have more regard for an animal in the wilds than I do the likes of Little Tommy Caldwell. At least an animal only kills to sustain itself. The Little Tommys of the world have no idea why they kill. They just do it."

"Maybe you're right. But what goes on in a mind like Little Tommy Caldwell's?" As Jimmy spoke, he once more glanced back at the limp dangling arms, the handcuffs still swinging from one bloody hand. A dark string of blood swayed from the hole above his ear.

"Who knows? Who cares? I've seen more than a few like him. I don't try to understand why they're the way they are—that would drive a man to distraction. I just know *how* they are. My only concern is to stop them, and as soon as I can. It's our job . . . we keep it simple." He shot Maria a glance and added, "Isn't that the way?"

"*Sí.* It is our way."

They rode on in silence until Jimmy French thought about it for a second and said, "For the life of me, I don't see how you two do it. Doesn't it ever bother you?"

The Ranger had taken off one of his gloves, and now he ran a hand back across the little girl's hair. "Oh? What?" He slid a knowing glance to Maria, then back to French.

"You know what I mean," French said, "this business of manhunting. Always tracking and searching . . . always finding yourself in a kill-or-be-killed situation."

"Didn't you tell me only this morning that you

wished you could be like us," Maria said to French. "Didn't you say it should be you and you alone who kills Doss Edding when the time comes?" She cut a faint smile, having a good idea what would come next. Beside her, the Ranger touched a fingertip to Justice's nose and smiled as well, listening for French's answer as he watched the child crumble most of a biscuit and let the crumbs trail away.

"Yes, I said that." French touched his fingertips to his swollen cheek. "And I meant it, at the time. I suppose a lot of people wish they could do something like this. But there's a big difference between wishing it, and doing it. Everybody who's been wronged wants justice . . . but there's few people who can stomach what it takes to get it. I thought I could, once I overcame my fear. But now that it's over, I wish to God I'd never laid hands on Little Tommy. Getting justice wasn't worth it."

"You've mistaken justice for vengeance. Vengeance is never worth it."

"But, I've never been a vengeful person before."

"And you've never been wronged in this manner before either, now, have you?" The Ranger looked at him. "When a person has an act of violence touch them, it's usually not justice they're after—it's vengeance. Most times they work out vengeance in their minds— play out what they would like to do until they're tired of thinking about it. Then they find a way to forget it. You took it a step farther. But when you went after Tommy Caldwell, to kill him, it wasn't for the sake of justice. Now, be honest."

On his lap, the little girl, having heard what she thought was her name being spoken, stopped chewing and looked up at the Ranger. He tapped a biscuit crumb from her cheek, winked at her, and watched the warm breeze play in her hair.

Jimmy French considered it for a second. Then he let

out a breath. "To be honest . . . I don't know. I was badly wronged by Little Tommy and Doss Edding—so were the folks in Cottonwood. I suppose you could say, I saw no justice in the Half Moon Gang getting away with it. So to that end, yes, I call that justice. What do you call it?"

The Ranger did not answer, but instead pretended to take a bite of the crumbled biscuit Justice held up to his face. When he'd pretended to chew and swallow it, then thanked her for it, he finally said to Jimmy French, "Are you still bent on killing Doss Edding?"

"No, not like I was before anyway. I'm not afraid of him anymore. If it came down to just him and me, I'd do it. But no, after what went on back there with Little Tommy, it isn't something I feel like I have to do now. Before, killing him was something that burned in my stomach. Now . . . I'd be just as satisfied to see the law handle him."

"Good, then," Maria said, leaning forward a bit and looking over at Jimmy from where she rode on the other side of the Ranger, "you have spent your anger and vengeance. Now you are only seeking justice and peace."

Once more, Jimmy French touched his fingertips to the gash on his cheek, to the mark of the chain across his swollen nose. "All I can say for certain is that I never want to go through something like this again. All this time, all I could think about was getting my hands on Doss and Little Tommy—but when it came down to it, fighting nose to nose like a couple of crazed animals, it flashed in my mind right then and there that no person should have to see that dark ugly side of their self."

The Ranger nodded, sliding a glance to Maria. "Then you've come out of this with the right frame of mind," he said to French. "For a while there, I was wondering if you would."

"Yeah . . ." Jimmy French breathed deep, feeling a

tightness that had pained him for days leave his chest. "I just had to get a handle on something in my mind. Still can't say I understand it completely. But I can at least put it away, hopefully never have to confront it again."

"Yep, that's best," the Ranger said. "In the heat of a situation, justice and vengeance are like mixing holy water and gun oil. When you shake them up, they come together in so fine a mix that even the sharpest eye gets lost in them. It's hard to see how the two will ever separate again." He allowed a tired smile. "But that's where the law comes in. When you set the mixture aside and let it settle . . . the gravity of law draws them back into their proper form."

Now Jimmy smiled. "Gravity of law? Don't you mean the law of gravity?"

"Nope," the Ranger said, "I said it the way it fits." He gazed ahead at the turn in the trail leading down into Cottonwood. Earlier, on his way out of town, Emma Frocke had run up beside his horse and moved alongside him. "You had Doss Edding in your hand! But you let him go!" she'd cried out, pointing a trembling finger toward where Doss Edding stood on the boardwalk surrounded by his father's men. "He's as guilty as Little Tommy! You could have shot him!" The Ranger had only stared straight ahead and rode on, not explaining to her that Doss Edding was the lesser of two evils right then.

But Little Tommy was dead. Now there was only Doss Edding, all that remained of the Half Moon Gang. The Ranger looked down at the child on his lap, Justice, with her curly hair and her eyes full of innocence. Justice, a child now forever scarred by this wild young land in its waltz with fate, both dark and light. He dreaded telling Judge Lodge of his daughter's death; and he wondered what the judge would do, now that this swirling mixture of holy water and gun oil was placed in his hands.

Maria saw the troubled expression on his face and said, "What if Doss Edding has gotten away—and slipped across the border into *Mejico* by the time you ride back to Cottonwood, then out to the Circle E ranch? Think of what this will do to the judge. If you left now, perhaps you would catch them along the trail."

"I know," the Ranger said in a quiet tone. He looked over at her, their eyes speaking to one another, neither of them needing to say the words. "But shouldn't I be the one to tell him what's happened, before I go after Doss?"

"Only if telling him is something you need to do first, to right the wrong you think he has done to you." Her eyes gestured over toward Jimmy French, then back to the Ranger, questioning him.

"To go by the book, the way the judge said he wants it, I need to bring Doss in alive," the Ranger said. "But if I do, what's changed as far as proving anything on him? He's been found innocent of bank robbery and murder—we have no witnesses to the stage robbery, except Two Dogs, and an Indian's words won't be accepted in court, not in Cottonwood anyway."

"What about me?" Jimmy French turned toward them in his saddle. "I can testify to what happened in Cottonwood. You have Doss's pistol. I'll testify to how I got it."

"That's over and done with," the Ranger said. "Even if it wasn't, Doss could say he had to go along with things just to keep you from being killed by the Half Moon gang. Once a lie like this takes root, it's hard to work against it. The judge let this get started in the first place. That gave Tommy an open door to stand up in court and let Doss off the hook."

"Jesus." Jimmy French shook his head. "Then . . . according to the law, you really have no reason to go after Doss Edding at all."

The Ranger looked down at the child in his lap, and pictured her mother's eyes, the way they'd pleaded with him before being swept away. "Yes, I do," he said. "When the law gets too twisted and snared to protect the ones it's supposed to, my boots aren't stuck to the floor. I'll step outside it."

"Just like that? You'll break the law? After everything you've just told me?"

"No, I won't break it. I'll bring Doss Edding in and dump him in the judge's lap. We'll see how he handles it."

"But you just said—?"

"I know. There's nothing that can really stick on Doss unless the judge throws the book out the window. But Doss and his father know he's guilty. The weight of that guilt is the one thing that will bring this thing to an end . . . if I play it right."

"I—I don't understand," Jimmy French said, his eyes searching back and forth between Maria and the Ranger.

"You don't need to." The Ranger stopped his white barb, Maria and Jimmy stopping their horses along with him. "Here," he said to Maria, lifting the little girl from his lap. He carefully passed her over. "There's a young man in Cottonwood by the name of Jesse Tiggs . . . fancies himself a gunman. I figure Matthew Edding left him behind to deal with me when I get back."

"Is he dangerous?" Maria asked with calm resolve.

"He wears a fancy pistol with a silver snake on the handle," the Ranger said, a faint smile on his lips.

"Oh, I see." Maria returned a faint smile. "Then, you don't want me to shoot him?"

"Not if you can help it. Just keep an eye on him for me. Crack his head if he gives you a problem."

"Of course. That goes without saying." Her voice took on a firmer tone. "Any more instructions before you leave?"

"Don't start on me," he said, still with a faint smile. "Isn't this what you wanted? For me to ride on to the Circle E . . . you tell the judge what happened?"

"*Sí,*" she said, adjusting Justice on her lap, placing an arm around her. "I thought it was the best way, to clear the air between you and the judge . . . don't you? After thinking about it?"

Without answering, the Ranger turned Black-eye, raised a hand, and lowered the brim of his sombrero. "Take Justice to her grandfather. Tell him Doss Edding is on his way."

Maria and Jimmy pressed on; and when the Ranger had ridden out of sight and no trace of him remained save for a drift of dust around a turn in the trail, Jimmy French asked her in a lowered voice how the Ranger could go off on his own to face all of the cowhands at the Circle E ranch. Wasn't she afraid for his safety? But Maria had shrugged and told him that of course she worried about the Ranger—what person in their right mind wouldn't?

"But if he thought he could not handle this alone, he would have asked for my help," she'd added. Jimmy French had only stared at her for a moment, and they moved on the last three miles toward Cottonwood, the afternoon sun leaning west, beginning to stretch long across the rise and fall of the land.

It was dusk by the time the Ranger slowed his white barb and eased it forward to the edge of a steep rock ledge overlooking the sparse grasslands. He'd flanked a rise of dust and followed it for the last two miles. Now, eighty feet below him, he spotted the riders where they'd stopped along the trail.

Matthew Edding stood beside his horse with Doss,

Carl Statler, and Joe Baylor gathered around him. They gazed back through the grainy darkness and talked among themselves. The Ranger watched Matthew Edding point a hand back along the trail, then face the other direction as if deciding whether or not to push on to the Circle E ranch.

"If you'd give me a gun, and leave me be, we wouldn't have to worry about the Ranger," Doss Edding spoke, making sure his voice was loud enough for the other hands to hear him. Wilson and Dowdy still sat atop their horses. So did the young Texas cowhands. They shot one another knowing glances—*this rancher's spoiled son talking tough now, trying to save face.*

"I've got an extra range pistol," one of them said in a flat tone, sitting slumped in his saddle. Matthew Edding glared at him. The young cowhand only smiled faintly, lifted his hat brim, and looked away. Beside him, Sanborn swayed in the saddle, his jaw the color of a purple sunset.

"We're going on to the ranch," Matthew Edding called out to them. "I know this business isn't what you new men hired on to do. So there'll be an extra five dollars for each of you this month, just to show my appreciation. Tomorrow we'll get back to the business of running cattle." He looked back at Doss, his voice lowering. "And you . . . get your arse back on that horse and keep your mouth shut. Come morning, you're heading out with Carl and Joe. Maybe a couple of years in *Mejico* will straighten you out." He shoved Doss toward the big paint horse, then turned and stepped up into his saddle.

Doss stood for a moment, his fists clenched at his sides. *Damn all this . . . !* His father had no right making him look like a fool in front of these men. He lagged back as the others moved forward; and when Matthew Edding turned in his saddle and started to say something, Doss stepped a couple of feet away from his horse unbuttoning his trousers. "I got to piss first! Can I at least do that?"

"Stay with him, Carl. Bring him up front." Matthew Edding turned from Carl Statler with a sharp yank on his reins, and heeled his horse forward, Joe Baylor following close behind him.

As they'd spoken back and forth, the Ranger had quietly cut his white barb away and eased along the rock ledge to where a narrow elk path snaked down through rock and brush to the grassland below. Halfway down the path, he stopped, slipped down from his saddle, drew Black-eye behind a bleached deadfall of juniper, and crouched there, watching the other riders file past along the trail. Then he eased down forward on foot, moving quick and silent, leaving the white barb loosely hitched to a dry sprig of deadfall.

At the rear, Carl Statler had lagged back and waited. When Doss finished his business and stood buttoning his trousers, Statler sidled his horse over close to him. "Boss is only looking out for you. Can't you see that, boy? I'd given anything for a pa like him when I was a young'n. You oughta try to go along with him on this."

"Shut up, Carl. I've watched you and Baylor kiss his arse my whole life. So don't try giving me your two cents' worth!"

At the lead Matthew Edding rode on, Joe Baylor beside him, and the others strung out, riding single file as they cut upward around a spill of broken boulders. "I hate seeing you troubled like this, Boss." Baylor spoke low just between the two of them. "Maybe there comes a time when a daddy has to pull loose some . . . let a boy go on his own. Nobody blames you that Doss ain't turned out the way you wanted him to. You've done all you could."

Matthew Edding stared at him in the closing darkness. Joe Baylor saw the look on his face, ducked his head a bit, and said, "Well, it's the truth. If I wasn't your friend, I wouldn't say it. Doss is just not what he—"

"Get this straight, Baylor." Matthew Edding cut him off. "You've worked for me for a long time. That might give you a little leeway as far as what goes on around the ranch when I'm not there. But this is a family matter, and Doss is the only family I've got. So go easy here. You're hired help, and nothing more when it comes to spinning an opinion on me and my son."

"Sorry, Boss.".

Matthew Edding turned in his saddle and looked back across the other riders. "Where the hell is Doss? I told Carl to bring him up here."

"I'll go see." Baylor cut his reins around. But before he'd heeled his horse back along the line of riders, one of the young Texans called out, "Hellfire! We got an empty saddle here!"

"What the—?" Baylor pulled up sharp on his reins, and Matthew Edding turned his horse beside him. They watched Carl Statler's horse trot away from the line of riders and cut out across the grasslands.

"Oh, no! Come on!" Matthew Edding yelled, spurring his horse hard, back along the line of riders. They, too, reined around and heeled their horses. Twenty yards back, Edding slid his horse to a halt, seeing Carl Statler rise up on his knees, wobbling, a hand held against the back of his head. "Spread out! Find him!" Matthew Edding only glanced down at Carl Statler, seeing what had happened. "Doss! Doss!" He rode along the trail, searching the darkness on both sides of him—there was no sign of his son or the big paint horse.

At the top of the narrow elk path, the Ranger slipped his white barb over the edge and up onto the rock ledge, pulling the paint horse behind him. Doss lay across the saddle like a sack of grain, knocked cold, his hat missing, his hair hanging down with a trickle of blood dripping from it. "Doss! Damn it, boy! Answer me!" Matthew Edding's voice resounded in the darkness.

"Boss!" Baylor cried out. "Carl's still got his gun in his holster! It wasn't Doss that hit him!"

Matthew Edding spun his horse, and kicked it back to where Joe Baylor stood, raising Carl Statler to his feet. The other riders had spread out slightly, but now they came back, sliding their horses down in a rise of dust. "I don't know what it was hit me . . . but it weren't Doss," Statler said to Baylor in a slurred voice. "Doss was standing right before me."

Matthew Edding heard him, and looked all around, up along the rock ledge and into the jagged rocks above them. He knew what had happened, and he cursed himself for having let his guard down for only a second. The Ranger had Doss; there wasn't a doubt in his mind. But which way had they gone? He spun among the cowhands. "Didn't I say spread out! What are you doing back here? The Ranger's got Doss! For God's sake! They haven't gotten far! Spread out and find their tracks!"

Two of the young Texans looked at one another. One turned to Matthew Edding and said, "To hell with your boy! I've had it with this crap. You ever decide to work cattle—let me know."

"You can't ride away on me! Not now, not like this!" He jerked the big Civil War pistol from his holster and cocked it. Dowdy, Wilson, and Sanborn all shied back on their horses. So did Statler and Baylor on the ground. But the young Texans only returned Edding's cold stare, their hands on their pistol butts, not backing an inch.

"We can't ride away, huh?" Now the Texan who'd spoken turned his horse slowly, his eyes still fixed on Matthew Edding. The others followed his lead. "You just watch . . . see if we don't start looking smaller by the second."

CHAPTER 24

Before the young Texans had ridden out of sight in the darkness, Matthew Edding turned to the others. "Baylor, help Carl go find his horse." He swung to the others, Dowdy, Wilson, and Sanborn with his pistol still in his hand. "The rest of you spread out! Find some tracks."

"I don't even have my pistol," Sanborn said in a slurred voice, through his sore and swollen jaw. "Dowdy said the Ranger threw it to high hell and away. I'd be better off going to the ranch, see if I can lay down and get my head cleared some before I—"

"Nobody else is leaving! Is that clear?" Matthew Edding's voice trembled with rage. "The Texans were only temporary. But you men are mine. You came onto my ranch saying you'd stick to the job, and, by thunder, *you will!* I'll shoot any of you who turn tail on me!"

The three men milled in place for a second, then eased away, spreading out, searching for the Ranger's tracks as Carl Statler swung up behind Joe Baylor in the saddle. They rode out on the double in the direction Statler's fleeing horse had taken. "Boss is getting plumb *loco* over this," Baylor whispered to Carl Statler over his shoulder. "We best keep on his good side. How the hell'd you let that Ranger catch you from behind anyway?"

"I didn't let him, damn it. I never heard nothing,

never saw nothing. Don't blame me. This whole thing is Doss's fault. I'm starting to wish they'd hanged him and been done with it. You know he's guilty, same as I do."

"I'll pretend I didn't hear you say that, Carl," Baylor whispered, shooting a glance back into the darkness toward Matthew Edding.

Atop the rocky edge of the slope and pounding hard across the sparse grasslands, the Ranger checked the white barb down, and pulled Doss's paint horse to a halt beside him. He slipped down from his saddle and listened to the darkness behind him. "You—you can't do this to me, Ranger." Doss Edding looked up at him as the Ranger stepped over and pitched him out of the saddle onto the rocky ground. Doss landed with a grunt. The paint horse sidestepped, but the Ranger caught its reins and held it.

"Keep your voice down, young man," the Ranger warned him.

"But I've been found innocent of all charges. I swear I have!" Doss rolled onto his side and looked up at the Ranger in the moonlight. "This ain't fair! It ain't even legal!"

"Sure it is. The judge told me about a Mexican rancher you bullied around. Said the charge was still open till he gets back and does something about dismissing it."

"That charge is nothing, Ranger. My daddy took care of it. He settled everything with Paco Flores! They've known one another for years."

"Nothing's settled until the circuit judge says it's settled. I think he'll be wanting to see that you pull a little jail time for it. While you're pulling it, I'll work things out with the judge on the Bannet stagecoach robbery, and see to it you hang for murder."

"How? What can you do? There's no witnesses, no proof. You can't pin it on me—"

"Shut up, boy." The Ranger kicked him. Doss let out a hard puff of air. "We've got nothing else to talk about, you and me." He stooped down, cuffed Doss's wrists, and dragged him to his feet. The Ranger had pushed hard across the rock land, putting as much distance as he could between himself and Matthew Edding and his men. He knew that by now they'd figured out he'd gone up into the rocks and headed back to Cottonwood. They could be as close as a mile or two behind him. "The best thing for you to do is keep quiet and help me stay ahead of your pa. If they pin me down, I'll put a bullet in your head, and that'll be the end of it. This time I've got you, one way or the other. I'm not giving you up."

"The judge will have to let me go. He won't throw the book at me for roughing up a Mexican. I'll pay an extra fine, maybe."

"You think so? We'll see." He hefted Doss, pushing him up into the saddle. "This will be as much of a surprise to you as it will be to Judge Lodge, but the woman and child on the Bannet stagecoach? That was the judge's daughter and grandchild."

Doss looked stunned for a second. He swallowed a lump in his throat. "I don't know nothing about the Bannet stagecoach. I swear I don't!"

"Yeah . . . you're swearing a lot of things all of a sudden. But you can save your breath on me. You're gonna hang, Doss. Your pa can't save you this time." He ran a hand along the paint horse's damp neck. "Although I should thank him for providing you such a fine animal as this. They won't catch us."

Leading the paint horse by its reins, the Ranger stepped back over to the white barb and slipped up into his saddle. "I do want to know one thing, though. Before Lew Harper died, he told me there was a sixth man in the gang—said this man quit you before the Cottonwood Bank robbery." He watched Doss's eyes as he asked, "Who was that man? Was he in on the Bannet stage robbery?"

"I don't know who you're talking about." Doss just stared at him, thinking about Jesse Tiggs, still back in Cottonwood, still wanting the rest of the money he'd get for killing the Ranger. Tiggs was his only play left in the game. He wasn't about to give him up.

"Suit yourself then. I'll find out sooner or later." The Ranger heeled Black-eye, pulling Doss along behind him.

Doss's voice lowered as he said, "Did—did you kill Little Tommy?"

"He's dead," the Ranger said, without going into details about who'd killed him.

"Did he put up much of a fight?"

The Ranger stared at him for a second. "What's the difference? He's dead."

"I just figured he did. The Half Moon Gang was his idea, you know."

The Ranger shook his head. "There's more craziness rattling around in your head than the world has time to deal with, Doss Edding. Of course Little Tommy put up a fight. He died hard. I believe he left here thinking him and this Half Moon Gang would go down in history."

"Maybe it will," Doss said, his voice low but defiant, still not admitting to anything. "The Half Moons made their mark. You've got to give them that."

"The Half Moons were fools. Even the name sounded stupid." The Ranger spread a thin critical smile. "Which one of you geniuses came up with that?"

"I'd like to see you do better, if you're so smart," Doss said.

"Shut up, boy. Try to calm yourself down and act like a man. We've got a hard ride between now and morning."

*   *   *

Jesse Tiggs stood in the dark twirling his pistol outside of the saloon, watching Maria and Jimmy French ride into town. At first, when he'd heard the horse's hooves, he'd thought it was the Ranger bringing back Tommy Caldwell. Now that he saw it wasn't him, Tiggs let out a breath and smiled to himself. He was glad it wasn't the Ranger because he didn't want it to be like this—at night, hardly anybody around to see it happen.

Besides, Tiggs had put in a hard day. He'd looked bad at the hanging, letting things get out of hand the way it had. How was he supposed to know to cuff Tommy's hands behind his back? Nobody told him anything. He shrugged it off. Hell, he was a gunman, not a hangman. What he really needed now was for everything to go just right between him and the Ranger. He still had a thousand dollars coming once he put the Ranger down—not to mention the big reputation he'd have from now on.

All in good time, he thought, spinning the pistol back down into his holster, seeing Tommy Caldwell's body lying over the saddle. He stepped down off of the boardwalk toward Maria and French as they reined over out front of the sheriff's office. From inside the sheriff's office a glow of lamplight shone through a dusty window. The town lay quiet now, except for the saloon.

"Evening, ma'am. May I be of service in some way?" Tiggs smiled, walking up to Maria, eyeing Little Tommy's body across the saddle. Behind Tiggs, the roar of drunken voices rolled out in a heavy wave. A bearded old man staggered out through the bat-wing doors and off along the boardwalk with a leather-bound collection of Edgar Allan Poe tucked up under his arm. On the dirt street lay another book with its cover open and its pages swaying in the air.

Maria eyed the glint of the silver snake on Tiggs' pistol butt as it moved up alongside her. "Oh—"she smiled, stepping down from her saddle with a rifle in her gloved hand"—you must be Mister Tiggs. I've heard about you." Her voice sounded impressed.

"Why, yes, ma'am, I am Jesse Tiggs, at your service." Tiggs hooked a thumb on his holster, jutting out his chest, so taken by the way she said it that for a second he'd lost all thought of why this woman came riding in with Tommy Caldwell dead on his saddle. "So, you've heard of me—?"

"*Si* . . . you are the gunman who works for Matthew Edding." She held her thin smile on him, but her eyes took on the impression of leveled gun sights. "I've been asked to crack your head if you cause me any trouble. Perhaps I should go ahead and do so now."

Tiggs stepped back, taken off guard by her words and the way she came moving toward him—the rifle barrel slightly drawn back. *A woman? For crying out loud!* What was he supposed to do? "Easy, ma'am!" He stepped farther back, glancing around the street, hoping nobody saw any of this. *What? Shove her back? Shoot her? A woman?* He back-stepped even more when she didn't stop for his raised hand. "I've no quarrel with you, lady." What was this? He was being backed across the street—by a woman! "Hold it right there, now! I'm warning you!"

But *still* she didn't stop. She stalked forward until Tiggs turned, on the verge of bolting away. Only then did she stop and relax the rifle in her hand. She grinned again, a tight taunting smile that told Tiggs she knew exactly what she was doing and that he'd been fool enough to fall for it. "There, see? Do you get my message—do we understand each other? I'm here to do a job. You keep a safe distance away, Mister Tiggs . . . and I will try not to hurt you."

To do a job? What the hell was all that? Who was she?

Where was the Ranger? Tiggs stood stunned as she walked back to the horses and reached up for the child on Jimmy French's lap. Then he shook his head a bit to clear it. *No, no, no!* He wasn't standing for this! He'd shoot her. She was asking for it! Did she think he wouldn't? "Lady! Hold it!" Tiggs spread his feet, taking a fighting stand halfway across the dark empty street, his hand poised near his snake-handled pistol. "You don't pull that kind of stuff on me and get away with it! Look at me! I'm talking to you!"

Maria turned, slowly, with the little girl on her hip, the rifle half raised in her hand. "Oh? There is something more you wish to say?"

Now, what was he supposed to do, shoot her with a kid in her arms? He stood rigid and boiling . . . feeling stupid . . . embarrassed. Jimmy French stepped down from his horse beside Maria as she stepped up on the boardwalk to the door of the sheriff's office. "Watch your back," French whispered to Maria, venturing a glance at the dark figure looming in the street.

She knocked on the door, then turned and looked out at Jesse Tiggs, just standing, seeming barely in control. As footsteps came forward across the floor of the office, Maria smiled back at Tiggs, and using her rifle barrel as if it were a broom, she swept it toward him. "Go on. *Shwoo* . . . go on, now!"

As the door creaked open, Judge Winfred Lodge gazed past Maria at Jesse Tiggs—Tiggs backing away quarter-wise, stumbling in a wagon rut.

"Is there a problem here?" The judge looked back at Maria and at the child in her arms. Something familiar struck him about the little girl.

"No problem, Your Honor." But then Maria's expression turned grave as she stepped inside, Jimmy French close behind her. "But I'm afraid I have some bad news for you."

"Oh? Really?" The judge spoke to Maria, yet his

eyes would not leave the little girl's face. In the passing of a second, recognition came to him; and before Maria could say another word, his voice trembled as he said, "Justice? My Lord, child . . . is it you?"

No sooner than the door to the sheriff's office had closed, Jesse Tiggs moved away in the darkness, angry, confused, shaken. He didn't quite know what to do with himself at first, being confronted like that by a woman—a beautiful woman at that. He walked to the livery barn for no particular reason, just settling himself down. There was no way a man could have done him that way and lived. But a woman? What else could he have done? His mind reeled.

He left the livery barn, a little more in control but still embarrassed, and walked all the way to the end of town and back, feeling eyes on him even in the darkness on the empty street. By the time he'd gotten back out front of the saloon, he'd gained a little more control. Okay, she'd caught him off guard. But woman or not, she better never try something like that again.

He couldn't just stand in the street and shoot it out with her. Of course not. But before he'd allow her to humiliate him again, he would—*what?* Tiggs stopped and took a breath and thought about it. Well, he'd ambush her if he had to. Shoot her in the back. He'd make sure no one was watching, and he'd sneak out of some dark alley or from around some deserted corner. *Jesus!* What a thing to have to do! He pushed up his hat brim and walked through the bat-wing doors.

At the bar he felt a few eyes on him, but when he glanced around they all seemed to have just turned away. *Settle down! Nobody saw anything. . . .* When ole Vernon stood a shot glass and bottle of whiskey before him, he poured one and tossed it back and looked all around again. No. The street had been deserted . . . no one knew what happened. He tossed back another drink and let himself unwind.

The drinkers had been talking about the hanging, and how Little Tommy Caldwell had gotten away. Now that Jesse Tiggs stood among them, talk of the hanging ceased and instead they shifted the conversation to the crime itself. Half of them agreed that Doss Edding was guilty as sin and should be treated no different than the others just because his father was wealthy and seemed to swing some weight with the judge. The other half believed the boy should be given the benefit of a doubt.

"After all, look at everything Matthew Edding is doing for this town," a voice said from within the roar of the crowd, "bringing in the railhead and all. And why in the world would Doss do something like that in the first place?" A rough hand waved away any possibility of it. "Naw, the Eddings are fine people. Don't you believe so, mister?" Bloodshot eyes turned to Tiggs, and the roar of the drinkers lessened a bit, waiting for his answer.

The couple shots of whiskey had cleared Tiggs' head a little. He turned back another, feeling himself gain control once more, and looked at the faces along the bar, cracking his easy smile. "Boys, whether Doss Edding is guilty or not, it doesn't make two hoots in hell to me." He patted the pistol butt on his hip. "Here's all the justice I believe in. For the right price I'd shoot him . . . and for the right price I'd set him free."

"Is that right?" A few drinkers edged closer along the bar, eyeing the silver snake on his pistol butt. "Aren't you one of the Circle E cowhands?"

Tiggs just looked at the weathered faces. "I work for Matthew Edding . . . but not handling cattle, if you know what I mean."

Faces looked at one another, then back to Tiggs. "So you're a paid shooter, are you?"

A shooter? Tiggs liked that. "Yeah, you might say."

He smiled, poured another shot, and tossed it back, feeling better and better. So what if the woman had rattled him for a moment? He was back to himself now, ready for anything. "Just think of me as the person Matthew Edding turns to when there's no place else to turn."

Tiggs let his words sink in while he took the bag of tobacco from his pocket and rolled a smoke. Then, as he struck a match along the bar top, he said to Vernon and Nick, "Bring all of these fellows a drink on me."

They drank and listened as Tiggs talked about the scrapes he'd been in and the men he'd faced down. He told them how the Ranger had stepped way over the line here, and if the Ranger came back causing trouble for Matthew Edding . . . well, it might just be the last trouble he ever caused anybody. He tossed back another shot. The drinkers did the same. When a few minutes had passed, an old man yelled across the batwing doors, "Somebody's brought in Little Tommy Caldwell! Deader than hell!"

"Lord have mercy! Ain't you coming, mister?" one of the drinkers called back to Tiggs as the crowd pounded out across the boardwalk.

But Tiggs only shrugged. "Seen one dead outlaw, you've seen them all." He reached out and poured himself another shot from the bottle.

CHAPTER 25

Near dawn, the Ranger led Doss Edding the last couple of miles into Cottonwood. He stopped both of their horses at the sound of a hoof scraping across rock off to their left. They'd pushed the horses hard throughout the night and had only now slowed down to a walk to rest them. They sat in silence, the Ranger cocking his rifle and lifting the tip of it beneath Doss's chin. A tense second passed until the outline of Two Dogs and his mule moved forward from within the sparse dry grass. Then the Ranger let out a breath. "Get on over here, Two Dogs. It's me, Sam, the Ranger. Maria told me what happened to your grandson."

"Yes . . . it was a terrible thing." Two Dogs rode forward the last few feet and stopped, facing the Ranger as if Doss Edding wasn't there. Giles Bertrim's rifle lay across his lap. "I could not find him. So now I must turn away from this . . . put it behind me, and go on." He took note of the Ranger's rifle as it came down from beneath Doss's chin. "There are men from the Circle E back there. I think they are searching for you."

"Yep." The Ranger swung his rifle back across his lap. "I'm just finishing up with the Half Moon Gang. If you're heading for Cottonwood, I welcome your company—provided that mule can keep up. I'd hate to leave you if they get close on my tail."

"This mule is old and goes the way he wants to go. If they get too close, I will disappear into the land."

The Ranger nodded, heeling his white barb along at a walk, pulling Doss's paint horse behind him. He nodded at the rifle across Two Dogs' lap as the old Indian pulled the mule in alongside him. "I've always considered you to be a man of peace, Two Dogs. Never known you to go armed."

"It is true, I am a man of peace. But these are bad times. For many nights I have dreamed of a mad wolf who springs out on people and devours them. I only carry this rifle until that dream fades from my memory. When I get back to people, where it is safe, I will give this to one of the young hunters."

"I've seen that rifle before," Doss Edding blurted out. "Look at the Circle E carved on it! This ole peckerwood stole that from one of our cowhands."

Two Dogs and the Ranger looked at him. Then the Ranger turned forward. "Pay him no mind, Two Dogs. He might well have been the mad wolf you dreamed about." He turned his gaze back to the old Indian. "Did you ever see what happened to the wolf in your dream?"

"No . . . and I don't want to speak about him until the dream is gone."

"Ask him where he got that rifle," Doss Edding said. "He's stole it off one of our cowhands, that's where."

Two Dogs stared straight ahead. "I found it on the trail. The land gave it up to me. There's not a man alive who can say I stole this rifle from him."

The Ranger heard something at work in the old Indian's words, but he let it go. "There . . . you see." He smiled, speaking back to Doss Edding. "The land gave it to him. How can anybody dispute that?"

While they rode on, behind them, less than two miles back on the rocky grassland, Matthew Edding slowed his horse to a stop and stepped down from his saddle. He bent down and touched his fingertips to the hoofprints left by the Ranger's white barb and

Doss's big paint horse. Then he straightened up and paced back and forth for a nervous moment, waiting for the others to catch up to him. "So help me, God—!" He raised a gloved finger toward them as they reined down around him. His face showed stark rage and tensed in the pale moonlight. "—If something happens to Doss because you men are holding back on me, somebody here is going to die! Do you hear me? I'm holding *all* of you responsible." His heated gaze moved from one to the other, then settled on Joe Baylor.

Baylor squirmed in his saddle. "Boss, we ain't holding back. These horses are blown on us. If we keep pushing, they'll die out from under us—"

"Shut up, Baylor! Damn you! My horse is just as blown as yours. We're pushing on! I don't care if it kills every horse in the bunch! Now, kick up the pace and let's ride!"

The men shot one another guarded glances, Sanborn wanting to moan from the pain in his shattered jaw. When Dowdy and Wilson heeled their tired horses forward, Dowdy said beneath his breath, "No, he don't mind killing a good horse at all . . . hell, he owns a few dozen." He rubbed a hand along his tired horse's withers, feeling the sweat and white froth there. "Ole Prince Albert here is the only horse I've got . . ."

In Cottonwood, although Maria had spent half the night trying to console the judge in his grief and attend to little Justice while the judge cried and cursed himself out loud, at the first hint of dawn she was up and on the street. She'd slept a couple of hours on a blanket pitched on the floor of the sheriff's office. Emma Frocke had come during the night and taken the little girl and the judge home with her. Now, Maria pulled on her gloves and stood huddled against the coolness of morning, gazing out through the grainy light in the direction the Ranger would most likely take into town.

"Why didn't you wake me," Jimmy French said in a sleepy voice behind her. She turned to see him standing in the street, two cups of steaming coffee in his hands, shivering a bit in the bite of morning air. He held a cup out to her, and she took it.

"Because you needed to rest. This is over for you, Jimmy. Now it is up to the Ranger and me." She sipped the hot coffee and turned from him, scanning the hazy horizon. "Go home . . . get some sleep."

"As tired as I was last night, I hardly slept a wink." He sipped the coffee. "And as far as this being over for me, it's not. You can't expect a person to get as involved in something as I've been in this, then just say go home and forget it."

"*Sí*, you are right." She looked at him as he stepped around beside her. "You are free to stay if you wish."

A silence passed, then French asked her, "How is the judge holding up?"

"He is out of his mind with grief, of course." She shrugged. "He blames himself, he blames God . . . he blames all things a person can blame when they are trying to deal with something like this. He will soon exhaust himself and regain his senses, I hope." She sipped the coffee and nodded toward the saloon. "What about Jesse Tiggs? Did you check on him this morning?"

"Yes. He was still going strong when I passed the saloon late last night—shouting about all the gunmen he's killed, about how he's going to outdraw the Ranger. When I just came past there a while ago, he was passed out across a table."

"Outdraw the Ranger. That poor imbecile." Maria sipped her coffee and gazed out into the grainy light. "He has apparently created some sort of stage show in his mind. The Ranger will not step out into the street and go along with it, of course."

"What makes you so sure?" Jimmy French held both hands wrapped around the hot tin cup, warming them as he sipped.

Maria shrugged. "Because the Ranger never fights the way another person wants him to, if he can keep from it. It would be foolish of him."

"You mean he will just back down? Refuse to fight him?"

"If he can, *sí*. What Tiggs does not realize is that this is strictly a job for the Ranger. And the Ranger will only do his job the way he sees fit to do it." She smiled a thin smile, gazing off into the coming dawn. "When and if the time comes, I'm sure he will fight Tiggs in such a way that Tiggs would never dream of."

A few moments passed; and before either of them heard a sound, a skinny hound perked up from where he lay curled up sleeping on the boardwalk. He growled low and stalked forward into the gray morning light. Maria set her coffee cup down on the ground and stood with her rifle poised until she caught sight of the Ranger and Two Dogs coming forward, the Ranger leading Doss Edding close behind him. The skinny hound shot forward off the boardwalk and spun and barked in the street.

"Are you being followed?" Maria asked as she stepped forward, looking past them, checking their trail. She kicked a boot toward the hound, just enough to shoo it out of the way. The hound backed off a couple of feet and kept barking.

"Yep . . . and they're pretty close," the Ranger said, stopping and stepping down from his saddle, keeping a firm grip on Doss's reins. He walked back and pulled Doss down from his saddle. Two Dogs swung a stiff leg over the mule and slid to the ground.

Jimmy French went to Two Dogs. "I hope everything worked out all right for you?"

Two Dogs looked into his eyes as he brushed road
dust from the front of his shirt. "I did not find my
grandson. But everything else went well."

The Ranger took note of the old Indian's words
while he shoved Doss Edding forward. "Let's get this
one in jail."

Jimmy French moved over in front of Doss, back-
stepping along toward the sheriff's office. "Remember
me, Doss? I bet you never thought you'd see me again,
alive anyway."

"Go to hell, sissy!" Doss growled, trying to stop, but
the Ranger pushed him forward. "I heard all the lies
you told me, Sweet Jimmy. When this is all settled—"

"That's enough out of you," the Ranger cut Doss off.
Then he said to Jimmy French, "We've got no time for
this. His father and his men will be here any minute."
He glanced at Maria, who moved along beside him.
"How's the judge?"

"As well as can be expected." She held the key to the
sheriff's office. "He gave me this . . . and asked for one
of us to come get him as soon as you brought Doss to
town."

"Then we're all set." The Ranger glanced around at
rooflines and alleyways; and they moved on to the
door of the sheriff's office as a few townsfolk came forward in the grainy light and watched them through
sleepy eyes.

At the saloon, the sound of the dog barking caused
ole Vernon to rise up from his blanket behind the bar,
where he'd slept with a copy of *Harper's Periodical*
spread open across his face. He kicked a boot to the leg
of a stool where Nick sat with his head bowed forward
onto the bar top. "Wake up, Nick. I believe we've got
a busy day ahead of us."

While Nick grunted and ran a hand back through his tangled hair, Vernon stepped over to Jesse Tiggs and shook him by his limp shoulder. "Hey, Snake Handle. You said to let you know when the Ranger got here. Now, wake up!"

Tiggs groaned and raised his head. "Leave—leave me alone."

"Leave you alone? Bull!" Vernon shook him harder. "You still owe me for three books and four rounds of whiskey. Now, get up, pay up, and drag your sorry arse outa here!"

Jesse Tiggs stirred, wiping his bleary eyes, and ran a hand down to the empty holster on his hip. "Where's my pistol?"

Vernon stooped down and picked up the snake-handled pistol with two fingers from amid scattered wet sawdust and flecks of soggy tobacco. He shook it off and pitched it onto the table. "The shape you're in, you better be careful you don't blow off a toe with it. Now, come up with some money. We don't extend credit here."

Tiggs stood up wiping his face, weaving back and forth, and running a hand down into his empty trouser pocket. "Where's all my money? I had it right here."

Vernon shrugged. "I don't keep up with other people's money. Last I seen, you had a wad of dollar bills out, showing it to that stranger in the silk vest. He lit out of here more than three hours ago, carpetbag and all."

Tiggs searched himself with shaky hands. "I . . . don't remember any stranger in a silk vest."

"I'm not surprised," Vernon said, holding out a palm and snapping his fingers toward Tiggs. "Now, pay up, before Nick has to wear you out with a bar stool."

Tiggs struggled with his thoughts, the rye still

swirling inside his brain. *Jesus.* . . . Things weren't going the way he'd planned! "You best go easy here, book peddler. I'm a gunman—a shootist, remember?" His hand went to the pistol on the table, but before he could raise it, Vernon clamped a hand down on his wrist.

"I oughta remember. That's all you said over and over all night long. But it wouldn't matter if you're Wild Bill Hickock. You still pay for what you drink . . . and the three books you tore up ain't free neither."

Tiggs looked over at ole Nick, who'd stood up behind the bar and now hefted the battered bar stool up on his shoulder and came moving around toward him. "Wait! Hold it. I've got a few dollars in my boot. Just let me get to it."

CHAPTER 26

Matthew Edding was the first to hear the sound of reins slapping and a voice yelling out at the buggy horse as it pounded along the rutted trail. He stopped his men and spread them out abreast, where they waited until the open-topped buggy rounded a turn in the trail, coming toward them fast, sliding a bit while raising slightly on two wheels. C. G. Hutchinson's red face looked up as the buggy righted itself. Seeing Matthew Edding and his men, Hutchinson laid back on the reins, yanking the buggy to a halt as it racked sideways in a rise of dust.

"Where are you off to so early, Banker?" Matthew Edding stared stone-faced, neither him nor his men backing an inch from in front of the halting buggy.

"Oh, Lord, Matthew! You gave me quite a start." Hutchinson tried to collect himself, offering a tight smile that did little to mask the dread and fear lying just one layer beneath skin level. Edding and his men only stared. "Why . . . I'm heading over to Circle Wells." Hutchinson ran a shaky hand across his reddened brow. "You know me, Matthew—the proverbial early bird, always searching for the worm . . . ?"

His words trailed beneath the sound of Edding's rifle cocking across his lap.

"Yeah? Well, that must be one terribly fast worm, the way you're driving that buggy." Matthew Edding's eyes bored into him as Edding stepped his horse up closer, the five Circle E men doing the same, until they'd surrounded the buggy. Hutchinson swallowed hard, glancing around at them, and instinctively moved his right boot over against the leather business satchel on the floor by his feet.

"I came to get my boy, Doss, back from that *loco* Ranger," Matthew Edding said. "I don't suppose you've seen them?"

"You know, come to think of it"—C. G. Hutchinson feigned a contemplative expression—"I did see the Ranger and an old Indian leading a prisoner into town only a few moments ago. But for the life of me, I can't say if it was your boy Doss with them or not." He gave a nervous shrug. "I honestly can't recall."

"I bet you can't, Banker." Matthew Edding leaned in his saddle, grabbed Hutchinson by his lapel, and raised him halfway up from the buggy seat. "But for the life of you . . . you better recall what I told you when this all started. If something happens to my boy . . . it's all going to be on *your head*."

"Please! Matthew! Mister Edding!" C. G. Hutchinson's heavy body swayed in Matthew Edding's tight grip. "I'm a businessman, nothing more! I live by what's in writing! I did what I could for you, of course, as your banker. But, my God, sir! I have nothing to do with how the law works. *I'm* certainly not responsible for that crazy Ranger . . . Who could have guessed he'd act this way?"

"By what's in writing, huh?" Matthew Edding turned him loose, shoving him down into the buggy seat. "Then you better write this down and keep it in a safe place. You're going back to Cottonwood with me. This was all your makings. You're facing it alongside me. Whatever influence you've got with Judge Lodge, you better hope and pray it's strong enough to get this whole thing straightened out."

"But! But!" Hutchinson stammered as Joe Baylor

reached out, took the buggy horse by its bridle, and started turning the buggy in the road.

"No buts, Banker! I'm ready to die if I have to." He gestured a hand taking in the others. "We all are. If I do, you're going to die with me!"

Baylor finished turning the buggy in the trail, then said to Matthew Edding, "We best keep around him, so he don't try making a run for it."

Matthew Edding glared down at C. G. Hutchinson with his pistol raised, still cocked. "I almost wish he would make a run for it. He wouldn't be my first banker."

They started ahead on the trail, covering the last couple of miles into Cottonwood with Matthew Edding in the lead, the buggy right behind him. Joe Baylor and Carl Statler rode on either side with Sanborn following, slumped in his saddle with a bandanna still pressed to his swollen jaw. Behind Sanborn, Dowdy and Herb Wilson lagged back a couple of steps. "Did you hear what Boss said back there?" Dowdy asked Wilson in a guarded whisper. "About how we all are willing to die if we have to?"

"Yep, I heard it." Wilson stared straight ahead. "But I can't say I necessarily agree with it. What about you?"

Dowdy glanced back along the trail with a wistful look in his eyes. "I wonder how long it would take to catch up to them Texans?"

"Forget it. You ain't leaving me stranded in this mess. Let's just stay calm. Don't forget, Jesse Tiggs is in Cottonwood. He's supposed to be a real gun slick. Maybe he'll have this whole thing shut down by the time we get there. If he does, we'll both come out of it looking good, making an extra five dollars next month to boot." He grinned. "You can't beat that, now, can you?"

"Naw, sir." Dowdy clucked his horse forward.

"Only thing better than that would be to get to town and see Doss's dead ass swinging from a pole." He snickered across the lump of chewing tobacco in his jaw. "Wouldn't it tickle the living shit out of ya?"

"Damn it! Keep your voice down, Dowdy, and try to look serious," Herb Wilson hissed, ducking his head. "We've still got to look concerned here."

Judge Lodge staggered back, his breath heaving in his chest, his hands gripping the edge of the battered sheriff's desk. The Ranger had shoved him back from the open plank door to the cell area, and now stood in the doorway with his rifle across his chest. "Let me! Let me kill him . . . with my bare hands, Ranger! Please!" The judge's eyes gleamed dark and cold—a man confronted by the torturing fires of hell throughout the passing sleepless night.

"Can't allow it, Your Honor." The Ranger shook his head. "If you want justice, you can press that old charge on him. If you want to hold him here . . . take Two Dogs' word as witness to the stagecoach robbery and charge him with it." His eyes fixed hard and cold on the judge's. "But if it's vengeance you're thirsting for, we're fresh out of it." He shook his head. "There's to be no murder here as long as I'm calling the shots."

"You're not calling the shots! I am!" The judge pounded a hand on his chest. "This is *my* jurisdiction! Not yours!"

"That's something we better get ironed out here in a hurry, then, Judge. Matthew Edding and his men are right on my heels. If you give me jurisdiction here, I'll take it. If not . . . you've got it all. I'll leave and let Matthew Edding tear this place to the ground. Maybe in a few years when Doss gets back from a nice long stay in Mexico, you can have him hunted down and arrested for spitting in public. It's your call. Now, what's it going to be?"

White spittle formed in a froth on the judge's lips. "For God's sake, Sam! That's my daughter laying out there in the badlands. Can't you understand that? My own flesh and blood—family!"

The Ranger stepped forward, his face close to the judge's, their eyes locked in a fiery test of wills. "They were *all* your family, Judge. The men who died here . . . the widows they left behind to mourn them. Their sons, their daughters. The day you took on the mantle of office, they *all* became your family. All those tortured faces you see day in day out across this territory. All the Emma Frockes of this country . . they came to you, trusting you, looking to you for justice. I'm sorry something this terrible has to hit you in the face to make you realize it. But if you don't realize it now . . . you best step down from the bench and find another calling. Your daughter will have died in vain."

Judge Lodge took a deep breath and let it out slowly. "I can't live with what's happened here, Sam. I've got to see Doss Edding dead. Help me, please. What must we do to make things right?"

Before the Ranger could speak, Maria turned from the dusty window and said in a grave tone, "Riders coming in. I see their dust."

"I have no idea how you'll ever right this in your mind, Your Honor." The Ranger jacked a round up into his rifle chamber and left the hammer cocked. "But you had the chance to work justice for everybody, and you let it pass. Now all we can do is take it to the street, and let justice work for itself."

The Ranger stepped back to the plank door and called back to Two Dogs, who stood beside Doss in a darkened cell. "Get him out the back way, Two Dogs. Take him to a room in the hotel and wait until you hear from Maria or me."

Two Dogs nodded. He'd tied a rope around Doss's neck and stood with the rest of the coil draped over his shoulder. The tip of his rifle rested beneath Doss's chin. On the other side of Doss Edding, Jimmy French stood waiting for someone to tell him what to do. Seeing the look on French's face, Two Dogs said, "Stay with me, Jimmy French"—he jiggled the rope in his hand—"in case this man gets to be too much for one old Indian to handle."

"You'll be a dead Indian before the day's over! You'll *all* be dead before this day's over," Doss hissed at them as Two Dogs shoved him forward from the cell. "You haven't seen my daddy in action once he gets mad."

Outside along the boardwalk, townsfolk hurried indoors at the sight of Matthew Edding and his men moving slowly abreast along the dirt street, ahead of C. G. Hutchinson sitting rigid in the buggy. Inside the saloon, Jesse Tiggs heard footsteps scurry back and forth out front. He limped over to the bat-wing doors, wearing one boot, and looked out at the riders. *Damn, it was too early for this!*

Behind Jesse Tiggs, ole Vernon stood holding Tiggs' other boot in his weathered hand. On the tabletop lay a few scattered dollar bills and some change. Vernon looked down at the money, shook his head, then lifted his gaze to Nick behind the bar. Each of them seemed to know what the other was thinking, and they nodded in unison.

Jesse Tiggs wasn't ready yet, feeling hung over, cotton-mouthed, and shaky. All the same, he managed a dry swallow and calmed himself. Okay, he could handle it . . . a thousand dollars coming his way, he thought. He was ready now—he could have used a stiff drink first. But the drink would have to keep until later. It was time to go to work now . . . get this job done. He was a gunman now, a paid professional killer of men. This was how it worked. This is what gunmen do.

In the sheriff's office, Maria took the glove off of her right hand and shoved it down inside her waist. The Ranger had slipped out the back door and began making his way through the alley. He would take position on them from behind, where they would least expect it. On his way he'd glanced up at the corner window of the hotel and saw Two Dogs' wrinkled hand lift the window open a few inches. He thought about the rifle Two Dogs said he'd found, and the way Two Dogs had answered Jimmy French about how things had gone out on the rock land. Something was going on in that old Indian's mind—the Ranger just didn't have time to consider it right then.

Through the dusty window, Maria watched the Ranger slip across the street behind Matthew Edding and his men. She'd jacked a round up into her rifle chamber and started to step back when she caught sight of Jesse Tiggs limping down the street from the saloon. He hurried forward in a wobbling gait toward Edding and the Circle E men. *One boot? What was this?* Maria cocked her head slightly, curious. "Your Honor," she called back over her shoulder, "stay inside until this is over. I'm going outside for a better look."

"But Sam told you to stay in here with me, Maria. Please . . . do like he told you!"

She smiled, half turning to him, her right hand going around the doorknob. "Aw, now, Your Honor, you must have misunderstood. The Ranger has never told me to do something in all the time I've known him." Then she opened the door and stepped out into the golden glow of morning sunlight, the rifle cocked, her finger on the trigger, the butt of it resting back firm against her thigh.

CHAPTER 27

The Ranger watched as he slipped closer to the street along the shadowed alley. He stopped for a second, seeing Matthew Edding and his men turn their horses toward the sheriff's office. They sat in the middle of the street. Matthew Edding stepped his horse a foot ahead of the others. Sanborn had backed his horse up beside Hutchinson's buggy, flashing a small pistol Carl Statler had given him on their way to town.

Everything was just about the way he'd planned it, the Ranger thought; he'd started moving forward once more when he stopped short at the sight of Maria coming out onto the boardwalk. What was she doing out there? Then he saw Jesse Tiggs limping hurriedly from the saloon toward Matthew Edding. *One boot?* The Ranger eased forward once more.

Seeing Maria standing there alone, Herb Wilson whispered to Dowdy under his breath, "This might not be as bad as we thought. Suppose she's all there is here?"

"Then where's the Ranger?" Dowdy asked.

"Tiggs, get up here!" Matthew Edding called out as Tiggs limped almost in a trot the last few yards into the middle of the street. But seeing Maria on the boardwalk, Tiggs veered slightly wide of her, keeping an eye on her as she smiled teasingly his way. "Where's that blasted Ranger?" Matthew Edding yelled down to him. "I paid you to do a job here . . . have you done it?"

"Well, no, I haven't yet. I was just on my way—"

"Where in the hell is your boot, man?" Matthew Edding fumed. Tiggs felt himself seem to shrink as the other riders cast their eyes away from him, looking embarrassed for him.

Back at the bat-wing doors, ole Nick and Vernon stood watching, Vernon with Tiggs' boot up under his arm.

"It's sort of a long story," Tiggs said, feeling his hangover boil in his brain. "I got robbed and had to hock it till I pay off a debt." He fanned a hand. "But it doesn't mean a thing. I'm here to kill the Ranger . . . we'll get Doss back, no doubt about it."

Matthew Edding's gaze went to Maria, her standing there cool, calm, confident. Then he looked back down at Tiggs. "Damn it, Tiggs! Where is he? Where's Doss?"

"Your son is in a cell," Maria called out from the boardwalk. "The Ranger is inside. The best thing for you to do is turn your men around and ride out of here."

"I'm not leaving here without Doss," Matthew Edding called over to her. "Tell the Ranger to get out here and bring Doss to me, or in about three seconds we'll ride right over this two-bit jail."

Maria shook her head slowly. "The Ranger can't come out now. He is busy . . . having his morning coffee."

Come on, Maria! Don't fool around out there! The Ranger winced, and eased forward to the edge of the alley. Matthew Edding glared at her for a second, then said, "So you think I came here to play games with you, little lady?" He shot a glance down to Jesse Tiggs. "Get over there and get her out of the way, Tiggs. Hurry up!"

"Sure, Boss." *Boss now.* Not Matthew, not even Mister Edding—just Boss, like all the other old thirty-dollar-a-month cowhands at the Circle E. *Jesus.* As soon as Tiggs said it, he felt his face redden. He took one step forward, then jerked to a halt, seeing the tight, thin smile on Maria's face. What was he supposed to do? He froze there. A tense silence passed. The other Circle E cowhands sat watching him, bemused, their hands on their rifles and pistol butts. Behind them, C. G. Hutchinson sat trembling in the buggy seat, too frightened to move.

"Well, Tiggs?" Matthew Edding called down to him, his horse taking a step sideways.

"Well, what?" Tiggs looked up at him, confused, not at all sure what he should do.

"Well . . . get on over there and remove her! What are you waiting for?"

Tiggs felt a cold sweat well up on his forehead. He wanted to raise a hand and wipe it away, but he dared not. On the boardwalk Maria stood with the same smile, the same expression on her face, something immovable and disarming about the woman. He looked back up at Matthew Edding, hating to ask, "Remove her how?"

Edding was ready to explode. "I'm paying you two thousand dollars, and you're asking me how? Get her out of the way, right now, Tiggs, or so help me God—!"

"But, she's got a gun." Tiggs' voice had a bit of a whine to it. He caught a glimpse of a couple of townsfolk who'd ventured forth from storefronts and watched. They were whispering about him. He knew it.

"Then, take the rifle away from her . . . she's only a woman! Get her out of the way!"

Tiggs limped a step forward, then stopped again, seeing Maria raise her free hand and motion him to-

ward her, taunting him, daring him. *Damn it!* He could
handle all of this if people would just act the way they
were supposed to. Okay. If she wanted to play it
tough, he would too. "Ma'am, you heard him. I'm giving you one last chance to get out of the way. You better take it."

"Or what?" Maria stared at him—that same smile,
same expression. What the hell was he supposed to
do? Shoot it out? Then he would. His hand poised near
his pistol butt. He stopped and spread his feet, getting
ready.

"I'm back here, Edding," the Ranger's calm voice
called out from behind the line of riders. "Now drop
your weapons, all of you."

Tiggs actually felt relieved for a second. He'd half
turned, almost facing the Ranger, who stood just inside the shadow of the alley. Matthew Edding started
to turn his horse and face the Ranger. But the Ranger
said, "Don't make a move . . . or I'll drop you."

"Where's my son, Ranger? You know there's no
way out of this for you or me, unless you turn Doss
free. I'll die right here with you if I have to."

"I know it, Edding," the Ranger said. "I've known it
would come to this the first minute I laid eyes on you.
But I've got to give you the opportunity to call it off
first. Now, pitch down your weapon. Tell your men to
do the same."

Here comes my chance, Jesse Tiggs thought. He was
the only one who could even see the Ranger! All he
had to do was get a little to the right, get Matthew Edding out of his line of fire. Then he'd have this thing
set up the way he needed it. He drifted one slow step,
then another. But then he froze when the Ranger
called out in a raised voice, "Have you got Tiggs,
Maria?"

"*Sí*, I've got him covered."

Jesus! Why wouldn't anybody give him a chance to do what he knew he could do?

"All right, Tiggs," the Ranger called out. "You get on out of here . . . you're no gunman. You've got no business in this. I know that woman. Believe me, she'll kill you and never bat an eye."

That woman? She'd kill him? No! No! How could they do him this way?

From across the street, Maria saw Tiggs starting to shake, going out of control, ready to either make a grab for his pistol or go running down the street screaming—she wasn't sure which. She raised her rifle to her shoulder and took aim.

"Now, drop those weapons, Edding," the Ranger said. "I won't ask you again."

Matthew Edding let out a tense breath. He'd had no idea that the Ranger was behind him. He'd have to get a better position somehow. "Will I get to see my son, then?" he asked, raising his pistol out to one side, his rifle out to the other, ready to let them fall to the dirt. Beneath him he steadied his horse in place with his knees.

"We'll see." The Ranger watched him closely, not trusting his move. "Now, tell your men to do the same."

"Boys, pay attention. Do like I tell you here." Matthew Edding called out to them; but the Ranger noticed he still hadn't tossed down his weapons. In the buggy, C. G. Hutchinson had seen all that he could stand. These people were crazy—all of them getting ready to die! Not him, though! As if coming out of a trance, he reached down slowly into his lap, lifted the reins, and as Matthew Edding's pistol and rifle seemed to be on the verge of dropping from his hands, Hutchinson let out a yell and slapped the buggy horse forward.

At the end of the line, Dowdy spurred his horse

hard, spinning it to the side to make his getaway, figuring Herb Wilson would do the same beside him. But
Wilson's horse spooked and reared high at the sound
of the Ranger's first rifle shot, and Dowdy's horse
plowed into its side. Both horses whinnied and tumbled backward in a spray of dust, catching the buggy
horse as it sped into the tangle of limbs and leather.
Hutchinson screamed, launching airborne from the
buggy seat, headlong into a high somersault.

Tiggs on the ground saw the play start, and
snatched his snake handled pistol just as the Ranger's
shot hit Matthew Edding from behind, high in his
right shoulder. Edding had just started to spin his
horse when the shot hit him. Now he reeled in his saddle, coming around, his pistol up, searching for the
Ranger.

Tiggs flinched as he drew. His pistol butt—the silver
snake handle still wet and slick with tobacco juice
from the floor of the saloon—slipped out of his hand
and tumbled to the dirt. He lunged out and down for
it just as Maria's shot whistled past his head. *Why, for
the love of God couldn't I get a break here?* He scrambled
along on his belly, Maria's rifle shots kicking up dirt
behind his feet. He snatched at the pistol, which
seemed to jump forward in front of him.

Above Jesse Tiggs, Matthew Edding's horse righted
itself facing the Ranger, who moved along the boardwalk now, pumping shots into the Circle E riders.
Tiggs got his trembling hand around the pistol butt.
All right! But as he raised it, Edding's horse swung a
nervous hoof, kicking Tiggs' hand, sending the pistol
spinning away in the dusty air. *Damn it all!*

From the window of the hotel, Two Dogs peeped
down on the street. "They are killing each other. It is
bad," he said over his shoulder to Jimmy French. He
saw the Ranger moving sideways along the boardwalk
as Joe Baylor spilled backward out of his saddle, saw

Matthew Edding firing on the Ranger as the Ranger dropped his rifle and brought his big pistol into play. Behind him, Two Dogs heard Doss Edding laugh. "Yeah, you'll be next, Sweet Jimmy."

On the boardwalk, the Ranger felt the bullet from Matthew Edding's pistol punch him hard, high in his chest. He slammed back against a window, feeling the glass shower down around him, but catching himself, getting off another round. This one caught Edding in his left cheek, taking out a chunk of meat and bone. A bloody ribbon twisted through the air as Edding went back out of his saddle.

A shot from Carl Statler's pistol hit the Ranger above his knee. He staggered, again nearly going back through the gaping window behind him. He got off another round, hitting Statler in the heart. At the same time, Maria's rifle shot exploded through the back of Statler's head and sent most of his face splattering across the boardwalk. Jesse Tiggs groveled in the dirt, helpless, whining, looking for his pistol . . . for something, anything.

Sanborn still sat his saddle, his horse spooked and prancing back and forth. Sanborn stared wide-eyed, his hand high in the air. The small pistol dangled on his finger. "Don't shoot! Please, God! Don't shoot me!" His voice slurred, muffled by his purple swollen jaw.

"Then drop . . . the gun." The Ranger's breath drew tight in his wounded chest.

"I can't!" Sanborn, on the verge of tears, shook his finger trying to get rid of the pistol. "It won't come loose!"

"Then . . . ride out of here." The Ranger staggered to the edge of the boardwalk, cocking his pistol toward Sanborn.

"Yes, sir, I'm gone." Sanborn spun his horse and batted it away, his one hand still high with the small pistol hanging on his finger. Across the street, the

Ranger caught sight of Maria down on one knee, a hand raised to a streak of blood on her forehead.

"Maria? Are you all right?" The Ranger stepped down into the street, but his wounded leg went slack beneath him. He faltered and sank, catching himself on the edge of the boardwalk.

"*Sí* . . . it is only a graze," Maria called over to him, seeing the blood on his chest. "Stay put, Sam. I'll come get you." Her voice sounded dazed.

On the street Tiggs crawled forward an inch, reaching out for a pistol in the dirt. "Don't . . . go for it . . . Tiggs." He looked over and saw the Ranger shake his head. "Face it. You just ain't . . . cut out for this kind of work, boy." The Ranger held the big pistol pointed at him. Tiggs slumped and rested his face in the dirt.

From the cloud of dust to the Ranger's right, Herb Wilson raised up with a moan. Dowdy lay limp and silent, his neck twisted at an odd angle. In the rising dust, C. G. Hutchinson limped forward holding his shoulder. The buggy lay upside down, the horse beneath it thrashing its legs. "Is—Is it over?"

The Ranger looked at him, letting his pistol sag a bit.

"Not yet . . . you . . . son of a bitch." Matthew Edding fired as he struggled up onto his feet, the side of his face a mess of dirt and blood. C. G. Hutchinson flipped backward with a bullet hole between his eyes.

The Ranger swung his pistol to Matthew Edding, cocked and ready. And Edding struggled, turning, facing him. "Let it go . . . Edding. It's . . . over." The Ranger forced himself up and staggered in place. On the ground, Tiggs crawled backward from between the two of them. Maybe the Ranger was right. Maybe he had no business here. Maria raised her rifle, aiming at Edding's back.

"Where's . . . my son?" Edding had a hard time raising his pistol, but still he did so, using both hands.

From the hotel window, Two Dogs called out, "Don't shoot! Let it end. I have your son up here."

Behind Two Dogs, Doss gave a smug smile and said to Jimmy French, "See? I told you about my daddy. He's been my ace in the hole all along."

"Send him . . . down to me." Edding called out, then stared at the Ranger and raised a hand to his shattered cheek. "You . . . fight, a hell . . . of a fight, Ranger."

"You too. I figured you'd be a . . . tough ole hoss to kill." The Ranger let his pistol lower. Across the street, Maria did the same with her rifle, the graze on her head causing her vision to blur a bit.

"Yeah? Really?" Matthew Edding slumped, but felt a little proud hearing it. "Well . . . I'm dead here . . . but I don't care. He's my son . . . you understand?"

"I understand." The Ranger turned his face toward the hotel window.

In the hotel room, Two Dogs and Jimmy French heard the Ranger's voice call out, "You know . . . what to do, Two Dogs. Send him down."

"Ha! Boy, oh, boy!" Doss Edding jumped up and down. "What'd I tell you idiots? Huh? Didn't I call this right or what?" He jutted his grinning face close to Two Dogs. "You sorry ass bag of dirt! I ain't forgetting you." He swung a cold stare at Jimmy French. "And you? You're gonna die for what you said about me. Hear me, you little sissy bastard?"

Two Dogs shook his head slowly, looked at Jimmy French, and said in a low voice, "This man's life is not worth the pain it causes others."

"You're right." Jimmy French returned Two Dogs' cold, caged stare.

On the street, Matthew Edding felt the ground sway beneath him, but he caught himself, holding a hand against the flow of blood from his shoulder. "Another time . . . another place, we might have been . . .

friends, Ranger. Who knows? Eh?" He tried to smile, but the missing gap of cheekbone wouldn't let him.

"Yeah . . . who knows." The Ranger felt his hand tighten on the big pistol, getting ready, waiting, the killing not over yet, but about to wind down any minute.

"I . . . always said, if . . . a man has good friends . . . to back him up . . . he'll never have to—"

Matthew Edding's words stopped beneath the long scream and the crash of glass from the corner room of the hotel. Doss came sailing out into thin air, his hands still tied behind him, his legs pumping, kicking, the rope uncoiling behind him. At the last second, Maria winced and looked away.

"*Nooooo!!!*" Matthew Edding bellowed, a tortured sound torn from low inside his guts as the rope snapped tight with a loud crack, then vibrated a deep hum—like the hand of God striking a heavy note on a bass fiddle.

A hot breeze lifted a low sheet of dust and swept it along the street. Except for the rustle of breeze, the world stopped and froze and tilted sideways for a second. Then Matthew Edding turned, his pistol coming up toward the Ranger. He pulled the trigger, but it only snapped on an empty cylinder. "Oh, God . . ." He stared at the Ranger, all substance and essence of hope gone from his eyes now. "You . . . do understand?"

"I do understand." The big pistol bucked once in the Ranger's hand, then fell. A ringing silence moved on the hot breeze along the dirt street. "It's only justice . . . taking its turn."

EPILOGUE

A week passed before the Ranger was back on his feet, and another week would pass before he was able to take up the reins to Black-eye and ride back to Bannet. During the first week, as soon as he was allowed visitors, Two Dogs and Jimmy French came to see him. They found the Ranger looking pale and drawn, propped up against a pillow in a feather bed in a room at the hotel.

Maria met them at the door, her head wrapped in a clean white bandage; and she moved to one side as they stopped and stood beside the Ranger's bed, both of them unsure of what to say.

After a brief silence, the Ranger spoke. "Well? Anything I need to know about how it happened? In case the judge wants to know?"

"He jumped," Jimmy French said in a clipped tone.

"He fell," Two Dogs said at the same time.

The Ranger nodded slowly. "That's simple enough."

"*Si*, he jumped . . . and he fell." A trace of a smile came to Maria's lips.

The Ranger glanced at her, then back to French and Two Dogs. He seemed to consider it for a second. "That would appear to be the natural order of things, I reckon." His eyes slipped across each of their faces. "The main thing is that neither one of you pushed him. Because if one of you did—"

"But they didn't," Maria said in a quiet resolved tone, cutting the Ranger off.

"I see." The Ranger nodded and let it rest. Then he said to Two Dogs, "There was a sixth man involved in the Bannet stagecoach robbery. Did you and your grandson happen to see him? Could you identify him?"

Something flickered in Two Dogs' eyes, but then he seemed to put it aside. Shaking his head slowly, he asked, "What would be the difference? The court would not take my word on it."

"But I would," the Ranger said. "Whoever that man is, I want him to account for what he's done."

Two Dogs leaned forward and said in a lowered tone as he adjusted the pillow behind the Ranger's back, "All men account for what they have done . . . one way or another. You must rest and find your strength. My mind is old and often forgets what I have seen."

The Ranger eyed him. "But will you try to remember?"

"I will try to remember." Two Dogs nodded, and he and Jimmy French stepped away from the bed and left the room.

The Ranger coughed a bit, then looked up at Maria. "I'm not going to ask which one of them pushed Doss Edding out the window. But I figure you know, don't you?"

Maria only smiled.

Later that same day, when the judge came by, Maria left the Ranger's room for a few moments to let the two of them talk. When she'd closed the door behind herself, taking little Justice along with her, the judge turned to the Ranger. "Sam, I don't know quite what to say to you. You were right, I was wrong . . ." His words drifted into a silent pause.

After a moment the Ranger coughed against the

back of his hand and looked at the judge. "There was
a sixth man involved, Your Honor. But with everybody dead, I doubt we'll ever find out who he is."

The judge let out a tired breath. "Then, so be it.
Whoever it is, he's probably long gone from here. He'll
pop up somewhere and get what's coming to him. I
need to put this thing behind me, Sam, and go on with
life . . . for my granddaughter's sake." He looked
down at the floor for a moment as a troubled darkness
moved across his brow. Then he looked back at the
Ranger and said, "I'm stepping down from the bench,
Sam. I want you to know that."

"You're a good lawman, Judge. I hate to hear that."

"But you said yourself—"

"I know what I said, Your Honor. But nobody's perfect. You broke no law . . . you simply didn't act in its
best interest this one time. It was a hard lesson for you
to learn." He ran a weak hand along the old scar on his
cheek. "But it's them hard lessons that stick with you
from now on. They make us what we are . . ."

By the end of the second week, the Ranger had managed to get around and walk the boardwalk with
Maria's help and the help of a hickory cane one of the
ole book peddlers had lent him. On the evening before
the Ranger would leave Cottonwood with Maria and
Two Dogs riding beside him, the stranger in a faded
silk vest showed up back in town and met the three of
them on their way to the hotel.

"There you are!" The stranger spread his hands and
smiled. "At last I get to meet you—the man who stood
alone here in this dirt street and faced that notorious
gang of killers! What an honor this is, sir!" He reached
out to shake the Ranger's hand, but the Ranger only
dealt him a puzzled look. "I really need to talk to you."

Alone? Facing a notorious gang of killers?

"I'm afraid you've been misinformed, mister." The
Ranger eyed him up and down as he spoke, and took

note of the silver snake on the butt of the pistol the stranger carried in the waist of his trousers. Maria and Two Dogs only stared.

"Come, now," the stranger said, dropping his hand. "Modesty is indeed a virtue . . . but you can't deny what a heroic thing you've done here." From out of nowhere a wrinkled business card appeared in his hand. "Let me introduce myself—" He held the card as if offering it to the Ranger, but then drew it back as the Ranger reached for it. "—I'm afraid it's the only card I have at present. I'm Jamison Lang . . . former Western News Correspondent, representing—"

"A newspaperman." The Ranger cut him off, let out a breath, and leaned on the hickory cane.

"*Former* newspaperman." Jamison Lang raised a finger for emphasis. "Now that I've heard about what has gone on here—you facing the Cowboy Gang and all, I've decided to write a book about it." He puffed out his chest and smiled, beaming.

"I didn't face anybody here. I snuck up behind them. And I wasn't alone—I had help, good help." He shot Maria and Two Dogs a bemused glance. "The only gang was the Half Moon Gang. I busted them up long before I got here. They weren't a part of what happened in the street."

Lang's face reddened. "Well, granted I'll have to make some minor changes . . . for the sake of good storytelling. Instead of the Half Moon Gang—which is perhaps the most ridiculous name I've ever heard of— I decided to go with the Cowboy Gang." He shrugged. "A much more dramatic ring to it, wouldn't you agree?"

"See there?" The Ranger smiled a weak smile. "You didn't really need to talk to me at all." Jamison Lang looked bewildered. But before he could say anything else, the Ranger asked, "Where'd you get the fancy pistol?"

"Oh, this? Why, I gave a young drunkard five dollars for it a couple of days back. The poor wretch was barefoot, said he'd had one boot but traded it for a shot of whiskey, although I can't imagine why anyone would want only one boot unless they already had another to match it." He shrugged. "Actually, he only wanted to sell me the silver snake inlay for three dollars—said he'd need the pistol once he got back on his feet. But my goodness, I told him, why ruin a perfectly beautiful gun? So I persuaded him to take five dollars for the entire pistol. Would you like to see it?" His hand went to the pistol; but if froze there when he heard Maria's pistol cock and felt it jam against his belly.

The Ranger raised a hand toward him. "No, I don't want to see it. Now, if you'll excuse us . . ."

"But—But—" Jamison Lang stammered, moving aside as the Ranger, Maria, and Two Dogs moved off along the boardwalk. "I have a tremendous proposition for you. This is the kind of story the people back East are going crazy over. It could make you famous! Make us both famous, I dare say! I'm going to write this story, sir, with or without your help. You might as well—"

"Then, do what you want," the Ranger called back to him, cutting him off. "Only leave my name out of it. Just refer to me as the Lawman, or the Ranger . . . or if you need to make up a name, just call me Sam Burrack."

"But, Sam?" Maria whispered, leaning close, steadying his arm as he limped along between her and Two Dogs. "You gave him your real name."

"I know it." The Ranger chuckled under his breath. "But you know how writers are. The Cowboy Gang?" The Ranger shook his head. "By the time he gets around to writing it, he'll be so full of himself that the name Sam Burrack won't be good enough for him.

He'll twist things around—probably call me Wyatt
Earp, call you Doc Holiday—" He looked at Two
Dogs. "Who do you suppose you'll be?"

Two Dogs stared ahead, a thin smile on his weathered face. "Some old Indian who saw the whole
thing . . . but nobody believed anyway."

That night, as shadows drew long across the dirt
street, the three of them sat at the window above the
town and sipped Duttweiler's Tea as they gazed on
the street below. They saw Jimmy French lock the
doors to the Cottonwood Bank and walk off toward
the sheriff's office. He'd agreed to stay and run the
bank until C. G. Hutchinson's estate was settled. But
afterward, he'd decided to move to Chicago and work
in a large dry-goods store. It wasn't the kind of adventure that could compare to what he'd been through,
but who knew? Someday, with a little luck, he could
see himself owning his own store, maybe more than
one—maybe several across the country. Couldn't that
be called adventure? He thought so.

As he approached the sheriff's office, Judge Winfred
Lodge stepped out with his granddaughter in his arm,
met Jimmy French, and shook his hand. A stack of papers came out of the satchel French carried. He passed
the papers to the judge, and with the touch of his hat
brim, moved off along the street. When he'd turned a
corner and out of sight, the judge stood for a moment
and gazed off toward the badlands, where the essence
of his daughter would lie forever.

"There's irony," the Ranger said in a reverent tone.
"Without that child, the judge's life would be mean-
ingless to him . . . yet for the rest of his life, he'll never
look into little Justice's eyes without remembering the
terrible thing that brought them together."

"*Sí*," Maria whispered; and the three of them
watched the judge draw the child closer to his chest
and turn away from the badlands sky. He walked back

inside the office, careful that the papers in his hand did not give way and go fluttering off on a breeze. When the door closed behind the judge, the Ranger asked Two Dogs, "Did you ever remember who that sixth man was?"

Two Dogs sipped his tea and ran a hand across his mouth. Down on the dirt street, Jesse Tiggs' bare feet shuffled across the boardwalk outside the saloon. He pitched a bucket of dirty water out into the street and stood there rubbing a grimy hand up and down his dirty trouser leg. "I have tried. But so far my old mind does not reveal a thing to me." Two Dogs stared down through the window.

Jesse Tiggs dropped the empty bucket and hurried down from the boardwalk when a passing horseman flipped a cigar stub to the ground. As the horseman moved away, Tiggs picked up the stub and drew on it until a glow of fire swelled and a thin stream of smoke curled from the side of his mouth. "Well, keep trying," the Ranger said to Two Dogs, raising his teacup and tossing back the last drink from it.

"I will," Two Dogs said in a low tone. But he didn't really need to think about it as he watched Jesse Tiggs step back through the puddle of mud he'd created in the dirt street. He watched Tiggs pick up the bucket and shuffle back across the rough planks of the boardwalk. At the bat-wing doors, Tiggs had to step to the side while four young cowboys filed out past him. They looked at him and laughed, and one shook his head and flipped a coin at Tiggs' feet. Tiggs only stood for a second, looking down at it with his head bowed.

"Well, what are you waiting for? Pick it up." The cowboy laughed. "It'll get you a drink, won't it?"

Tiggs bent down, picked it up, and without facing the men, hurried through the bat-wing doors into the glow of light and the sound of a twangy piano. At the bar, Tiggs would drink his rye and look around for someone who might buy him another. He would learn to tell tall tales to pay for his drink . . . and in time, he would be known far and wide as the man who'd faced Sam Burrack, the Ranger, and had lived to tell about it. *You oughta hear it,* one cowboy or drifter would say to another, *it sounds almost like the truth.*

But, naw, I doubt it, someone would reply, *that old man ain't nothing but a drunk—been one all the years I've known him.* This they would say among themselves years later, Two Dogs thought, gazing down on the darkening street below. And seeing the justice in this no less than the creak of a hangman's rope or the bite of a lawman's bullet, he smiled to himself.

"If the truth's known," he could hear voices say, "I'd bet it was a woman that did him in." Women can break a man, they'd all agree, tossing back their drinks while drunken old Jesse Tiggs lay on the floor. And one might laugh and say, *Ain't it the truth. A man can kill you with the drop of a hammer. But there's women out there can break a man in half—never laying a finger on him.*

Two Dogs, still smiling to himself, leaned back in his chair. The Ranger looked at him, and asked with a curious expression, "If you do ever remember . . . you will tell me the truth, won't you?"

Two Dogs looked from one to the other as Maria refilled their teacups from the pot on the table. She lifted her cup as they sat in silence, her dark eyes meeting Two Dogs' for only a second. Then she sipped the tea and gazed across the far purple horizon.

"Have I ever lied to you?" Two Dogs asked.